HATE
F*@K

Cole and Hailey

the complete story

a serial romance in
The Horus Group series

by
Ainsley Booth

www.ainsleybooth.com

Warning: This is just the start. This doesn't end well. And it's going to get much worse before it ever gets better.

Cole:

I push her buttons. I *want* to push them in the good way. Dirty, up-against-the-wall, my-hand-in-her-pants kind of way.

But that's not possible, because I'm dark and she's light, and we both know it.

So I push her buttons in the bad way, making her hate me.

Hailey:

If a genie granted me three wishes, I'd ask for Cole Parker to never look at me again, that I'd forget the dark promise in his eyes, and that just once, before he vanished from my life completely, that he'd push me up against a wall and fuck me.

Then I'd go wash my mouth out with soap.

This is the complete story of Cole Parker and Hailey Dashford Reid. The Horus Group series will continue…

—cast of characters—

The Horus Group
Cole Parker

Jason Evans

Wilson Carter

Tag Browning

The Reids
Morgan Reid — *m* — Amelia Dashford Reid

Taylor Dashford Reid

Hailey Dashford Reid

Morgan Dashford Reid II

Alison Dashford Reid

HATE F*@K

Cole and Hailey

part one

one

Hailey

I pick at the blueberry muffin on my desk, which my friend Taryn gave me out of pity since I can't go outside. I have two monthly reports to run and a mile-long, hand-scribbled list of fixes for our website from my boss, but I can't concentrate on work right now.

My co-workers all understand, which makes me feel all the more guilty for bringing this shitstorm to their doorstep. These are good people, regular middle-class, law-abiding folks. None of them have a sister who is stupid enough to believe a powerful man when he promises no-one will find out about their affair.

Newsflash. People always find out.

Long story short, my family is a freaking train wreck, and I was an idiot for thinking I could have a regular job and pretend I'm a regular girl.

My phone vibrates in my purse, and my skin crawls. I don't want to answer it. There is literally not a single person in the entire world I want to hear from right now.

"Hailey?" I glance up at my boss, standing beside my cubicle, and wince at the look on her face. A mix of pity and annoyance which I understand and resent at the same time. I didn't blow the Vice President. This isn't my fault.

"I'm so sorry, Ellen. They'll go away soon." I'm talking about the various scuzzy photographers and videographers from media outlets camped in front of the converted townhouse that houses the employment agency I work at. This is new and awful and unexpected for my co-workers, and I feel like shit for bringing this into their lives.

Me? I know the drill. They don't care about me, but they want a sound bite, and I'm the rebel. The only member of the family not holed up at my parent's estate—again.

Jesus.

It wouldn't be a Friday morning if I hadn't already considered changing my name at least once.

Because being a Reid? It sucks.

She leans against the fabric covered half-wall in a poor attempt at nonchalance. "Will you hate me if I suggest you work from home this week?"

Yes. I bristle at the totally reasonable suggestion because, like so much of the drama in my life, I feel like it's not fair. Which is petty, so I suck it up, because my boss is awesome for knowing that I'd rather just keep going on as if my family isn't on the national news. "No. I get it."

The truth is that there isn't anything for me to do at home. I'm an intern. The whole point is that I'm on the job site, soaking up the knowledge and expertise of those around me.

"You can finish knitting those socks you brought in yesterday." She offers a weak smile, knowing that I'm miserable. "And as soon as it is safe for *you*, we want you back here. You're a hard worker, Hailey. Don't let this be anything other than a momentary blip."

I take a deep breath and nod. What else is there

to do? Ellen pats my shoulder and drifts away.

Against my foot, my purse vibrates again. I want to kick it. I don't.

It is *not* a genetic requirement that I have no self-control. Just because my father and my sister have both caused national scandals in the last six months doesn't mean anything other than Fate has a gross sense of humor.

Beside, I have two other siblings and a mother who *haven't* caused national scandal—that I know of. So only thirty-three percent of Reids are morally reprehensible. So far.

With a thunk, I drop my forehead to the desk. Fuck. My. Life.

I only wallow in self-pity for a minute. My boss is right. I can go home and knit, and at least if I'm there, my co-workers will be able to come and go as they please. It's not like I'm being super productive or anything. I yank my bag out from under the desk, stick Ellen's list of website fixes into the outside pocket, because those I *can* do from home, and slide on my oversized, extra-dark sunglasses. No way are those assholes getting a picture of my whole face.

I don't bother to say goodbye. I just power down my computer and head for the back staircase. There's a gated backyard that leads to an alleyway, and I can dash across it into the back of the import/export shop across the way. From there, I can get a cab.

It's a great plan, but as soon as I swing the door open, I know it's not going to happen.

For one thing, there are a couple of photographers sitting on motorcycles on the other side of the gate.

But even worse than that, Cole Parker is standing on this side of it, and he looks *pissed*.

Cole Parker. I think of him as the CFO of The Horus Group—CFO standing for Chief Fuck-You Officer. I don't actually know his title. The Horus Group probably doesn't do titles.

The four men came out of nowhere two years ago and buzz quickly swirled around them, branding them as the go-to crisis management team in the city. Probably got that reputation by getting bad people out of even worse situations. Hardly noble heroes, even if they look the part.

There are four of them, all various shades of bad-ass super soldiers who turned in their uniforms for suits and smooth lines. Cole and Jason, both ex-Navy SEALs, according to my brother. Tag, an ex-cop, local to the Metro DC area. And Wilson…he looks like a computer nerd on steroids. Obviously a CIA hacker gone rogue.

And one of them is standing between me and freedom.

Part of me knew Cole would be waiting, because my father has them on speed dial. I just didn't expect him to be mad at me, which he clearly is.

Angry Cole is still incredibly good-looking, so I'm tempted to stand there and just look at him vibrating for a minute, but the last thing I need is a picture taken of me anywhere near Washington's favorite fixer. I grab the door before it even slaps shut behind me and as quickly as I stepped out into the damp January dreariness, I'm back inside.

But of course I'm not alone. That would be too

easy.

Because this is the thing about Cole Parker. He's a fucking pit bull, and sometimes that's good, temporarily, when he's on your side. When you've pissed him off, though, it's downright scary. He'll rip the heart out of anyone who crosses him, backed up by a carefully constructed non-disclosure agreement.

I should know. He made me sign one. It was the closest we've ever been, him leaning across the conference table pointing out the various places I needed to initial and sign. The delicate hairs on my arms had stood up as if they knew I wanted to say, *Take Me, Mr. Parker.* Totally inappropriate on a million levels, and the way he glowered at me, I knew he was thinking the same thing—*never going to happen*.

Six months, I've known Cole Parker. Well, *known* would be an exaggeration. My father hired The Horus Group to get him out of "a bind", as my mother would call it. Bile rises in my throat at the willful blindness there. A bind. For fuck's sake.

Six months, I've lived with the twin reactions of disgust and something…quite different than disgust. I don't want to name it, the way my skin prickles when he's nearby. The way his dark gaze gets under my skin and takes up residence, leaving an itchy awareness that Cole Parker is not like other men. Not in general, and not for me.

So I should keep walking, up the stairs, through the office and out the front door, cameras be damned.

Instead, I stand there like a chump, waiting for him to lay into me. It doesn't take long.

"You're not answering your phone," he growls, and I jam my sunglasses on top of my head so he can see me roll my eyes and know that I'm not impressed. "You're out of your fucking mind if you think I'm letting you be chased down an alley by thugs on bikes."

"I was just going *across* the alley, and if my safety is at jeopardy, you could have called the police." I take a step towards the stairs and he moves with me, closing the gap, so I stop. The last thing I want to do is get any closer to the coiled snake that is my father's personal crisis management expert.

"Ms. Reid, this is not a time to be principled."

I'm sure that where Cole Parker is concerned, there's never a time to worry about such things as principles and morals and laws. "It's okay. I'll go out the front."

He narrows his eyes—still hazel flecked with gold, just like my stupid memory recorded them from our previous encounters—and backs me up against the wall. "I've got men out front. We're taking you home, one way or another."

"That's *not* my home."

I'm pretty sure I can hear teeth grinding as he glowers down at me. "Fine, then to your apartment."

I'm the second of four children born back to back to back. Staring contests? Ha. Fuck Cole Parker. I've got this in the bag. I tilt my head to the side as if to say, *bring it, pretty boy.*

He really is. Pretty, I mean, in a masculine, made of steel kind of way. Dark brown hair, thick dark lashes around those tiger eyes of his. A chronic case of sexy stubble that a really good razor could probably fix, but wouldn't that be a shame.

If he was anyone else, I'd take this staring contest as an opportunity to eye fuck him. Run my fingertips along his jaw and—

"Stop it." He jams his hand on the wall next to my head and leans in close, his harsh words reverberating between us. Close enough that I get my first whiff of his spicy sweet cologne. It brings with it the dawning realization that I did exactly what I really meant not to do—I let him get close.

Fuck me. I swallow hard and pretend I don't care. "You blinked."

"This is not a game, Ms. Reid. You might not like the drama that your family members face from time to time, but my job is to make sure you're safely escorted home."

"I thought your job was to—"

"Uh uh uh." He shakes his head as he presses his index finger against my lips. A shiver wracks through my body at the touch, and I fight to keep my eyes their normal size. Controlling my pulse is a lost cause, it's hammering away like a Habitat for Humanity crew on speed. "You keep your feisty little comments about what I do to yourself. I do the job that needs to be done, regardless of whether or not I like it. And I don't blink. Let's go."

He drops my sunglasses back into place on my face, then somehow he wraps his arm behind me and is easing me out the door before I have a chance to protest again. Since we're in view of the photographers, I give up the fight. He can take me

15

to my apartment. Point, Cole. I'll slam the door in his face as soon as I'm inside. Future point, Hailey.

I slide a neutral mask of indifference over my face as Cole maneuvers me around the cameras and motorbikes, keeping his body between me and anyone else at all times. He's tall enough that it literally feels like I've got my own brick wall around me. I hate to admit how nice that is for a change, not having to construct one out of wishes and denial and principled hot air.

He gets me into the passenger side of a giant black SUV and before I have a chance to take a breath by myself, he's around to the other side and we're off.

"You don't listen to music?" It's weird how quiet the car is. And how clean. It looks like a rental car on the inside, but it doesn't smell like one.

No, Cole's car smells like the man himself. Sinfully delicious. *Stop it, Hailey.* I can't. Desire is apparently my stress response, because I'm not normally like this. But every six months, my family hits the evening news, Cole storms into my life, and I get all achey in the good places.

"Not when I'm escorting a client."

"I'm not a client."

"Same thing."

"I don't need your help."

He doesn't answer.

"Are you afraid I'm going to make fun of your terrible taste?"

He stares straight ahead, as if my question has no effect, but after a beat he taps his finger against the stereo. Nine Inch Nails. Okay, he doesn't have terrible taste. Point, Cole. It's a good thing he doesn't know I'm keeping score.

I give him a sideways glance, which I'm sure he notices but doesn't acknowledge. He's driving quickly, not speeding exactly, but moving faster through traffic than I feel should be possible. And he does it with ease, which is...concerning. And hot.

He cuts around the university and heads north. Of course he knows where I live, but I'm annoyed that he didn't even bother with the pretense of asking for my address.

Out the window, everything is cold and dreary. I hate January. Even though it's mid-morning, it doesn't feel bright out yet, like the day is sluggish to get started. Ridiculous, because so much has already happened today.

I know what we'll find at my apartment — another minor swarm of photographers. I must have just missed them this morning because I went to the gym before work. Taryn dragging me to early morning yoga finally paid off. But I've been through this once before, although six months ago I didn't decide to ride out the drama in my own space.

This time would be different. I clear my throat and brace myself for opposition. "I'm not going to my parents' estate. You can't make me pack a bag and leave again."

He doesn't say anything, but he doesn't need to. Disapproval rolls off him in a palpable wave, making the last minute of the car ride incredibly uncomfortable. He parks half a block up from my low-rise apartment building, turns off the SUV,

17

and just sits there.

Being all big and angry. And disapproving.

"You should go for some variety. Crack a few jokes when you take people hostage," I say into the silence, and he flexes his jaw. Maybe that's not funny.

"We're going to get out and walk at a normal pace to your apartment," he says slowly.

"Normal for me, or normal for you? My legs aren't as long—"

He cuts me off with a stare, as if to say, *are you always this mouthy?* I'm not. He brings it out in me, and I'm not sure what he'd do with that knowledge. "Give me your key."

I take a breath and hold it, thinking about arguing, but it's not really worth it. I hand over the bundle of keys, and he looks at the knitting needle fob hanging off the ring. I wait for him to crack a joke—*deadly* or something like that—but he just points a finger at me and tells me to stay.

Like I'm a fucking puppy.

Since I was thinking about hopping out of the car, the reminder wasn't entirely off base. But *still*.

He comes around to my side, opens the door, and we're off. A few questions get tossed my way by the waiting media crew, but I genuinely can't hear them because the blood is pounding so hard in my ears. *Whomp. Here we go again. Whomp. At least it's not a murder investigation. Whomp. Maybe it's time to move.*

Wilson is waiting in the lobby, which surprises me in an uneasy-making way I don't like, and Cole mutters a question I don't catch, which I like even less.

"Yeah, all clear. We've installed a level two security system. She's good to go."

She's *what*? I clear my throat, and Cole slowly turns back to look at me. He knows what I'm about to ask, and the look on his face says *don't even bother*, but you better fucking believe I'm going to bother. "Did you break into my apartment and install a security system?"

"Upstairs, Hailey." He reaches out and curves his hand around my upper arm. Oh, hell no.

"What gives you the right? Was there anyone *inside* the building? No, right? So you've just gone crazy pants overboard, and invaded my privacy—"

"Technically *I* haven't invaded your privacy yet, I just had Wilson do it. Upstairs." His grip tightens, and my back prickles with the awareness that we're standing in front of a plate glass door, and ten feet on the other side, photographers are crowding on the sidewalk.

I shake his hand off my arm. "I'm going upstairs. Alone. Make yourselves useful and get rid of some of those vultures. They're bothering my neighbors."

"If you think I'm not seeing you safely locked behind a door, you're crazier than I thought. Up. Stairs. Now."

I'm not sure why *he's* getting mad, other than angry seems to be a permanent state of being for Cole. He's not the one whose life is turned upside down.

"Back off." The words rip out of me, and I realize I've shifted from annoyed to furious without realizing it. I feel like all the blood in my veins has been replaced by burning acid, and I literally want to stomp my feet and yell about how unfair life is.

I need some perspective. My life is just peachy. But I can't keep that front and center with Cole standing in front of me, all judging because I won't just do what I'm told.

Pressing my lips together, I hold up my hand and walk to the stairs. "Follow at your own risk. I've had enough of this for one day."

—two—

Cole

I start after her, because I'm not thinking clearly. I never do when it comes to Morgan Reid's second daughter.

Wilson jams his hand out in front of me. He can't actually stop me, but the thud of his palm against my chest is enough of a distraction that I stop long enough for him to talk. "Let her be. It's clear up there."

It better fucking be, or I'll kill him. I say as much, then spin around and glare at the photographers on the sidewalk. Hailey wants them gone, I can do that. Then I'm going upstairs so we can have a little talk about safety and common sense.

Hailey Dashford Reid, with her silky brown hair and big, smoky blue eyes, all prim and proper and so fucking sexy it makes my nuts ache. Also, totally off-limits.

For one thing, she's the daughter of a client. And she hates her father, so that's...messy. But I've fucked messy before, that doesn't usually bother me.

That it would bother me with Hailey is the biggest reason I need to stay away from her.

Of course, I could have sent Jason or Tag to pick her up, and I didn't. I wanted that privilege for myself, because if I can't have her bent over my bed, I'll take her spitting fire at me. Not nearly as satisfying, but it's something.

I was happy to let Tag run lead on this current drama with her sister because I'm done with their shit. I'm not entirely convinced that Taylor Reid wasn't the one who leaked the story to the press. Only in this twisted fucking family would fading from the media spotlight be seen as an unfortunate turn of events.

"Two years from now, Taylor's going to have her own MTV reality show," I mutter, and Wilson laughs behind me as I push my way back outside.

I recognize one of the photographers, and I pull out the pack of Cuban cigarillos I always carry for just such moments. "Walk with me, Clark."

He walks with me. I let him offer me a light, setting the tone. I'm about to do him a favor, and we both know it.

"Listen, she's in for the day. And night. I'm here, I'm not going anywhere, unless she's going with me. She's not going to give anyone a statement. Got it? She has no knowledge of the veracity of any allegations."

"What do you know?"

"Fuck you, that's what I know."

"I want a quote from a Reid girl about the VP breaking someone's heart."

"*This* Reid girl is off limits."

He takes a long drag. "For real?"

I turn around, looking for someone else to give my scoop to.

"Fine. Sorry. Shit. What you got?"

"The Senate Majority Leader's in a private meeting with the Democratic Senator from Maine as we speak."

"Seriously?"

"You haven't heard the rumours?" Of course he had. They'd been swirling for weeks, but both parties had done a good job of pretending the defection wasn't going to happen. Liars, every single last one of them.

"You got an address?"

I hand over the card from my pocket. "Both arrived there about an hour ago. You don't have a lot of time."

"You going to tell everyone else?"

"In about ninety seconds."

Nodding, Clark slings his camera into his backpack and heads for his bike. One down, seven to go.

Correction, five to go. Two of them take off after Clark, figuring something is better than the nothing they're going to get out of Hailey now that I'm here.

Having the reputation of a ruthless motherfucker comes in handy.

I kneel and stub the cigarillo I didn't really want against the road side of the curb. I send most of the others on their way, except for one stubborn dick who doesn't know what's good for him. Back inside, I toss the butt in the trash can beneath the mailboxes, send Wilson out to fuck with that guy's cell phone in the creepy blackhat way he does, and head upstairs.

Hailey Reid and I are going to have a little chat about behaving.

—three—

Hailey

It's not that I didn't expect him to come back. I did, at some point. Maybe when I try to sneak out the fire escape to get groceries or if I order in Thai food, he'll be there to intercept either me or the delivery person or both.

But I've only had ten minutes to breathe, and now he's knocking at my door. I know it's Cole, because he as much as said that he wouldn't let anyone else get to me.

I want him to go away, because if he does, that would mean this whole thing would be over. It's not, so he's still here. And I want him to go away because…I'm torn between this irresistible tug and my better judgment. I like things I can control. I like things I can put in boxes.

I can't put Cole in a box. There's no duct tape strong enough.

The silver lining of him still being here is that I can look my fill of him, even if it incites rioting feelings of guilt and disapproval at myself. Cole Parker in a suit is definitely a guilty pleasure, but a girl's gotta take what she can get.

I open the door. "Back so soon?"

"This will all go away if you just lie low for a couple of days," he says as he stalks into my apartment. He stops suddenly, and I enjoy the almost invisible double-take he does at the unusual structure in the middle of my living room. Well, at least I know this is the first time he's been in my place. So it's only his co-worker that's invaded my privacy.

"It was here when I moved in," I breezily lie, because *yes*, that's my stripper pole, and no, I don't need to explain it to the seething beast. I wonder for a second what Wilson thought, but I have it for shock value, so I hope he did a double-take, too.

I'm not whatever they think I am, that's for damn sure. I wave my hand toward the couch. Might as well sit and pretend to be civil. "Would you like tea or coffee while you yell at me?"

"I'm not going to yell at you."

"So when I say that I've got a date Saturday night—"

"You can't go." Okay, that was more of a growl than a yell.

"It's for a special performance at the Kennedy Center. Of course I'm going. There will be all sorts of famous people there—"

"—Including the Vice President, and if you say anything—"

"I've never met the man. I'm not going to meet him tomorrow night. And just because my sister gave him a blow-job doesn't mean I *care*, about him, or her. I'm certainly not going to make a public scene."

"It wasn't just a fucking blow-job. It's practically a professionally made sex tape. He's going to be impeached over this. It's going to drag on for *months*. And they're going to need all sorts of B-roll to run behind the endless commentary."

Not for the first time this morning, I consider the possibility that my sister leaked that video herself. The thought turns my stomach. Who would want to forever be associated with a video of themselves on their knees, face buried in an old man's crotch?

Cole glares at me like I'm an idiot for not getting this. "Hailey, you need to lay low."

I decide I need tea, and head for my kitchen. Since I live in a tiny two-bedroom apartment, that's only ten feet away from the living room, but he follows me anyway.

"I get that I'm being petulant, but this sucks."

He doesn't say anything. I glance over my shoulder at him. He just shrugs. "I'm not going to say I'm sorry, princess. Tell your date that you need to stay in. He can bring you ice cream and you can watch Project Runway together."

I squint, trying to imagine how that would go, suggesting to Trevor Waters that we hang out on my couch for the night instead of being seen. Nope. Never going to happen. A weird, icky feeling twists in my gut at telling Cole that Trevor doesn't like me enough to bring me ice cream.

That's okay. I'm only going out with him so I don't have to go to the opera alone. And I *am* going. Cole can stuff it.

"If you—" He jams his hands into his suit pants, shoving his jacket out of the way. Scowling, he mutters something under his breath that I don't catch.

"If I what?"

"Nothing."

My first instinct is to push more, needle him to say whatever was on his mind, but maybe some of the knee-jerk reactions between Cole and me should stay silent.

"Look, I get the rules, okay? No comment, ever. Not even if they say something about Morgan and Alison." My younger siblings live at home. Morgan is twenty-one going on fifty, a total businessman just like our father, except he's not evil. And Alison…God, my nineteen-year-old sister is so freaking innocent it hurts. But I'm not an idiot. There's no upside to engaging with a scummy reporter if they try to bait me with a disgusting rumor. "I'm not going to cause any problems."

Cole stares at me, his eyes flicking up and down my face, and he yanks on his tie. "Fuck. You're such a distraction."

His tone does something to my insides that I don't like. I bristle and point at him, as if my wagging finger could ward off the accidental hurt he just piled on me. I want to tell him I'm just as important as anyone else in my family, but that's digging deeper into a situation I want nothing to do with. So I tell him off in as light a way as I can muster. "Hey, that's seriously enough name-calling for one day."

His fingers freeze at the top button of his shirt. I curse myself for interrupting, because I really want to see the sliver of chest he was about to reveal. "When did I call you a name?"

I stare at that spot instead of answering, and with an exasperated sigh he yanks his tie fully off and stuffs it in his pocket. Then he flicks open the neck of his dress shirt, the crisp white fabric giving way to darker skin stretched taut over muscle and tendon and fantasy fodder. Shadows play along his collarbone and I wonder what the skin there tastes like, and if that subtle cologne he wears smells

28

even better up close.

Clearing my throat, I turn away and grab my kettle to fill. Busy-work might distract me from how good he looks in a suit. I wonder why he's wearing one if his job today is just to corral me—he doesn't always suit up. I've seen him in khakis and a polo shirt—a more disingenuous outfit for him I can't possibly imagine—and jeans and a t-shirt, in which he looks most at ease. That was my first glimpse of him, in the middle of the night when we were all sequestered at my parents' house months ago. Your father boinks a call girl and she turns up dead in the Potomac, you set aside your dislike for the family and crawl inside the castle.

And Cole shows up soon thereafter, his perfect body stretching the limits of denim and cotton, and you decide to stay a while just to look at him.

Even when I realized he's amoral and has only casual respect for the laws of the land, he's still nice to look at.

Sometimes I disgust myself. Disgust might be a strong word. Disappoint, maybe, because instead of wanting someone else, someone normal and healthy—an average Joe with a 401k and a Volvo—instead of that, I'm captivated by *this* man. By brooding eyes and broad shoulders, dark secrets and sharp commands.

Nothing wrong with fantasies, Hailey. I'll keep telling myself that, because I've got a lot of Cole Parker fantasies, including one where he slowly strips out of a suit in my kitchen. Right now, my back is to him, and I'm quite sure he's not actually taking his clothes off, but he's prowling around and he *did* just undo that top button, so this still feels

29

weird and dangerous. And maybe a little bit of a turn-on.

Ugh. "Do you like tea?"

"Sure." His voice is *right there*, behind me, and my breath catches in my throat. "What name did I call you before?"

My voice cracks as I answer him. "You said I was crazy."

"What?"

"Earlier, you said—" I clear my throat and drop my voice an octave. "'You're crazier than I thought'. So, why do you think I'm crazy?"

When Cole laughs, it's ripped from him like he's truly surprised. I know he's ex-military, and he sees the worst sides of some scary people, but Jesus, life is too short to not laugh regularly. So even though I don't like him laughing *at* me, I bite back the snarky response that slides so easily to the tip of my tongue. Maybe if I'm nice to him for a minute, he'll get the hell out of my apartment and leave me to my quiet fantasies, where Dream Cole laughs all the time. Naked.

"Hailey." His voice roughs up a bit as he says my name, and I turn around. He's not as close as I thought—a solid three feet of empty space sits between us, but he's leaning forward just a bit, and it's enough to make me shiver. He lifts his phone, all business again. "I called you twice this morning, so I know you've got my number. But you didn't answer." He swears under his breath. "Use it. We don't need to talk, you can just text me. But don't leave this apartment alone, or there will be hell to pay."

"That's ridiculous."

"And right there, that's why I think you're crazy."

"Well, I think you're crazy for thinking you can somehow determine that there will be 'hell to pay'." My voice raises toward the end of that, because fuck it, I'm back to being mad again. "Did you stop for a second and think that maybe you think I'm crazy and a distraction and whatever else because I don't play your fucking Men in Black games? But news flash, buddy—that's not my world. I'm not a celebrity, and I'm not a politician. I'm just Hailey Reid, who had the misfortune to be born into a fucked up family. I'm smart enough to see the problems that raises, and for the last time, I'll be a good girl, okay?"

My chest is heaving as I finish my stupid tirade, and all of a sudden I realize he's breathing hard, too. He's glaring at me, like my words wound him up but good, and then he's in front of me, *right* in front. Close enough I can smell his cologne and the bare skin beneath it, and then I feel him. It's weird that I don't feel him first, because he's pressed hard against my body, arms bracketing me against the counter on either side of my hips. But once I do, I can't *not* feel him. All of him. And he's big, and hard, and definitely turned on, which I don't expect. Oh, sweet mother of all that is holy...

"Cole—" I breathe, and he cuts me off.

"When I say you're a distraction, I mean I can't get you out of my fucking head. I wonder what the inside of your mouth tastes like and if you'd pull my hair when I go down on you."

"No." My voice has dropped to a bare whisper, because *holy fuck* and *how is that possible?*

31

"Yes," he growls, and I make a noise that sounds suspiciously like a whimper. This is a disaster. It's one thing for me to covet Cole from a distance. He's beautiful. It's something completely different for him to want me.

For a second, I revel in that. I let my mind go blank and roll around in what it's like for Cole—of the mad driving skills, angry thousand-yard stare, and legendary reputation for all manner of dangerously delicious things—to have a hard-on for *me*. It's better than a million dollars, and for the rest of my life, I'm going to remember this moment when someone that out of my league pressed his cock against my belly and growled at me.

But in the next second, I remember all the reasons this is a bad idea. When I'm not looking at him, I don't *like* Cole. And I can't kiss someone I don't like. I definitely can't rub up against them like a cat in heat. And right now, he should be doing something else. Getting my sister out of trouble, for example. And then after that, he probably has a hot date with a supermodel.

I plant my hand firmly in the middle of his chest and push.

He doesn't move.

"Cole…" Damnit. My voice is not on board with the whole *tell him no* plan. Instead it does a very uncharacteristic breathy sigh thing that sounds like a completely fake admonishment that's not-so-secretly an invitation to be bad. Very, very bad.

There are a lot of layers to how fucked up my feelings about this moment are.

"I know," he rasps. "Just…shut up for a

minute."

He drops his face toward my neck, and as he inhales next to my ear, my insides light on fire, like his breath is a lit match and my blood has been replaced with gasoline. No one has ever done that before, and I want him to do it again, consequences be damned.

Saying my name on a long, slow exhale, he drags his cheek against mine, lining up our faces.

Shut up for a minute. How the hell does that line work on me?

Because it totally worked. Like panty-melting magic. My nipples are tight, my breasts heavy, and my thighs ache.

"This isn't a thing, got it?" He grinds out the words, his lips now perilously close to mine.

I can't handle whatever is going on, not straight up, so I get lippy. It's my way. "Yes. Totally forgotten already. This is nothing."

"It's not fucking nothing, Hailey. Jesus." He pulls back just enough to look at me. Great, now I've said the wrong thing and he isn't going to kiss me. Which should be the right call, but damn, my body is protesting. "It just can't be more than this." He drops his gaze to my mouth, and that look feels almost as good as a kiss. It's deep and probing and hungry.

I don't like Cole. But I do like his hungry gaze.

I think I like it a lot. So I lick my lips.

His mouth crashes into mine at the same time as his hands slide through my hair. He's shaking as he tastes me, and I have this vague realization that he's holding back. Screw that. If this can't be anything more than a one-time-only taste, I want all of him. I nip at his lower lip, which I think he likes because he makes this grunting noise that my body responds to on a primal level.

My nipples tighten, making me aware of how heavy my breasts feel against my bra. Deep inside my pelvis, something tugs, freeing my inhibitions.

I bite him again and he rewards me with the same noise, louder and longer this time. He rocks me backward, sliding one leg between my thighs, and I can see how biting him might have been a mistake.

The kind of mistake that leads people to get naked against their better judgment.

Cole shudders, then he's all over me, like he needed that second sink of my teeth into his flesh to confirm consent. I get that. He kisses in a way that needs consent, that makes you feel like you've been stripped bare and fucked hard. This kiss is going to leave me achey and satisfied, even though the bare part can't happen.

It can't happen. I'll keep telling myself that.

Our tongues tangle as I wind my arms around his neck, and his hands start to roam. First his fingers drift along the V-neck of my sweater, raising goosebumps across my chest. I desperately want him to cup my breasts and thumb over my nipples, but I know that's beyond the boundary he's set. I shudder as he slides his knuckles down the outside of my shirt, blazing matching trails along the sides of my boobs that I very much want him to re-trace with his mouth.

As his hands land on my hips, I'm suddenly self-conscious about how wide I am there, but he's squeezing and it feels good and he's still kissing me.

My mind flashes to that glaring look he gave me right before we collided, and instead of casting doubt on what we're doing, it revs me up.

"Fuck yeah," he mutters, his voice gravelly and deep as I slide my mouth to his neck, tasting the warm, tight skin. I want to devour him, and he seems okay with that. His breathing slows, like he's trying to control it. I want to make him lose that control, but I'm not the only one playing with fire. His fingers toy with the bare skin at my waist, between my sweater and my generic stretchy black dress pants. Big hands. Strong, warm, calloused fingers. I almost wore jeans today. Never before have I been so lucky in a wardrobe choice, because I can feel all of him pressing into me and it's burning me up in the best way imaginable.

Tentatively, I lick down the valley between his Adam's apple and the corded muscle that flexes as he tips his head to the side. Between my legs, his thigh bunches and shifts. His hands slide back over my hips and onto my butt, and all of a sudden he's lifting me.

I'm a big girl. People don't just hoist me in the air, but Cole's got me settled on the counter before I can say, "Don't strain your back," so I don't. Instead I give in to the delicious thrill of being kissed like he just can't help himself.

He settles into the V of my legs, his erection throbbing between us and he slows his kisses as if to say, *if we were two other people, we'd do a hell of a lot more*. But we're not.

"You're still distracting me," he says quietly after tracing my lower lip with the tip of his tongue.

"I don't mean to…" I trail off, leaving my lips parted in invitation, but he just looks at me instead of closing the gap again. Fear holds me back from pushing in for another kiss. I'm not sure what the rules are here.

"I have to go." He's got me securely in his arms, but I feel like this is the end, that he's rocked my world with the sexiest kiss ever and that's it, and all of a sudden, I'm filled with a different kind of emotion.

Sadness.

Fuck off.

I shove that prickly bitch back into the pit of my stomach where she belongs, and I nudge his face with mine. He nudges me back, heat zinging between us, and then it's all wet and hot and delicious again.

But there's more this time, it's hot but it's also heavy. Too heavy, and I feel myself getting mad. Who the fuck is he to kiss me like this, make me feel like this, when it can't go anywhere?

I pull back, my lips still swollen from his bruising kisses. He chases my lips for a minute, not realizing that we're done, but we are. I need to be the one to stop this time.

It's like dragging myself blindfolded through mud. Putting distance between us is strangely disorienting when sparks are still firing in all directions and every cell in my body is saying, *ditch work and drag him into your room before he realizes what he's doing.*

"I didn't mean to—" he starts at the same time as I make a dismissive sound and cover my face with my hands.

"Don't worry about it, faces bump all the time," I mumble through my fingers. "You should go."

He makes a noise I can't quite decipher, and after a beat I feel the absence of his body heat as he moves away from me, then the door knob turns, the hinges squeak, and he's gone.

I said it. And yet I'm standing here, wishing like hell I hadn't just pushed him away, because kissing Cole Parker was like winning the make-out lottery.

Too bad I'm never going to do it again.

—four—

Cole

Outside Hailey's apartment, I stand on the landing for thirty seconds. Twenty to get my shit together and will my erection away, and the last ten talking myself out of heading back inside.

Kissing her was a stupid move. I didn't mean to do it.

I've thought about it for months and done everything I can think of to cock-block myself. Dated other women to drive the thought of her mouth from my head. Stepped back into the shadows at the handful of events we'd happened to both attend. Watched her with other men—men nothing like me—and told myself to get a fucking clue.

Downstairs, Wilson is patiently waiting for me. He looks up from his phone and smirks. "Did you forget we agreed on video surveillance for the apartment?"

Fuck me. Not patient at all, the fucking perv. "Destroy that." I close my eyes. "No. Download it onto a USB stick for me. Then destroy it."

"Seriously, you want to wank off to it? You're an idiot."

"Fuck you." I take a deep breath. I don't know why I want it. I don't need video of what is probably just her heels on my ass to get off. I've got the memory of her tongue licking along my lips and her teeth against the skin on my neck. I'm good. But I still want the video.

"And stop the video surveillance."

"You trust her?"

"More than I trust you, asshole." It was a lie. I'd trust Wilson with my life, as much as I would Jason or Tag. But it scrapes at me that I forgot for a second that his eagle eyes were always watching —that just a few hours earlier, I'd asked him to put that surveillance into place.

And all it took was Hailey yelling at me across her kitchen for my blood flow to head south and make some dumb-ass decisions.

I'm not going back to her place. I do have will power, and I'm able to bury what I want when it's for a greater good. What's good for Hailey is me, far, far away from her.

But just in case. "And sweet talk yourself back in there and remove the cameras."

"And what should l tell her…?"

"Tell her nothing. Tell her you want a fucking knitting lesson. Tell her you need to babysit her until after we figure out a plan of attack for the media. I'm heading back to the office to meet with Jason."

Wilson shrugs, his slightly-too-long hair flopping in his eyes. He does apathetic disturbingly well, part of his everyman presentation. I've seen him be everything from a gamer geek to a blue collar construction worker. I've also see him in the underground fighting rings. Nothing everyman about how he pummels bulkier men into the mat.

Floppy hair my ass.

"Thanks," I mutter, shaking his hand.

Twenty minutes later, I pull into the underground parking garage beneath our offices.

We have the second and third floors of an office building between Dupont Circle and Adams Morgan. Shiny enough to impress our clients, but not quite institutional K Street. Also, close to my condo, which is really all I care about. I stop at the coffee shop on the ground floor and get lunch, telling myself I'm not postponing the inevitable lecture on professionalism and priorities from my business partner.

I'm lying, because Jason is waiting to pounce as soon as I step into our reception area on the second floor. I should have just gone straight up to my office on the third.

"What the hell were you thinking?" he spits at me, and I ignore him.

Instead I nod at Ellie, our receptionist. She gives me a wincing smile that says he's been pissed for longer than the half hour it took me to get here from Hailey's place. I let out a long, slow breath, and wag my coffee at the stairs. "Let's go do this in private."

He waits until we get upstairs, then lets loose. "Tag? You gave Morgan Reid to Tag?"

Oh. "That's what you're pissed about?"

"Tag's a fucking bull in a china shop. Shit. I spent most of the morning apologizing for him."

"Did he make Amelia and Taylor happy?"

"Only because one or both of them want to fuck him."

I sigh. "And we know that's not going to happen, right? So who cares how pissed Morgan gets?"

"He's the one paying our bill."

This is delicate ground. Jason's half-brother

41

Mack is a silent investor in our firm, and Jason has a legit oar in wanting to always stay in the black. On the other hand, I don't give a fuck about money, not the same way he does. Plus we're plenty profitable. "Then you should have gone yourself."

"I did. But he's your client."

"I don't want him as my client." The half-year-old tension simmers between us. Truthfully, neither of us is right or wrong. It's fucking shades of gray and Jason wasn't pushing me for selfish reasons. Between the two of us, he's more the good guy. Hell, he's still working for Uncle Sam, even if it's in a dark and unseen way.

But it wasn't fucking right, what we did. Not then. And that truth has eaten at me for six long months.

I don't care where the order came from.

Jason grits his teeth and glares at me. "Is that why you're fucking his daughter?"

I don't even feel my coffee slip out of my hand. He says the words and I'm in motion, one fist grabbing the front of his shirt, the other cracking against his jaw.

He's like a brother to me, so I stagger back after that one shot. One too many, but I couldn't help myself.

"You done?" he asks slowly, glaring at me from under pulled together eyebrows. His voice is quiet as he rubs his jaw. Nobody does *Disappointed Dad* quite like Jason.

"It was one kiss and Wilson has a big fucking mouth." There's no point in staying pissed about it. Part of me knew I'd be coming back to this conversation. But I'm prickly—too prickly, which would be Jason's point if I let him make it.

"No secrets, remember?" It was our promise to each other when we started the firm. It's how I know that Jason still does covert work and Tag has a sometimes on-again, mostly off-again affair with his ex-wife. Wilson…well, the no-secrets rule has weird asterisks when it comes to our resident spook. But he tells us what he can, and Jason vouches for the rest.

"Fine. What do you want to know?"

"Why her?"

I can't help myself. And that's the problem. That's always the problem with relationships. They're a distraction. They make men weak.

"Fine, don't answer that. Is it out of your system?"

Memories from that first night we were called to the Reid estate slide forward in my mind, offering themselves up as if I need a reminder that Hailey's been under my skin for six long months. I don't. "Leave it alone."

"She's not your type."

I clench my fists, and shove them in my pockets so I don't punch him again. Jason's known me for eleven years. I know he's not talking about her curves, because in that respect, she's definitely my type.

He's talking about her heart. And he's right.

"You'll break her."

"I know. I'm not going to kiss her again." But that's not good enough, just saying it. I have to push her away, and I know exactly how to do it. "Really. I'll take care of it." By being a bastard.

43

"Tell me about the plan of attack for Taylor."

Reluctantly, Jason lets me change the subject. He outlines the interview with *People* magazine —"the fewer words the better"—and the lawyers are already on retainer. Unless the Vice President was completely honest about the affair, it'll be likely that the House of Representatives would find a way to impeach him.

Taylor Reid, Washington party girl, might bring down the man who thought he was eighteen months away from being the next President.

It was a good thing the Reids didn't have any political aspirations, because they'd just destroyed their own political party with what would surely be a protracted scandal.

"Please tell me we have a plan to find other women he's slept with."

"Wilson's got his interns on it." Three computer nerds at Georgetown who'd latched on to our friend after he'd spoken to their class. Whatever turned their crank.

"Not a bad day's work before lunch, then." I vaguely point at my desk, only now remembering I dropped my coffee. I swear under my breath and Jason laughs at me. "I'm not sorry I punched you."

He sobers up fast. I've said too much, because I'm restless and frustrated, but that's the thing about the brothers you choose. They forgive a lot, and they understand you better than you understand yourself. Thank Christ for that. "You *can't* start something with her, Cole. There's no way that ends well. I'll take a few more hits if that's what it takes for you to remember who you are."

"One step up from a hired gun." I can't keep

44

the resentment out of my voice.

"We're fighting the good fight."

I shake my head. I'm not sure there's any good left in this world, except for in the beautiful delusions of the innocent. Like Hailey.

And that's why I need to break her heart now. Not because of what I am, but what I believe—and what I can't because I've seen too much.

Done too much.

Hurt too many.

Been hurt. I shove that thought away even as I recognize that's probably more true than all the other shit. Hailey's the kind to *care* with a capital C. That the thought makes my hands tremble and my stomach turn is even more reason to slice the ribbons of want between us before she gets any crazy ideas.

five

Hailey

The last few days have spun past in a blur. Taylor's been on TV a lot, but the press has lost interest in me. I even went to work yesterday, and spent earlier today at the spa with my baby sister Alison.

We didn't call Taylor.

Alison wanted to. I gave her my best stink eye and she changed the subject.

Now I'm on a date, although Trevor Waters, junior advisor for the junior senator from Texas, has spent more time in the lobby on the phone than next to me in our seats at the Kennedy Center.

I know I'm privileged to be here, that this isn't a once in a lifetime experience for me. But I can't help long for more. Something hot and intense, but a little less fucked up than whatever I'd flirted at with Cole.

This is a date set up by my well-meaning but not-really-thinking friend Becky. Just because Trevor and I both like opera doesn't make this a good idea. For one thing, it could only be a good idea if both of us were actually present on the date.

A date I'd gone all out for, even though my heart wasn't in it. Black velvet halter dress, tight through the waist, thanks to the best corset money can buy. My boobs look great, not that Trevor would notice.

I sigh to myself. The truth is that he's missing in body. I'm checked out mentally. That's not better. I don't even care if he's into me, because even though he's attractive enough — tall, slim, nice haircut, good teeth — he's just not my type.

It's a sad state when my only nerves about going on a date are whether or not the press will hound me with annoying questions, and not whether or not there's going to be kissing at the end of the night.

I applaud with the rest of the attendees as the lights go up for intermission, then head out to the terrace in search of my absentee date. Or alcohol. I'll take whichever I find first.

It's cold outside, and I don't see Trevor anywhere. I head inside, hoping he can find me at the bar, when my skin prickles with awareness. I sense Cole a moment before he speaks, and it bugs me how I suddenly don't feel alone. Annoyed. Alive and raging, sure. But no longer lonely. It's an awful trick my mind is playing on me, because if there's anyone who will abandon me, guaranteed, it's the man behind me.

"You've got your socialite rags on, Hailey."

I whirl around, telling myself it's to lay into him. How dare he slide that silky voice all over me like we're intimate. But when I collide with his gaze, I'm the one left doubting…because he sure looks at me like, at least on some level, we already are. My lips certainly remember something that felt like a hell of a lot more than an accidental collision of mouths. My ears remember his filthy words lighting me up from the inside out.

He wants me. Why, I can't quite understand. How, when we don't even like each other, we can be ten feet apart and it already feels like we're halfway through foreplay…I don't understand.

I don't like not understanding. I don't like anything about this, especially the part where it ends. I like the absence of our vicious dance even less than the mess of it. How screwed up is that?

I square my shoulders and let my inner bitch take over my voice. "What are you doing here?"

He raises his eyebrows in vague disbelief. Well, okay. So he's wearing a tux. Clearly, he's here for the opera just like me. "I need to play this game for clients. Network. That kind of bullshit. You've opted out of this life, so the bigger question is, what are *you* doing here?"

I bristle, because what the hell does he know about the choices I've made? "I'm on a date. Wait. I *told* you I was coming here."

I didn't think it was possible for his liquid gold eyes to burn cold, but I was wrong. Cole hates that I'm on a date, and the thought gives me an illicit thrill. Good. He needs to know that not everyone jumps at his command. Not everyone is within his realm to control.

He steps closer. "Pretty romantic first date, the Kennedy Center."

"Who said it was a first date?"

"Since your date isn't at your fucking side, making you feel like the most beautiful woman in the world, I should hope it's not a repeat."

He's not wrong. I don't say that, though. I don't say anything.

"Who's the fuck up?"

"None of your business."

"Does he kiss you like he could get drunk on your mouth?" He dips his gaze to my lips, which

49

part as if on command. *Fuck off, lips, don't be difficult.* I lick them in a nervous attempt to get my body back under my own control, but that just makes his pupils dilate. Like the *promise* of my mouth is enough to make him drunk.

I don't tell him I haven't kissed Trevor, and I won't be. Unfortunately for me, the bar for kissing has recently been raised to impossible heights.

I might need to become a nun. I shake my head and give him my haughtiest stare, left hand firmly on my hip. "That was a mistake."

He glares at me, like I'm making him be a jerk and he resents it. "Doesn't mean I don't want to do it again."

His words blast through me and I reach for the railing to steady myself. "Don't. I'm on a date, for Christ's sake."

He swallowed hard, and my gaze slides past him to a woman fast approaching. *Holy shit.*

"You're not here alone, either."

"No."

She's beautiful, and I'm filled with irrational jealousy. I'd just finished telling him I was none of his business. But I selfishly still want him to be my guilty something. And the way she's sauntering over…my stomach turns. I tell myself not to ask the question, but it spills out anyway. "Who is she?"

"My girlfriend."

I didn't hear that right. I couldn't have, but when I meet his gaze, it's suddenly cold and unwavering.

"But you came over…No."

He lifts one eyebrow. "No?"

"You kissed me," I hiss under my breath. It sounds catty and I don't care.

He drops his voice, too, but it just sounds sexy. "I kiss a lot of women, Hailey."

That doesn't sound sexy. Fuck him. It's my standard refrain. "Like, this week?"

I can't swallow and my mouth is dry. I can't believe I let him touch me, and now she's beside him. Blonde, thin, pale in a pretty way. Ugh. I hate her and hate myself for hating her. I smile and offer a hand. "Hi, I'm Hailey Reid."

"Penny Kristoff." Her grip is sure, and I want to ask her if she knows her *boyfriend* apparently *kisses a lot of women*, but I'm afraid I might vomit all over her Donna Karan gown if I open my mouth.

So instead I press my lips together and nod and smile through some lie Cole tells her about what we were talking about—a charity connection we discovered over the last few days, because "I'm a cheating scumbag who can't keep my tongue in my mouth" probably wouldn't go over well. I make a noncommittal noise when she asks me…something, and then finally my good for nothing date shows up and I escape.

The next hour passes by in an angry blur. It's like there's a slideshow of our kiss playing over and over again in my head with an awful National Geographic narration. *The alpha male, ever alert for an opportunity to rut with a willing female, pounces at the first sign of vulnerability.*

By the time the performance is over, I'm beyond ready to go home, but there's a talk after the performance that Trevor wants to stay for. We file out to the foyer with everyone else.

"Would you like a glass of wine?" Trevor murmurs, touching my elbow.

I shake my head, then change my mind. Sure, whatever. "White, please."

I excuse myself to the ladies room where of course I run into Cole's girlfriend. Because Fate clearly hates me.

She's at the mirror, touching up her lipstick, and I decide to do the same. There's no way my bladder can perform while she's in the same room, and it was really just an excuse to get away from Trevor anyway.

"Lovely performances tonight," she says with an authentic smile. Sure, why shouldn't she smile? Blissfully ignorant of how gross her boyfriend is.

"Yes." I apply a careful layer of Barely Red, and as I do, she watches me. Not suspiciously. Not innocently. Something else I can't quite figure out is playing in her eyes. I cap the lipstick and tuck it away.

I've got two choices here. I can run and hide, or stick my toe in the water and find out what's what. It's very unlike me, but Cole's lit a spark inside me. It's dangerous and crazy, and I'm perilously close to not giving a fuck. "You're Penny, right?"

She steps closer, tipping her head to the side. "I am."

"Cole didn't mention you..." I leave that trailing. I don't want to be a bitch here. I'm done with him, so it doesn't matter—except it does. Ugh.

"No, he wouldn't." Her lips plump and curl at the corners, like she's got a secret that pleases her.

I don't want to get sucked in, but that smile has

52

a million questions racing through my head. "What do you mean?"

Another secret smirk, and I want to smack her. No, I want to walk away, but I can't.

And then she turns and looks at me, and everything shifts slightly as her voice turns overtly friendly. "That's a great shade on you."

So much for me being brave. I take a mental step back into the protection of my ingrained graciousness. "Thank you. It's a favorite."

"I can see why Cole likes you." She leans this time, not actually moving closer, but the room feels smaller. And hotter. "You're luscious."

Whoa. "Pardon?"

Surely I've misheard her. But then she tugs her lower lip between her teeth and glances down my body, and *nope*, I'm pretty sure she said I was.... Wow. So maybe Cole and his girlfriend *both* kiss random women. That didn't make me feel better.

"You're very much his type." She says it almost under her breath, and I wish I could say that I don't like hearing that. I'd wondered, over the last hour, why he'd kissed me when he was with this woman. Of course now I wonder if he has some kind of fetish for thick thighs and soft breasts.

And since I don't like that idea at *all*, I feign my last vestige of ignorance. "Excuse me?"

She pinks up, finally cluing in to the fact that we're very much not on the same page. "You know..." she says softly. "Don't you?"

"No, I really don't." My voice is high and wavers a bit, but I stand my ground.

"Oh." She presses her lips together, pink cheeks now ruddy with embarrassment. "Then let's blame this on champagne and a long work week."

I'm not sure I can. She knows something about Cole that I don't. Hell, what she knows about her boyfriend that I don't would probably fill a stadium. But right now, her words are ringing in my ears.

"Listen, this…" She lifts her hand and hovers her fingers between us for a minute before ever so lightly touching my collarbone and exhaling as she does. "I know he's difficult. But the way he was looking at you." She makes a warm humming noise. "I'd like to watch him fuck you."

Oh. My. God.

"I have to go," I squeak, and spin on my heel in the world's fastest and least elegant bathroom escape ever.

In the foyer, Trevor is waiting a few yards away, holding two glasses of wine. An usher opens the doors to the hall again, welcoming us back for the talk, and all of a sudden I just can't.

I fumble at my purse, pretending that it just vibrated. I quickly hand back the glass he'd just slid into my fingers, and look at my dark phone. "It's my sister, do you mind going in without me?"

He better not mind. He spent most of the first half taking work calls on a Saturday night first date. And of course he doesn't, because whether or not I'm on his arm really doesn't matter to him.

I watch my date disappear, toss back my wine like it's water, and look for a place to stash the glass before I disappear into the sad, cold night. I feel a momentary pang of guilt, but I can text him an apology. Family emergency. He'll believe that.

Cole's hand is *not* the place I wanted to dump

an empty glass of wine. But there it is, reached out in front of me as he comes around my body. "Long night?"

"Something like that. I need to leave, so if you could give that to a waiter," I murmur, not looking him in the eye.

Without breaking eye contact with me, he finds a surface I didn't notice and disposes of the glass. "We need to talk, beautiful."

No, I need to knee him in the groin, then go home and take off this stupid gown.

"Why does your girlfriend think she might be able to watch you fuck me?" I hiss under my breath, barely taking a beat to appreciate the way he blanches ever so slightly. Good. Fuck him.

"Penny told me she said too much. She's sorry."

"She doesn't need to be sorry. You do, for kissing me. And calling me beautiful. Totally uncalled for." My words are coming out in short, sharp, staccato bursts. I wish they'd land half as painfully as they rip from me, but Cole seems unaffected.

"Fine, then *I'm* sorry. It was inappropriate for me to kiss you." He moves closer as he says it, and as much as I want to knee him in the junk, there's a part of me that gets warm. *Stupid girl* warm, with the goose bumps and convenient memory loss that ensures that assholes like Cole get to keep spreading their DNA through the population.

But this isn't the first time I've mistaken attention as something more. And it wouldn't be the first time that attention would be purposefully misrepresented as something more.

"There's nothing hot about being used," I say

quietly. It doesn't sound quite right as I say it, and the flare in his eyes says I'm wrong. If I am, he needs to fix that impression, because he kissed me when he had a girlfriend, and he sure as hell acted like it was a dirty little secret.

I slap myself back. No. It doesn't matter if he had twisted good intentions when he kissed me.

His lips tighten and he clenches his jaw for a minute, like he's at war with himself. I know the feeling.

Finally he drops his chin, staring at me with his magnetic eyes. His voice, low and rough and intimate, does dangerous things to me on the cellular level. "I wasn't using you, and that kiss was fucking hot. You can't deny it."

I can't. Doesn't mean I won't try. "Wow, mixed messages much, Mr. Parker? It can't happen again, you've got a girlfriend, a convenient omission of fact the other day...but you sure seem obsessed with my mouth."

I think he's getting taller and wider and angrier as he stands in front of me, but I'm not afraid. I'm fired up, and so is he. "Not at all, *Ms. Reid*. I didn't realize that I needed to spell out the details of my personal life before I reacted to you eye-fucking me in your kitchen. It was a kiss. Get the fuck over it."

"Oh, I'm over it." Another lie. My nose must be a foot long.

"And if it seems like I'm obsessed with your pretty little mouth, it's because you keep licking your lips." His gaze drops to my mouth again, and I laugh.

Then I lick my lips.

"If I wasn't working for your family right now…" His voice is still low and tense, but we're starting to attract some attention. Just enough that people might wonder what we're talking about.

I should shut up. I should walk away. I don't do either of those things, because I can't let him have the last word, especially when it's a lie. "What? Nothing, Cole. You'd be working for some other scum bag. Tell me — how many murders have you covered up this week?"

Eyes dark, nostrils flaring, he looks every part the affronted party. Torn between disappointment and relief — because I've pushed him away for a reason, and not just because I'm frustrated and feeling scorned. Cole's no good for me on any level.

But his words, when they come, aren't angry. They're *taunting*. And he takes his sweet time delivering them. "You don't know what you're talking about, beautiful. And that's okay. You have a right to be pissed at me, because I live in a world of secrets and lies that, God help me, you'll never understand." For a second, I think he's going to stop there. When he starts again, his voice has changed. Shifted, like he's lost a tug-of-war, and his eyes glint in a new and thrilling way. "But when you say shit like that, it makes me want to put that mouth to work doing something more…satisfying."

Heat crawls up my neck, then down between my aching breasts and into my belly. Sucking him off is *not* a turn on. Stop it, body. You're fired from the What's Best for Hailey Committee. "Surely you can find someone else who doesn't object to you being completely amoral to give you a blow job. Like your *girlfriend*."

"Haven't you figured out yet that I don't want anyone else?" He shakes his head, clearly frustrated, and before I can process what he's saying, he's slamming even more at me, his words coming fast and furious now. "I want you. On your knees, your lips wrapped around my cock."

I gasp. "What the hell happened to *it was a mistake* and *this is nothing*?"

"Oh, it's still a mistake. But I was kidding myself about one taste being enough."

He has a girlfriend. And I'm not into threesomes. Plus he'd said *cock*, like that was something one just said in the foyer of the Kennedy Center. My cheeks are hot and I know that as soon as I open my mouth again, I'm going to be stammering.

But before I can react, before I can grab on to the shitastic pile of truth he just dumped between us, he makes an amused face, as if to say, *see? We're playing in different leagues, little girl*, and turns on his heel, quickly striding toward the Hall of Nations.

He's pulled back behind his curtain of lies. More to the point, he's had the last word.

"Get back here," I whisper, my voice stolen by white-hot rage. I literally feel tipped sideways, but this isn't over. I get to end it, I stubbornly insist in my head, even though it feels completely laughable at the moment.

I stare at his retreating back, righteous indignation coursing through my body. I want to run after him, leap on his back and pummel him about the head, but my heels preclude the running and the fact that we're very much not alone precludes the rest.

But we are so not done with this conversation,

so I follow. Slowly, but he knows I'm behind him. I can tell from the extra-square shoulders and the way he *isn't* looking around.

And it's not until he takes the sharp turn about ten feet in front of me that I realize this is a trap.

I slow. Eight feet. Six. If I turn that corner, he's waiting for me.

Two feet.

I take a deep breath, ready for whatever Cole has in mind, and step into an almost empty hallway. Definitely empty of Cole and his raging energy.

Spinning, I ignore the hurt slicing through my chest. He's playing a game with me, and it's not one I'm up for.

Trevor has our coat check tickets.

Maybe I don't need my coat. I step into a nook and pull out my phone. I'll just text him and beg off. Whatever. I don't care what he thinks, it's not like we're going to do this again.

I bump into the wall as I step back, but then the wall gives way in a smooth, swinging motion, because it's a door. Cole's on the other side, and he tugs me into the dimness of another concert hall.

Before I can protest or yell at him again, he has me pinned against the wall, his mouth on mine. Teeth clashing, tongues sparring, I pour as much anger into this kiss as he does. Maybe more, because I hate how good he tastes and how perfect his hands feel, one gripping my wrists and holding me against the wall. The other is tracing my collarbone, making my nipples tight from five inches away.

"I'm going to do a lot more than kiss you. Tell

me to back away and I will." He devours my mouth again, making every cell in my body pulse. I lazily consider the fact that he's not actually giving me a chance to tell him anything, but his tongue is like a magic wand that makes me wet and wanting. "But you don't need to. No one will ever know. It'll be our dirty little secret that I know how sweet you come on my hand."

I swallow a moan as Cole jerks the bodice of my dress down, freeing one of my breasts. He cups it from below, his thumb teasing at my nipple in a way that makes me want to beg for his mouth right there.

Another reason we can't do this—he could have me on my knees, desperate for scraps of his attention, with no effort at all. That's the stuff of fantasies and dirty books, not real life.

Can't do it *again*, I mean. Because Cole slapped a pause button on real life when he dragged me in here. We're definitely doing this. He's promised me an orgasm, and I want him to deliver.

And then I'll get on my knees for him, just this once.

six

Cole

I've jerked off to the fantasy of Hailey's tits more times than I can count over the last six months. She was wearing a V-neck t-shirt that first night I saw her, and a necklace that dropped straight to the top of her cleavage. Soft and sexy, they have captivated me ever since, and now I know what it feels like to have her flesh filling my hand. Fucking amazing.

I brace myself tight against her body, relishing the tension in her arms as she strains against me, her creamy skin dancing under the dim pot light above us. I wish we had time for me to explore every inch of her body with my tongue, from her delicate wrists to the soft dimples I imagine are at the base of her spine.

We don't. I can't. Her weenie-assed date is going to be looking for her soon, and I just got a 911 text from Wilson that one of our clients has been busted for a DUI. He has it in hand for now, but we need to meet back at the office soon to put together a statement.

Stolen moments, that's all we get. But I'm done thinking that Hailey and I can't happen. We just can't happen in a healthy, functional way.

Good news is, I do dysfunctional like a fucking pro.

"Cole," Hailey pants my name as I drag my mouth down her neck. "This is crazy."

It's insane. "Tell me to stop, then."

"Don't you dare stop." She sighs and arches her back as I latch onto her swollen nipple and suck her hard into my mouth. The taste of her and the way she jerks against my body drives me crazy. Her dress is soft velvet, and it folds easily in my fist as I pull the fabric up, baring her leg. She's wearing stockings attached to a garter belt, and as my fingers hit the pillowy skin at the top of her thighs, I curse the fact that I don't have a condom on me.

I took it out of my wallet, knowing it was the only way to keep myself from fucking her if given half a chance.

Hailey arching her hips into my eager hand definitely counts as a chance, and now I'm hating myself for not being ready for it.

I tease my finger under her garter, savoring the feel of her body bared to me. Her pussy is mere inches away, but as soon as I get there, it's going to be game over. I'll be lucky if I remember any of this beyond the animalistic memory of being inside her. Already I feel lightheaded and drunk on the delicate scent of her skin.

I've got a reputation as a tough guy. Ex-Navy SEAL, nothing fazes me. But if anyone wanted to undermine me, all they'd need to do is throw Hailey Reid in my tracks. This woman turns me into a simpering idiot. And if she'd have me, I'd give it all up and try to be a better man for her.

Like she knows I'm over-romanticizing this moment, she licks up my neck and sinks her teeth into my jaw. "Having second thoughts, tough guy?"

With a growl, I jerk my head down and capture

her smart mouth with mine. She tastes like champagne and innocence and warm, sexy woman. "Just trying to decide if I want you to come on my fingers or my face."

She whimpers at my words, pressing her face into my cheek even as her lips part and her tongue sneaks out to taste me again. I said them to be rough, to tip her sideways a bit in an effort to regain control over the situation, but it makes me hard as nails that dirty talk works for her.

Willing myself to hold my shit together—and remember to keep my dick in my pants—I slide my fingers up the garter to where the ribbon meets lace. Where her leg meets her hip in a crease I want to get up close and personal with, but we're in the back of a mostly dark concert hall and time is of the essence.

I find her pussy wet and swollen, and at the first slippery touch, all control disappears. I hike her leg up onto my hip, pressing hand between her hot, hungry cunt and my own hip as I rock my erection against her.

My hand is drenched, but I still start with one finger, gently easing into her. She's ready and willing, bucking against me, and I slide two in on the next thrust, cupping all of her wet heat in my palm. Her clit bumps against the heel of my hand as I finger her, slow and deep and hard, and with each surge her hitching breath gets more ragged.

Her hand curls around my neck, her grip alternating between tight and fluttery as she works against my body, and my dick is fucking begging me to be let loose. It would be so damn easy to lift her up a few inches, rip open my fly, and sink inside her. She's tight as fuck around my fingers, she'd milk my cock like nothing else I'd ever felt.

Literally, because it would be the first time I'd ever fucked someone without a rubber.

I need to get my cock away from the soft cradle of her thighs.

Swallowing her moaning protest with one last, rough kiss, I slide my fingers out from her lace panties, replacing that pressure on her clit with the iron rod in my pants—just for a minute, safely on the other side of thin suit pants. I can feel how wet she is against me, and I don't care that I'm going to smell like sex when we leave or that I'll need to head out the back exit. Fucking worth it to grind into her just once.

I bring my glistening fingers to our mouths, breaking our kiss just long enough to slide the taste of her over my tongue. She stares at me for a beat, her eyes wide and her chest heaving, and then her mouth crashes into mine, my hand barely getting out of the way in time. She groans into my mouth as I roll my hips and my tongue at the same time, sharing the taste of her.

In my thirty-one years, I've had a lot of sex. Dirty, vanilla, familiar, anonymous. I thought I'd experienced it all, but Hailey going nuts as I lick her wetness off my fingers? Hottest thing I've ever experienced.

As of this moment, my ill-considered arrangement with Penny needs to be drowned in the Potomac, because I've tasted beautiful and I'm not letting her go.

seven

Hailey

This is so much better and so much worse than I imagined it would be. My head is swimming and I ache for more of Cole—more of his mouth, his fingers, and that impressive erection I can feel between my legs.

I want that so much, I hurt.

"Fuck me, Cole," I beg, not caring that it's stupid. I want him to take me right here, hard against the wall, consequences be damned.

"Can't." He kisses down my neck, although *kiss* is a strangely polite word for the way his mouth is devouring my skin. "You're going to come on my face, beautiful. And you've got to do it fast."

Before I can protest, he drops to his knees and lifts my left leg over his shoulder. I slam my hands back against the wall, a futile effort to brace myself for the onslaught of sensations.

I'm expecting hard and fast.

I get slow and lazy, and it's so much better.

It's like he can bend time to his will, because the world ceases around us. It's just the two of us at the back of an empty concert hall, me pressed against the wall, Cole between my legs. His tongue licking me like an ice cream cone, and his hand...

Oh god.

Cole's fingers are heading up the back of my thigh, toward my ass. I arch away from them, because my ass is not my best feature. His hands should be on my boobs, or my calves. I have very nice calves. Curvy, long, and delicate at the ankle. Very little about me can be described as delicate so I take extra pride in how nice my ankles are.

As if he knows I've gone into my head a bit, Cole sucks on my clit hard, and that works. I moan and sink into his mouth a bit, relaxing.

And that's when he slides his fingers between my rear cheeks, just a tease. My face burns because I'm mortified, but it also…

"You feel amazing," he murmurs against my thigh, pressing a kiss there before covering my sex with his mouth again. This time it's the hard and fast I expected, and I lose my mind. The most beautiful pressure ever builds in my lower belly, and I stop feeling embarrassed about how good Cole's fingers feel as they stroke all the nerve endings between my pussy and my ass. I don't care that his face is wet because of how wet I am, or that I'm panting and whimpering like an idiot as he tongues me to a crashing orgasm.

I blank for a second, a moment of bliss after Cole pushes me into a sensational free fall, and then it's this pulsing that seems to have no end, like a perpetual motion machine in my womb, each throb rubbing those nerve endings in just the right way all over again.

In the aftermath, as my pussy clenches at the empty air, and the spots clear from my vision, as Cole presses the top of his head to my belly and uses his pocket square to clean me up before setting my panties back into place…in that moment, I think about inviting him back to my place.

A stupid thought. I push it away as readily as it

comes, and I tell myself to keep it meaningless. He's good at sex. So what. I can give him a blow job that would make his head explode, and we'll be even.

I'll get right on that, as soon as all the nerves in my body stop firing off at random, sparkly intervals. It's like there are a million fairies gallivanting through my body having a freaking May Day celebration.

I close my eyes and take a deep breath as Cole settles my skirt back to the floor and rises in front of me. I don't want to look at him, although I can't quite figure out why. It's not that I don't want him still. I do.

I reach for him, my eyes still closed. He braces his arms on either side of my head and kisses me, long and slow and deep, as I slide my hand against the front of his pants, up and down his straining cock.

"Open your eyes, Hailey."

I shake my head.

"I have to go."

Damn. My eyes fly open. It's bad form to beg to suck cock, right? "But you—"

"I'm a big boy. I'll be fine."

"I don't mind," I whisper, gripping him tighter. "I mean, I want to return the favor. You made me feel so good, it's your turn."

He presses his hips into my hand and kisses me again. This brush of his lips has a painful taste of finality. "I mind. When you suck my cock, it's going to be in private."

When.

Holy shit.

"Go find your date and get home safely." His words roll over me like gravel. We're both here on dates with other people. And just like that, the spell is broken.

"Right." I stare at a spot over his shoulder as I squeeze my hands together, wondering where the hell I dropped my purse. "Excuse me."

"Hailey." He says my name like it's the start of a bigger statement, but no further words come. That's just fine. There aren't any words that can excuse participating in cheating.

"Go find your date." I repeat his words back to him, but where his were accidentally rough, mine are deliberately sharp.

He grips my jaw, turning my face toward his. "She's nothing to me."

"She's your *girlfriend*, Cole. Your word, not mine."

"Not anymore."

"I'm not sure she knows that."

"She won't care."

"That's…weird. And *I* don't care."

"No lies between us, beautiful."

I stare at him. At his gorgeous face, the hard lines and piercing gaze. There are so many lies between us already. "Except about your work, right?"

Tension crackles between us. After a beat, he steps back, releasing me. It's like we didn't just share a spectacularly intimate moment. I'm frosty, he's pissed…order has been restored to the universe, and I'm alone again.

Nothing new.

But for the first time, I'm not sure that solitude

is better. Cole has the same drama spilling around him that my family does, but walking away from him? A million times harder.

I still do it, though. I'm not an idiot.

— —

I tell myself to stop thinking about Cole's fingers inside me. His steely gaze piercing my soul as he watches me come undone for him. His taunting words sliding under my skin as I rail against him. My hate should push him away, but it just seems to turn him on, like I'm a challenge he can conquer.

I don't like to think about how easily that's proven true. So I need to move on.

It's been a week. I can still taste myself on his lips. That's hardly progress.

I make lists of all the reasons I should never see him again. For one thing, I'm Georgetown and he's Dupont Circle. Actually, more the scuzzy K Street type. Even before the fifty shades of moral gray area behavior, we're already two very different people.

And there was the girlfriend, or whatever Penny was to him. Some kind of complicated relationship I can't wrap my head around.

The murder cover-up.

How bossy he is.

But that just leads to a pros list, because he might be bossy in the bedroom.

And he seems to like how soft I am, all over, and my gigantic boobs.

Plus, no matter how hard he drives against my

69

body, how firmly he grips my wrists as he pins me in place and rips pleasure from my body, I know he'd never hurt or embarrass me.

But he'll always be an enigma, and orgasms — even earth-shattering ones — can't make up for secrets and lies.

As if the mere thought of amoral behavior is like a Bat signal for my older sister, my phone pings at me. An email from Taylor.

I stare at the screen for a minute. The subject line is blank because she knows if she gives the topic away, I'm less likely to click. Ha. Joke's on her. I'm not going to click anyway.

I'm not going to delete it. It'll sit there, forever, a little bolded electronic line to remind me of how far we've drifted apart. We've never been close, not like the relationship I have with Alison, but this is my big sister. Up until high school, she was my closest friend, by virtue of sharing a playroom.

We definitely don't share a playroom anymore. Sometimes it feels like we're not even playing in the same arena.

I tuck my phone back in my purse, slap on a baseball hat and oversized sunglasses, and head for the Metro station. There haven't been any photographers bothering me in weeks, but covering up is a better-safe-than-sorry plan.

It was good to get back to work this week, and today Taryn and I are going out for sushi at lunch to celebrate my return to normalcy — all I have to do is pretend my scandal-loving sibling doesn't want to talk to me for some reason.

At the staff meeting, Ellen announces that the budget looks like it might have room for a new hire in the summer. She doesn't look at me, but Taryn does, and I bite my lip to keep from grinning. I'd be thrilled to keep working at the employment agency after my internship is over.

I'm floating on a cloud as we head for lunch, but it doesn't last long, because Alison texts me as we arrive at the restaurant. I shoo Taryn inside and take a deep breath before reading the message. **Did you get Taylor's email? Family meeting tonight.**

I feel a momentary stab of guilt over the tentative way my siblings tiptoe around contacting me. On the other hand...I did *see* Taylor's email and I didn't open it. So there's some responsibility for the dysfunction sitting on my shoulders. That uncomfortable fact isn't easily shook off. **Haven't read it yet. Probably can't make it.**

Alison calls me next. I take a deep breath before answering on the third ring. "Hey. I'm on my way into lunch, so..."

"Don't *hey* me." For a nineteen-year-old, my baby sister is such an old soul. A little mother, always has been. A refreshing change since our actual mother never cared for that role. "This is important."

"I don't care. I know that makes me an awful person, but I just don't."

She sighs. "*Vanity Fair* wants to do an article on Taylor."

"Yep, don't care."

She keeps going. "The article is about Washington as the new New York for young adults of privilege, some bullshit like that, and Taylor's lawyer thinks it would be good if we all cooperate."

71

Because my straight A's baby sister, nose-to-the-grindstone brother, and my own track record of actually working for a living would make our oldest sister look like something less than the horrid slut she actually is.

How I hate that word. Hate myself for using it. But she wears it like a badge of honor, brassing out the media coverage of her indiscrete blow job as if it were any other party girl oops. Would have been less of a big deal if the pants she'd snaked her tongue into hadn't belonged to the Vice-President of the United States.

"You guys can do it without me. Tell the reporter I'm a massive bitch."

"You're not…" Her voice drops to a quiet plead. "Come on, Hailey. There's no downside to it for us, just an interview. And if it helps show Taylor as a normal girl who was taken advantage of…"

"Alison, you're barely old enough to even know about what Taylor did, but we both know she *wasn't* the victim. I mean, there wasn't a victim. She had an affair with a married man. A *famous* married man. Let her wear that."

My baby sister doesn't answer, and for a second, I think maybe she's hung up on me. She's quiet, in general, but she has a decent bite when she wants to dole it out. "Go have lunch," she finally says. "We can talk about this later."

"Except I'm busy later, rememb—" I huff out a breath as she disconnects the call on me. This isn't over, I know that, but I shake it off. Crispy spicy salmon rolls are calling my name.

One giggly hour later, I'm back at work and

Ellen has left a note on my desk to come in and see her. Taryn gives me a thumbs up as I swipe on fresh lip gloss and brush my hair. Ellen doesn't care, but I do. It's about being professional.

She waves me in before I even knock. "How was lunch?"

"Delicious." I smile. "You wanted to see me?"

"Have a seat." She launches into some nice things, then pauses and crosses her hands. "I hope you'll apply for the job in the summer."

"I will." I press my thumbs into the palms of my hands, two sharp anchors in reality. *Be cool, Hailey*.

"And hopefully there won't be any more drama between now and then, right?" She smiles, but all of a sudden, I'm less enthusiastic. It could be nothing. People say things with smiles on their faces, right? And don't mean anything by it? I'm talking about normal people.

Because *my* people don't. Not my people by choice, but the ones I'm genetically connected to — and fatally attracted to. Those people lie through their teeth as often as they order martinis and put on suits. All with a smile and a *trust me* glint in their eye.

I smile again, more weakly now. "Would it help if I change my name?"

She laughs, then stops and stares at me. Then laughs again, tipping her head back. "Oh, Hailey."

I don't know how to take that. "I would. If it would help."

"Hailey, your last name is as common as apple pie at a Fourth of July picnic. Don't worry about it."

But I do, all afternoon. I worry about it so much that I forget about the stupid family meeting, because I'm so focused on separating myself permanently from said family that it drops from my mind completely that they're trying to suck me back into their drama.

It all slams back into me as I step outside at the end of the day and find Cole waiting for me, leaning back against his giant black SUV like he owns the street. He's big and scary looking, tall and tough and dressed to impress, but no amount of silk suiting can contain his badass self.

I stomp up to him and prop my hands on my hips. "Oh for fuck's sake."

"Excuse me?" He smirks and leans in close. "Nice to see you again, beautiful."

"No, it's not nice. It's awful. Why are you here?"

"Would you believe me if I said I want to take you for dinner?"

"Not even a little bit, unless dinner is at my parents' estate."

He shrugged. "I hear they're serving salmon."

"I'm not going."

He makes a regretful face. "Ah, but you are."

Blood rushes through my ears like the Pacific surf slamming against the beach at dawn. "You did not just threaten to kidnap me *against my will*."

He laughs. "All the magic words there. Got it. No, I didn't threaten you."

"Good. I'm going home."

I've barely turned before he loops his hand around my upper arm and spins me against the truck as people walk by. He leans over me, looking every bit the part of the adoring boyfriend I'm sure —I know he's just doing it to hide my face, a weird protective reaction that doesn't mean anything. He nuzzles my neck and I concentrate on how much I hate the game playing. And him.

I need to keep reminding myself of that fact.

"I hate you," I whisper, because saying it might make it true.

"No you don't," he mutters against my ear. "Because I'm going to take you to this family meeting, but I'll also get you out of there as quick as I can. Promise."

"I don't want to go."

"We don't always get what we want." He says it so authentically, for a second I think he's on the same page as me, wishing this was a real embrace, but he glances around—we're alone on the street again—then shoves away from the car and slides his hands into his pockets. He gives me a cold, dismissive look. "Now get your ass in the car."

"This isn't going to go well, I'm warning you." I'm ramping up fast now, and I'm not sure if it's the rejection I'm feeling or my general frustration about the situation. "This is beyond the pale, Mr. Parker. Seriously, fucking off-side move."

His eyes glitter like smoky quartz set in chiseled granite. "Just doing my job, *Ms. Reid*."

"Don't say my name like that."

"You're the one who brought back the formal address."

"You're the one who's acting like a prick."

"You have a potty mouth."

"Excuse me? *A potty mouth?*"

"It's true."

"So I swear. It's the twenty-first century, women are allowed to do that."

"Allowed? Yes." His gaze drops to my mouth. "I didn't say I had a problem with it."

"Then what's with the commentary?"

He barks out a cold laugh. "You're such a good girl. I didn't expect you to have a filthy mouth."

"Maybe your expectations were all wrong." And maybe mine were, too. Because the way he's looking at me…it's anything but cold. But as quick as I see that flash of heat, it's smothered again.

He swears under his breath.

"Now who has a potty mouth?"

"Come on. The sooner we finish this up, the better."

"Why?"

"Hailey." That's it. He just says my name without any inflection or implied further statement. What the hell am I supposed to do with that?

"Cole." I say his name loaded with meaning. Cole, you're inscrutable and don't think for a second that's a good thing. Cole, stop dancing around the issue. Cole, please finger-bang me again, I really liked that.

He laughs again, his voice strained now. "That's why. Get in the car."

—eight—

Cole

Hailey's glowering at me from across the sitting room, probably wondering if I'll notice if she tries to escape.

I will. A dark, hungry part of my soul leaps at the idea of prowling after her, caging her against a window just before she tries to climb out. Licking my way down her neck and under that blue blouse she's wearing. She looks like a sexy librarian.

A pissed off, sexy librarian, because we still haven't gotten to the meeting part of the evening. Her father is drinking port and watching Taylor hit on Tag. I don't like the gleam in his eye, because I know he doesn't like Tag, so that's some fucked up shit if he's enjoying whatever game Taylor's playing there. Of course, it's not a hard leap for me to make to think the man's a pervert. I don't like anything about Morgan Reid, or our dealings with this family, except for Hailey, who doesn't belong.

Dinner was stilted, awkward and fake. I don't blame her for not wanting any part of this world. I'm used to the passive aggressive layers of this social class, but it's different with her here. I'm not used to being judged for merely being in their presence.

She may have been born with a silver spoon in her mouth, but Hailey's shucked the trappings of her wealthy upraising. Tonight she's wearing knee-high brown leather boots, tights and a jean skirt that had me taking notice of her legs as soon as she walked out of work. A button down shirt makes it a work outfit, just barely, and the lace top of her cami underneath makes me think of all the ways I want to get her naked.

She's got curves that just won't quit, and now I know how fucking sweet and soft she is under those layers. I have this fantasy of her, naked in my bed, clutching a sheet in front of her as she yells at me. Her hair tumbles down around her breasts and her eyes will do that thing where they turn to emeralds when she's pissed off.

Maybe I could drag her to a back hallway somewhere in this palace and tell her how her black and white view on the world is ten kinds of fucked up. That there's no good and bad, just bad and worse. She'd yell at me at the same time as she arches her pussy into my hand, hating how wet she gets when we fight.

I'm a fucking asshole for wanting to needle her, make her spitting mad, then slide my hand between her legs and get her off. And I don't really want to do that, because she actually is good, the exception that proves the rule. Beautiful and innocent, and I want her to stay like that for the rest of her life. She can't see what I see, it'll break her heart.

One of the hardest adjustments for me in moving from the military to the private sector was adjusting to clients like Morgan Reid. If Jason didn't have his own agenda, I'd never have taken him on as a client.

If Jason didn't do what he did, I wouldn't be in this line of work. I'd be on a beach somewhere, teaching Hailey how to surf and making love to her in an outdoor shower.

But in the hierarchy of what really matters, my base urges don't rank anywhere near international security.

I shutter my filthy thoughts as she makes her way around the room. By the time she's in front of me, I'm back to the cold motherfucker she's used to. I give her a feral smile, because the best defense is a good offense.

"Why are you smiling?" she asks, rightfully suspicious.

"Thinking of ways I can torture kittens," I mutter under my breath, keeping my eyes on her sister as she talks to Tag on the other side of the room. The last thing I need to see is Hailey blushing if she gets it—or the adorable frown between her eyebrows if she doesn't.

"I'm not surprised." A long pause, then she sucks in her breath. There it is. "Wait, was that a pussy reference? Do you want to fuck my sister? Because that's disgusting. Which I guess would be par for the course for you."

Fuck. There's a part of me that wants to leave it at that, but her voice catches on the idea that someone would prefer Taylor—with the fake boobs, fake laugh and fake food, no calories please —to Hailey's depth and sexy-as-hell natural beauty.

"I wasn't thinking about your sister. Not now, not ever."

"Then..." She trails off, and I glance sideways at her, unable to resist. Her cheeks are in fact pink, her lips slightly parted, and I'm totally screwed.

I turn toward her and drop my voice, ensuring

that my words are for her ears only. "Your pussy is the only one I want to devour. I want to lick you up and make you scream. Have you come all over my face and then drive my cock so deep you'll feel me for a week."

"That doesn't sound like torture," she whispers.

"My plans always have a way of going off the rails around you. But if you want me to, I could bend you over that wingback chair, slide my hand up the back of your thighs and tease you while your family drones on about meaningless bullshit. Make you wet and aching, and leave you like that until I take you home."

She gasps, her lips dropping into a perfect 'O', making my nuts ache and my dick throb at the promise of her sucking me into her hot little mouth. A promise she didn't make, I need to remind myself. Even though we've shared a kiss and I've gotten her off, most of the time she doesn't like me.

With good reason, because I'm about to tell her she should do something she really doesn't want to do—put herself out there, give up some of her privacy, and all for her family, who don't seem like they'd do shit-fuck-all for her.

I'm not a nice man. I don't deserve to have her mouth anywhere near my dick, that's for damn sure.

As if we've arrived at the same conclusion at the same time, she tightens her face into a smooth mask that would rival a Kennedy and steps away from me. "No, I don't think that would be a good idea."

No fucking shit. "And yet you're going to let

80

me drive you home."

"Do you still have a girlfriend?"

Regret pangs through my chest at the memory of hurting her like that. "That relationship—and I use that word loosely—has been terminated."

"Because of me?" She asks the question quietly, face still blank, but her lips are a bit darker. Her eyes a bit wider. Just enough that I think, she has no clue how much she affects me. She's full of hope, has no clue, and I'm a fucking asshole for playing with her heart.

"Yeah."

She stares straight ahead and slowly bites her lower lip. And I get a fucking hard-on again. "Then maybe you can take me home," she drawls with unexpected sass. "If you're a good boy and get me out of here quickly."

I clear my throat and step into the center of the room. "Shall we talk about why we're all here tonight?"

— nine —

Hailey

I'm a complete idiot. It's like my panties just take themselves off as soon as Cole wanders past and whispers something filthy in my ear.

Good girl rule number one: distance yourself from the family without morals.

Good girl rule number two: don't take your panties off for someone who will sell you down the river for a pay check.

Technically speaking, I haven't actually taken them *off* for Cole yet, he just shoved them aside last week. And ground against them before that. And made them wet tonight.

Holy crap, I need to stop thinking about Cole and my underwear, because he's currently outlining a plan that is the complete opposite of what I want.

"The focus of the article shouldn't be Taylor, or any other partier. Let's sell the reporter on Alison and Hailey," he says, repeating the suggestion that has me steaming mad. He blithely ignores the daggers I'm shooting his direction with my eyes. "Get some good press for the family for a change."

Ali gives me a nervous look, because she knows I won't go for it. I won't. I absolutely, under no circumstances…

Cole turns and pins me with a hard look. His dark amber eyes say a lot of things, including *trust me* and *I've had my mouth on your pussy, stop looking at me like I'm evil.*

83

Evil might be too strong a word, but he's not the type of guy I ever thought I'd find myself falling for. Because I can't trust him, and like he knows it, he narrows his eyes and spins back to the group. "Fine, Alison and Morgan Junior, maybe."

At the loss of his gaze, I feel bereft, and for a foolish minute I consider standing up and pledging that I'll do the interview after all.

"No, that's not interesting in the least," my mother says from the corner. Nobody else reacts, not even Morgan, which makes my heart break a little. Cold slithers up my back as she continues, not looking at my brother. "Of course Hailey will do it. It might even give that charity she works for some visibility."

I know she's doing it on purpose, but I still snap back. "It's not a charity. It's an employment agency. And there's no *of course* about it. My life isn't for public consumption, in the first place, and it's not that interesting, in the second place."

"You're such an ungrateful brat," Taylor whines, and I want to slap her.

"There's a difference between being ungrateful, and refusing to be forced to *be* grateful. I pay my own rent, I buy my own groceries. I put up with this bullshit—"

"Language, Hailey." Like my mother doesn't swear. Except she doesn't. I sigh. "Think of what will make your grandfather happy, perhaps?"

He'd have been happy if you hadn't gotten knocked up twenty-six years ago, I think to myself. But she's not wrong. My maternal grandfather, who paid for my university tuition and has never asked for anything in return, would tell me this is a

84

moment to be selfless and the only cost would be momentary discomfort.

And maybe it would get them off my back for a while. A girl could dream.

"Fine. One interview. Not here, they can come to my apartment or meet me at Starbucks." My voice is strained as I agree, and I can feel Cole looking at me. Screw him.

And just to show him that I'm fine with the moral gray area, I might just do that.

A meaningless fuck with a bad boy.

Watch out, world. Hailey Reid is turning over a new leaf, and it's going to be good and dirty.

As the conversation swirls into the nitty gritty details—the "talking points", Tag calls them—my attention turns to the specific bad boy I have in mind. The only bad boy who's ever caught my eye. Why does he have to be on my father's payroll?

He doesn't seem to notice my observation of him, but when he pulls his vibrating phone from his pocket and excuses himself into the hallway, I decide to follow.

I give him a head start, which is stupid, because I'm not stealthy in the least—Taylor smirks at me as I excuse myself like she knows I'm going to play slap and tickle with the butler. I narrow my eyes and throw a silent *fuck you* in her direction.

It's also stupid because now I can't find him. I grew up in this house, but it's massive and I can't guess at where he's gone. There are four bathrooms on this floor alone, but if he wanted privacy, he might have headed upstairs or to the library.

I take a wild guess at the last option and head

in that direction, but I don't get that far. I find him standing outside the door to my father's home office. He's got his phone in hand, but something isn't quite right.

"Hi," I say quietly, not sure how I feel about... any of this. The evening. Following Cole and finding him here, quietly not doing whatever it was that he seemed to excuse himself to do.

"Ready to go home?" he asks, cold and distant again, and that's okay. I'm used to this fire and ice routine now. That's probably the first sign of Stockholm syndrome setting in.

"Soon, yes." I hesitate, then ask the question that's on my mind because other than a guilty one-night stand, what do I have to lose? "What are you doing here?"

"I got a call."

"You weren't on the phone."

Ice turns to granite. "You ask a lot of questions."

It's the kind of answer that bad guys give in movies, and a frisson of fear skitters through my body. I'm not afraid of Cole, but I am suddenly afraid of whatever is going on, because nothing seems quite right. Cole's not a natural PR guy, not really. His edge is too sharp, his world-view too rigid, even when he pretends it's not.

All of a sudden, I'm *sure* something is going on, and I don't like it.

I excuse myself to freshen up, scurrying off before he can read anything into my expression, and when I return to the sitting room, I'm settled and more calm on the outside.

I keep the rest of my questions for when we're

86

in the car, heading back into the city. But as we drive through the night, they all spill onto my tongue and over my lips. "What's really going on?"

"What?" He glances my way, reading my face. What does it show him? Doubt? Distrust?

I take a deep breath. "You don't kiss like a sleazy lawyer."

His lips twitch against his bland mask. "Maybe because I'm not a lawyer."

"You're not sleazy, either."

His lips turn down at that. "Don't, Hailey."

"Don't what?"

"Don't turn me into a white knight. I'm not a good guy."

"You used to be."

"Not really." He sighs. "Even the good guys do bad things for good reasons."

"Like what?"

He laughs, rough and hollow. "That's classified."

"Just how much of a bad guy is my father?"

"Don't go there."

"That sounds vaguely like 'Don't worry your pretty little head about it.'"

"Well, your head is quite pretty. And I don't want you to worry."

I let out an exasperated groan. "It's not like I'm going to say anything to him. I'm not —"

He sighs, interrupting me. His next words come out a weird mix of a command and a request, like he's trying to be polite and failing. "Let it go."

"You were in his office tonight."

"That's not letting it go."

"You're a lousy spy."

This time his laugh is warmer. "I'm not a spy."

"I bet that's what all the spies say."

"Probably."

So Cole's not just a Washington fixer. Maybe this is why they can charge so much money for "PR expertise", because they're all secretly spooks and assassins.

On the one hand, that's ridiculous. But for a second, I think, oh God, I made out with an assassin.

I let him go down on me. And enjoyed it.

If given half a chance, I'd probably give this assassin a blowjob because I can't stop thinking about how big his cock felt and what it might look like. Did he have a tattoo of a sniper rifle on it or something freaky like that.

The James Bond fantasies were piling up like crazy. I needed to put a lid on them, but Cole scaling a building...Cole in hand-to-hand combat...Cole jumping out of a plane...

"Jesus, Hailey, what part of our conversation put that look on your face?" Cole roughly jerks the vehicle around a corner and accelerates out of the turn. He slides his hand over my knee, tugging my legs apart.

"I don't have a *look* on my face," I whisper, but my cheeks are hot and my lips are wet, because I just licked them, and Cole's staring at me like he's remembering our conversation at the Kennedy Center. I know I am.

I lick them again.

"I'm not a good guy," he repeats, rubbing his fingers up the inside of my thigh. A searing brand I readily accept, because his touch sparks me like

88

nothing else ever has.

"I don't think I care." My words are breathy, desperate. I don't sound like myself at all. I don't care about that, either.

"You should."

Another turn, another hot press of his fingers against my leg. Another brain cell gives up the fight. Ha. I'm not fighting this. I want this more than my next breath.

As soon as he parks in front of my apartment building and puts his SUV in park, before I even have my seat belt undone, his hands are in my hair and his mouth is all over mine.

"I'm not a spy, you silly girl. But it's complicated," he rasps as he pulls away from a long, slow, deep kiss that leaves me breathless and aching for more. "It doesn't have anything to do with how much I want you. I'm not going to hurt you."

I laugh. "Sure you will. Don't lie to me to get in my pants."

He strokes his thumb over my cheekbone, his gaze hard and piercing as he parses my words. A nervous, guilty weight tugs in my chest, because I'm asking him for something that's so far outside my realm of experience, it's possible that it's just not done. *Hey, dangerous man. Wanna use each other for the night?*

But it never takes Cole long to read a situation, I've learned, even when the situation is made up and in my head.

He squeezes the back of my neck, harder than I expect. Harder than is polite.

It makes me moan, and his eyes go dark. "Fine.

This isn't going to end well. And it's not your pants I want to get into, but your hot, tight, sweet-as-fuck pussy. I've had my fingers inside you. You clench so tight, beautiful. You've got such a hungry little cunt, it's gorgeous. And it tastes like the best kind of sin. Is that what you want me to say?"

I don't answer him. I don't have to. He's on top of me again, pressing me back against the passenger door, licking his way into my mouth. He's still stroking my cheek with his thumb, and his fingers curled almost painfully around the nape of my neck. The combination is intense and I want more of that.

"Yes," I gasp, pulling at his jacket. "Say it. Do it."

"Dirty girl," he mutters, rocking his other hand against my tights-covered clit. "Let's get you inside, then. Inside and on your knees. You owe my cock a long, wet kiss."

— ten —

Hailey

Cole keeps one hand on my hip or the small of my back all the way up to my apartment. He opened the front door for me, because of course he knows the code, but when he pulls out his keys, and I realize he has *a key* to my apartment, that I *did not* give him, I open my mouth to give him an earful.

Before I can get even a single word out, he's kissing me, hot and hard. And I'm kissing him back, because he tastes like man and mint and power. But then I bite his lower lip, because invasion of privacy and principles.

The conflict annoys me. That he's not kissing me anymore annoys me, and that he's laughing at me, his eyes raking down my body like he's already got me naked and spread wide for him...that annoys me, too. And turns me on.

"Cole!" I shove against his body. He doesn't move, but he does take off his jacket. I'm a complete idiot. It's like my panties just take themselves off as soon as Cole wanders past and whispers something filthy in my ear.

"Get naked, beautiful." He grins at me, another wolfish look that melts my insides, and peels off his tie.

I take off my coat, then cross my arms in front of my body. "You just let yourself into my apartment."

"Your ass was in my hand and your mouth is

bruised from my kisses. I assumed I had your permission to enter."

"You had permission to enter after *I* opened the door. And invited you in."

"An invitation is for coffee or a fucking board game, Hailey. I have a key, I used it. It was the fastest way to get my cock inside you. Which, by the way, needs to happen now. On your knees." His hands go to his belt, and my womb tugs. My fucking womb. What the hell.

I lift up a hand. "Hold on, I think we need to establish some boundaries. You can't have a key to my apartment."

"If you let me keep it, I'll wake you up with my tongue between your legs."

Yes please. I can feel myself get wet at the mere thought, and I press my legs together in weak resistance. "Do you know how crazy that sounds?"

"Fine." He pulls his keys from his pocket, stalking toward me as he strips one from the silver ring. He tucks it into the pocket on my jean skirt, then hooks his fingers into my waistband and slams our bodies together. "You make me crazy. I don't need a fucking key. I can pick your lock anytime I want a taste of your pussy, but tell me more about these boundaries you want to erect between us."

He tips my head to the side and blazes a hot, wet trail with his mouth down my neck. His fingers go to work on the buttons of my shirt, and I can't think clearly. I want his thumbs on my nipples and his thigh between my legs, and I don't have to ask. As soon as he gets a few buttons open, he's teasing me through the lace of my bra, working me like a fine guitar as he grinds me against the door we've

92

just come through. We fit together like the most fucked-up puzzle pieces, but maybe that's the point.

Maybe I'm fucked up, and Cole is just what I need to not feel so completely alone.

I wrap my arms around his neck and imagine for a second he might just take me right here. But I'm wearing tights, and boots, and there's nothing sexy about a chubby girl peeling herself out of spandex and leather.

"Hey..." I sigh as his mouth makes its way past my collarbone, raising goosebumps across the sensitive skin of my chest. "I'm going to get more comfortable, hang on."

"Is that girl code for give yourself time to talk yourself out of this?" Cole opens his mouth, covering my nipple through the bra, and only sort-of gently scrapes his teeth over my flesh.

"Promise it's not," I whisper.

He steps back and waves his hand as if to say, *go do your thing.*

I scurry to my bedroom and flip on the lamp, grateful for it's attractive-making glow. Kicking off my boots and tights, I shove them and the small pile of laundry in the corner all into my closet. My bed is made, check, and I double check I've got a box of condoms in my bedside table. Wishful thinking finally pays off.

I stare at myself in the mirror on the back of my door. My hair is mussed up, my lips are swollen, and my shirt is hanging open. I'm a hot mess, but...it's kind of sexy. I grin at myself, do up two buttons to try and make the most of my curves. I think about taking off the skirt, but it's better that Cole not see the full extent of my thighs until after we've had sex.

Plus I'm cute.

You're cute, I mouth at myself in the mirror.

The chubby chick stares back, not quite believing me.

You give Cole Parker a hard-on.

That works. She flashes the world's biggest smile back at me.

Stepping back into the living room, I find Cole bent over my knitting basket. "What is it with you guys? Wilson had a million questions about my knitting when you made him babysit me that day."

He shrugs as he turns, and I almost miss it.

Almost.

My blood runs cold. "Cole?"

"Come here." His voice is rough. Distracting.

Almost. "What's in your pocket?"

"Nothing."

"Tell me something about knitting."

He stalks toward me, and I know he's going to change the subject to sex.

"You can't distract me with your tongue. Stop it."

"I can, and I will." He stops a few feet short and looks at me from head to toe and back up again. "Look at you. Jesus. It's a fucking miracle I didn't fuck you that first night."

"I bet you say that to all the girls you bug."

"It wasn't a bug, and I really don't." He laughs. "Do you want me to tell you about all the women I fuck and how none of them get under my skin the way you do, in your jean skirt and white bra peeking out like that?"

"What was it then?" I'm ignoring the part where he says I get under his skin. I know all about that, the strange hold someone can have on a heart and soul and how unnerving it is.

"Nothing."

I make a harsh buzzing noise. "Wrong answer."

"When Wilson was here that day, you probably couldn't stop talking about your knitting, right? I bet you curled up right there in front of the basket and talked his ear off about it for an hour."

I flush. "He was asking me a million questions!"

"He probably panicked. Fucking amateur. I'll kick his ass for that." Cole pulls out something that looks like a webcam from his pocket. "He was looking for an opportunity to take this back."

It's official, I'm not getting laid tonight. I sigh, surprised I'm not more pissed. I mean, I'm plenty mad, but now it's mostly frustrated disappointment. "Seriously, Cole? Get out."

"I'm not hiding it from you."

A hysterical edge takes hold of my laugh. "Oh my god, like that makes it okay. You bugged my apartment. You bugged my apartment? What the hell?"

"For your security."

"You cut a key for yourself."

"I gave it back."

I dig in my pocket, and pull out...not my key. The silver shape is too long, and it's got the wrong number of bumps. I glare at Cole, who just shrugs.

"Okay, so I didn't give it back. But that's the key to my apartment. In case you ever need it."

He lied to me. He's always going to lie to me. I

want this man more than my next breath, but I can't trust him. I stare at him, my vision growing dark around the edges.

"Hailey, you need to breathe."

I suck in an angry draw of air, then let my words fly. "I don't need it. I'll never need it. That's not my world! And I don't know where you live! This is beyond fucked up."

He starts to say something, but I storm past him. I don't get very far. He grabs me by the waist and hauls me into his body, my back to his front. His arms around my waist. His mouth against my ear. "Beautiful. I'm not a good guy. Right? You know that. But I'm not going to hurt you. And someday, you might need me for more than this. No matter what, you can always come to me."

I shake my head, not wanting to process what he's saying. It's crazy.

"If we met at a different time and place, I'd want you to teach me how to be good. Because you're so good it makes me wish I had a heart. For you, I'd try to be an average man, with feelings and everything."

But that's not going to happen. He's right. It doesn't matter. All we have is the raging heat between us—and right now, hearing him promise shit I'll never get, there's an extra dose of rage in me. Luckily, we don't need to like each other to satisfy our physical hunger.

"Shut up," I say, struggling in his arms. "Shut up! Stop being so calm and distant."

He grinds his erection into my ass at the same time as he slides his hand inside my shirt. "Does this feel distant? I'm here, Hailey. Bad idea and everything, I'm here to screw you because it's what you need. I'm calm because I'm trained to not give a fuck. Sorry, babe, that's just how I am."

His words and his actions don't match up. He's holding on so tight, but touching me so gently. He might be trained not to give a fuck, but I'm not the only one who needs this. A tear slides between my eyelids, burning my face, and I shake my head. No. I'm not going to be sad. I'm going to be sexy and brave and selfish.

Because I want him, however I can get it. And maybe it's for the best if he slides out of my life once tonight is over.

I wrench myself out of his arms and twist around, my fingers feverishly working at the buttons on my shirt. Undoing them, for him. For his hungry, dark gaze. For the way he stalks toward me, backing me into my bedroom.

He pulls a gun from a holster on the back of his dress pants and clunks it down on my bedside table. Then he strips off his own shirt, and I take in the sight of his big, broad chest. His rippling shoulder muscles, one covered in faded ink, the other decorated with more horrifying scar tissue. I gasp and fly to him, touching him there, and he mutters into my hair, something about shit I don't need to worry about. God.

My breath is ragged and harsh as he kisses me, slowly stripping both of us of the rest of our clothes as we sink into a bittersweet exchange of unspoken wishes.

For everything to be different.

For this night to last forever.

For me to not be quite so painfully innocent, or

Cole to be so brutally cold. Maybe we could meet in the middle if I wasn't such a Pollyanna, or if he didn't carry two—no, three guns. Jesus. I stare at the collection growing on my bedside table and wonder just what the hell he was armed for when he went to my parents' estate.

With me.

He curves around my back, shoving my torso forward onto my bed.

"Such a princess, with a big tall bed like this," he mutters, his hands skimming down the line of my back to my ass. "Just the right height for a bad man to bend you over and fuck you hard."

"Do it," I urge, pressing into his touch.

"Is that what you want, beautiful princess? For the bad man to just do what you say?" Cole trails his fingers lower as he taunts me, finding me wet and ready for him. "I don't think so. And frankly? I don't care."

"What are you going to do?" I ask this breathlessly, because I'm game for anything. Anticipation skitters beneath my skin, heating me from the inside out. I arch my back, shamelessly presenting myself. "Are you gonna spank me, bad man?"

Cole groans and smooths a palm over my ass while the other hand still strokes my pussy ever so gently. "That's a good idea."

My breath slows, or maybe I hold it, as he nudges my legs further apart. He rocks against me, his own inhales not as steady and *calm* as I'm sure he'd like them to be. I like that. I raise up on my tiptoes, giving him more of me. I'm slippery now, sloppy even, and his fingers feel so good. I could probably come just like this, just from rocking myself against—

Nothing. He pulls his hand away, making a disapproving sound. That makes two of us, but my whimper turns to a strangled gasp as his fingers return in a whip-fast spank.

Against my fucking *pussy*.

"Ow!" I'm panting now, trying to catch my breath, but I can't figure out why. It's not like that hurt. It just…I grind back at him, and he does it again, making me groan and press my face into the bedspread. Jesus. I'm so close to coming, hard, and all he has to do is tap me once more…

So of course he doesn't. Bastard. He flips me over like I'm a fucking waif, and climbs on top of me. "Is this what you want, Hailey? You want some dirty sex with someone you don't have to look at ever again?"

"I'm pretty sure the fucked up track record of my family guarantees I'm going to have to see you again."

He braces his arms on either side of my head and brushes some hair off my cheek. His eyes are dark, almost black in the dim light of my room, and a nerve is twitching in his cheek. Between us, his cock rests heavy on the soft of my belly. His thighs press my own open, and it wouldn't take much to bring us together.

I stare up at him, my breath slowing. I want it, in a deep, aching kind of way. But now I'm scared again, because this is too much. Too intimate. I'll want *this* over and over again, for the rest of my life. Cole, hard and big and on top of me.

Safe and sexy and real.

No. This can't happen. I want *this* too much. Something else needs to happen instead. I lick my lips, what's become our shorthand for a blow job and wiggle beneath him. "I thought you wanted me on my knees?"

"I think I want you just like this." Husky and rich, his voice undoes me. "Can you handle it?"

Not even a little bit.

"Please," I whisper. "Just a taste. Come on. Don't you want to fuck my mouth, bad man?"

"Stop," he grinds out, even as his cock pulses against me. A dirty fight between good and evil was playing out inside him, and I can't handle Good Cole. I'd fall in love with Good Cole in a New York minute, so we need Bad Cole to come out and play.

"Hold my hair. Make me choke. Paint my face with your—"

He cuts me off with a hard, punishing kiss. So I bite him. It's become our way.

Or maybe just my way.

There's a definite possibility that I'm the fucked up one here. Not a surprise. I'm a Reid. It was just a matter of time for my defects to show.

"Not on your knees." He rolls onto his back, pulling me with him for one more kiss before he wraps my hair around his fist and holds me in place as he props himself up against my pillows. I get my first look at his cock as he shifts me between his legs. Thick, long, blunt, and covered in the softest looking skin, even as it's stretched tight. It lays to the left, against his hip, bobbing in the air a bit, giving me a clear look at his sac, too. I breathe in his scent, clean with a musky maleness

100

that makes my mouth water.

He laughs, soft and slow, a quiet rumble. "What are you waiting for, an invitation?"

I giggle at the unexpected tease. This isn't going as I expected at all. Intense one minute, funny the next.

"Just taking my time," I breathe, turning my face toward his cock, now pointing right at my mouth. Perfect. I stick my tongue out and swipe at the bead of pre-come waiting for me, enjoying the way that makes him hiss.

Enjoying the taste of him on my tongue.

I want more.

I lick around the thick crown, savoring the taste of his velvety skin, before sliding my whole mouth over the head and bringing him deep. Well, deep-ish. He's big and my mouth isn't.

"More," he growls, and then it turns out that there is in fact more, and I can in fact take it. He lifts his hips slowly, at the same time as he guides my head lower, his hand alternating between pressing at the back of my neck and stroking my hair.

It's the stroking that does it, that unbearable softness. I need him hard and rough, and he knows that's what I want. He knows I'm trying to fit him into a stereotype.

But *this*, the gentle touch and push and all of a sudden his cock is buried in my throat, and I'm struggling to breathe through my nose...this is what I need.

Cole drifts his free hand—the one not fisted in my hair, guiding me as I suck him off—over my cheek and down my neck, finding my swinging breasts. He groans again as he cups one of my boobs, and that simple touch topples the last of my defenses. I can try to orchestrate dirty sex with him, or we could just *have* dirty sex.

I pull back, pressing a sloppy wet kiss to the end of his cock as I rock back on my heels. "Condoms are in the top drawer."

"Thank Christ," he mutters, yanking one out. I watch as he rolls on protection, then crawl on top of him. He palms my ass as I reach between us and sink onto his length.

It takes three slow presses to take him fully, and by the time he's deep inside, I'm halfway gone again. I tip forward, resting my hands on his shoulders, and his solid arms wrap around me, holding me there. He's staring at my tits, which is good, because I don't know how much eye contact I can take while I deal with the fact that nothing in the entire world has ever felt as good as Cole Parker filling me up.

He says my name, so quietly I almost don't hear it. Almost. Not quite. And that's when I realize…it's too late. I'm not fucking Bad Cole. That asshole took a walk when we got naked, and the man inside me thinks I'm beautiful and loves the look of my breasts floating in front of his face when I ride him. He might not be a good man all the time, but there's nothing but goodness here between us.

I coast on that realization for a minute, trying hard not to fight against it. Wanting to be okay with it. I say his name, and he grins up at me, but when I say it again, I think he gets that I'm on the edge of freaking out. He tightens his grip, as if to say *I've got you*, and despite all the mistrust outside of this space, I know he does.

He sticks out his tongue, long and brazen, and pulls one nipple into his mouth. Like a lightning bolt to my clit, the strong tug makes me grind against him and arch into his mouth.

"So pretty," he mutters, replacing his tongue with his thumb as he moves to the other one. "Fucking tasty, and pretty, and I want you to come on me, Hailey. I want your little pussy to grab onto my cock and fucking milk it, you hear?"

"Uh huh." It's all I can manage, because his words are like magic fingers, working with his pulsing cock and his dangerous tongue to blow me apart.

"You need to come, beautiful. I'm going to start fucking you so hard. I'm going to bury myself deep, and blow my load inside you. But I can't do that until you've gone over. I can't do that until you're good."

"So close," I pant, rolling my hips as I sink onto his shaft again. "I'm good. I promise. Just…harder. Do it harder."

With a jerk, Cole tumbles us sideways, sliding our limbs together as he stretches out on top of me, pinning my hands over my head with one hand, pressing one of my knees up and away with the other, so he can do it harder.

He surges into me, stealing my breath. I roll my head back, overcome with sensation, and I barely notice him find my face with his until he's right there.

And his eyes.

Oh my god.

"Don't look at me like that," I whisper.

"Too late."

He slows his thrusts, dragging his thick cock through my folds like he's dragging my heart through the jagged rocks that surround him. Falling for Cole Parker is the worst possible scenario. It can't happen.

But he's inside me. Deep.

And it already happened when I wasn't looking.

I cry out, and he covers my mouth with his, a furious kiss as we come together. I swear I black out for a second as every bit of me spasms around every bit of him, and he jerks hard above me, driving his hips into me and holding them there.

There's a moment, right after my vision returns, when Cole's forehead is pressed against mine and I can still taste the sweet maleness of his tongue...I arch my back, and my nipples rub against his chest, and I'm totally ready to go again. For that second, it feels perfect and easy and...fucktastic.

And then reality crashes into me.

We didn't just fuck. That wasn't dirty—except it was. That was...more.

That was dangerous in a whole different way that I did *not* sign up for.

"Oh my god." I say it out loud this time, because it's all I'm capable of, and the silence is too much.

"Don't freak out," Cole mutters, his voice rough and dry. And laced with something suspiciously like humor.

"Are you laughing at me?" I cover my face, then realize that leaves my naked body sprawled

104

across my bed. Fuck it. It's my bed, and the light is pretty. I'm going to hide behind my hands and my hopefully golden skin—there's a lot of it, maybe he'll get distracted.

"This isn't a big deal. I'm still the bad guy you hate."

I sigh, and shift my hands enough to uncover my mouth. "I don't really hate you. Not in here. In here, you've got a nice cock and a talented tongue."

"Okay." His voice has warmed up a bit, and the word rolls out easily.

I peek through my fingers as he shifts his weight, rolling off the bed to deal with the condom. I slam them shut again as he turns back, so I just feel him tuck back in next to me. "What does that mean, okay?"

"It means, go to sleep, beautiful. I'll be gone in the morning."

"Oh." I don't know if I like that.

"And maybe I'll use that key to let myself back in from time to time. Middle of the night, secret-like."

"Oh." I think about that for a minute, then smile. "Okay."

— eleven —

Cole

My phone rings at quarter to four. Jason's ring tune. For the first time in three years, I'm tempted not to answer.

Good news for Jason, my sense of duty overrides everything else. Motherfucker.

"What?" I mutter quietly, rolling away from Hailey's sweet warmth.

"We've got a major situation, all hands on deck."

"If it's a Reid, I'm going to murder someone. If there's anyone left to murder."

He doesn't answer right away. Shit.

"No, it's not a Reid. But there's a situation. Can you meet me at the home of Representative Brian Fletcher?"

My phone vibrates with the address. "Sure. I'll be there in ten minutes."

I tug on my undershirt, boxer briefs and dress pants. I holster my weapons, the Browning last. I stand there for a second, holding the weight of it in my hand. Fuck. So much for being a good guy in this room.

Reality has a way of settling in, and my reality is that rich people call when they've done bad things. And I'm extraordinarily good at getting them off the hook.

I pick up my dress shirt just as Hailey stirs. Her long brown hair glints with subtle gold highlights in the moonlight, and her soft, pale skin glows like an angel. I drop to my knees next to the bed.

"Go back to sleep. Work calls."

"No…"

I laugh softly and lean in. "Here, I'll take a picture of us, you can sleep with that."

"K. Good deal." She smiles sleepily for my phone and lets her eyes drift shut again as I text it to her. "You come back again sometime, ya hear?"

"I will. I'll wake you up with my tongue next time."

She makes a throaty sound that gets me half-hard and I press a quick kiss to her lips before I say anymore. I tuck my shirt into her arms and head for the living room. If Rep. Fletcher thinks I look more badass in a wifebeater and leather jacket, that's only to my advantage.

Any asshole who wakes me up at four in the morning and drags me from the warmest, sweetest bed I've ever slept in had better have a good fucking reason, or there'll be hell to pay.

—twelve—

Hailey

I've been upright for seven minutes, but I'm still waking up. I'm standing in my kitchen, wearing Cole's shirt that he left behind, waiting for the coffee maker to fill my mug. I wandered through the living room on my way to caffeine and flicked on the morning news, but all I can hear right now is The Black Keys still strumming away in my bedroom from my alarm clock iPod dock.

I need to have a shower. I press my fingertips to my lips as I blush over the memory of how Cole talked to me last night. How I talked to him. The taunting and the teasing and the little snippets of sweet in between.

This is a disaster waiting to happen, I know that, but for the next little while, I'm going to enjoy being ravaged by the big, bad wolf. Or maybe he's a tiger, with those amber eyes, flecked with gold. He's definitely something, that's for sure.

I take a long, slow sip of coffee as I sway my way into my room. I turn the music off and stand in front of my closet, drinking my coffee, thinking about what to wear.

Mostly thinking about Cole.

But when I hear his name, it's not in my head.

It's on the TV in the living room.

This is Washington. Cole could be on TV for any number of reasons. I put my coffee on my bedside table and shake off the remaining cobwebs as I look for the remote to rewind the new story.

109

My heart starts thumping painfully as I watch the double fast rewind on the screen. Cole in handcuffs…somewhere. My thumb slips on the play button, missing it, and I go too far.

My mouth falls open as the newscast begins. "Sad news for residents of Kentucky this morning as the wife of Representative Brian Fletcher was shot and killed in an apparent lover's feud. Arrested without incident at the Fletcher home early this morning was her lover, Cole Parker. In an ironic twist of events, Mr. Parker first met Anabeth Fletcher when his crisis management firm was hired by her husband last year. The two struck up a friendship. Photographed together here at the National Gallery earlier this year…"

My Cole. Photos flashing on the screen aren't unfamiliar to me, of course. He's been with a lot of women, mostly casually non-relationships. Sometimes as a polite escort. He's a good looking man, trusted by their husbands.

I sink to my knees. Oh my god. My chest hurts.

This is a mistake.

Surely this is a…

I flash over the last month. Cole's sudden interest in me.

His surveillance of my apartment, totally unnecessary for my sister's drama.

My conveniently public show of jealousy and his subsequent breakup with Penny.

Last night.

My stomach turns over.

He knows how much I hate the public scrutiny, how I've hidden from the spotlight of being a Dashford Reid. Fuck, I don't even want to be a

Reid, no matter how common a name it is.

And he did this to me anyway.

He slept with me, knowing…

I gag on that thought as my attention is dragged back to the TV.

"An autopsy will be performed later today to determine an exact time of death. Mr. Parker, seen here earlier in the day wearing a dress shirt the police are now searching for…" The words all run together again in a maddening buzz as I look down at the blue shirt I woke up to. That I rubbed my face in and wrapped around my naked body with a smile.

That's when I really get it.

I'm his alibi.

HATE F*@K

Cole and Hailey

part two

—one—

Hailey

I have never been so worried and so pissed off at the same time.

It takes me a solid half-hour to climb up off my living room floor. In the shower, I scrub my skin raw, getting the smell of Cole off me—and then I instantly regret the loss of him. Which only makes me cry again, because he was just *arrested* and that can't be good.

I need to tell someone he didn't do it. I mean, he *can't* have done it. Right? The man who made love to me—or at least, fucked me with a crazy level of intensity and all the feelings—just hours before did *not* leave my apartment and shoot a woman.

He has to be covering for someone.

It has to be a mistake.

I scrub myself all over again.

Out of the shower, I call in sick to work. I'm already late, but they don't seem to mind—big surprise, Hailey has another drama. I will never get the permanent job at this rate, but somehow that doesn't seem quite as important as clearing Cole or protecting my quiet, little life. After I change my name, I can start job hunting again.

After carefully choosing my best trying-not-to-be-noticed outfit and finding my biggest, darkest sunglasses and matching baseball hat, I head out the door. I can't go to the cops. There's no press here, but there will be at the police station downtown.

And I'm still a Reid. It's not in our nature to voluntarily talk to the authorities.

No, there's only one option.

I get in my rarely used car and head for the offices of The Horus Group.

I remember from our very first briefing with them, they chose their office building for a few reasons, including the fact that the underground parking garage has three entrances and the entire space is covered by video surveillance.

Cole held my gaze. It was the middle of the night, and we were in full panic mode. If my father was arrested...

"If anything ever happens, and you're scared...you come to us. The press can't come into the parking garage. Circle the block and call us. We'll make sure you can get in safely."

The next day, my car was taken for window tinting.

Today's the first time I'll actually need to do this spy routine, and I can't even pretend I'm not nervous.

It's a slow drive, being rush hour, and sure enough, when I finally get there, cameras and people are blocking the first entrance to the parking garage, the one beside the main doors to the building. But around the block, the back entrance looks unobserved. I pull in to the gate then press the code I've memorized.

My heart thumps painfully as I get out and head for the elevator. Nerves prickle my skin, and I have a little freak-out when I press the button for the second floor and nothing happens. All of a sudden, a small screen above the buttons lights up, and I see the receptionist for The Horus Group.

"Ms. Reid, my apologies for the elevator being locked down." The second floor button lights up, and the car starts to move. "See you in a minute."

I nod mutely before she disappears.

When the doors slide open, she's waiting with a bottle of water for me. "I'm Ellie, by the way, if you don't remember me. I didn't know we were expecting anyone."

I look around.

"They're not here. There's been an incident." She looks so calm.

"Yeah, I saw the news. I need to talk to..." Well, Cole probably isn't an option. "One of them. As soon as possible. It's about what happened."

"I'll let Jason know you're here. I'm sure he'll be back soon. Do you want to wait in a meeting room? Can I get you anything?" She's moving toward the desk, totally efficient. Not freaked out in the least—I don't get how she can be calm.

"No, thank you." I watch her for a moment. My age, probably, maybe a year or two older. Pretty. Capable. Does she know she works for soulless bastards? "I'll just wait here."

"Okay." She offers me a quiet smile and picks up the phone.

Twenty minutes later, Jason walks in from the stairwell. He looks intent, busy. Uncharacteristically dressed-down in jeans and a black t-shirt, and I realize that he too probably got out of bed in the middle of the night.

"Hailey!" His voice is friendly and welcoming, but his gaze is hard and flat.

My pulse flutters in my neck, and I'm not sure I can actually form words. Maybe this is a mistake. "Where's Cole?"

He pulls his brows together.

"Maybe we should go up to my office," he says, pointing to the third floor.

Upstairs, there's a large conference room in the middle, across from the elevators, and offices are at the front and back of the building. Jason's is at the front, looking down at the main entrance. I walk to the window. What looks like the entire Washington press corps is now amassed out front.

Jason doesn't bother to follow my gaze before saying dismissively, "More of them followed me here."

"I got in the back entrance no problem," My voice trembles, and it's so quiet I'm not sure he can even hear me.

"We'll make sure you get out without being noticed, one way or another." When I turn around, he's still standing beside his desk. He waits until I settle in the chair opposite before he sits down himself. "You saw the news today?"

"I did. That's why I'm here."

"Cole didn't kill that woman. He arrived at the Fletcher house after I did."

"I know. He…he was with me before that."

Jason's dark eyes turn black as I speak, sending icy cold fear down my spine. But when he speaks, his words surprise me. "I'm sorry."

I wait for more. He doesn't give it, and I don't know what to say. What is he sorry for? He didn't do anything. If anyone needs to be sorry, it's Cole, but even then…he's never hidden who he is. I went

118

into last night with my eyes wide open. A meaningless fuck with a bad boy.

Obviously, that's exactly what I got.

If I'm a suck who can't handle that, it's on me.

"I'm prepared to make a statement to the police." My entire body is shaking now, but it's the right thing to do. "I'd prefer to do it as discretely as possible, of course, but—"

Jason stands suddenly and I cut myself off. He starts pacing as he shoves his hands into his pockets.

"I mean, the discretion isn't as important as clearing Cole's name," I continue, my mouth dry. I remember the bottle of water Ellie pressed into my hands and I twist off the cap. "It's just…"

"You don't need to do this," Jason says, now staring out the window. His voice is strong and clear, showing none of the nerves rioting through my body. "If it's too much of a bother."

"Excuse me?" I push myself to a stand. "It's not a *bother*. It's the right thing to do. But I have a right to try and protect myself." Someone has to. Cole certainly didn't think about me before walking into the middle of a crime scene and making himself the prime suspect.

Jason shrugs, and white hot rage replaces the nerves inside me. I cast about for the right words, but none come. I don't understand what it is we're doing here, and as mad as I am at Cole, I wonder if *anyone* here has his back.

After a beat, Jason turns around, his t-shirt pulling against his straining biceps. Even at rest, he's a pit bull. Where Cole is big in a safe, protective way, Jason is scary looking. The pissed-off look on his face doesn't help.

"Maybe it would be best if you leave before he gets here."

"He's coming here?" I squeeze my hands together, distracted by the thought that Cole is, at least temporarily, free. "So…what does that mean?"

Another shrug. I really hate Jason's shoulders right now. "Tag and our lawyer are at the station now. He hasn't been taken to central booking, as far as I know. He might not be charged with anything today."

I don't understand. Hasn't he been arrested?

"All of this is beyond me, and I don't get why you're *mad* at me, when I haven't done anything, but if I can move that *might* to a *definitely won't be*, I want to help."

Jason opens his mouth and pauses before saying something obviously different from his first thought. "Look, you don't need to worry about Cole. He's a big boy."

Fuck that noise.

"I'm not going anywhere until I see him." I sit down and pull out my phone.

It's a long, silent minute before Jason grunts. "Fine. Suit yourself."

two

Cole

Jail would be better than sitting across a desk from Detective Kendra Browning in the middle of the precinct like I've been brought to heel.

A Russian gulag might be better. Kendra makes my nuts want to crawl back into my body for protection.

Sure, she's beautiful. Smart. One of the good guys.

The problem is, I am not.

"Mr. Parker, you need to answer my questions."

I only want one woman calling me Mr. Parker, and it's not Kendra. I stare back at her, confident in my Miranda-protected right to shut the fuck up. Being under arrest is a pain in my ass. And she won't even put me in an interrogation room so I can demand my lawyer and be left alone.

I've been here for an hour, after being transferred from another precinct. I'm not sure why Major Case wasn't involved from the start, and I don't really care. I just need to hang tight until one of my partners shows up with a lawyer, then I can go and find the asshole who killed Anabeth Fletcher.

If it's my client, that's going to be awkward, but I don't think it is. We only had just over an hour with him before the police showed up — presumably called by someone who knew there was a dead body in the house.

Someone responsible for that death.

The entire time we were there, he was in shock. Real shock, not an act.

That'll happen when you don't remember falling asleep, then wake up in your den, a gun in your hand and a dead wife upstairs in your bed.

As soon as we all got there, we knew something didn't add up—right now, Wilson is getting a private lab to run Fletcher's blood, find out if he was drugged. The scotch he swears he was drinking before he fell asleep is gone—the decanter, the tumblers, the original bottle in the bar. Vanished.

So when the cops showed up, I made a gut decision to complicate the scene. I picked up the gun. Maybe it was the wrong call, but it means my client's not in a cell right now.

And all of that is none of Kendra's business, because whatever is going on here is way over the pay grade of a DC cop. She couldn't unravel this even if she believed me, and she wouldn't, because she thinks I'm as crazy as her ex-husband.

When she sighs and looks back at her computer, I reach for my pocket out of reflex. But everything—my keys, my phone, my wallet—is currently on a tray on her desk.

She notices me eyeing my phone, because I didn't hide it. She picks it up and twirls it slowly between her fingers.

"Drop it and I'll send the department a bill for a new one. Actually, I've been meaning to upgrade, so go the fuck ahead."

"So you do speak, after all." She leans in,

flashing just a bit of cleavage, which doesn't work —even if I weren't mad as hell at how this has gone down, she's not Hailey. And Kendra's not available, either. Not really.

Her tits are nice, though, and so is the try, so I give her the slow, appraising look she wanted. Then I close my eyes and tip my head back against the chair.

"Who have you been texting, Cole? Mind if I have a look?"

"Get a warrant, Detective. It's got a password on it for a reason."

Her laugh turns to a sigh as heavy footsteps sound behind me.

"Oh great, the cavalry's arrived." She pushes back from the desk, shoving it against my arm in the process. I don't react. "Who let this guy past the desk sergeant?"

I recognize the hard-edged laugh as belonging to one of my business partners, Tag Browning. Kendra's ex-husband. "Time to let him go, baby. You don't have anything."

"Don't call me baby. And I don't have anything because you guys tampered with a crime scene. And since I have *that*, it's not nothing after all."

"If that was the charge, you'd have arrested us all. Instead, one of your goons paraded Cole in front of the media—"

"I think your partner likes the cameras just fine. This morning's stunt will bring you more clients hungry to cover up murders—"

"You should worry more about the wide-spread corruption and uniforms on the take than—"

"Than a woman's murder? You've lost all

perspective—"

I stand up, shoving my chair back hard enough it bounces off the desk behind me. "Enough!" I yell it, because seriously, these two need to find a fucking room. "Am I free to go?"

"We want to question you…" Kendra purses her lips. She's killing time.

I brush past her and scoop up my belongings before I point to John Grant, our entirely respectable attorney standing a few feet behind Tag. "Contact my lawyer when you figure out what it is you want to ask me. I don't suppose I can have my guns back?"

"Ha. We're going to be running those ballistics through *all* the systems before you ever get them back." She sighs. "Cole…" Frustration rolls off her. She wants the Assistant U.S. Attorney on duty to charge me with something—anything. But there's nothing that will stick because I haven't done anything wrong.

Today.

She sighs. "We used to be on the same side. If you guys tell me what happened, I'll probably understand."

Not a chance.

I nod at Tag. "Let's go."

Outside the station, we say a terse goodbye to John, who is, of course, unimpressed with my stunt. Once we're alone in the car, Tag starts talking. "You need an alibi."

I have one. Not for the first time this morning, I worry about Hailey—what she's seen, what she's thinking. If she's worrying about me. God, I don't want that. But I've brought it on myself. *You knew*

124

you were going to hurt her. Bravo for being a fucking fortune teller. I'm not going to use her again, hurt her again. Hailey won't be how I get out of this, no matter what. "This'll go away."

"Kendra's out for blood."

"Not as much as the truth. We just need to find it for her."

Tag's phone beeps, and he glances at the screen. "Wilson's got something."

I nod, then pull out my own phone. I can't really say anything, but I need to send her *something*. When I type in the password, her photo is on the screen. Just hours ago, and everything has turned upside down since. **Are you okay? I'm going to work now. I won't be long. I'll find you after that.** I can't tell her it's all going to be okay. I won't make a promise I can't keep.

We drive to the office in silence. It's past breakfast time, I barely got two hours of sleep last night, and haven't eaten yet. I insist on grabbing food in the lobby, and ignore Tag's scowl. "Fuck you, I'm hungry."

"Fuck you, I'm interested in getting you out of this jam as soon as humanly possible."

"Your wife flashed me her tits just before you arrived."

For that, I get the door whipped into my shoulder as we arrive on the third floor. I probably deserve it.

"I didn't enjoy the view, if that's your problem."

He doesn't answer me.

We find the other guys in the board room. Jason is pacing in front of the large screen on the far wall, every inch the patriotic warrior. Wilson's

125

sitting at the head of the conference table, scrolling through something on his laptop. He glances up as we enter, then presses a key, making the screen come to life.

It's exactly what I expect to see—a black and white video of me, leaving Hailey's apartment. Time-stamped ten minutes before four in the morning.

I don't sit. "Turn that off. Where's Fletcher?"

Jason turns around slowly, facing me across the center of the table. "He's at home with his family, and one of Grant's first year associates standing guard." He points over his shoulder where my face is frozen on the screen, a clear shot because *yes*, I looked at the camera. I always do. It's an unconscious move now, making sure I'm seen when I want to be, and not seen when I don't want to be...*Fuck.*

I'm a hypocrite, thinking in one breath that I won't use Hailey as an alibi and yet obviously my sub-conscious has no problem. Too fucking bad. "No, we're not using that."

"That's not your call."

"Yes, it is."

"As soon as the medical examiner determines time of death, this clears you."

"That's the wrong move." I sift through the possibilities, weighing the risks and benefits. Hailey's off-limits, but I'm not sure how that's going to be received by my partners, knowing the lengths I'll go to protect her. How much she means to me.

Jason narrows his eyes. "Is this about the girl?"

Anger thumps through my veins. *Yes.* I've

126

exposed her to too much already. "No. Clearing my name too quickly could shift the focus to any one of you. Or Fletcher. Let's never forget the client, right? I know I didn't do it. And since I have a history with the victim, this is perfect."

A soft gasp comes from behind me, a breathy sound filled with hurt and confusion that I'd recognize anywhere, anytime. I want to punch Jason for asking me that when he knew she was standing behind me. And I curse myself for not hearing her.

"Hailey…"

She shakes her head at me and takes a step back.

Fuck me. I point back at Jason. "You're a fucking asshole, and this conversation isn't over. Don't do anything with that video. It might clear me of murder, but it implicates me in tampering with a crime scene, since I picked up the gun. Silence is our best course of action while we find the motherfuckers who did this. That's where we need to focus our energy."

Hailey's standing in front of the elevator by the time I finish yelling at my partner. "Where the hell do you think you're going?"

She looks back at me over her shoulder, her body shaking but her voice clear and cold. "This was a mistake."

"A *mistake* would be running away before we have a chance to talk. My office."

"Excuse me?" Her eyes narrow but she doesn't resist when I slide my hand over her hip and guide her down the hall, my arm locked around her waist.

127

I feel reckless. Out of control. *Not scared*. No, I'm not scared of anything.

Except losing Hailey.

I'd have to have her to lose her, and I'm not sure she's mine.

Not sure that's on the table—now, or ever. It shouldn't be. I should push her away right now. I just don't know if I can do that, either.

As soon as the door clicks shut behind her, I have her in my arms, my hands in her hair. I kiss her hard, and she whimpers against me, her arms tightening around my neck as I consume her.

Her lips are faintly salty, like she's been crying. That rips me up inside. I did this to her.

She kisses me back as we desperately hold on to each other. It's a long time before we break apart. Her lips are swollen and wet. My chest aches. We're a mess, and I'm more settled than I've been in hours. I never want to let her out of my arms.

"I'm glad you're not in jail," she whispers, hugging me tight for a second before pressing her hands against my chest.

I don't let her go. "You shouldn't be here," I mutter against her lips. "Someone might see you."

"I drove and parked underground. I needed to tell you that I'll talk to the cops."

"No."

"Yeah, I heard you say that to the other guys." Her body tightens inside my arms as she says it.

"You heard some shit out of context."

She sighs. "I'm not sure there's enough context to make me understand your life."

What the fuck? "It's not my *life*, it's my job."

128

Another sigh. She tips her forehead against my shoulder. "No, what *I* do is a job. Working at McDonald's is a *job*. Leaving my bed in the middle of the night and getting arrested for murder...that has to be more than a job or you shouldn't do it."

That had been the wrong word choice, but I can't explain the difference to her. I focus on what I can say. "I didn't want to leave your bed."

She tenses again, pressing her hands against my chest. Trying to push me way. *Not going to fucking happen.* I lean into her, over her, moving her back the few inches until she's pressed against my door. I grab her hands and press her arms over her head. She glares up at me as I dip my head to kiss her again.

"What? You don't believe me?"

She gapes at me for a moment. "I don't know what to believe," she finally says, her voice strangled.

Fuck.

I'm not going to hold her against the door—kiss her, fuck her, make her scream—if she doesn't trust me.

I drop her hands and take a giant step back, my brain scrambling to catch up to the strange feelings coursing through me—possession and fear, yes, but also something else.

Something dangerous. Something I can't name.

129

three

Hailey

Cole steps back from me, his expression shuttered and his body tense.

I've made a misstep, I can sense it in the air.

I go for a flippant response, even though it feels wrong as I say it.

"You know, for someone who's become famous for being able to talk rich people out of almost any kind of trouble, you're not doing a good job of it for yourself." I wave my hand at his face. "Pull your shit together, Cole."

Like a cat, he moves fast and without warning. He grabs my waving wrist again, and we stand there. Me, in shock, him…I'm not sure. He takes another step back into my personal space, and his other hand slides around my hip, twisting me until my front is pressed against the door. It's not a *slam*, per se, because it doesn't hurt, but he's holding me there. I suck in a breath and hold it, not sure what the hell is going on. I'm not *scared*, but I'm something. Full of feels, Alison would say.

"I'll pull my shit together before we leave this office." He spits the words out between gritted teeth, and it should be off-putting, this ridiculous testosterone dump. It *is* off-putting to my head. Much lower in my body, I'm consumed by a strange sensation to arch into him and make him feel better.

I start laughing at the absurdity of the notion that sex would help. He'd been *arrested*. Lawyers make that better, not fucking. I sigh and twist my head to catch his gaze. "What are you doing? Why did you drag me back here?"

"Stop talking, Hailey." A thrill runs through me at the sound of my name on his tongue and the look in his eye. He loosens his grip, leaning his forearm on the door next to my head, his fingers just loosely circling my arm now. His thumb rubs back and forth over the pulse point on the inside of my wrist, making my skin tingle in a strangely soothing way. "I'm not doing anything."

I let out the breath I was holding, and it rattles between us in a shaky exhale. "Then…maybe you should let me go." I pull my hand free from his grasp and turn to face him. I press my palm against his chest. Even vibrating with tension, touching him feels good. *Right.* Even as I shove against him, pushing him out of my way, I relish the contact. He lets me shift him out of the way. "Whatever is on your mind…just say it."

He turns his back to me, staring intently at something on his desk. "Now's not the time."

I glare at his rigid spine until my eyes burn, which doesn't take long, then I glance down. There's a big coffee stain on his carpet, I notice randomly. He should have that steam-cleaned.

Three deep breaths, and I look up. He's turned back, and whatever that little outburst was all about seems locked down again. Maybe. Barely.

We stare at each other for a minute. I should tell him more. Tell him that I know he's a good man, deep down, and that I trust him.

132

But I'm not sure I do. The fear inside me is a sharp, stabbing pain. It feels wrong to doubt him, but within hours of sleeping together, he dragged me perilously close to the edge of scandal.

Not on purpose. I close my eyes, not wanting to see how he clenches his jaw and guards his gaze as he takes in my silence.

From the second he saw me, I've known Cole is pissed I'm here. But then he kissed me, and for a second I thought it might work out somehow.

"I didn't want to leave your bed," he repeats his earlier statement, his voice rough and raw.

My eyes snap open. "But you did."

"It's what I do. I fix shit. Sometimes that means I leave in the middle of the night."

"And get arrested?"

He shrugs like it's no big deal.

I shrug right back, my eyes narrowing because it's totally a big deal. "Now I'm your alibi for last night, aren't I?"

He snaps to his full height and glares at me. "Nobody needs to know that. I would *never* drag you into this shit."

"You don't think anyone's going to find out you're sleeping with Morgan Reid's daughter? You think you're the only team who can hack into digital data streams?" My voice lifts as I wave my arm over my head in Wilson's general direction. "The cops—"

"Don't have the budget for someone like Wilson. And nobody else cares. *We* care because we want to find out who killed Anabeth Fletcher."

I close my eyes at the name of the poor woman who died.

"We weren't…She and I…" he trails off, and I stare at him, incredulous.

"Seriously? She's *dead*, Cole. I don't care if you fucked her."

His eyes flare at that. "Really? I'd care if I heard on the news that you were having a secret affair with someone. That's the story that's being spun, right?"

I can't help it. My voice raises itself, and all of a sudden I'm yelling at him. "I'd never *have* a secret affair with someone, you asshole! I *date* people, and only one at a time. I don't have *affairs*. I don't do anything illicit, or dirty, or *wrong*."

He doesn't even blink at me calling him an awful name, even though I already regret it. "Really, beautiful? Because last night you were all over me being your dirty little secret."

"That was a mistake."

He's across the room before the words fade into the air between us. He stops an inch short of slamming me against the door again. "Nothing about last night was a mistake," he grinds out. "And I'm not complaining about being your secret anything. I'm not sleeping with anyone else. Anything you see or hear, if it's true, belongs in the past."

"The recent past?"

"The *past*," he repeats, this time with emphasis. "Once we're not yelling at each other and I don't need to get back to work to solve a fucking *murder*, you can have as many details as your delicate little ears can handle."

That shuts me up, because no, I don't want details. Not now, not ever. I don't want the images

134

of Cole and other women in my head. Multiple women at the same time. Damnit. It doesn't take much to poke the green-eyed monster inside me, and I don't have that right.

He drops his forearms against the door, bracketing me in place without touching me. He glares at me. "What we have, Hailey...it's different."

"We don't have anything," I whisper. *Lies*. My skin itches for him to touch me.

Like he knows what I need, he slides his hand around my neck and holds me in place as he presses his forehead to mine. "Would we? If everything was different? If you weren't innocent and light, and I wasn't darkness and—"

"I'm not as innocent as you think." And he's not as dark, either, but I don't care about that fight in the same way. "I can handle the truth. What happened last night?"

He shakes his head. "No. You don't need to know anything about that. You're not involved."

"You made me involved when you made me your alibi."

His hand tightens around my neck. "I didn't do that on purpose. I didn't know I'd be called out." His thumb traces a slow circle on the sensitive skin behind my neck. "I want to protect you, Hailey. If I had my way, you'd never know anything about the ugliness I see every day."

That's incredibly sweet, but Cole doesn't do *sweet*. And despite his good intentions, the impact is that my life has been flipped upside down, all because I slept with a crazy man. So there's only one thing to say. "That's stupid."

135

Another long, pregnant pause. "When it comes to you, I'm a stupid man."

I can't break his gaze. I don't want to. We're both spitting mad, but this connection between us still feels...good, somehow. Maybe because he's secretly sweet. Maybe because he's working that spot on my neck better than any man has ever worked my g-spot. My head is swimming and shivers ripple out across my skin from that slow, circling thumb.

But I'm not a stupid woman, no matter how much I want him, so I pile on another lie. "You might be swayed by the chemistry between us, but I'm not."

"Give me some time to fix this." There's a weird catch in Cole's voice, and for a second, I believe him. I *want* to believe him.

I press my lips together and try to calm my racing mind. "How?"

Instead of answering, he kisses me. Slower this time, his lips parting mine so softly it barely feels like anything. But in the absence of hard thrusts and greedy licks, something else forms. A bittersweet connection, wet and warm and fleeting.

He doesn't have an answer because there is no fixing what isn't broken. This isn't a temporary state for him. This is who he is.

We're incompatible. And this might be the last kiss we share.

Well, screw him.

Now is not the time for sweet. I never wanted sweet from Cole. I wanted real and honest, and if I can't get honest, at least our goodbye can be real.

I nip at his lower lip and he freezes, his breath

hot against my mouth. I do it again. *Come on.*

"We always knew this wouldn't work." I ignore the catch in my throat. Sure, I thought we'd have a bit longer. But it would never be easy to let him go. This is for the best.

"Don't speak for me," he growls, dragging his lips up my cheek. I close my eyes and he kisses my eyelid, then my nose, then my lips again. "You're deep inside me, Hailey. That's all I know. And this scandal will fade away, replaced by something else. And you'll still be inside me."

Oh God. His words blast through my defenses and I scramble to recover. I shake my head, going on the offense. "I can't. It's too much." I wind my arms around his neck, bringing his lips back to mine. "Thank you for last night," I whisper against his skin, all out of lies. "And I'm so, so glad you're not in jail."

He kisses me again. More sweet. Tears prick at my eyelids.

"Stop kissing me like that," I hiss. I can't leave him like this. I already doubt this move and I'm not even out the door.

He tightens his arms around me—a steely embrace I've never experienced before, and will never again. It's such a cliché that he's ruined me for other men, but right now it feels painfully, brutally true.

He drops his face to my neck, his next words muffled and quiet. "I'm not going to play the bad man for you now."

"It's not...I'm not asking..." But I am. I'm asking him to play a role that will allow me to walk away without guilt or worry.

Still more lies, but at least that one is just to myself. I'll always worry about him. He's a lunatic with a death wish, and I care about him despite myself. But I need to be done with this.

I nod silently and hold him tight for a minute, kissing his hair. He hasn't showered yet, and he smells like himself. Stripped bare. Vulnerable. And suddenly, I can't let go. I squeeze him even harder, and he groans against my neck.

"No," I whisper, the tears *so* close to falling again. "No. Don't be stupid. Let me tell the police you were with me."

"I can't." His response is immediate. Without hesitation. "I know you don't understand." He swears under his breath, a harsh combination that sounds like *fuckthisshit.* "I don't need saving, Hailey. This is just a regular day at the office for me."

I nod again, but this time I don't say anything. I'm out of words that might work.

"Come here." His voice is still soft, and rough, but there's an edge there, a command. Old Cole. Before-we-fucked Cole. I slowly peel myself off him as he rubs his thumb along my jaw, tilting my head so we're staring each other in the eye. "Last night wasn't a mistake."

My breath hitches in my throat.

"Tag is going to follow you home."

I nod.

"And we're not fucking done."

I shake my head, and his nostrils flare for a second before he crashes his lips against mine. I give him as good as I'm getting, swallowing his rage. *Yes.* I want him to sear my soul, to mark me

138

with a hate I can handle. I dig my fingers into his back as he thrusts his tongue against mine, instantly making me wet.

I'm awful for wanting him right now.

But at least I'm in good company. With a grunt, Cole slips the button loose on my jeans and spins me around. "Put your hands on the door, Hailey."

With a cry, I close my eyes, pressing them shut as I do as I'm told. Anticipation pings through my entire body. *Yes*.

He jerks my jeans down my hips, taking my underwear with them.

"We're not fucking done." He smoothes his hand over my bare ass and I whimper as he dips lower and finds me slippery and ready for him. "You have a problem with that?"

"Yes," I grind out.

"You have a problem with this?" He swirls his fingertips around my clit before teasing my opening.

I'm breathing hard. *No*.

"You need to say it, Hailey."

"No, I don't have a problem with this, you bastard. I want you."

"Then we're not fucking done." He thrusts one finger deep inside me, then adds another on the second slide, stretching me wide. I clench around his fingers, needing more.

He gives it to me. Swearing under his breath, Cole unzips, and the next thing I feel is his cock, big and hard, pressing against me from behind. With one hand, he jerks my hips an inch higher and I press onto my tiptoes as I arch my back, desperate for him to slide inside.

We both groan when he gets the angle right and surges into me. He fills me right to the point of gasping. Pleasure isn't the right word—I'm still aching from the night before, and in this position he feels bigger than ever before. It also feels different. Hotter, rougher, and more intense. So good.

I never want him to stop.

He slowly drags in and out, his ragged breaths matching my own as I press back against him on each thrust.

"Mine," he says so quietly I barely hear him. The single word is as erotic as any kiss or caress, and a fresh flood of my arousal lubricates his erection, making it easier for him to fuck me. He repeats the word, a little louder this time, and I cry out when he grabs my hips, hard, and drives even deeper than before.

"Don't stop," I beg.

He doesn't.

His brutal rhythm makes my eyes water and drives my pulse into my throat.

I love it.

I need it.

And I'm so damn close, but he's fucking me against the door in his office.

Coming is easier said than done. As if he senses that I'm riding the edge and can't get high enough, he slows down. He squeezes my hip, then shoves his hand under my shirt and cups one breast as he leans over my back.

"Please make me come." I say it quietly, but then he tweaks my nipple and I gasp his name, louder this time.

"Hush, beautiful."

"Shut up and fuck me," I gasp, the command roaring out of me in a very un-Hailey-like fashion.

He does just that, stroking my breast and using his words to add that something extra I need to the perfect penetration that's gotten me so close. "You're mine, Hailey," he growls in my ear as I press my lips together to keep from screaming as I come hard.

As soon as I finish spasming around him, he pulls out and jerks himself off against my ass, the wet slide of his hand on his cock and his increasingly fast breaths the only sounds in the room as I stand there, bare-assed and shaking, leaning against the door.

The hot, wet splash of his come hitting my lower back is a surreal cherry on top of the angriest sex I've ever had. It's made worse by the fact that I think the anger was all one-sided.

I slide a glance over my shoulder as he wipes me up with something. His undershirt. At some point he took off his jacket, which is on the floor, and now he's bare-chested.

I turn around and wiggle back into my pants, trying hard not to touch him.

Why does he have to be so disgustingly beautiful? All chiseled muscle. And deep in the middle of that perfectly carved chest is a heart. Black and brittle on the outside, but there's a tiny part of him that calls me *his*.

Damn him. I can't handle being his.

"We done here?" I pour as much disdain into those three words as I can muster. Turns out, I can muster a lot.

His head snaps up at the ice in my voice. He stares at me for a minute before turning and going to a closet in the corner, where he pulls out a dress shirt and puts it on. "Sure. I should get to work. Give me a minute to wash up and I'll get Tag to escort you home."

"I can find him."

He nods, not looking at me. "I didn't use a condom. I'm sorry. If you need something…"

"Yeah, I noticed. Thanks for asking. I'm on the Pill. I assume all of your secret affairs put you in the high-risk category, so —"

"I've never done that before," he says, cutting me off, but he doesn't match my pissed-off tone. "I get tested. I'm clean."

I sigh. I'm not really mad about the lack of a condom. Cole would never put me at risk, and I could have told him to stop. I would have if I wasn't protected against pregnancy. "I'm sorry. I trust you." It takes all my effort to force myself to add something that will push him away. "With my body, anyway."

He stiffens, and I turn away. It's time for me to leave before I do any further damage.

"Hailey."

I look back at him, keeping my hand on the door handle. I *am* leaving, no matter what he says.

But he just steps close enough to hold out a hard plastic card. "Take this. It's a pass card to the office. It works on the elevator and in the stairwell. Access to both floors. If you ever need…"

I stare at the unmarked white card that tells me he trusts me with *everything*. My heart cracks. "I can't take that."

142

"I can't let you go unless you do." He presses it into my hand, his fingertips grazing the inside of my wrist as he flattens his palm against mine. "Up to you if you ever use it."

"You already gave me your apartment key," I whisper.

"So you've got some options."

I wish I didn't know a dozen ways I might need those options some day. I stare at our hands, just barely touching. Cole's entire world between our palms.

—four—

Cole

"That was really uncalled for," I spit at Jason as I storm back into the conference room. I'm talking about the stunt he pulled by asking me about her when she was right fucking there, but from the look on his face, he doesn't care.

I don't care about him right now, either.

Waiting until Hailey cleared out of the building was one of the hardest things I've ever done. I have no idea how long it will be until I can see her again, until it's safe to bring my shadow into her light, even in secret, and now I'm *pissed*.

"How long you took to get rid of her? Yes, it was." Jason scowls at me, but since we need to stay on the same side today, I hold myself back from punching him. Just barely. "I thought you said you'd handle it. She says you were with her last night."

Last night. Ten minutes ago. "She's none of your business."

"No," he barks, taking me by surprise. I know he's not pleased, but the look on his face is murderous. "She should be none of *your* business, for her sake. And the sooner you remember that, the better it will be for *her*."

I stare at him, pulse pounding. He's not wrong. "Well, maybe I need to reconsider what business I'm in, then."

"Right now?" My best friend and business partner slides his usual calm mask into place and smirks at me. I want nothing more than to punch that smarmy look off his face. "Sure. We can discuss that right after we figure out who murdered Anabeth Fletcher."

I twist to glare at Wilson, who just hunkers down behind his computer and doesn't say anything.

Jason continues as if I haven't just threatened to quit. "Tag is going to stop and talk to the medical examiner on his way back. Hopefully he can get an exact time of death."

I take a deep breath. *Focus*. "Fletcher didn't do this." I say it as a statement of fact, but none of us know for sure.

Jason frowns. "Unless he's the world's greatest actor, no. I was heading home when he called me, already in my car, so I was there fast. Ten minutes after he woke up, maybe? And you guys all got there fifteen minutes after that. And I didn't see anything that made me think he knew what the hell was going on."

Jesus. A man wakes up next to his dead wife, a gun in his hand…if you have our number, you call it. You don't call 9-1-1. Not if you've got enough money or power to know better.

I wish we'd had more time to clean up the scene. But no sooner had I arrived than the police were knocking on the door, and I only had one option. I wiped down the gun and picked it up, dropping it as soon as the uniformed officers came through the bedroom door.

Our client didn't need to be arrested for the

murder of his wife. I spared him from that. I can't spare him from the months of rumors and speculation, but I could keep him out of handcuffs this morning, so I did.

"Then we need to dig into their backgrounds, figure out why someone would want Anabeth dead." I lean forward, bracing my hands on the coffee table. "Brian had me escort her to a few things last year. He never gave me a reason, and at that point, I was just happy to make the contacts. We need to ask him why."

Jason nods. "We'll go over there later today. Once we know more."

Wilson clears his throat and the screen flickers to life. He's got a macro running on that laptop that auto-fills a fancy looking presentation with data from a number of databases he shouldn't have access to.

Shouldn't have access to is like catnip for Wilson.

So Anabeth's deepest, darkest secrets scroll across the wall.

"That's it?" Jason shakes his head. An abortion when she was twenty-two. A few parking tickets. An audit five years earlier that carried a small tax penalty. "So this isn't about her."

"Not unless she was leading a double life we don't know about." Wilson's voice says it all — not likely.

I frown. "What about Fletcher?"

We already know his dossier from when we accepted him as a client. None of us need to look at the screen. Jason makes a *beats me* face. "We took him on as a client because of who he knows, not who he is. He's on the Education and the

147

Workforce committee. Not a threat to anyone. Might be a good future leader, but that's two or three election cycles away."

"Huh." Wilson squints at his screen and types a few quick keystrokes, then another round of lightning-quick taps. "Well, two months ago he started making noises about an anti-sex slavery bill. It was shot down by the party leadership staff. Twice."

"What? Why?" Jason asks the question that's on both of our minds. That sounds like an easy bill to support.

This is our area of weakness. None of us are Washington insiders. It's an advantage because we're truly non-partisan. On the other hand, parsing shit like this makes all of our heads hurt.

"Searching…hang on." A few more key strokes, then he stops and stares at the screen. "Holy shit."

"What?"

"The poor bastard." Wilson narrows his eyes as he punches a finger at the keyboard. The large screen flips to a projection of an email account. The recipient is Fletcher's chief of staff, an experienced Hill veteran.

Is there any way to get Fletcher out of the way? Something that might remove his wife as an option, too?

I stalk around the table and stab my finger at the sender's email address on the screen: **syst34@xmail.com.** "Who in the *hell* is this?"

"Hang on…" The email zooms to the corner of the screen as Wilson brings up a black search box and starts typing. IP addresses whiz by on the screen until one flashes and stops.

"Jesus Christ. The email was sent from a server inside the Russian embassy."

We all curse at the same time.

"Wait. Look at his history. Fucking hell, this motherfucker gets around. The Turkish embassy. Iranian. Practically everyone except the Chinese."

Well, no shit. Nobody asks the Chinese embassy if they can just hop on their wifi and send murder plot emails from their Hotmail account.

I look at Jason. He looks at Wilson. "You sure? This isn't some teenager pranking?"

Our ex-CIA hacker doesn't even blink. "Nope. These emails were legitimately sent from those locations. I don't see anything else that interesting, so maybe he slipped up. Hopefully there's more — maybe in code…it'll take me an hour or two to read through all of these."

I cross my arms and narrow my eyes at Jason. "Time for you to call the puppet master."

He looks back at me blandly. He's always so sure he's on the side of good, no matter how fucked up things get. I haven't had that confidence in years — the primary factor in my decision to leave the SEAL teams.

I still don't really understand why Jason left with me. He'd been tapped for the secret squirrel, black ops team. Although we play at that, most of the time we're exactly what we seem to be — fixers, up-and-coming bachelors of Washington society. Professional assholes.

Not superheroes. Not even anti-heroes.

Nothing heroic about what we do, even if there's a shadowy organization that keeps telling

Jason we should keep doing it.

And I'm the number one asshole who *does it*, without an ounce of belief.

No wonder Hailey wants nothing to do with me — she can see my true character.

But right now…this might be one of those moments when the other side of what we do might actually make a difference. Too late for Anabeth Fletcher. Hopefully not too late for her husband.

"First, call Tag. Tell him to pick up Fletcher and bring him here," Jason says. "He can stay with me while you two figure out what someone might want Fletcher to lose his seat in the House." He rubs his thumb between his eyebrows. "And yeah, I'll go make a call."

He disappears to his office. This is the deal. He's the only one who talks to his PRISM contact.

Project **R**esponsible for **I**nternational **S**ecurity **M**easures.

It sounds so…reasonable. And compared to the forces of evil in this world, it is. But the powers-that-be who formed the alliance are ruthless. They wouldn't care about an individual murder. Not of Anabeth Fletcher. Not of a hooker who made the mistake of saying no to Morgan Reid six months ago.

My stomach turns at all the blind-eyes that have been turned in the name of international geo-political stability.

But if the take down of Representative Fletcher is a lead domino, intended to start a chain reaction that culminates in World War III…that, they care about. That, we can demand support on.

And if this turns out to be nothing? Then

they'll turn a blind eye to the justice we administer.

— —

We wait four excruciating days before making our move.

Word came back from PRISM that they were concerned, but had no immediately relevant information to share. Whatever the fuck that means. So we did our thing.

Wilson read every single email he could find. We talked to people. Found out that Fletcher's bill was shot down after lobbyist intervention. What lobbyist? No one would say.

Tag gave Kendra what we had. She said it wasn't enough, and she was right.

So now I'm waiting in an alley a few blocks from his house in the early evening. There aren't any cameras nearby. Tag dropped me in a visual dead zone, and he'll pick me up again in the same spot in a different vehicle.

Wesley Perry, Fletcher's snake of a chief of staff, is walking toward me. Face down in his smart phone, because he's an asshole and unaware of his surroundings.

It gives me a decent amount of pleasure to yank him into the dark alley and send his phone flying toward the brick wall. "Oops."

"Hey!" His fists come up too late. I've got my forearm pressed against his neck, up into his chin. He scrabbles his hands against me, his eyes wide with fear.

Good.

"Two options here, motherfucker. Talk or die,

got it?" My breath puffs in his face.

He kicks at me and I step back, letting him trip himself. Down he goes and up I drag him, slamming him against the bricks again, my fists holding him so tightly his coat tears at the seams. The rip makes me grin.

"Next thing to break is your face."

With a whimper, he presses his legs together and my nose tells me why he's crying. He's pissed himself.

Of course he has.

"I haven't even hit you yet."

"Don't hit me," he says, his eyes pleading for mercy.

"No, I'm definitely going to hit you. I'm going to leave you battered and bruised, so you never forget that I'm more terrifying than the asshole you've been working with. Who is he? Because I'm not scared of him."

He shakes his head. "I don't know what you're talking about."

"Wrong answer, Wesley." I drive my fist into his guts. "Try again."

"You've got the wrong guy," he gasps.

"So you didn't exchange emails with **syst34@xmail.com**? Because I know that you did. And I don't like being lied to."

He groans as I thump him against the wall again, but he still doesn't talk.

"*Is there any way to get Fletcher out of the way?*" I recite the email from memory. "And you responded. **He needs to be disgraced. Ruined forever. Maybe he could off his wife**."

"I didn't mean it," he whispers, which is

152

pathetic if it's true. I don't fucking care.

"But she's dead, isn't she? An innocent woman. You did that. Who were you talking to?" I release him, and he staggers towards me, putting his hands up. I jab twice, quickly, before delivering a roundhouse to his jaw. It's barely fair.

Good thing I don't believe in fair.

"I don't know his name."

"Wrong answer." Another jab to the gut. I'm done hurting him now, because I'm not a murderer, but I don't have a problem bruising them up when I come across them in an alley.

"I think he goes by the name Andre. I heard him answer his phone that way once."

"Where did you usually meet him?"

"The Mall. A coffee shop near the Hill sometimes. I haven't seen or heard from him since Anabeth—"

Blood sprays the wall as I thud my fist into his jaw. "Don't fucking say her name."

He sags against the brick, and I step back, my chest heaving.

Ten seconds pass. Thirty. The chill of the cold February night is getting to him. He's been pummelled in an alley. Any second now…

His shoulders slump, and I lean in, gripping his jaw in a painful hold. "Physical description. Anything you remember. I want it all. Give me everything, and you leave here alive."

He spits out more than I expected. Enough that when he's done, and I've whispered a promise to make the injuries permanent if he doesn't quit and find another job in another city doing anything but power-play politics, I saunter out of the alley, leaving him standing.

More than he deserves.

I'm getting soft.

I shove that thought away. I know why. I don't want any thoughts of Hailey in my head while I do what I've gotta do.

Tag pulls up ten seconds late and I get in. My hands are freezing and my knuckles hurt, but I've got what I need. As soon as we pull away, he gives me even better, unexpected news, as he hands over a tablet.

I hit play as he explains. "Brian Fletcher's neighbour to the east has video surveillance, after all. Kendra doesn't have this yet, I assume, because she's still sniffing around us covering this up for the good representative."

"Why are we just getting it now?"

"Their system went offline before Wilson started looking that morning. It just blipped back on and he snuck in through their digital backdoor tonight. Two masked men scaled the wall into their backyard twenty minutes before Fletcher called Jason. No great shot of their faces, but we've got build, height. And one of them has a slight limp."

"You gonna suggest she get a warrant for this?"

"Already done."

I nod and pull out my phone. I replay the voice recording for Tag. We listen to it twice on the way to the office, and by the time we get there, we already have a plan.

— five —

Hailey

A week without Cole has meant a week of thinking.

I want to scrub him from my brain, and my heart, but he's in there. Stubborn bastard.

I keep coming back to memories I didn't even realize I had, and each time they replay in my mind, I'm reminded that he's wanted me just as long as I've wanted him. It's bittersweet and totally unhelpful.

Five months ago, I was summoned to my parents' estate.

At the time, I convinced myself I was going to be a good daughter.

Now I know I went to see him again.

— —

Five months ago

It's embarrassing, how my face flushes as I walk into the library where they've gathered to talk about who-knows-what. Something to do with Georgetown, I guess, which is why I've been called, since I just graduated. But my face is hot because *he's* here. Cole of the thousand-yard-glare, who turns me on and repulses me at the same time.

Who are you? I want to ask him. How can you be so soulless and so freaking captivating at the

155

same time? Why the hell won't you get out of my fantasies and let me dream about a nice quiet life that doesn't have any drama in it?

I bee-line for the bar, because I could use some liquid courage for whatever this is, and for ignoring the uncomfortable tension seething my way from Cole's corner of the room.

Right away, my mother is in my face, and against my will, my eyes dart around her to find his face.

I don't know why I do. He's obviously pissed at me.

I get it. I'm so useless when it comes to this society stuff.

"Did you give a quote to the campus paper detailing that you're not close to your family because you're trying to be an upstanding citizen?" My mother's voice is shrill. Migraine-inducing. Completely un-maternal.

"That sounds like something I'd say *inside my head*, but no. I know better than to talk to anyone." I barely even have any friends who would know that about me. I just started an internship at this employment agency and got all excited when this girl Taryn asked me to have lunch with her. I'm an island of silence, because of my family. I shake my head and repeat the denial. "Definitely didn't say that."

My father rises, a smirk on his face. "It doesn't matter, Amy." My mother stiffens. She hates that he calls her that. Amelia Dashford Reid doesn't do nicknames. "It's just some socialist kid trying to make trouble before the unveiling of the Reid Steyner Center next week."

156

That's something Cole and his group of evil minions managed to do. A month after my father narrowly missed being charged with murder, they've orchestrated a major donation to the business school that will see a think tank named after my father's company.

It makes me sick.

But that doesn't change the fact that I didn't have anything to do with the article my sister must be tapping against her knee. Taylor doesn't willingly read anything—unless it's about herself.

After another short yelling match that one of the other Horus Group guys—Jason—deflects into a more productive conversation about something else I don't care about, I head outside for some fresh air. I need to clear my head.

I want to convince myself to run screaming and never look back, but that leaves Alison all alone with them. And I love my baby sister. I'm willing to do *anything* to protect her.

It's dusk, a lovely summer evening that I'd enjoy if I didn't have to go back in with the vultures soon.

And if I were alone. Because when I look up again, Cole is a few yards away.

Watching me.

For a second, his gaze is hot and dangerous. Like he sees me as a woman, and the cold anger from earlier is gone.

"Ms. Reid?" And just like that, bam, he's back to being a suit.

My sisters all have first names. Me? To Cole Parker I'll always be *Ms. Reid*. Held at arm's length like *I'm* the problem.

I'm a twenty-three year old intern at a disability employment agency. Between me and Cole "No Comment Motherfucker" Parker, I'm not the problematic one.

I live in a small two-bedroom apartment and refuse to touch my trust fund. I volunteer at a food bank, and in my spare time, I spend too much time on Ravelry. I'm pretty sure Cole spends his spare time cage match fighting and seducing the wives of Washington's most powerful men. We are nothing alike.

If I keep telling myself that, maybe it'll start to feel true.

"What is it, Mr. Parker?"

His eyes glitter for a second. "That went off the rails back there. We wanted to ask you if you'd attend the dedication ceremony with your father."

"I work during the day."

"Yes, I understand congratulations are in order on your internship. The dedication is at the end of the day. I'm sure your manager—"

My eyes narrow and I cut him off. "I'm sure you also understand I don't want to ask for any special favors or treatment. I work until five every day. If it's after that, I can come, yes. It takes me about thirty minutes to get to campus on the Metro."

"Tag or Wilson could pick you up." He shifts his gaze over my shoulder, looking out at the rolling lawn.

"Not you?" I don't even realize I asked that out loud, because he doesn't respond. He just stares over my shoulder. But then I hear the question, like on a weird delay, bouncing around in the air between us, and I try to take it back. Because mortifying—even before he ignored it. "Never mind. I don't need a ride. I prefer to find my own way."

"I know." He flicks his gaze back to my face, and I regret wishing for it, because his attention, hot and piercing, burns me from the inside out.

"Someone inside has the details?" I edge toward the door. "Because I need to go." *Right now*. I can't handle being alone on a patio with this man. What was I thinking, asking if he'd be the one to pick me up?

If Cole Parker ever showed up at my office, I'd kick him in the shins and run as fast as I could in the other direction.

"Yes." His eyelids drop and his lips part, drawing my attention to them. Perfectly carved from granite. Perfectly surrounded by rough five o'clock shadow that makes me shiver at the mere thought of it scraping along my skin, because the man is built for sin.

And I'm so secretly fascinated by him. By the promise of his hard, muscled body, and wicked mind. By his reputation. Whispers of his prowess have reached even me, hiding as far as I can from Washington society.

"Hailey," he says as I turn. And later, I'll wonder why he doesn't just let me go. No...later, I'll wonder why he doesn't haul me into the shadows and kiss me until I'm begging for more, because in hindsight, it's what we both want.

But he just shakes his head. "Don't come to the dedication if you don't want to."

I hold his gaze, letting him singe me. Just a

159

little. "It's okay. I'll be there. It's the right thing to do."

— —

God.

I shake off the memory and pace across my living room. I'd shoved that conversation away, forgetting it under a pile of dislike and resentment, because when I went to the dedication and Cole wasn't there…I was pissed. I'd felt tricked.

That was nothing.

Now it's so much worse. Now I've had him, in my body and heart and mind. And I still feel like everything between us is lopsided.

Cole has all the power. All the knowledge and control.

He could destroy me.

Because after everything that's happened, after walking away, all I want is another moment with that hot, burnt-amber gaze on me.

— six —

Cole

Our work is done. Tonight the Metropolitan Police will be making arrests — good ones that will stick, with loads of legitimate, legally obtained evidence — in the murder of Anabeth Fletcher.

A man named Andre Beauchamp was the money. Shadowy money, and Wilson and I don't think the buck stopped with him, but it's what we've got for now. Two hired men led us to him, and all three were arrested.

I'm glad.

I'm also fucking tired.

After a while, beating people up gets old.

Especially when the adrenaline rush can't be worked out with a good, hard fuck, which is exactly the wrong thought to have while I'm in the shower.

I tip my head back, letting the hot water hit the bruise forming on my jaw. That asshole's head was made of fucking bricks.

Wincing, I grab the ice pack from the tile shelf and hold it in place as I turn and put my back under the steady stream.

My preferred therapy: hot, cold, and beer. I've already finished one bottle, and the next is sitting next to the other ice pack. I came into the shower fully prepared to stay here for a while.

But now I've thought of fucking, which makes

161

me think of Hailey.

I should feel like an asshole for taking her against my office door. I just want to do it again.

Too bad she's off-limits right now. It's better for her if she's insulated from this bullshit, although I've wanted to go to her, every single night.

I take my cock in hand, already throbbing at the memory of sliding into her without any barriers.

That was fucked up, that I didn't even think about a condom. I'd been so sure she was going to tell me stop, and when she didn't, I lost my mind. Standard operating procedure for me and the delicious Ms. Reid.

It's all her soft curves and endless sweet skin. *No, it was the thought of never having her again.* I needed to claim her, to mark her as mine. It wasn't enough to say it. I needed to see in her eyes that she'd heard me. *Mine.*

When this is all over—when I've fulfilled my promise to Jason, and closed the case that made me take on Morgan Reid as a client in the first place—I'm taking Hailey away from all of this. Finding that private beach we can surf and fuck and laugh on. Not a care in this world except for each other.

Hailey in a bikini. In nothing at all, just the world's softest sand pressed to her hips and breasts and ass. I squeeze my eyes tight, holding on to that fantasy as my orgasm builds. I'm squeezing my dick hard enough it might hurt if I didn't need that tightness.

Laughing. Her modestly covering her breasts as she stumbles through the surf, me chasing her.

Grabbing her and rolling together in the waves until I find my place between her legs. Hard against soft. Tough against sweet.

That's the part that turns me on the most about her. More than how sexy she is, it's her fucking sweetness. I've never had anyone like Hailey in my life before. *You don't have her now, asshole.* No, right now I've let her go, but I'm still watching her. Still aware of her, constantly.

She's alone right now, in the bed I want to be in more than I want my next breath. In the morning she'll get up and go to work. In a few days, she'll have her Vanity Fair interview, and I should be there with her, but I can't be.

One day, I'll be good enough for her. One day, I'll be able to be in the same room with her and not threaten the fragile goodness she's constructed around her.

I jerk myself more roughly now, so close to release. Regret morphs to something less-definable, leaving an angry edge on the usually simple *feelsfuckinggood* of masturbating. There's nothing simple about my fantasy of Hailey. Nothing easy or possible about getting the woman of my dreams alone, safe, and all mine on a beach in Hawaii. Fuck, I can't even have her in an apartment in Washington for more than a few hours.

And even that was perfect. Hailey begging me for more. Fucking her face. Spanking her pussy. *Fuck me.* I need her. Need to spread her legs wide and feast on her wet, swollen cunt. Drive deep and blow my load inside her.

Fuuuuuck.

I fall forward, wincing as my palm slams

against the shower wall, some of the cuts on my hand screaming in protest. With my other hand, I slow my strokes, milking my cock as the last spurts fall to the drain below.

With fantasies like that, I need to stay as far away from Hailey Reid as I can get, for as long as I can.

We both know it won't be forever. I'm not that strong.

seven

Hailey

I didn't have any doubt that something would slam Cole and me back together.

I just assumed it would be another mistake. Another scandal in my family.

Not something even darker. Totally random. And utterly terrifying.

— —

Two weeks after Cole was arrested, the Metropolitan Police Major Case unit executed a raid on a condo near The Hill and arrested two men for the murder of Anabeth Fletcher, and at the same time, a simultaneous warrant was being served in Virginia on a third man, whose name never made it to the papers.

I was dying to ask Wilson about it.

I didn't.

Not when he came over the next day to do my prep for the Vanity Fair interview, and not three days later when he showed up twenty minutes before the reporter in case I had any last minute questions.

Instead, I made him knit me a scarf.

"You're getting pretty good at that." I peer over his shoulder. Only two dropped stitches that row. "You can give that to Jason for his birthday."

"I don't know when Jason's birthday is."

"Seriously?"

"Correction. I don't *care* when Jason's birthday is."

"How about Cole's birthday?" I'm not sure why I bring that up. I walked away. I don't care about him. *Liar, liar, pants on fire.*

"June tenth."

I freeze. Somehow Cole having an actual birthday—a date on which he was born, once helpless and small and probably very cute—makes him more human. "How do you know that off the top of your head, but not Jason's?"

He ducks his big, blond head and stares at his knitting.

"Wilson?"

"I thought you might want to know. I can also tell you his favorite foods, total net worth, and the results of his last physical."

In broad strokes, I think I know the answer to the last point. I don't care about the middle one. But the first... "Uhm, okay. What kind of food does he like?"

Wilson twists his head and looks at me. "If I tell you, can I stop knitting?"

"Nope. It's going to impress the reporter, and if I'm lucky, distract her. The ladies love a man who's good with his hands. Maybe if *you're* lucky she'll want to nip the interview short and drag you back to her hotel room."

"I think she's married."

"Too bad for you."

"Too bad for *you.*" He shoves the world's ugliest scarf attempt back into my knitting basket. "Why did you agree to this interview if you don't want to do it?"

Because I don't like to be selfish. "I couldn't think of a good reason to say no."

"Pretty sure 'my life isn't for public consumption' is a perfectly acceptable reason." He stands, filling the space beside me, and for a second I think he's going to hug me. That would be weird, but he doesn't. Instead he skirts around me and pulls his computer out of his backpack. "Do you remember what I told you the other day?"

"From her previous stories, you think she really wants the hint of taboo. She's going to keep coming back to Taylor and the Vice President." I nod. I can do this. "But instead I'm going to give her the estranged sister story."

It's not a lie, and it's a part of my life I don't mind sharing. I won't make Taylor look bad, but it's to my advantage that the world knows we aren't close.

"And if you can find a way to talk about sexual assault on campus..." he trails off as I snap my gaze to meet his. I'm scowling, because we've been over this. "Okay, fine. I'm just saying, it's a sexy story." He turns a faint shade of red. "Jesus. Not sexy, that's not what I mean. Sensational. It'll sell magazines."

I roll my eyes and head into the kitchen to make tea.

"I'm really the wrong person to be doing this with you," he calls after me.

Too bad I've banned the right person. Cole would just *get* my boundaries without these awkward conversations, but he's off-limits because if he helps me with this, we'll end up naked in my

167

bedroom before the interview is over.

No, Cole is not an option.

And I refused to have Jason do it. I'm furious with him, even more so than with Cole. *Because you're not really mad at Cole.* No, I'm just trying my best to move on from an ill-advised fling. But Jason, on the other hand—I saw the way he looked at me, like I was a problem that needed to be dealt with. I get enough of that bullshit from my family. I don't need it from their hired muscle, too.

I lift my voice. "Why are you here if you don't like stuff like this? Didn't Tag volunteer? He likes pretty reporter ladies."

"He did. Cole wanted me to do it."

You're mine. His words roll unbidden into my mind, and I stare blankly at my tea cupboard before grabbing four random boxes and sticking them on a tray with a tea pot of hot water.

Now I'm grumpy, because how can I move on when he's all but here in person?

I set the tray down a bit harder than necessary on the coffee table.

"You didn't need to make tea if it's pissed you off."

I shoot Wilson a death look.

"Oh. Not the tea?"

"No, not the tea."

"Me?"

"Shut up."

"Ah. Cole?"

I sigh and sit down. "I'm not mad at him."

He hesitates, then looks at his computer before talking again. "But you were."

"Yes. No. I wasn't mad. I was scared." And I

168

still think Cole came perilously close to using me. But I'm not going to tell Wilson that. It feels like a betrayal to even think it when Cole's actually been pretty steadfastly on my side.

Again, I think about asking Wilson about the arrests. I go half-way there. "He's okay, then? Not under investigation for…anything?"

"He's fine. Kind of pissed, still. Stomping around like a hungry bear." That makes my heart ache, that Cole is out of sorts and I can't soothe him, and Wilson must see that on my face, too, because he shakes his head. "I'm not helping, am I?"

"It's okay," I whisper.

"It would be best if you forget him."

"We'll put that on the long list of things that would be best for me. Right below having a different family and moving to another state."

"Why don't you?"

"You're all full of questions, today, Wilson." I narrow my eyes at him. "Why?"

"Good for you to get this shit out now, realize it's all there on the tip of your tongue."

I stare at him. "You're doing this so I don't say it to the reporter."

He blushes, which is weird. The more I learn about Wilson, the more I'm using that word. "She's going to be a pro at pulling this shit out of you. That level of honesty would sell a lot of magazines. So when she gets here…you need to know where you might go, so you can *not go there*."

"You're evil." I take a deep breath. "Okay. I won't get tripped into talking about why I still live in Washington."

"What about dating?"

"I date. I'm young. I'm not looking for anything serious."

"Good. Career plans?"

"I love the non-profit sector, and consider it a real honor to work hands-on with people who are working hard to get ahead in the shadow of all this wealth and power."

"Great."

He takes me through ten more questions before the reporter arrives, then excuses himself to the kitchen to give us privacy. Ha. Like he can't hear everything from ten feet away.

She introduces herself and tells me to call her Leanne. I make the same request for her to call me Hailey and she sets a voice recorder next to the tea.

She starts with easy questions, letting me orient her to my life.

When she finally asks about Taylor, I spill my guts about going in different directions in high school, and slide in honest praise for my sister's creativity and social prowess. I talk about my little sister and my brother, too, all approved talking points, and the whole time she nods and smiles. On the more dangerous points, I keep to the canned answers, and after a few runs at me from different directions, she gives up trying to get more.

After an hour, I'm pretty sure we're done. Wilson moves closer, and I think he's going to shut her down when she leans forward. I can hear the shift in her voice, and it scares me, because I don't know where she's going with what she asks me next.

"Did your father ever sexually abuse you,

170

Hailey?"

I gape at her, speechless. No. I hate my father. He's an asshole, and now that I'm an adult, I've come to understand him as a sleaze. But if he'd ever touched me inappropriately, I'd have…God. I can't even imagine what I'd have done. Stabbed him in his sleep, probably.

Wilson joins me on the couch, but he doesn't stop the interview. "Are you okay?" he asks quietly.

I nod. "No, my father didn't abuse me." I say the words slowly, staring at the reporter. "Really, he didn't. Why are you asking me that?"

I want to know if Alison said something in her interview. I can't remember if that's happened yet. I can't think clearly about anything, actually, and all of a sudden I want both the reporter and Wilson out of my apartment.

I want to call Cole. And then I want to call my sister and make sure everything is okay.

Because even though my father never touched me, a cold realization slithers through my gut that I can't entirely rule out that he didn't touch one of my sisters. I can't say he's not capable of that.

"Do you know Gerome Lively?"

I shake my head. Beside me, Wilson doesn't move—and that's a big tell, because he's actually a pretty twitchy guy. Constantly in motion, even as he's hunkered down behind a computer. His head bobs and his fingers tap. But right now, he's an ice giant.

"Have you ever been to a private resort in the Bahamas?"

I turn to Wilson and silently ask him with my

171

eyes if I can answer that.

"Have you?" he mutters, his brows drawn tight.

"No." My mind is racing as I turn back to the reporter. "What is this about?"

"Something that has come up in the course of my interviews. Gerome Lively—" Leanne glances at Wilson, and I follow her gaze. His face is an unreadable mask. "He's a British financier with property around the world. Your father has visited his compound in the Bahamas many times over the last ten years."

Memories flash. My parents fighting when my father returned from a business trip. My mother, half in the bag, tossing words at him that shocked and scared me, so I shoved them out of my head until now. "I've never traveled with my father out of the country."

"Have your sisters?"

"No." The denial comes fast. I don't actually know if it's true about Taylor, but I'm certain Alison's never gone to the Caribbean with him. My mother prefers Hawaii and Europe, and both of my parents prefer not to take children on their separate vacations. We're inconvenient. My stomach turns at the new implications of that long-accepted reality.

Did my father just have a general disdain for us all, or did he actively hide a gross part of his life from his family for all this time?

I want to throw up. Instead, I smile, not giving a fuck if it reaches my eyes. It doesn't.

Leanne pauses before lifting the recorder and turning it off. "If you think of something along those lines…please get in touch with me."

"I will." I say it automatically, being polite to the person who's just quietly blown apart my world. I should be used to having the unthinkable dropped in my lap. I'm not. And I won't contact her again, no matter what. But I lie and promise I will because it's the right thing to say.

After she leaves, I shove Wilson's knitting project back into his hands and tidy up the mugs, then go to the bathroom and splash cold water on my face. When I come back, he's added two inches of perfect rows to his scarf. Interesting.

"You've gotten quite good at that all of a sudden. Who is Gerome Lively?"

"You heard her. He's one of the richest men in the world." The needles clicked and his fingers flashed as he whipped through one last row before casting off as I stared at him. "Here you go. A present."

I scowl at the knitted square. "She wasn't asking about a society puff piece. Who is he and what does my father have to do with him?"

"Your father is also one of the richest men in the world."

"And?"

"And they're both dangerous. Kinky as fuck, and not in the good way." He shoves himself up to stand. "I shouldn't be the one to tell you about this."

"I'm not sure anyone else will." Cold, slimy revulsion squirms through my gut. "Like, more of what my father did last year?"

"Probably."

"And you guys help them?" My voice is

fluttery, full of panic and disgust.

"No. No! What happened six months ago… that was a…" He clenches his jaw and presses his lips together. "I can't tell you anything about that, but no, we're not on the same side of anything as Gerome Lively. He's a vile human being."

"And my father vacations with him."

"No good comes from you asking more about that."

"Do you know more?"

He doesn't answer, and my blood boils.

"Does *Cole* know more about that?"

I want to hear *no*. Instead, he doesn't say anything. "Fine. Be difficult. But be difficult somewhere else, we're done with this nonsense. I'm going back to my regular life now."

He makes a reluctant face and tucks his computer away in his bag. "Are you okay?"

I think about lying, but he already knows the truth. "No. I need to talk to my younger sister."

"Do you want her to come here?"

I nod.

"I'll go and get her."

"Seriously, Wilson, you can go back to whatever work you're doing. This is…" The usual Reid bullshit. "This is beyond the scope of whatever it is you guys are doing to rescue Taylor's reputation."

He frowns at me. "Cole's not going to like that."

"Well, bully for him. This is my personal life, and until it hits the pages of a magazine, I'd like to keep it that way. Personal. Private. Family only." It's kind of a ridiculous thing to say to a hacker. I'm sure Wilson knows all sorts of things about me that

I don't even know myself.

He just shrugs, like that's my fight to wage with Cole.

Maybe it is.

Bring it on.

—eight—

Cole

Wilson knows something he doesn't want me to know.

He doesn't have a lot of tells, but this is one that he hasn't been able to shake—dropping into stealth mode. I'm pacing in the conference room, waiting for him to return, and he slips right past me. I don't see him come in. But I do hear his computer power up in his office.

"What's wrong?" I ask as I stride into his office.

He doesn't look up. "Hang on."

"No. You knew I was waiting and you snuck past me like a ninja. Obviously the interview didn't go off without a hitch. Spill."

"Wow. You used your keen observational skills to deduce that I was in my office. Lights on, door open." He punches in his password, then starts scrolling through a blur of files on his desktop. "We need to talk, I just need to find some information first." He glances up and blinks at the expression on my face. Then he throws me a bone. "Hailey is fine."

"I wasn't—" I cut myself off. "Shut up. You're not Dr. Ruth."

He frowns. "She's a sex therapist, not a relationship expert. You meant—"

"Again, shut up. What do we need to talk about?"

He pulls out his phone and texts someone. Jason or Tag, presumably. "Gerome Lively."

Fuck. I knew this was there, in the background. Eventually, Morgan Reid's friendship with Lively would bite him in the ass, as it should, because they're both twisted fucks. But not yet. "How?"

He grabs his tablet and brushes past me. He talks as we walk to the conference room, and by the time the big screen lights up, I'm fuming.

"So, yeah. Vanity Fair is digging into him. She didn't say either way, but I'm sure they're going to talk to the Feds, so Jason needs to talk to his guy. Find out where this puts Reid and the others we're watching here."

"It could take years to unfold. Fuck. I mean, this could be the break we need, but PRISM isn't going to be happy if someone shows their hand too soon and he manages to cover his ass."

With the flick of a finger, Wilson throws ten pictures of teenage girls on the screen. He doesn't need to explain them to me. All missing. All flew out of the country on business class tickets to various points on the globe and then bounced out of sight.

It's a case we've been working for nine months. It's why I took Morgan Reid's case. I need him to lead me to Lively.

Nothing else matters.

Nothing else mattered.

I'm not giving up on the mission because of Hailey, but I can't pretend my loyalty isn't divided.

It's divided as fuck. And if push comes to shove, she wins.

178

I'm not even sure she likes me, unless I'm naked in her bed, and she still wins. She'll always win, because the only thing I've truly believed in in *years*, is her goddamn earnestness. Her righteous indignation over the shades of gray that rule my world and how she doesn't hesitate to tell me I'm full of shit.

She's fearless. I keep thinking of her as innocent, but only in spirit—pure, good. Lightness and grace. She's not innocent of the evils in this world—even less so today, apparently—but she still believes that's an aberration, an *other*, in a world of order and justice and common decency.

Hardly.

I know better than anyone how that darkness lurks under the skin of so-called good men and women everywhere. And when those people have power, it's my job to take that knowledge and use it when necessary. Hoard it when it's not.

"It'll be good for *them* if this cracks now." Wilson says it quietly, but there's an edge to his voice.

I glare at him. "What does that mean?" I know full well he means the girls. I want him to have the fucking balls to say that to my face, because I would never choose to keep them in peril if I had choice in the matter.

It turns out the edge is something else. "This isn't convenient timing for you."

"That's bullshit," I grind out. "And if you think for a second Hailey would want me to avoid dealing with this, you underestimate us both." I flick my gaze away from him and look back at the screen. "It's only bad if he scuttles under a rock."

179

Wilson pauses before changing the subject slightly. "That new bug you put on Morgan Reid's cell phone is giving us some information."

Morgan's company had changed cell phone service providers right around the time his oldest daughter, Taylor, decided to blow the Vice President and record it for posterity. Or publicity, the jury was still out on her motivation. I noticed he didn't have it on him when we were there last time, discussing the magazine article. Took a chance he charged it in his office and won.

I'd just managed to place a listening device in it and slide back into the hallway when Hailey found me. The one and only night I've spent with her.

We'd been a little distracted the last two weeks, but Wilson had been digging shit up on the sex tape Hailey's sister had accidentally-on-purpose starred in. It wasn't looking good for Taylor Reid, but since we're bastards, that would stay our secret.

It never ends.

"What do you mean? Texts? Phone calls?"

"Both. Regular travel plans at first blush. It didn't click for me until the interview this afternoon, but Morgan is going to Miami weekend after next. For four days."

Which meant a helicopter ride to Lively's private island. "Disgusting."

"You should go with him."

I recoil as if Wilson's physically hit me. "No."

"Yes."

"It's a good thing you're not my fucking boss."

Behind me, Jason laughs as he enters the room and paces to the head of the conference table.

180

"None of us would ever try to own you, Cole. You have a tendency to turn rabid too often. What does Wilson want to make you do?"

"Go to Gerome Lively's Bahamas compound with Morgan Reid."

"That's a good idea."

"Fuck you, too." I can't. Fuck me, I didn't think this choice would come this quickly. But I choose Hailey, no second thoughts. "Whoever goes will have to fuck the women. I can't do that."

The temperature in the room drops ten degrees as Jason says nothing. His silence says it all, but then he opens his mouth and makes it so much worse. "You've never had a problem with orgies in the past."

Before I can launch myself at him, Tag is there, holding me back.

"Get off me," I spit, my muscles clenched and ready for battle. "When the hell did you get here, anyway?"

"Just before Jason decided to masterfully push all your pervert buttons, you idiot. Stop."

"It's not the same thing," I growl, as surprised as my friend that I'm on edge about my sexual history now. Anything—everything—I've ever done has been with consensual adults. Sometimes more than one at a time. *Often more than one at a time.* Until Hailey, I'd never wanted anything to be private. Personal. Intimate.

"He knows that. What the hell is wrong with you?" Tag shoves me again for good measure and turns to the others.

Seething, I back off, but I'm not listening to them anymore. I'm rattled and edgy, and ready to

181

just bring in the FBI or the CIA. Anyone who will take this filth and put it in jail where it belongs.

I pace back and forth, stopping just shy of Tag each time. He's planted himself between me and our other partners, and he's waving his hands in the air. I suck in another lungful of air and try to dial down the asshole-reaction long enough to hear him. It's fucking hard.

Tag ends his tirade with a summation that I appreciate, since it means at least half of us are on the side of me not getting too friendly with Lively. "This is not what we are. We don't go undercover and we don't *ever* suggest to each other that we do anything illegal."

"He picked up a fucking gun and happily got himself arrested for murder the other day. He's not a fucking fragile flower." Jason glowers in my direction as he says this. "Until it comes to a woman he has no business fuck—"

"Finish that thought and Tag won't be able to hold me back," I grind out.

Wilson rolls his eyes and stands up. "Okay, let's wind this back to what needs to be done before deciding who will do it."

He catches up Jason and Tag on what we know, and what the Vanity Fair reporter said to Hailey during the interview. My skin crawls at the thought of her and her sister processing this shit all alone right now.

"So shit's about to hit the fan for Lively."

"About to...or will in a few months...or maybe never. Who knows who he has in his pocket? Isn't that why we're on it, too? Because PRISM doesn't trust that he'll ever be prosecuted, and he can

182

bring down too many big fish?" I shake my head at some of the names we're protecting. "Seriously, you don't want to send me to the Caribbean with Reid. I may just massacre the lot of them."

Jason snorts. "Wouldn't be the worst idea I've entertained, except for the whole global destabilization thing."

"Hell of a side effect to justice." Launching us into World War III is exactly what PRISM is trying to avoid. The true cost of that disgusts me, but I understand their mission. I don't always understand the domino effect of things that they think they can see. Jason does, more than me. Instinct? Intuition? Sometimes I act on them, when I'm not thinking too hard. But I never trust my gut, not really.

I learned early on how emotional responses can lead people to devastating consequences.

It turned me into the hard-ass motherfucker I am today, and usually, I'm just fine with that. Not so much tonight. It feels like I've got razor blades under my skin and a fucking marching band of monkeys inside my chest.

Wilson points at Jason. "You need to get us some direction. Figure out what the puppet masters want us to do. Then we can decide who should do whatever it is that needs to be done." Now he's pointing at me. "You need to admit that you're not just sleeping with the Reid girl."

I shift uncomfortably and cross my arms. "I have no idea what I'm doing with Hailey." God's honest truth, right there. "I swear. I haven't shared because…"

When I trail off, Tag clears his throat. "I get it.

Shit gets complicated, it's hard to talk about."

"Oh, for fuck's sake. Seriously?" Jason shakes his head. "No. No relationships, no women, no falling in love. Cole here is proof positive that it makes men weak."

"Distracted, maybe. Not weak." Tag shrugs. "If someone threatened Kendra, I'd rip them apart, limb from limb."

"You know she divorced your sorry ass, right?"

Another shrug. "We don't live well together. Doesn't mean she's not important to me. Doesn't mean I can't still do my job while wanting to keep her safe."

I want to ask Tag how to balance this shit out, still care about the job and care about the woman at the same time. Because I feel fucking tilted. Instead I nod. "Yeah. What he said."

"He loves Kendra. Is that how you feel about Hailey Dashford Reid? Sweet, good girl daughter of the rich and famous, who has rejected everything your sexy ass in a tux represents?" Jason snorts. "You know there's not a chance in hell of that working out, right?"

Is this love? If it is, I fucking hate it. It's painful and uncomfortable, distracting and not nearly naked enough.

"Little early to call it anything. I care about her. More than I expected to, I'll grant you that. You saw that coming, I guess." I'd wanted her for months. Thought that if I had her, I could get her out of my system. Turns out I wasn't the only one in the equation, and Hailey wanted more. Fuck me, I *needed* more. We both did. And do.

Two weeks might be my limit.

Jason just shakes his head. "It's almost morning in Geneva. I'll stay up and make some calls. What we need here is some cooling off time. Take the night, get your head on straight, and let's discuss a game plan over breakfast tomorrow. Deal?"

We shake on it, and I go back to my office. At the other end of the hall, Jason closes his door without looking back at me. Beside him, Wilson leaves his door open, but flicks off his light. He's about to fall deep into a pile of computer code and probably won't sleep before breakfast.

Tag just shrugs at me, apparently his favorite gesture today, grabs his bag and hits the stairs.

I should leave, too. Instead, I log into my computer and pull up the video feed of Hailey's apartment. We have cameras on the front entrance and her door. I choose the latter and hit rewind. Two hours back, I see Hailey and Alison leaving together. I immediately flip to the front door camera and time synch the feeds, to get a clue as to where they're going, but Hailey just waits for a town car to pull up for Alison, hugs her goodbye, then heads back inside. I watch her climb the stairs, and if she just locked herself into her apartment, I'd have powered down and gone home.

Instead, she stops on the landing outside her apartment, her hand on the handle, and looks up at the camera.

The look on her face—tight, drawn, *sad*—destroys me.

And I head for the door.

nine

Hailey

It takes me a minute to realize why I've woken up. It was the creak of the front door that did it, or maybe the beep of the alarm system as he turned it off. I'm not sure, because my first fully conscious observation of the apartment is total silence.

What the hell just woke me up?

Then I hear footsteps.

He's not trying to be quiet, not really. I have no doubt, if he wanted to be quiet, I wouldn't know he was here until he was on top of me. I shiver against my will, hating how much that excites me.

"Get out." I want him here, like crazy, but all of a sudden, the emotions of the last few weeks crash inside me and I'm *angry* at him. Pissed that it took him so long to come. That it's in the middle of the night and I know he'll be gone again before dawn.

Livid that we both need this to keep going.

He pauses in the doorway for a second before prowling closer. "I'm not here."

"And yet obviously…" I sigh as he steps into the moonlight streaming through my window. God, he looks good. Rumpled. Tired. But hard as fuck and sizzling with energy. I want to touch him all over, absorb that intensity and sooth the raging beast inside him. My reaction isn't selfless, though — not at all.

While we were apart, I could pretend I was getting over him. Now he's here, and my chest hurts at how much I need him. Emotionally and physically. I press my thighs together, a futile effort against the instant ache he creates inside me.

"In the morning you can pretend this was just a dream. Or a nightmare."

I shake my head. "Never that. But will this just torture us more? Because tomorrow you'll be gone again, and we'll start this cycle all over."

His eyes glitter in the dark, his teeth flashing white as he grimaces. "Wilson told me about the interview. Is your sister okay? Are you okay?"

"Seriously? You break into my apartment to ask me if I'm fine?" I'm shaking with relief that he's finally come to me, and angry that it took so long. And I'm still pushing him away. "I don't know what kind of monster my father really is—I won't be surprised if it turns out he's the worst kind—but he never hurt us like that. Thank God."

"I'm sorry anyway."

"Why? It has nothing to do with me." I prickle at the conversation. I don't want to talk. I want to touch and hold and bite and cry from pleasure, but I don't want to talk anymore.

"You found out some shitty fucking news today. That kind of thing can mess with your head."

He would know, I'm sure. The last shitty news he got nearly landed him in jail. Which reminds me... "I'm not your problem anymore, Cole. Remember? I never was, not really."

"You don't think you're my problem?" He slides out of his jacket and unbuttons his shirt. "You don't get to decide that for me. You can push me away and tell yourself that I'm not *your* problem. That's fine." He strides toward me, and I'm so glad my drapes are open and we have a full moon tonight. Cole stripped down to just dress pants, his thick, muscled torso twisting in the moonlight is the prettiest thing I've ever seen. He climbs on top of me and shoves the blankets out of the way. "But *you* are *mine*. My problem, my concern, my fucking constant worry because I'm not good enough to be in your bed and at your side, keeping you safe."

His words are heavy and sharp, and they land on me like that, but they don't hurt. I can feel them, though, pointy and meaningful, and if I fight against them...that hurts. A part of me wants to relax, and let him slide closer. Slide inside me the way he's said I'm deep in him already.

He's already there. And it's too much, so I'm in denial.

"This is crazy." When he's this close, I can't remember all the reasons we shouldn't be together. All I can feel is how right it is when he's touching me. How perfect it will be when he thrusts himself inside me and claims me the only way I'll let him. I'm wet. Ready. Swollen and aching and hot for him. Only him, spoiled for all others.

"No shit." He rolls his face against mine, forehead to forehead, nose to nose...lips to lips. I whimper as he kisses me. I've missed him so much. Needed this so much. "Good crazy or bad crazy?"

"Don't stop crazy," I whisper, arching into his hands as they move over my body. He strips me out of the tiny sleep shorts and tank top I'm wearing. Was wearing, because now they're on the floor, along with the rest of his clothes.

"I'm sorry," he mutters after grazing his teeth over my bottom lip. "I should have called you. Tonight. Before. You deserve more than this."

"No." I shake my head. "I'm not the princess you think I am. I won't pretend I'm happy about all the rest, but this is…fine. I'd rather have you in the middle of the night than not at all. Even when I'm upset with you…I want you."

"God, I've missed you, Hailey." He kisses me so hard it hurts. I wrap my arms around his neck. I want more.

"Shut up and fuck me, okay?" It's the wrong thing to say. It's flippant and dirty, and he deserves to know I feel the same way. *I missed you, too*, I say in my head. But when I open my mouth, no words come out. So I kiss him back, then bite his chin on my way to his neck. His Adam's apple bobs under my tongue as I lick him there, savoring the taste of his skin. "I'm still on the pill. I'm such a good girl, I take it every day."

"Jesus, I'm sorry about that." But his cock flexes against my inner thigh. *Gotcha.*

"Really? You didn't like being the only man who's ever been bare inside me?" He tightens all around me, and I throb for him everywhere — heavy, sensitive breasts. Wet between the legs. Hungry mouth. But this isn't quite right. "You don't need to be sorry." I drop my voice, dropping the act. Dropping everything, including the mask. "I missed you, too. So much."

Another growl, and he surges over me. For a second I think he's just going to drive his cock into me, and God knows I'm wet enough, but he just rocks above me on all fours, stretching out this moment like it's made of bubble gum or something similarly nice and sweet and not at all the brittle, desperate desire threatening to crack inside me.

"You are *not* a good girl. You're a goddamn vixen." He rakes his gaze down my body, writhing beneath him, and exhales slowly. With intent. Like that little bit of honesty was enough, and now we can play again.

I shiver again, impatient for more. "Misrepresenting myself...that sounds punishment-worthy."

He laughs and crawls back a few inches, dropping his face to my neck. His breath brushes against my skin. "Is that what you think I should do? I come to you because I need you, and I think you need me, and you want me to spank you again?"

"You didn't really spank me the first time," I say, panting, because *yes*, I want his hand print on my ass. I want that sting, that sharp bite that fades into the most delicious warmth. I only got a taste of it, and I want more. "Did you come here for something else?"

He skims his cheek over my collarbone and down my chest, inhaling deeply as he buries his face between my breasts. The scruff on his jaw tells me he hasn't shaved in a few days, and I never want him to shave. I want everything about Cole to have this edge — sex with spanking, kisses with beard burn, and our words to never, ever have whatever softness is about to come out of his mouth.

Not just because I can't handle it — although the last time we were together kind of proves I can't. I'd fall for this man in a heartbeat. *You've already fallen for him.* Right. I've fallen for a man I can't have except between the hours of one and four in the morning every few weeks. And I can barely hang on to being cool with that, but I need to. So he can't be lovely. He just can't. It's not allowed.

Plus I *like* the bad boy thing. I didn't know I wanted it until I wanted *him*, and maybe I only want it because it's him.

But I don't want him ever thinking that I want him to dial back the dirty.

"Cole?"

He looks up at me, his mouth wet and his eyes glazed, and my stomach drops. He doesn't need to say anything, after all. A single look does it.

I shake my head. *Please don't make this heavy.* I can't say it out loud, because if he needs that, I'll give it to him.

I'll give him my heart even if it means tearing it out of my chest while it's still beating.

He licks his lips and blinks, and the look is gone. "I had something else in mind for tonight," he says, his voice all husky and sexy and not at all needy. Like he knows. "Something I've been thinking about since you leaned against my door and wiggled that gorgeous ass of yours at me."

I don't remember wiggling anything, and I tell him as much.

"Hmm." He sucks one of my nipples into his mouth as he thinks about this, and it's like an electric current straight to my clit. Oh God. He releases it with a wet pop. "It was something incredibly tempting, anyway." He curves one hand under my body as he's talking, cupping his hand over my ass, his fingertips teasing at the sensitive tissue in the middle. "Have you ever had anyone here, Hailey?"

I shake my head, my heart pounding a mile a minute.

"Too much?"

Is it obvious on my face? "No," I squeak, because while it's much more intense, more intimate, than anything I've experienced before, I don't want him to stop.

I never want him to stop.

He hums against my sternum as he moves slowly down my body. "Is it okay if I touch you like this?"

"Yes." Definitely yes. I squirm inside the warm, safe circle of his arms, but yeah, it felt good. Surprisingly good. Like I might kick him if he stopped.

"Don't think about it. Just feel."

Oh, I'm feeling. And reacting. My pussy clenches, demanding to be filled, or licked, or both. Yes, definitely both.

"This was worth me playing burglar, yes?"

That reminds me. "You're lucky, you know. Another day or two and you'd have been out of luck."

"Why?" He licks a lazy circle around my belly button, and my eyes roll back in my head.

This has to be why I share what I say next, because I'm *not* thinking clearly. He's worked his way behind all my filters and censors and good girl nonsense, and now I'm going deep in the TMI zone. His finger is circling the inside of my ass cheeks, it's his own damn fault. "My period's due later this week. You really should schedule your break-ins in advance." He bites my belly and I squeal. "You know," I continue, more breathlessly this time. "To avoid inconveniences."

"I'm pretty sure I'm not so much of a jerk that I'd call that an inconvenience." He clearly thinks the label applies in other ways. Maybe it does.

The sum total of what I know about Cole — really know, truly in my heart — is how right it feels when he's between my legs. His hands, his head, his cock.

Right now, it's his head, and I'm in heaven.

In the morning? Maybe hell. But it'll be worth it.

With his free hand, he squeezes my inside thigh as he presses it up the bed, holding me wide open for his questing tongue. And fingers.

I whimper as his thumbs stokes over my perineum, sliding into the slippery wetness that proves I like exactly what he's doing. And then he pulls that moisture back and —

"Oh!" This time it's more of a gasp than a whimper as he uses my own arousal to ease his fingertip into my tight rear hole. Just the tip. Just enough to make it burn. The muscles there clench and relax on their own, blooming in arousal, and I wiggle — okay, now I'm wiggling, damn him.

"Yes," he mutters, his gaze hooded and heavy, fixed on the spot where he's just barely penetrating me. "That's so fucking hot. You are unbelievable, Hailey. You'll take anything I give you, won't you?"

I nod and push against his finger, not even

194

realizing I'm doing it, but as I press, I open for him, and his finger slides slowly into my body. Where nobody has ever been before. I'm going to die, and it's not from embarrassment, because it feels too good. Intense. Almost painful. Burning, yes. But so damn good, I never want him to stop touching me there. I gasp again, that's all I'm reduced to now, noises and mewling, as my hands grab at the bed beneath me.

He dips his head, dark spiky hair covering my view of his mouth as he begins going down on me, but I can feel it. All of it. The licks. The sucks. The swirls that make my legs tremble. He kisses every bit of my pussy, and with each sizzling contact, my world narrows to the push and pull of impending climax. I rock my hips under his face, and at first I try to hold on to the bed, to contain myself, but then I'm sliding my hands into his hair and it's so much better.

Restraint is totally the wrong way to go when the man of your dreams is licking your pussy like it's made of spun sugar.

And finger-fucking my ass. I can't forget that. He won't let me, because as he slowly twists me towards what feels like it's going to be a heavy, layered orgasm, he's still talking. Individual words like "tight" and "wet", "sweet" and "hungry."

Then his thumb takes over, sliding deep into my pussy before lazily rolling up and around my clit, a slow slide of thick flesh on lubricated skin. And that frees up his mouth for full-on sentences again, and I die and go to heaven, coming all over his hand as he presses his rough cheek against my thigh and tells me I'm beautiful. "You come so sweet, Hailey. Jesus, I need you."

"Take me," I pant, flopping my hands wide on the bed. I'm boneless, my brain cells scrambled but good, and he could fuck me like a speed demon right now and I wouldn't care.

That's not Cole's style, though. He grins at me, all feral animal, and ever so slowly slides his hands under my hips and flips me over.

Like I'm a fucking pancake. Except…yup. I pretty much am.

This works too. Not sure it's my best angle, but he likes my butt.

"I told you," he whispers in my ear as he looms beside me, his erection pulsing heavy against my hip. "I need you, and not for a quick fuck. I don't want to just take you. I need you writhing beneath me. I need you digging your heels in my ass, fucking back at me as I sink balls deep into your hot, wet, *delicious* pussy."

"Okay," I breathe, not entirely sure how that's going to happen because *boneless*.

"We've got all night," he says, laughing under his breath at me.

I smile despite myself. "You don't need to sleep?"

"An hour or two, maybe. *If* I get my fill of you." He kisses my shoulder, then sinks his teeth gently into the fleshy part of my back as he trails his hand down my spine, his fingertips the only point of barely-touching contact on my skin. Smoothing his palm over my ass, he lifts his torso up as if by magic—or impressive abs, because he has those in an eight-pack—and keeps stroking down my legs, raising a trail of goosebumps in his wake. My

196

pussy clenches at the promise of more. "I love how soft you are here," he says, curving his fingers to the extra-fleshy part at the top of my generally heavy thighs. "Spread."

One word, and I instantly comply. But instead of thrusting his fingers inside me, or teasing my sensitive, still nerve-twitchy flesh, he just cups my pussy in his big hand and lifts my pelvis into the air. I scramble onto my knees, keeping my cheek pressed against the bed.

He settles behind me, those hands spread across my butt. I wish I had some lube. I wish I was the type of girl to look over my shoulder and say, *"Hey, I've got lube in the top drawer of my dresser. Feel free to fuck me in the ass."*

But I'm not that girl. I'm not a prude, not anymore, but I don't have lube on demand and my sex talk is going to need a few practice rounds before I'm tossing out the backdoor invite with ease. So instead, I wiggle my butt.

And Cole laughs.

This I can do.

"That was fun," I whisper, loud enough that he can hear me, but quiet enough that my voice doesn't waver and crack.

He sucks in a breath. "You have no idea how much I want to do more to you, Hailey."

"Tell me." I close my eyes and arch my bottom into his touch.

Instead of detailing all the depraved acts on his mind, he drags the head of his erection through my wetness, my swollen labia parting for him as he presses into me, just an inch. Just enough to stretch me around his girth and make me want more. "This, for one thing." He strokes in and out, shallow thrusts that have me arching for more. "And this." Deeper now. Harder. "I want to tie you up. Cuff your hands behind your back so I can hold on to them as I fuck you like this."

"What else?" I pant the question, eager for more.

"Everything. I want you to ride my lap as I pull your hair and suck on those pretty pink nipples."

I groan at that image, and Cole pulls me up onto my hands, then higher, so I'm unsteadily on my knees, but he's got me, one of his forearms banded around my torso beneath my aching breasts. He drives his cock up and into me, this angle sharper and more intense than before. And his other hand is twisting in my hair.

Pulling.

I whimper, and he nips at my earlobe. "Sweet Hailey likes to be fucked hard, doesn't she?"

I nod. I do. "By you. Only you."

"Because you're mine."

My breath hitches in my throat. "Yes."

"I like to play games with you. It's unbelievably sexy because you are sexy. But don't use games to put distance between us, beautiful."

"No…." He's literally inside me. The distancing will come later. By him. Not me. I'm just trying to hang on to my hat.

He grunts in my ear. "Too late. Time for the good girl to get her punishment."

Oh. I try—fail—to suppress a grin, because that sounds awesome.

"It's hardly punishment if you enjoy it," he growls, pinching my nipple at the same time.

I lean into his hand, making him cup my entire breast, as much as he can hold. Inside me, he's still moving, slow drags in and out of my slick pussy that make it hard to think. "I don't think there's anything you could do that I wouldn't like," I sigh, rolling my head back against his shoulder. His grip tightens on me and he flexes his cock deep inside me, reminding me just how full he makes me.

How empty I am when we're not doing this. So there is a way he can hurt me.

"Don't leave me again for weeks," I whisper, and I try to turn my face to look at him, but he jerks me forward, tumbling us both onto the bed. He slips out of me as we fall, his cock slapping the inside of my thigh with a wet, taunting whack. I growl at him, and he wraps his hand around my jaw, his thumb playing at my bottom lip.

"I'm no good for you," he mutters. "I don't want you to know how I deal with murderers and perverts."

"I can guess." I shove up onto all fours, presenting myself to him. Demanding he keep fucking me.

"Don't." He lazily slaps my ass as he finds my entrance again and thrusts deeply. Leaning over me he grabs my hair again. "Stay innocent of all that, Hailey. I'll give you as much of this—" He slams his hips into mine. "As much of this as you want. As often as I can. But out there? Pretend you don't know me. Go to work and be a good girl, for real. I love that about you."

Oh my God. He's moving over me, into me, faster now, and the thick crown of his cock is hitting a spot inside me that is obliterating all higher function, but Cole Parker just used the L-word in the same breath as saying he doesn't want anything to do with me in daylight hours, and I'm mad and happy and turned on and it's not fair.

Nothing about this is fair.

Including how fast I'm rocketing toward an orgasm.

Cole's hand slides down my sweat-slicked back to grab my hip, his other hand drifting up and down my neck, between my jaw and my collarbone, before he settles it heavily where my neck meets my shoulder.

And then the talking is over. Cole's pounding into me, holding me in place as he pistons his hips at an unbelievable pace that drives me into the stratosphere. My hands slip on the sheet as he drives me up the bed toward the headboard, the only sounds in the room now grunts and slaps and moans.

Feelings take over as I fragment into parts. Inside, he's stretching and filling me, rubbing exactly the right spot that makes my eyes roll back in my head and the most unholy noises rip from my mouth—*oh yes, right there*, I think, or maybe I say it, I can't be sure. I'm definitely saying things, babbling and moaning for more because I'm aching and it's *right* there. So close.

I hear myself, from a distance, as that narrowing sensation returns and I'm just nerve endings and sound.

Holy shit, I'm loud, I think abstractly as Cole launches me into a spectacular, blinding orgasm.

Above me, he's swearing as he jerks hard against me, filling me up with his come.

Oh, that's going to be so messy.

He pulls out and rolls me onto my side, and I slide one hand between my legs — to hold it in. To just hold it, the tiny bit of Cole that I get.

He disappears for a second and comes back with a washcloth from my bathroom and cleans me up, finishing with an open mouthed kiss to my pussy that makes me want to climb on top of him and do it all over again, but it's so late, and he's climbing into bed next to me.

Sleep sounds just as good as sex right now. And if he's still here when I wake up, that'll be even better.

ten

Cole

My phone chirps at five thirty in the morning. It's still dark outside, but Hailey's not in bed.

How the hell did she get up without me realizing?

I leap out of bed before I hear her clinking dishes quietly in the kitchen. Since I'm up, I make the best of it and go find her.

She squeaks as I wrap my arms around her from behind.

"Good morning." Her voice is warm, her body soft and relaxed as I kiss her neck, but something is off.

I bring my lips to her ear. "It's the middle of the night."

"I figured that was your morning and decided to make coffee."

"Why are you up?"

She shakes her head and doesn't look at me. "Just couldn't sleep."

"You conked out quickly last night."

"You mean three hours ago, after you ravished me?"

I laugh against her. "Ravish? I think I fucked your brains out."

"Yeah. That. It was good."

I brush my lips against that spot behind her ear. "Better than good."

She nods. "Much better."

"So?"

A shrug. I don't like shrugs. "So nothing. Here. Coffee."

She hands me a cup over her shoulder, full of my favorite black liquid, and I sip it. "Nice. Come back to bed."

"No, I want to be awake when you leave this time."

"I'll be back." I take a deep breath. "Maybe not for a few days. A new case has come up at work and I don't know what's going to happen exactly. If I disappear, that's why." I take another deep breath, realizing that no matter what Wilson finds, I need to make contact with the FBI closest to Lively. Find out what they know and where they might be at on an investigation. *Please let there be an open case.* "Might need to go to Miami. But soon."

She pours herself a cup and slowly turns in my arms. She's wearing that tank top and those tiny shorts I found her in last night, and they're hot. Everything about her is hot. Her curvy legs, from her long, sculpted calves to her soft thighs that feel so fucking good around my head. Her belly. Her waist and hips, curvy and tight in all the right places. Her tits, swinging free in this tank that I can totally see her nipples through. Driving me crazy already.

And her pretty face. But right now, her lips are twisted in worry, and her eyes...I like the way her eyes turn into happy half-moons when she laughs and widen when she has a dirty thought. I like everything about her eyes except the way her gaze cuts straight through my bullshit. Like it's doing right now.

"Miami?"

"Yep." This is one of those things I don't want her to know about, but thanks to that reporter, I can see her putting two and two together.

"Awfully close to the Caribbean. Is this a business trip?"

"I'm not leaving the country. And the rest isn't for good girls to know." I say it softly, but there's enough steel in my voice, she should take the hint.

Of course she doesn't, at first. My girl isn't a pushover. Fuck me. But she just stares at me, knowing enough to be wary, before brushing past me and heading for the living room space. Knitting basket. Stripper pole. And in a large wooden armoire, a small TV. She turns it on and CNN immediately appears onscreen, which surprises me.

I go to the bedroom long enough to pull on my boxer briefs, then join her on the couch. "News before six in the morning? Black coffee? There are many layers to the Hailey onion." I play with her hair while she ignores me, her eyes glued to the stock ticker at the bottom of the screen. "Do you trade?"

She nods, her lips moving unconsciously.

Is it weird that I'm getting half hard at the thought of Hailey being a money wizard? It's not surprising, given her genes, but her very public rejection of the business world her family is steeped in on both sides makes me wonder... things. All sorts of things I want to know about this woman.

We finish our coffee in silence as she watches the numbers and I watch the B-roll behind a story on a riot in Cairo, then an interview with someone

205

from the United Nations. It's all just noise, distracting the world from the real shit going down behind the scenes that never makes it to news desks, but it's good to know what everyone else is being told.

"Do you want another cup?" I kiss her bare shoulder, my few-days-of-stubble catching on her smooth-as-silk skin. "I should shave before I come over next time."

She whirls around, our heads almost crashing into each other. "Don't you dare." She licks her lips and glances at my jaw. "I like it rough."

Jesus Christ. How the hell am I supposed to leave for work when she says shit like that? "I bet you do."

Her eyes go wide at the rough note in my voice. *Really rough.* God, I'll never get enough of her.

I grab both mugs and shove them on the coffee table before hauling her into my lap. "Are you done watching that stuff?"

She nods, and I make the most of the next twenty minutes, first on the couch, then in her shower.

It barely scratches the surface of my itch for her.

— —

Ellie is setting a tray of fruit in the middle of the conference table when I arrive.

"Seriously?" It's a good job I scarfed an Egg McMuffin on my way in.

"There are bran muffins, too." She points to the side table where a coffee carafe and the world's tiniest muffins sit pertly on a plate.

"We're not girls."

She rolls her eyes as she walks past me, which I wouldn't catch except she whirls around. "Speaking of girls, you smell like one."

"Shut up."

"That's rude, boss. I'm guessing you don't own vanilla body wash."

Fuck my life. "Sure don't."

"I'm guessing Hailey does."

"You know, my private life could be left as private, and that would be totally fine."

She wrinkles her nose as she taps her chin, faux-thinking about that for a second. "Probably the wrong place to work for that strategy."

"Get out." She laughs as she heads for the door. "And come back with bacon."

"I like her!" she hollers as she hits the stairs, heading back to her desk.

That makes two of us.

Right on cue, Jason appears. "I see you didn't take my advice."

"I don't remember hearing anything other than 'sleep on it'. I did that. I want to go to Miami."

He gives me a look of genuine surprise. "Oh?"

"And meet with the local FBI there."

"Oh." He shakes his head. "PRISM is concerned the Feds won't move quickly enough."

"Meet with, and help them find what they need quickly. Maybe in a way that forces their hand."

"I like the sound of that better." He leans over the table. "Melon. Yum. Let's see what Wilson says."

"About what?" Our ninja hacker strolls in just

as he hears his name. He's wearing yesterday's t-shirt and jeans and his hair is standing on end — I'm guessing he never left last night. The lack of sleep has clearly futzed with his testosterone levels because he too gets excited about the melon, grabbing three pieces before he flops into a chair. "Nice fruit tray. Good idea."

"Never mind about the damn fruit. We need something to shut down Lively this weekend. Before Morgan Reid goes there. Before…" I sigh. No, that's not right. "Or maybe at the same time. Jesus. Maybe I need to step away from this, I'm not objective anymore."

"Finally. I'm glad you see that." Jason grabs a strawberry and points it at me. "Now we can use that power for good instead of evil."

"I'm not following." I scowl at him before turning to pour myself a cup of coffee and grab a teensy-ass muffin. I start pacing back and forth as I consume both. "I don't have enough distance from this to make the hard decisions."

"Or maybe you've finally found something to believe in and now you can fight for what you feel is right." Jason and I both swivel our heads to look at Wilson, who yawns. "What? Aren't we the good guys, deep down inside?"

I'm really not sure anymore.

"Listen," Wilson says, scrubbing his hand through his hair. "I know I'm the last person in the world to talk about doing the right thing, but there are young women, right now, trapped in a sex slave ring for dirty motherfuckers who are too powerful to be taken down by conventional law enforcement. And we're sitting on our hands because the timing has to be just right."

"Well, it does," Jason said drily. "If we take things into our own hands and take out the wrong peg at the wrong time, it could spell disaster on an international event kind of level."

"Could." Wilson snorts. "I *could* be one of those crazy conspiracy theorist guys, spouting predictions and nonsense. Or I could stay up all night combing through the internet history of teenagers who have no idea they're a breath away from being kidnapped because they look like Britney Spears or Kate Middleton, which is what I *did* do, and I gotta say, after that dark fucking shit, *could* doesn't sound nearly strong enough to keep me from blowing this asshole into a million pieces."

Tag comes in just as Wilson says that, and despite the tension that's twisted my shoulders into a solid block of granite, it's funny as fuck that he doesn't even blink before saying, "Good morning to you, too, sunshine."

"I'm in the middle of something here, douche nozzle. How about you show up on time for once?"

"I was too busy kissing your mother goodbye." Tag chuckles as he helps himself to some breakfast. I'm not even surprised for a second when he makes positive noises about the fucking fruit tray. No doubt Ellie will be pleased it went over well, and next meeting we'll have smoothies.

Wilson shoots him a dark glower, but continues on his original tack anyway. "So I've been thinking about Cole going to Miami. What he could deliver to the Feds that would bring down Lively, save those girls, and not destabilize the global financial markets in the process. And I think I have a lead.

209

Actually, two of them."

He swipes at his tablet, sending a picture we all recognize to the large screen on the wall.

"Tabitha Leyton?" We all lean forward. The twenty-something singer-songwriter is every marketer's wet dream. She's drop-dead gorgeous... and notoriously private, even though her dark red hair and swollen lips are plastered on billboards all across the country. I frown and look back at Wilson. "What's going on?"

"She's one of two women I think we should talk to," he mutters, his lower lip caught between his teeth as he taps at the tablet. Another picture appears, and below both, dates and cities. Different dates, different cities. The other woman is blonde, gorgeous, and a complete mystery. Wilson doesn't leave us hanging. "And this is Clara Forrester. She's an artist, lives in New York City. I think both of them have spent time with Gerome Lively. Enough time that they would know things. Probably have seen some of the missing girls. Rumor has it, he doesn't hide them.

And both women have stopped visiting Lively —I spent hours tracking through their travel records, and the common points with Lively stopped three years ago for Leyton and eighteen months for Forrester."

"Where are they?" I'm ready to run for the door. The chance to help a witness come forward about Lively...my heart is pounding.

Wilson grins, a rare expression for him. "You and Tag will go to New York to talk to Clara Forrester. Jason and I will go to L.A. and track down a rock star. And then we'll need to sit on

210

whatever they tell us—their security has to be our highest concern. But hopefully by the time you go to Miami—and I think you *should*—one of us will be able to escort a reliable witness there as well."

Jason nods, then pins me with a stern look that he doubles up in Tag's direction as well. "No telling your women."

Like I would ever in a million years involve Hailey in this. "Of course."

"Tag?"

He shakes his head. "Like Kendra would believe me even if I told her."

"I'm sorry, man." Wilson gives him an exaggerated look of faux-sympathy. "Must be hard to be used for your body by someone who doesn't even like you."

My lips twitch, because actually it's not so bad.

Tag just tosses a chunk of melon in the air and snatches it in mid-arc with his teeth. "Meh. Whatever. At least I'm getting laid without having to pay for it."

"All right, kids, that's enough squabbling." Jason claps his hands together. "Let's book some flights, yes?"

eleven

Hailey

The knock at the door the next night isn't a surprise, really, but it still throws me for a loop.

It's so soon. So normal.

So completely out of character for the brooding man on the other side of the door that I'm instantly wary, reverting back to the comfortable armour of a good scowl.

"I'm not giving you a blow job."

It's only been thirty-six hours since I would have happily sucked him off, and maybe I still will —seeing Cole looming in my doorway has a way of chasing the pain of cramps away, at least momentarily—but I'm a different woman.

A hormonal, cranky woman.

He just grins from the other side of the threshold. "Wow, you've got a low opinion of me."

I don't. I'm just bitchy and may have lost my filter. Plus I had a shitty day at work. "God, no. I'm sorry. Hi."

He doesn't look offended, but he doesn't make a move into my apartment. Maybe he forgot I was going to be indisposed for a few days. I did tell him in the middle of sex, in the middle of the night.

"I have to warn you, I'm not very good company tonight. Lady problems." I step back, giving him the option to stay, because he's big and strong and smells good, but I'm wearing leggings and an old oversized t-shirt and a scowly face.

I'm genuinely surprised when he steps inside

and holds up a brown paper bag. "I thought you might like some vanilla bean ice cream. With chocolate sauce."

"I don't understand."

He leans in, pulling me close. He stares at me for a beat before groaning and kissing me softly on the nose. "That's fucked up shit, right there. You don't understand why a guy would bring you ice cream when you're having your period?"

No, I really don't, not even as one does. That's the stuff of rom-com movies and married people. My heart swells a bit. "Okay, you have a secret sweet side and I'm a bitch for assuming otherwise."

"Don't apologize too quickly. Now I'm trying to figure out what I'd have to do to get that blow job back on the table."

"Wait a few days." I grin.

"Noted." He kisses me again, this time on my cheek, but right on the corner of my mouth. A stealth near-sexy kiss. He's good. "Have you eaten dinner yet? Should I put this in the freezer or serve it up immediately?"

I tilt my head toward the kitchen, and he follows me. "I just made a BLT, do you want one?"

"Definitely." He sticks the ice cream in the freezer, then leans against the counter as I prep the sandwiches. "I'm sorry I didn't call you yesterday."

"I asked you not to ignore me for *weeks*, not hours. You said you might be busy." I shoot him a smile. "You brought me ice cream within a very reasonable time frame of using me for filthy sex. No worries on staying in my dirty-secret good books, okay?"

He narrows his eyes at me, like I chose the

214

wrong words, but he doesn't say anything, so I just turn back to the sandwiches. "Mayo?"

"Please."

"Salt and pepper?" I glance at him out of the corner of my eye and he nods, smirking.

"Two slices of bacon or three—ee!" I squeal as he shoves the sandwich fixings further onto the counter and spins me around, pressing his entire body against mine. "Enough sandwich talk?"

"Like three questions ago, beautiful." He kisses me slowly, a belated, extended greeting that warms me from top to bottom. I open for him, and he strokes his tongue against mine, his solid, commanding thrusts silently rewriting our narrative.

He's not my dirty secret.

This isn't just sex.

The truth is, as crazy as it sounds given that this is Cole and me, I'm just making my man a sandwich and he's just glad to see me at the end of a long day.

He still kisses like a bad-ass, though, leaving me breathless when he finally relaxes his embrace. He stares down at me for a second before smiling just a tiny bit. "Missed you last night."

"Same." I don't ask where he was. I have the feeling that if he was free, he'd have been here, and since he wasn't, he was doing something he doesn't want me to know about. "I'm glad you came over, even though I'm a bit of a dragon lady."

"Love it when you spit fire at me." He winks and spins me around. "Keep cooking."

"Yeah, real fancy dinner." I finish up, Cole's hands on my hips the whole time, his chin against my hair. This is *nice*. Dangerously lovely, in fact, and I want to guard myself against letting it get too deep, but it's probably too late. Two nights, a few heated encounters, and I'm hooked on him.

"Go sit," I whisper, and he kisses my hair.

"Can I grab us some drinks?"

"There's beer and wine in the fridge. Some Perrier—I'll have that, please—and OJ? But it might be past its prime."

"Beer it is." He grabs a bottle for himself and the sparkling water for me, and leads the way to the couch.

I flick on the television and look over at him, taking in his fitted black suit and tie, and white shirt. He's even wearing dress shoes instead of boots. "You're all dressed up. I feel like I should offer you a martini or something."

Cole closes his eyes and snorts, then slowly undoes his tie as he tips his head back against my couch. "I know it goes against my James Bond image, but I can't stand martinis."

My breath catches in my throat because I hate his James Bond image. Even though it's hot, I want him to secretly be different. "No?"

"Beer and a burger kind of guy. Beer, burger, and babe." He looks at the sandwiches in my hands, then flicks his gaze to my face as he gives me a big, sexy grin. "Or sandwich and babe. Come here."

"I'm all schlubby." But I put the plates down because I'm being silly, and we both know it.

"Do I look like I care? You look comfortable. You know who's not comfortable? Me. I need a warm woman in my lap and a sweet mouth to kiss for a minute. Get your ass over here."

I climb into his lap, loving the way he spreads his solid, muscled thighs wide. How his arms easily wrap around me, and the hungry way his hands glide over my curves. We kiss again, this time more playfully, before I slide over to sit next to him. We eat our sandwiches together in silence, watching the news, then he takes our plates away and returns with two bowls of ice cream and the bottle of chocolate syrup.

The top of the hour headlines have just finished, so I turn the volume down and curl into his side. "This is really good."

"You deserve good. You deserve the best."

I want to sink into this warmth. I want this moment to last forever, except for the whole cramping-and-having-my-period annoyance.

And when we finish our ice cream, Cole takes the sweetness to the next level. "I want to take you on a date."

"What?" I twist to look at him.

"A date. You. Me. A movie and popcorn."

God. I can't even handle this. Time for snark. "I like junior mints."

"Good. We'll get those, too. And I'm going to hold your hand."

The way he says it makes me laugh. "Are you warning me?"

"I don't want it to be too much in the moment." He says this straight, and for a second I'm not sure, but the way he pulls me close, like he might not want me to see his eyes crinkle...that has to be a tell.

"Shut up." I mumble that into his chest. Never

mind being too much then…this level of boyfriend behavior might be too much right freakin' now. We sit there for a minute, me buried in his chest, before I slowly prop myself up on his lap and try to be real for a second. "We don't need to go out. I like you coming over with ice cream."

Cole clearly doesn't like me compromising on this point. He narrows his eyes. "Your last date before me took you to the Kennedy Center."

"Yeah, but it wasn't really that great to begin with, then some asshole kind of interrupted it and…" My cheeks turn pink. I can't help it.

His hands tighten on my hips. "Say it." He dropped his gaze to my mouth. I lick my lips. It's like a reflex, I can't help it, and I like how his eyes darken in response. "Wicked woman."

I slide my arms around his neck and cuddle closer, bringing my lips to his ear. "My last date was interrupted by a sexy bad boy who went down on me in an empty concert hall while Washington's snootiest milled about in the lobby."

"That's better," he mutters, squeezing the back of my neck. This is the wrong conversation to have when indisposed. We are both getting worked up, I'm all tight and achey inside, and, well, his arousal is obvious on the outside. The solid length of him is pressing insistently against my thigh. As much fun as flirting and cuddling is, I'm leading him on.

I shake my head. "This isn't fair, I'm sorry."

"Don't do that."

"What?"

"Don't assume that I'm a monster who can't contain himself." He rocks against me. "Neither of us needs to get naked or come to have a good time.

We don't need to talk about sex, but I gotta say, doing a recap of the first time I tasted you sounds like a great way to spend some time. Builds a nice slow burn of anticipation for the next time we do that."

I must be dreaming. That's the only reasonable explanation.

"Who are you and what have you done with Cole Parker?" When he just smirks at me, I slowly kiss him, languid and tender this time, just touching and tasting until we're both warm and drowsy and we slip sideways on the couch. Cole tucks me in front of him and we watch the next set of headlines—how has an hour slipped by?—and then he tucks a lock of my hair behind my ear and quietly asks if he can stay over.

Seriously. I never want to wake up. This is like some magical alternate reality where Cole and I can actually date and be a normal couple.

It's the best thing I can imagine.

I find him a toothbrush and we take turns washing up, then snuggle in my bed wearing just our underwear. I was going to find a t-shirt to sleep in, but as I got down to my panties, he tugged me into bed, and now we're wrapped around each other. His phone blows up a few times, but he never takes long and when he props up on one arm and asks me what I'm thinking about, I take a chance and tell him the truth.

"Help me understand your job."

He blinks at me. "Not sure that I can, but I'll try."

I roll onto my side so we're nose to nose, and he wraps his arm around me. "Why do you do it?

You could do anything else, right? Regular old security. James Bond stand-in. Grumpy old man lessons."

He laughs. "None of those sound like fun."

"Neither does what you do—I mean, you don't seem to enjoy it." I hold my breath after the words rush out of me, because it's entirely possible I'm way overstepping the bounds of our fledgling relationship.

The seconds stretch as he looks at me, a long, thinking-man's pause before he cocks his head to the side and gives me half a smile. "No, my job isn't fun, either. But it brought me you, and this, right now? Is the most fun I've ever had in my entire life."

I laugh, because that has to be a lie. "More fun than what we did at the Kennedy Center?"

"That was hot. And fun, yes. But this..." He shakes his head as he strokes a hand up and down my spine. "I didn't know this was possible for me. Dinner on the couch, talking about work. Laughing together. It's..."

"Weird? Freaking? Scary?"

He sticks his tongue out at me, a playful gesture that punches me right in the ovaries. "It's fun."

Oh.

But I still don't get the job thing. And it's none of my business, but I keep asking because I feel like I *can*, like he'll let me pick at this scab until I'm satisfied. "Then *why?* Why not do something more satisfying?"

"I'm not sure what else I would do, for one thing. I joined the Navy right out of high school.

And also because I can do this stuff. Because others can't, and someone has to. We have a certain skill set that is in demand."

"Okay." I still don't like it, but I get it now.

"What else is on your mind?"

"That's probably enough for one night." I smile up at him.

"I don't want any doubts between us. If you've got worries about me, I want to hear them." His eyes glow as he squeezes my hips. "I can deal with any obstacles between us, but I have to know what they are."

"I'm not going to ask you what you were doing last night…" I trail off, wanting to get these words just right.

Cole misunderstands my slowdown, and he shakes his head softly. "I can't tell you. You don't want to know, I promise."

I frown. "Okay on the first point. Totally okay. I started saying the wrong thing there, give me a second. But on the second point? Don't shield me from the ugliness of life, Cole."

He presses his lips together like he wants to argue that point but thinks better of it. "Go on." His eyes soften. "Please."

"I'm not going to leap to any conclusions, but I have to know…That first night, when we slept together here. When you left. You put yourself in the middle of that investigation because you knew you had an alibi, right? You knew you had me?"

He shifts beside me. We're almost naked, except for underwear. There's literally nothing between us but secrets. My pulse picks up, because I didn't mean to make this a turning point in our relationship, but now it just might be exactly that.

Can I handle whatever answer he gives me? I want to think I can, but my pulse says otherwise. *Please be my white knight.* I hate that I want him to be good.

It should probably be enough that he's good to me.

His arms tighten around me. "I knew I was on camera. I knew my cell phone would place me not at the scene of the crime. I never intended for you to be involved."

"What about after? I was so scared. It's hard for me to wrap my head around it being no big deal to you."

"You being exposed to something like that is a big deal. Will always be a big deal. But I'll never be the one to show it to you."

He's right. And I can't very well tell him he can't keep secrets from me—a conversation he's neatly avoided, because he's going to keep doing just that, damn him—and in the next breath complain about being touched by some of the drama in his life.

"You're a bit bossy, you know that?"

He kisses my forehead. "How I've gotten through life."

I burrow my face into his bare chest. He's turned over a new, sweet leaf, but this is still Cole. Locked up tight and always in charge.

One deep and meaningful conversation isn't going to change that.

Probably a lifetime won't change that.

And here I am, cuddled naked in his arms, sleepily wondering if that might just be okay with me. I'm probably ten kinds of foolish, but in this moment, I've got more than I ever dreamed possible. It's not the future I imagined for myself, but now it's the one I want more than anything.

— twelve —

Cole

We've spent the last week and a half together. Nights wrapped around each other and days spent busy getting shit done so we can do it all over again.

It feels normal. And so fucking fragile I'm a little scared to breathe the wrong way, because when I'm not with her, I'm buried in a mountain of twisted depravity that makes me sick and it has no end. Clara Forrester has agreed to talk to the FBI, and Tag will fly her to Miami after I get confirmation that the Feds have enough of an investigation to make an arrest after her interview.

Because she's got a lot. Dates, times. People. A Danish prince and an Australian politician. Business leaders. Some people, like Morgan Reid, the FBI might be able to flip into witnesses, because Clara Forrester has *pictures*.

And now we have those pictures, too. But without context, those pictures mean nothing.

We can't let her down, so we dig and document.

At the end of every day, I feel sick.

Two decades of Lively entertaining men with young women he lures into his world and holds captive. A gilded cage, apparently, but a cage nonetheless. And sex acts that change them forever.

Even Clara, who was a willing guest, was coerced into acts she didn't want to participate in.

225

It makes me want to tear Lively apart.

But when I come back to Hailey's place, all that fades away. She smiles brightly at me and welcomes me into her heart and her body, shows me how good love can be, and all is right for a few hours.

I'm being selfish, and she doesn't even know it, so tonight is our first official date, and it's all for her.

After a debate on what movie we should see turned into sex against the wall and no agreement, Hailey suggested we do something else, which is how I've ended up in a fucking hipster dive bar on H Street.

My woman is in her element, gleefully ordering a third round of a drink called Awesomeness, which tastes too good to not be dangerous. I'm on my second gin and tonic, and I'm nursing it because any second this place could get shut down for a health code or safety violation.

"Isn't this music awesome? Like the *drink?*" she yells, pressing herself into my side.

I have to admit the music is good. Hard and loud. Not exactly romantic, but it does give me other ideas. "You want to dance?"

Her eyes get all big and round and she licks her lips. "Really?"

Fuck yes, if the mere suggestion gets her worked up. The actual thing will be our quickest ticket back to her place.

It's entirely possible that I'm the worst boyfriend in the world. I don't have a lot of experience, not that it's an excuse. It doesn't take a genius to understand that dating is about

226

showering attention on a woman while she has her clothes on, because you like her and want to burrow yourself deeper in her life, and obviously you aren't good enough for that, so you need to earn your way in.

And since this is Hailey and me, I've got a long fucking hill to climb, and I'm not good at this. I should be—it's not far off from the shmoozing that I so unexpectedly took to like a fish to water when we moved to D.C. But the stakes are different with that. Those people need me more than I need them. There's always another sorry loser fucking up his life.

With Hailey, the shoe is on the other foot. Any second, she's going to realize I'm not good enough for her. That I'm a professional liar and a cheat, and no amount of financial or political security will make up for that in her eyes.

Just my luck to fall for a woman with an unwavering moral compass and the internal fortitude to walk away from wealth and power because it's the right thing to do.

Of course, that she did that just makes me want her all the more.

She twists in front of me, swivelling her hips through the drunken crowd. She's wearing dark jeans and knee-high boots with a sparkly tank top under a tiny jacket. I can't keep my eyes off her.

On the dance floor, I grab her close and spin her around so my front is pressed against her back.

I grind my cock into her ass as she tips her head back against my shoulder. I want to hold her here forever. I get her for a minute before she spins away. As the music pulses through the air, she

227

peels off her jacket, baring the long smooth expanse of her arms, golden pink under the dance floor lights. I grab the loose end of the jacket, reeling her in for a quick taste of her mouth.

"This isn't dancing," she says, her face still pressed to mine, close enough I can't see the smile. But I can feel it.

"This is better," I growl, banding my arms around her waist as she slides her fingers through the short hair at the back of my neck. I move us to the heavy thump of the music, my thigh sliding between her legs, and we kiss again, over and over again until she's panting and I'm ready to find a dark corner.

But this is our first date, and I want to earn — legitimately, for once in my life — the right to a second. And a third. And a tenth. So when a couple beside us bump us apart, I keep the few inches of distance and actually start dancing.

This isn't a bad move, because although I'd rather be kissing Hailey, I actually do know how to dance.

And she's impressed, but so am I, because where I've got some moves, she's got more, and they're *good*.

She rolls her body, mirroring what I do, and we flow together, almost meeting at the hips each time before sliding away. I keep one hand on her at all times — my fingers grazing down her arm, then my other palm cupping her waist as she twists in the other direction.

Her gaze is glued on me. Always dark. Pleased, with an edge of wanting more. I can't keep my eyes on hers, because the rest of her is shimmying in ways that jack up my blood pressure, but every time my roving gaze finds her face again, she's still looking at me.

And her smile gets a little bit bigger. More teasing.

I spin her around, touching more of her now. She glances back at me over her shoulder, her hair swinging away. I can't resist the bare neck, and I press my face into her slightly damp skin, tasting her briefly before pulling back. "Another drink?"

She nods, and I will my dick to hang on, but then she breathes four little words that make my night. "Back at my place?"

I have her out the door and in my waiting hired car before she can change her mind. I've never been more grateful for a privacy screen in my entire life. I tersely give the driver Hailey's address before slamming the little sliding door shut and hauling her into my lap.

"Uhhhn," she mumbles as I jerk her tank top up and her bra down, baring one breast. I kiss her hard on the mouth again before whispering that she needs to be quiet, then I dip my head and suck her nipple into my mouth in a harsh, hungry pull.

She pants my name, barely more than a breath, and it bounces around us in the quiet of the moving car. Up front, the driver is listening to something. Talk radio, maybe, or an ad. Outside, there's end of the evening traffic noise.

But right here, it's just Hailey and me, my name on her lips and my mouth on her body.

The nervous tension I'd been feeling is gone now, replaced by something more familiar—the need to possess her, to mark her soul as she's marked mine.

"You were beautiful tonight, dancing for me." I free her other breast and roll the second taut peak over my tongue, savoring the unique taste of her skin and the still fresh scent of her vanilla perfume. "You're always fucking beautiful."

"But you liked the dancing?" she whispers, sliding her hands over my shoulders, her words slurring slightly. "Maybe I'll be your private dancer when we get up to my place."

I chuckle and kiss the inside of her bare arm, pebbled with goosebumps. "Almost there. You want your jacket back on, drunk girl?"

"Nuh-uh." She shakes her head vigorously as she fixes her bra and top. "I'm going to take them all off...soon enough anyways."

She tips her head to the side, like she's thinking about the words she just said and wondering if they made sense, and I kiss her cheek, then her mouth, because it's right there.

The intoxicated cuteness continues on the slow, hip wiggling climb to her apartment, but as soon as the door closes behind her, she zips into efficiency-mode, going to the stereo on a bookshelf in her living room.

There she starts rifling through her CDs. She waves her hand over her shoulder. "You should take your clothes off, I might want to violate you after I find this album…"

I slowly strip off my dress shirt, but I leave my jeans on, and settle on the couch. I like this bossy, drunk Hailey. I'm not going to leave her in charge for long, but as long as she's got a plan, I'm game to see where it goes.

230

She puts on some sultry R&B from the seventies and turns around, right hip cocked and her boobs deliberately on display.

"Close your eyes."

"Seriously? I want to watch you strip for me."

"Serious as a heart attack." She smiles as she slowly unzips her jeans, then stops before I get to see the good stuff. "And I'm not going to strip for you, but if you're a good boy, and close your peepers, I will dance for you."

Her warm, husky laughter surrounds me as I drop my eyelids and tip my head back against the couch. I've wanted to see her use the pole for weeks. I'll take it however she wants to dish it out. The music is a promise of something seriously good —better than good, because Hailey just hopping out of her jeans on a regular night is enough to get me hard.

She moves closer, warm air swirling around me, but then she's gone again on another laugh, leaving me a frozen statue of barely contained sexual frustration. She could torture me for hours, but she doesn't. Fabric rustles, then I hear a soft sound that I assume is her jeans hitting the floor a split second before she breathes the word I've been waiting for. "Open."

I blink twice, taking her in. She's wearing my shirt, barely buttoned, and her curvy legs are bare and she's posed against the pole like a pin-up model.

Jesus. Blood rushes through my head on its way south to my cock. "Wow."

She plumps her lips in a naughty-as-fuck pout as the music changes to something slightly more upbeat—and decidedly dirtier. As the singer sighs and moans her way through a chorus about motions and notions, Hailey steps around the pole, one hand holding on above her head, her body angled out and away. Her hair swings wide as she launches herself into the air, twisting one leg around the pole as she slides down, twirling effortlessly.

I can't breathe.

My shirt. Flashes of white lace underneath. The music. Her damn smile.

"I've been thinking, Cole…" She drops, inch by inch, into the naughtiest squat I've ever seen and presses slowly onto her tiptoes before rising and circling the pole again.

Flying.

"This thing between us. Maybe I didn't just want you to be my bad boy fling…" She bites her lip, and I just about lose my mind. Keeping my gaze glued on her painfully slow twirl around the pole, my shirt riding up on her hips, I ease my fly down and wrap my fist around my aching cock. She flips her hair over her shoulder as she glides her left foot up her right leg, stretching her thigh wide open and flashing those impossibly innocent panties at me. "Maybe I like being a little bad, too."

Jesus. She's going to kill me. "Take your panties off."

She winks at me. "I will. When I'm ready."

"I want to see your pussy."

Another slow twirl, and this time when she comes around to face me, her free hand is working on the buttons of my shirt. "Why?"

"Because it's beautiful."

"Mmm. Try again."

"It is," I growl.

"What else?"

"Because it's mine." Her lips part and her eyes sparkle. Good. I stand and pace around the coffee table, stopping just short of her. "You're mine. And if I tell you to show me how much you want me, you'll do it."

She slides her back against the pole, my shirt now fully open. Her breasts and belly jiggle as she works herself up and down, her mouth shiny and wet from her licking her lips. "And if I don't obey you?"

I step closer. "You like being punished far too much."

"I know," she breathes as she drops again, one arm stretched above her head, her circled fingers controlling her descent on the pole. She stops with her mouth just inches from my throbbing dick. "It's so naughty."

Fuck. Me.

"You want this?" I jerk myself in front of her face and she nods, sticking out her tongue to catch a drop of pre-come.

"Yummy."

I curse as I grab the pole above her and drive my cock into her eager mouth. She swallows me straight into her throat, her lips sealing around me as she sucks. Hard.

It's too much and not enough at the same time. The perfect wet heat, the soft pulling of her mouth, begging for me to spill myself down her throat.

"You're so naughty," I groan, smoothing my free hand over her hair and then her cheek, ending up with my fingers stroking the soft skin of her throat. "Such a good cocksucker, Hailey. Just for me, on your knees. So hungry for me, aren't you?"

She nods as I thrust in and out of her mouth.

"Take me deep again. I want your nose against my belly, beautiful. God, yes. Like that. Fuck, you're so perfect, Hailey. Fuuuck-ck." I hold myself against her face as I come on her tongue in heavy blasts—and she swallows every last drop.

She holds me in her mouth until my cock stops pulsing, then waits at my feet, eyes glazed as I do up my jeans again.

"Up, beautiful." She glides onto her toes, stretching as tall as she can go, and I curl my hand around the back of her neck. "Thank you."

Other words pound in my chest, words I can't bring myself to say just yet. But I feel them. I lick my way into her mouth, kissing her and tasting the faint remainder of myself on her tongue.

Peeling her panties low on her hip, I stroke my fingertips through her wetness as I keep kissing her. She whimpers as I slowly circle around her clit, her hips shamelessly rocking against my hand.

"Tell me what you want."

"Your mouth." Barely a whisper, her request makes me hard all over again. "Lick me."

"Come with me to Miami," I murmur against her skin as I kiss her neck. She's all soft and she smells like vanilla musk and woman. Turned on woman, and I can't let go of her. Not for a night, not for a weekend.

"I have to work," she groans, tipping her head back to give me more skin to lick as I fuck her ruthlessly with my fingers.

"I bet you have a week of vacation time you have no intention of ever using," I rumble against her belly as I drop to my knees and strip her out of her panties. "Hold on."

She grips her hands tighter around the pole and watches, eyes dark and pleading, as I lift one of her legs and then the other, draping them over my shoulder.

"Ahhh," she cries out as I press my hands under her ass and lift her hips, bringing her pussy to my mouth.

"Tell me you'll ask for a day or two off and I'll make you come."

"Mmmm." She rolls her hips and I twist my face, kissing her inner thigh. "Cole!"

"Promise me you'll ask, beautiful. Say it, and you can have my tongue buried deep inside you."

"And if I don't?" she asks, gasping as I puff hot air on her exposed cunt.

I groan regretfully, enjoying this way more than I should. "Then I might need to put you down and go find some ice cream."

"Won't you be busy with work?"

"Little bit. Lots of time to lie on the beach with you. It's not Hawaii, but it's not here, either."

"Not here sounds good." She tips her hips again, and I lick her almost where she wants it. Almost. Not quite. She growls at me.

"Hey, growling is my thing."

"Licking my pussy is your thing, and you're not doing it!"

"Miami."

"Yes. Damn you, yes." Before she can protest again, I close my mouth over her cunt and show

235

her in a filthy kiss how grateful I am she's bowed to my will.

Usually I take my time. Fuck that shit. I want her come on my face and I want it now. I want this orgasm, then I'm carrying her to her bed, where she's going to come again on my dick. Make me come inside her, and then I'll hold her until she's ready for me to do it all over again.

I'm a fucking beast, devouring her, and she's humping against my face, desperate for more.

"Come on, Hailey," I croon as I slide two fingers deep inside her. "You've got the tightest, sweetest pussy. Jesus, yes, come for me."

She clenches my fingers as I part her pussy lips, giving me more space to lap up her slippery sweetness. Her scent, the swollen plumpness of her cunt, the little moans as she grinds against me...it's the best thing in the entire world.

As soon as she explodes, pussy fluttering and legs shaking, I have her in my arms.

I lay her on her bed, spreading her luscious legs so I can be inside her, and she wraps herself around me, pulling me in deep.

I say it then, the secret I've kept inside. I say it so quietly she doesn't hear me, I'm sure of it, because she doesn't react.

"I love you," I breathe into her hair as she digs her heels into my ass. She moans my name and I thrust again, this time the words just in my heart. She kisses me as I pin her down, fucking her harder and faster until we come together in a sticky, perfect mess.

—thirteen—

Hailey

For someone raised in a wealthy family, I don't have a lot of experience flying on private airplanes, and it's pretty sweet. We're twenty minutes away from landing outside Miami, I have a happy buzz from some very expensive champagne, and I'm sitting sideways in the comfiest chair ever while Cole's rubbing my feet. The flight attendant just cleared our plates and left us with warm, wet hand towels.

"This might just be heaven," I muse out loud, giving him a lopsided grin.

My big, bad, scary beast flashes a happy smile right back at me. We haven't worked out all our issues—haven't talked about what comes next, or later on down the road, but I'm not thinking too hard about that. I'm just happy that I've let myself have him, for now or for however long he'll have me, and I'm not overthinking it.

Too much.

I mean, I *worry*. He's insane, and something is happening at work, something huge and dark that makes him restless. It's why we're going to Miami, but he keeps saying he just has a couple of meetings. And when I showed him my bikini, he promised to make them as short as possible.

Three days away from Washington. Away from my family and press that recognizes me and mostly away from work.

This foot rub is just the beginning of what is going to be the best weekend ever.

Cole lifts my right leg, smoothing his big, rough palm up the back of my calf.

"Stop looking up my skirt," I grumble.

"Stop wearing bright blue panties that scream 'rip me off'."

"We don't have enough time…" I whisper the denial at the same time as he tugs the fabric aside, totally revealing me for a liar. I'm aching for his touch, my sex swollen and wet, and we both know it won't take long to get me off.

"Hold this," he whispers right back, a wolfish expression on his face as he wraps my fingers around the embarassingly damp crotch of my underwear. I grip it tightly, watching from under heavy eyelids as he presses my thighs further apart, putting me on display for him.

Over his shoulder, I see a shadow move in the hallway to the galley kitchen where the flight attendant has been this whole time.

"I think someone's watching," I whisper, a nervous thrill rocketing through me.

"Is that a problem?" Cole asks, his voice low and rumbly. He doesn't look back, or up at me.

"No," I breathe, surprising myself. I'm not sure if I like it for me, or for him. "Do you like that idea?"

He slides first two, then three fingers into me, stretching me wide. "Only if you do."

"Just watching?" My voice cracks as he strokes me inside, rubbing my G-spot with each thrust of his hand.

"Definitely." He glances up at me, his face all

seriousness now. "I don't think I'd share well. Not when it comes to you. This pussy is all mine."

"Okay."

He smiles at me, pure sex now, as he twists his hand, bringing his thumb to my clit. "Let her see you come, Hailey. Let her see how much you like riding my hand. Let her see how fucking beautiful you are, spread open like this."

I arch my back, rocking my pelvis against his thumb. "That feels *so* good."

"It looks good." He leans over me, taking my mouth in a kiss. "Come on, beautiful. Feel even better."

"I do," I pant as the screws twist inside me. Higher and higher I climb, rocking against his thumb, pushed by the insistent rhythm of his fingers deep inside my body.

"I'm going to fuck your ass tonight, Hailey." Cole's breath is coming as fast and hard as mine now, and this is just for us. His words are just for me. "I'm going to finger you like this, in your ass, until you're loose and ready for me, and then I'm going to fill you with my come. I'm going to mark you as mine, everywhere."

That visual burns me up, because I know what that feels like now.

When he came inside me the first time, I hadn't expected how long it would still be running out of me.

Or how hot I'd get when I thought about it after the fact.

"I am yours," I whisper. "Always."

"Love that, beautiful." He nips at my lip. "Love that so much. God, look at you. Glazed eyes. Wet

239

pussy. My good girl…" His voice drifts as I seize around him, coming hard and fast in the end.

He kisses me again, over and over again as he cleans me up. I wriggle out of those bright blue panties that started it all, because they're soaked.

"Your turn," I murmur, reaching for the erection straining at the front of his cargo pants.

He snags my hand and brings my fingers to his mouth. "No time now. Besides, I told you. I've got plans for you later."

"I can't wait." We exchange a secret smile as the pilot's voice crackles through the intercom, instructing us we're about to begin our descent and we should buckle up.

Once we land, the jet rolls right up to the small airport office. We step onto the portable staircase, Cole first. I stop at the top, tipping my face to the sunshine.

"It's so lovely and warm," I gush at the bottom as Cole takes my hand.

"I should have a car waiting on the other side of the building," he says, grinning. Behind us, a staff person collects our bags and follows along.

I'm painfully aware of the fact that I'm not wearing any underwear, and as we step into the modern glass building, the air-conditioning brushing against my bare skin *everywhere*, I squeeze Cole's hand. "I just need to freshen up a minute, okay?"

We're almost at the concierge desk, and I blush when the pretty dark-haired woman behind the counter looks at me. Can she tell? God, I need to get better at this good girl/dirty girl routine.

Cole waves his hand and the cart behind us

240

stops. I snag my carry-on bag, which has an emergency change of clothes in it, and dart into the ladies room, which is just as nice as the rest of the private airport—two big stalls and a shared sink area.

Just in case my boyfriend might get any ideas in the car ride, I swap out the jean skirt I was wearing for a pair of white capris that go just as well with the turquoise tank top I've got on under my linen jacket.

Back at the sink, I pull out my make-up bag. I'm retouching my lipstick when the concierge lady comes in.

"Hi," I smile at her.

She smiles back. "Hello, Ms. Reid."

"I'll just be another minute."

"Take all the time you need. He'll appreciate the effort."

I resist the urge to eye-roll at her. Polite conversation is one thing, but really, that's none of her business. I lean forward, taking one last quick inspection look in the mirror.

A weird feeling slides through my gut at the same time I see her edge toward me. But when I glance her way, she just smiles and murmurs something about the towels on the other side of me.

I don't notice the needle, but I sure as hell feel the pinch as it slides into my arm. I just have enough time to think about yelling, but it comes out like a deadened cough before the syringe bounces to the floor and her hand slides over my mouth.

"Hush, baby girl," she whispers as my eyelids flutter shut. "The Master is waiting for you."

HATE F*@K

Cole and Hailey

part three

— one —

Cole

Something isn't right.

I'm standing alone at the concierge desk, because the ground crew guy wheeled our bags out to the front and the brunette behind the desk headed into the washroom a few minutes after Hailey.

I stare at the bathroom door.

The hair on the back of my neck stands up.

The concierge couldn't have waited? We'll be out of here in a few minutes. Wealthy clients prefer to piss in private. Either she's brand-new, or…

I take a few steps toward the washroom before stopping myself. Hailey will flip if I storm in there, worrying about her.

My gut tightens. *Fuck*. Better to beg forgiveness.

If I embarrass her, I'll be more than happy to grovel. I like nothing more than being on my knees in front of her.

I stride across the empty lobby and shove the door open, holding it with my outstretched arm. "Hailey?"

Nothing. The silence inside blares inside my head like a fire alarm. I twist, scanning the lobby once more before I slide inside. With my back to the wall, I pull my weapon from my concealed hip holster and creep around the privacy wall. I find an empty room and an ugly mix of adrenaline and fear dumps into my system.

Fuck, fuck, fuck. Kicking open the two stall doors, I confirm the room is empty, and my brain stutters to a stop. Hailey's gone. Hot, pounding rage pumps through my veins as I rip through a door tucked behind the second stall, bursting into a storage room with an exterior door.

Safety off on my pistol, I kick that door open and brace myself for shots, but there's nothing.

I'm standing in an empty alley beside an empty private airport.

She's just gone.

Wilson answers on the first ring as I run back to the lobby, phone to my ear. "How's Mia—"

"Hailey's been taken." My voice is ragged, my words spitting out in a staccato burst as I report and scan the scene at the same time. "Two suspects. First is female, brunette, early thirties, maybe a hundred and forty pounds, five and a half feet. Second is male, younger than that, maybe early twenties, just shy of six feet, one hundred and seventy pounds. Both were masquerading as airport staff, so I'm sure the real staff are here somewhere, bound or drugged. You need to call the FBI. I won't be here."

"Whoa, hang on." I can hear him typing, but I don't care. Nothing he can say will keep me from finding Hailey and ripping her captors apart with my bare hands.

My bags are abandoned outside. A town car is pulling up. My car?

"Shit. Hang on, Wilson."

I need back up. I wheel around and sprint out

246

onto the tarmac, where the pilot and flight attendant are having a laughing conversation in the open door of the private jet. It's surreal, like the last ten minutes didn't happen.

I don't know these people well, but Jason's brother, Mack, owns the plane and employs them. We've flown with them before, and I wouldn't say I *trust* either of them, but there's no way Mack Evans and Gerome Lively are even on speaking terms, let alone collaborating to kidnap my girlfriend. And I need someone who might know Mack's Miami driver.

There is no doubt in my mind who is responsible for this. I need to find out where he is.

"Wilson?" I bark into the phone.

"Yep, here. There aren't any traffic cams near the airport."

"What about around any properties that Gerome Lively owns or leases? Does he have an estate here?"

More typing. I grind my jaw and stare at the pilot, who is still eye-fucking the flight attendant. He's going to be practically useless as a back-up, but a second body is better than nothing. "Hey, you," I yell. He glances my way. "Need your help, bud."

My voice is shaking, but he doesn't seem to notice. He waves the flight attendant back into the plane, and jogs down the steps.

I nod my head toward the terminal, not trusting myself to speak again. I've got one hand on the phone pressed to my ear, the other wrapped around a gun in the pocket of my cargo pants.

He walks with me.

In my ear, Wilson whistles. "Yeah. You're not going to like this. They're getting on a boat."

"Fuck. I need images, now. We'll find a helicopter."

"We?" Wilson raises his voice, calling out for Jason. "Don't do anything stupid, Cole."

"Gotta go."

"The FBI—" A face full of protocol-obsessed suits is the last thing I need.

"They can catch up. I'm taking the pilot with me. Try to spin that into something other than a second kidnapping, got it?"

As the man besides me reacts—too slowly for my liking, but at least this time it's to my advantage —I grab his arm and drag him across the lobby and out the front entrance of the terminal.

I point with my phone at the suited, sunglasses-wearing man standing next to the waiting town car. "Who is that?"

The pilot, whose name I should really get at some point, clears his throat. "Mr. Evans' driver."

"You know him?"

"Yeah." He twists away from me, but doesn't move far. Maybe he has guessed I've got a gun in my pocket. "Look, Mr. Parker..."

"Get in the car." I grab him again, shoving him into the back seat, following him in. "Where can I get a helicopter flight to the Bahamas?"

"For real?"

"Yes, motherfucker, for real. My girlfriend, who you just flew here, because of *me*, has just been kidnapped. So I need the questions to stop and the help to start. Got it?"

"You have a strange way of making friends."

"We're not fucking friends. What's your name?"

"Harry. We should call the cops."

"Someone else is doing that, Harry. But we don't have a lot of time."

"How do you know that?"

I glower at him. "Can you find me a helicopter around here? You know a guy, or a place?"

"Yeah."

The driver's door opens and the chauffeur slides into his seat. "Where are we headed?"

Cool as a fucking cucumber. Maybe he could be my back up.

The pilot sighs. "Palm Beach Sky Tours." He rattles off an address, then looks at me. "Can I call this guy and give him a heads up?"

"Make sure he's got a bird ready to go in the air. No other details."

"What are we going to do?"

"Rescue her."

—two—

Hailey

The unmistakable salty scent of the ocean wakes me up, but it's the most reluctant wake-up call of my life.

Groggy and disoriented, I fight against consciousness. *A few more minutes.*

But now that I'm half-way awake—or a quarter of the way, maybe—confusion is setting in. And still sleep tugs me back, seducing me into its dark embrace.

My next conscious thought—a few minutes later, maybe, but I'm not sure—is, where is Cole? I miss his big, heavy body behind me. I'm not sure what happened last night, after all his big talk… but now I'm sleeping alone, and I don't think he was next to me at all. Unless I passed out? Maybe he's working.

My head *aches*. Like I drank too much and maybe have the flu at the same time. Did I get food poisoning?

I let out a small groan, testing my vocal cords. My mouth is dry, but my voice works okay. My eyelids are too heavy to open, so I roll onto my side and press my face into the pillow. At the least the bed is really nice.

Five more minutes of sleep, then I'm getting up. And as soon as Cole gets back from his meeting, I'm demanding a re-do on the crazy hijinks, minus the champagne.

"Get up," a harsh, female voice barks, and my

breath catches in my throat as hot panic floods my body. Dragging my eyes open, I scramble onto my knees, the room spinning around me.

I'm not in a hotel room. From the bright blue water out the window and lack of city noises, I don't think I'm in Miami, either.

And the gun currently pointed at me is *not cool*. Not cool at all.

"I'm up," I stammer, cursing myself for showing my fear. I repeat the words as I breathe shallowly, trying to take in every little clue I can see without looking too obvious.

Big bed. En suite bathroom. Lock on the door. And a woman who looks mad at me, which is weird, because I'm pretty sure I didn't just kidnap *her*.

A breeze from the window is cool on my skin — all of my skin. With a squeak, I realize I'm naked, and I snatch the bed sheet, pulling it up in front of me.

"The Master is waiting for you," she says, flipping her long, shiny dark hair over her shoulder like she's not holding a deadly weapon. "You need to take a shower."

New memories slam into my brain. The bathroom at the airport. *Cole*. What happened to him while I was being drugged? How much time has passed? Where the hell am I, and how the hell do I escape?

"Hey, honey," she sneers. "Shower."

Her voice grates at my skin and I shrink back, bumping into the wall behind me. "I don't understand what's going on."

"You don't need to. Get up." She waves the gun

252

at me for good measure and I ease off the bed. Okay, I'm not going to stretch time with a Q&A session.

"Shower."

"A *quick* one," she hisses.

My heart thumping and my face burning up, I skitter around her, clutching the sheet around me, and dash into the bathroom. It doesn't have a door, so barricading myself in isn't going to work.

I stare at shower stall. Rows of shampoo bottles line the ledge. A white bathrobe is hanging on a hook. Everything looks brand new and unused. Small comfort when I'm being held in God-knows-where for God-knows-what-purpose. Shivering as I consider the possibilities, I turn on the shower, wondering how long I can make this last.

My mind races.

It's daytime. Is it the same day as when I was drugged? I don't feel like I've been drugged forever and ever. For that matter, I don't even feel that unclean. Maybe it's only been a few hours.

I just need to find a phone, or a computer, or something to light on fire. Some way to raise the alarm, because if I do, The Horus Group will come for me.

Relief slams into me at that realization. Of course they will. It's just a matter of time. Because one of them—Cole—has branded me as *his*. Fair enough. He's *mine*, too.

And Cole Parker is a bad man.

Okay, when he's inside my bedroom, when we're making love, he's the best man in the world.

But here? In the outside world, with good and bad forces at work? Here it's a bit more complicated. I've never been completely comfortable with the fact that some of the time, they also work for the scum of the earth—but I can't think about that right now. Because right now, knowing they'll do absolutely anything to win is to my advantage.

Whoever it is that has me—chances are Cole knows all about them. As soon as he figures out where I am, he'll come for me.

I just need to hold on long enough, and deal with whatever faces me outside this suite.

Whoever *The Master* is...and whatever he wants me for.

— —

Hoping to put the robe on for modesty was foolish. My shower ends when the scary woman stalks in and points the gun at me again. She's a different person than my first kidnapper, I've realized now, although they share a common look.

She allows me to dry off, but when I reach for the robe she slaps down my hand, instead wrenching my arm behind my back and marching me butt-naked into the bedroom again—where the first woman, the one who stabbed me with a needle of some kind of noxious shit, is waiting.

"Oh baby girl," she croons with a creepy smile. "Are you all squeaky clean now?"

I shrink from her touch, but it does no good. Together, they seat me on a padded bench.

"Who are you?" I ask, my voice cracking.

"I'm Kimber," the creepy sweet one says softly as she starts to comb my hair. "And that's Regan.

She's annoyed because we didn't include her in your rescue."

"Rescue?" I almost choke on the word.

She leans over and licks my earlobe. Bile rises in my throat and I force myself not to react. "Your boyfriend is a lousy lay. The Master will take much better care of you."

If I wasn't naked and there wasn't a gun pointed at me right now, I'd kill her.

So this is how good and bad fade to shades of gray.

Shaking, I stand when told to, and tell the normal, embarrassed part of my soul to curl up in a little ball and cover its ears. *This is like a doctor's visit or a sorority initiation.* Nothing can hurt me if I'm not available to be hurt. Good Hailey cowers in the pit of my stomach, but somehow my legs are walking and my head is holding itself high.

I repeat all points of orientation to myself ten times in quick succession. The room we've just left, it faced west. The sun was bright, and sinking but still high, so it's mid-afternoon. There are—holy shit. Many bedrooms on this level. Eight doors that I can see. The tile floor is cool beneath my feet, but it means that everything echoes. Maybe I can use that.

How, Hailey? With your advanced knitting skills? Fuck, I don't know. Panic swells in my chest and I shove back against it.

That won't do any good.

Regan turns to me as we reach another hallway, one that leads outside at one end, and she sneers. "Just remember, it hurts more if you're not turned on. Find something to like about it."

I don't know if she's telling the truth, or if she's

255

trying to play with my mind, but if she is, it works. My knees give out and they scramble to catch me as I drop.

I've never been so happy about being heavy in my entire life, because they can't. Regan's gun skitters across the tile as I scramble away from them, and I'm on it before she is. I don't really know how this thing works, but I point it at her and pull the trigger, because nobody is going to fucking rape me today if I have anything to say about it.

It feels like I've been punched in the hand and my arm swings wildly in the air, the force of the shot sending me back a foot.

Regan gapes at me as she looks down at her chest, where a big red spot is blooming, then she collapses just as the hallway fills with people.

My mind blanks as I stare at her body. *I just shot someone.* Thunder rushes through my head and my hands slick with sweat. I'm hot and cold. Killer and prey.

I stumble backwards, running into Kimber, and she screams, which makes me scream, but then I remember I have the gun. So I put it to her head, and twist around her body, making her my shield.

I'm breathing so fast I think it's possible I might pass out soon, but before I do, I want to get some clothes on and maybe find a boat or a panic room or something.

This is a lot harder than it looks in the movies —doubly so because I don't even watch these kinds of movies.

Who knew I'd need to star in my own horror film?

"Ms. Reid," a confident, warm voice says from behind the swarm of men, and as they part, I see Gerome Lively step forward.

After that Vanity Fair reporter mentioned him, and I knew Cole was working on something related to him…I did some Googling.

I even went into the dark corners of the Internet that Cole would rather pretend I don't know about.

Revulsion rises in me. This man had me kidnapped. Planned to rape me—or let his friends rape me. All because of Cole, or my father, or both of them. Nothing to do with me.

"You don't want to do this," he says, fake charm oozing off him.

"I don't know what you think I want to do, but —" my voice cracks, and I tighten my grip around Kimber's neck, making her groan. "Shut up, bitch. You stabbed me with a fucking needle. On his order?"

She cries, and maybe she would nod, but she can't move her head.

I twist the gun toward Lively, my hand shaking. "Get out of my way."

"You're not going anywhere. This is silly."

I fire at him without waiting for another word, but unlike the point blank range where hitting Regan was easy, this bullet ricochets off the ceiling.

His cool demeanour slips a bit and he steps into a hallway or a nook, something just off this corridor, and he waves his goons back, too.

"Not good enough," I scream, losing my shit now. Good. Maybe scary Hailey can kick some ass, because scared Hailey isn't doing so well. "Get out of this hallway!"

They slip away, and I edge Kimber forward, painfully aware that my naked butt is hanging out behind me and I have no clue where I am or what's between me and freedom. Or even what direction freedom might be in.

"Where are they going?" I hiss in her ear, and she gurgles at me.

Oops. Strangling a hostage…never a good idea. I ease up enough to give her some air, but it's a total waste. "You'll never escape," she wheezes and I roll my eyes.

Maybe not, but if I go down, I go down fighting.

I didn't know I had that in me, but apparently I do.

I'm still shaking and ready to pee myself, but I push us forward. The outside that I'd glimpsed at the end of the hall looks like it's actually a second or third story balcony. Maybe not my first choice. But before we get there, the hall opens up to the right to a large common room.

Where Lively is waiting with what looks like a small army.

Okay, maybe it's just six guys. Or eight. I can't count.

I can't *think*.

"I told you this is silly, Hailey," Lively says, smooth as poisoned silk. "Because of the special relationship I have with your father, I'll forgive you this indiscretion. I should have welcomed you to the island myself. I apologize."

I stare at him, dumbstruck. I just killed a woman. I'm holding another one hostage. I'm buck-fucking-naked,, and he's talking to me like he's just been a bad host for a weekend away.

My skin crawls as it dawns on me that maybe this is all this is to him. Murder? No big deal. Drama? He eats hostages for lunch.

That shallow breathing thing gets me again, and I wobble on the spot. *Damnit*. I was so close, and now it's all slipping away.

Literally, as one of his armed guards approaches and my hand shakes too hard to pull the damn trigger. *No!* I did it twice, I can do it again...

But I can't. Hot tears splash on my cheeks as I realize I'm done for. Kimber is wrenched from my arms, and as the guard takes the gun from me, twisting my arms behind my back, the window shatters and he drops to the ground.

I stare at him for a second—because *I* didn't just shoot him, and then I know.

I feel Cole the second the doors crack open. He's like a hot Caribbean wind, swirling in, wrapping around me, ready to suck me back out again. Because I'm his, even from across the room with a dozen bad guys in between.

And like a hurricane, he's an unstoppable force, taking out the two men closest to him with his bare hands, then shooting the guards at the other entrances.

Behind him, a man I don't know comes in, and Cole issues him terse commands as he sprints toward me, reaching me at the same time Lively does.

—three—

Cole

Hailey calls out my name, and for a split second, I can't see anyone else.

I leave the round-up of the incapacitated men to Harry and his helicopter pilot friend, who, it turns out, is ex-military and far more switched on than Harry is. And right now, they just need to hold rifles straight.

It takes me three seconds to cross the room and get my shirt off and around her naked form. Another millisecond to realize that Lively has a gun, and it's pointed at my head. I drop, swinging my leg around in a vicious sweep that brings him down, then I'm on him like a cage fighter.

"Break into my house and attack me? Prison orange will look good on you —" I slam my fist into his jaw.

"Deluded motherfucker," I growl. "You think you can stop us? You're the one going to prison. And any other guests you've got here, too. Every single last one of you will fry for taking her."

Lively sneers up at me. "At least she was a decent fuck. Chubby girls are always gagging for it."

Slamming his head into the ground isn't nearly as satisfying as I want it to be. I drag him back up onto his knees. Seeing the blood drip from his battered nose onto his pristine tennis whites? The snot and tears as he gags on his pain?

That's better.

I zip-tie his wrists, then haul Hailey against me. "Beautiful," I rasp.

"I'm okay," she says, her chest heaving and her body shaking. Her hands scrabble at the sleeveless shirt I'm left in.

"He had you naked."

"Just that. He didn't…what he said…" She starts crying. "I shot someone. In the hallway."

"Good girl."

"I knew you'd come, but I didn't…I couldn't let him…"

"I know. You did the right thing." I kiss the top of her head, and look across to Harry. "You guys should call this in, then get the hell out of here."

"How many people are you going to get tangled in the law with you today, Cole?" a familiar, disappointed voice says from the terrace we just came in from. Jason steps into view and nods at Harry and his friend, gesturing for them to scram. "Step away from Lively."

"Fuck off, Jason. If I was going to kill him, I already would have." I cock my pistol and jam it into Lively's temple, just for fun. "Or maybe I still will." I glare at my best friend.

"He isn't worth it. And the Feds are two minutes behind me, so how about you let him be arrested without incident, yeah?"

I set my jaw and grit my teeth. He's right. I'm not acting under the protection of any arm of the US Government. We might be on a private island, but the Bahamian police would arrest me for murder in a heartbeat.

And I'm no longer the guy who doesn't give a fuck about that.

Jason looks at me, then back at Lively. He slowly turns and slides his Glock into its holster. "Put it away, brother."

I kick Lively hard in the back, making him fall forward onto the tile floor. I stand there, seething, my boot on his spine, my weapons securely tucked away as men in windbreakers and hats clearly labelled as the good guys swarm the room.

Hailey cries as I'm handcuffed and shoved against the wall, but I know this is the easy part. They're just securing everyone. Ten minutes, tops, and I'll have her in my arms.

It's only eight, and it feels like a lifetime.

A female officer brings her a blanket, which gives her more coverage than my shirt, and I pull her closer.

But she's in shock—there's no embrace tight enough to hold her together right now. And that's okay. We've got all the time in the world to make this better.

It's late when we're escorted onto a US Coast Guard vessel. I still don't know how Jason arrived, but he smoothed over a lot with the Feds and now, as we head back to Florida, I know something needs to be said.

But there's a lot of other stuff that's already been said, and one good day of making bad people pay doesn't negate all the shit that's come up between us in the last while.

So I stick with something safe. "How were you so sure I wasn't going to shoot him?"

"We've got our problems, but you've never been as far on the wrong side of right as you think you've been."

263

I'm tired, and I ache in a million different ways. "That doesn't make an ounce of sense."

"It does to me," Hailey murmurs, tightening her grip around my waist. "You saved the day."

I stare over her head at Jason. We both know that it's only the day that I've saved. Lively still has a million ways to get out of this.

When Hailey falls asleep, wrapped up in a fleece blanket and three layers of FBI-branded clothing, Jason clears his throat. "You know what he's going to do."

"He'd hire us, if we were available. So we need to figure out who he'll go to."

He nodded. "Wilson was already watching for noise in that direction before I left. We didn't know how fast you'd get to her."

"Not as fast as I wanted. Turns out your brother's pilot has a conscience and so do his friends. They made me verify a bunch of shit and make sure we were properly armed before taking off, and we did a couple of high passes before figuring out where to land."

"Safety bullshit?" He laughs with me, but it feels damn hollow.

"I did this to her," I say roughly, looking down at the woman I love. Whose safety I'd risked without even thinking about it.

"You didn't know he was watching us. None of us did. Wilson is beside himself with guilt. You're not alone in feeling like you failed her." He grimaces. "But your girl…she's tough."

"Yeah."

"We'll get him."

"*I* will."

Jason narrows his eyes. "This should be a team effort."

"Some of it will be."

But before I leave Miami, there are some conversations in the shadows that need to happen, to ensure Hailey's never touched, ever again.

—four—

Hailey

I wake up as the boat docks at an official looking port in Miami.

"Shit," I whisper. "I don't have my passport."

Cole laughs, holding me tight. "Really?"

"What?" I scowl at him. "Oh, ha ha, sure. Joke is on the girl who's never been kidnapped before. You re-enter the county, you need your passport."

"First of all, beautiful, your passport will be waiting for you in there. And second...come here." He pulls me up and kisses me on the lips. It's soft and chaste, but it rouses my usual desire for him that constantly hums just beneath the surface. He smooths his hand over my cheek, sliding his fingers into my tangled hair. "This shouldn't be anything but a quick bureaucratic paper stamping thing, okay? There will be a formal interview tomorrow, but we're probably only half an hour away from a hot shower and bed. Promise."

Twenty-four minutes later, he's sliding a keycard into the door of a top floor downtown hotel room. We came straight up from the parking garage, driven here by a hired car, and Cole promised the room was under someone else's name.

Nobody knows we're here.

For the first time today, I don't need to hold myself together.

Even while I slept, I was keeping a lot of shit at bay.

Now it starts to fall away, and before I realize

it, Cole's got me in the bathroom. His hands freeze at the hem of my shirt. "Can I?" he asks, and that just makes me sob harder.

Of course he can.

But of course he has to ask.

I hate that I need him to, that the little kiss we shared and the little sparks I felt have vanished. His hands on my skin are now strictly functional.

I still his movement, sliding my palms over the backs of his hands. Up his arms, over his shoulders until I'm wrapped around him.

"I just need a hug," I whisper, and he holds me tight.

He starts the shower, and when he turns to leave, I pull him in with me. He washes my hair and I lean against his chest, and when we get out, he dries me off, then holds me as I fall asleep.

— —

The next morning, we're summoned to the regional offices of the Federal Bureau of Investigation and separated for hours while I'm grilled on what happened.

I tell my story, over and over again until my heart aches and I'm physically shaking. First, I give my statement to a nice guy in a dark grey suit, then again to two agents, a woman and a man. Two more grey suits. Neither quite as nice as the first one.

The questions are harder. More pointed. They won't stop asking me why Cole brought me to Miami. I hate that they won't accept the weekend trip answer.

It has to be the truth.

"Can I have something to drink?" I ask at a pause between questions.

The guy looks at his watch. "It's actually lunch time, can we get you a sandwich?"

My stomach protests at the thought of anything solid. "Water is fine."

"We might be here a while."

I give him a tight smile. "Hopefully not."

A knock on the door comes quickly, delivering the water that I've asked for, and my eyes dart to the mirrored glass on the wall.

"You made a tempting target for Lively," the female agent finally says after I drink half the bottle of water.

"Really?" I ask, my voice clipped and cold now. I'm so done with this. "Obviously I was a poor choice for a sex slave."

"You think your boyfriend knew that when he flaunted you in front of his nemesis?"

I bang the water bottle on the table, my hands shaking so hard it barely stays upright. "I think you're focusing on entirely the wrong villain in this narrative. *I* didn't know I had it in me to defend myself. I'm quite certain Cole didn't, either. And I hardly look like that bastard's preferred type. So whatever you're alluding to? It's dead wrong."

"Dead is the operative word, isn't it, Ms. Reid." That was from the male agent. I stare at him, cataloguing him. Greying hair, lined face.

"It was either me or her. You wanted me to make a different choice?"

They glance at each other.

"Can I talk to Cole Parker, please?"

269

"He's being interviewed," the woman says. "Can I get you some lunch?"

Hell no. So I say six words I never imagined crossing my lips. "I think I need an attorney."

— —

Apparently Jason was waiting in the lobby with lawyers, and I should have said the magic words sooner. We finish up pretty quickly after that, then go to the law offices of the firm Jason and Cole have retained to protect my identity in all of this.

They order food in, and the strategy talk continues. Most of it goes in one ear and out the other because my brain is fried with stress and stimulation overload and the lies and innuendos that had been shoved at me all day.

I'm so done.

We don't leave until it's dark, so I fall asleep on the drive back to the hotel, and I'm all groggy when Cole wakes me up before easing me out of the back of the hired car.

"Come on, I'll get you settled."

"Wait," I protest as he guides me into the elevator. "What do you mean?"

He gives me a look I can't decipher as the car stops on the mezzanine level and a group of business people get in. Always a bodyguard, Cole's stance shifts slightly—he does this thing where he looks like he's relaxing, but really he's a coiled snake, ready to strike at the slightest threat.

I hold my tongue until they get off a few floors below ours.

"I'm not a child. You can't just tell me it's bedtime."

His nostrils flare and his jaw clenches, but he just moves me out of the elevator and down the hall toward our room. "I need to go out for bit," he finally says as I start undressing. "I won't be long."

"And I shouldn't ask were you're going?" I yank one of his t-shirts off the chair in front of the window and pull it on before I shove my pants to the floor, my back to him the whole time.

I don't hear him cross the room, so I shiver as he grips my shoulders. He jerks his hands away, but he doesn't move.

"You have every right to be afraid of me," he mutters into my hair.

"I'm not." It's the truth. I turn and try to catch his gaze, but he holds himself rigid and straight, staring out the window at the city below.

Pressing up onto my toes, I part my lips and trace a cord of muscle up his neck with the tip of my tongue.

His hands slam onto my hips and he rocks me back against the window. I arch against the cool glass, but I can't catch his gaze.

"What's wrong?" I ask as I wrap my arms around my waist, all sex kitten impulses vanishing at his lacklustre response.

"Nothing." But now I can see he's shaking, and what I thought was just him being on high-alert in the elevator is really him being on edge around *me*.

"Fine," I mutter, shoving past him. "Go out. Do whatever dirty work you need to do to make yourself feel like you've got this under control."

I don't know if I shoved him to goad him into

action—wouldn't be the first time—or if I actually thought I could stomp to bed and he'd just leave it be.

But of course he doesn't. Before I get two steps past him, he's lifting me around the waist and carrying me to the couch as I kick half-assedly and protest more vigorously. "Put me down!"

He does—sideways on his lap. His eyes burning dark, he glares at me as he rubs his hand lazily over my ass, hanging out in the open space between his spread thighs.

I love it when he holds me like this. I can feel his muscles bunching beneath me, and I'm hyperaware of each powerful shift as he holds me. We're both restless. If we weren't twenty-four hours out of him rescuing me from being used as a sex slave, I'd have thought this was the start of something hot. Cole the Dom.

Where the thought should make me giggle, or pant because bossy Cole is super-hot, it just makes me sad.

The way he's practically vibrating to get away from me, I think it's more Cole the Emotionally-Unavailable-Can't-Handle-Shit Guy.

Doesn't quite have the same ring to it. Fuck. I want to cry, but that'll just make Cole feel worse.

And there's *always* this chemistry between us. He can't help but squeeze my flesh, but he doesn't want to do anything else. That's crystal clear.

Even knowing that, I still press close, feathering kisses over his jaw as he holds still as granite. He groans as my lips find his, and he holds me tight, but his lips leave mine at the first opportunity.

So I stop trying.

Cole hugging me has never felt so much like a rejection before. In my head, I'm convincing myself to get down off the ledge, using all the talk therapy tricks I've picked up over the years.

Surviving a childhood steered by Morgan and Amelia Reid has made me a self-talk ninja. *This is hard for you both. He's been at your side the entire time. He's given you no reason to doubt him. You fell apart last night, maybe he's confused about the mixed messages.*

"Do you want to talk about the interviews today?" he asks, his voice a sudden grate of sandpaper in the quiet of the room.

"No," I say, laughing without humor.

"It's their job to poke in all directions."

"I know," I snap, harsher than is needed. "I don't need to talk."

Something shifts then, something that gives me reassurance and hope. He relaxes beneath me and I feel his erection, heavy and solid and growing.

Point, Hailey. Or at least my naked ass.

"What do you need?" he asks quietly, his lips brushing against my hair.

I squeeze my eyes shut and bury my face in his neck. "You," I whisper.

With a groan, he slides his hand up my thigh, rucking his t-shirt up to my waist. I go to turn, to get on my knees and straddle him, but he tightens his grip, holding me in place with my side against his chest. "Don't."

"Let me touch you," I beg.

"Shhh." He rubs his thumb across the top of my thigh, making me moan despite myself. "This is just for you."

He skims his hand under my shirt, over my belly, then back again. Lower this time, and firmer, right where my belly meets my mound—my on switch. I twist, pressing my face into his neck as I spread my legs for him.

Point, Cole.

First he circles my opening, a teasing rub that makes me squirm and murmur achingly for more. Then he strokes me more deliberately, gathering the wet evidence of how quickly he can turn me.

Spreading it up to my clit, he rolls his thumb over that spot as he twists his hand and thrusts into me.

Sweet one minute, hard the next. Why did I expect anything different?

Two fingers drag out of me, slow enough I can feel every single inch. I shudder as his knuckles slide out of my entrance and I rock my hips, inviting him back in.

"Fuck my fingers," he growls, tugging on my hair, giving himself more access to the sensitive bits of skin he likes. My ears, my mouth, my neck. "Be greedy. Get yourself off on my thumb. Take it, beautiful."

I roll my pelvis in a shameless echo of his words, sliding my pussy all over his hand. I like the heel of his palm best, and when I find it and start whimpering, he takes over again.

"Yeah? Do it," he whispers, his tongue licking along the curve of my ear as he talks me straight into coming on his hand. "Grind on me. Look at you go. You're so fucking gorgeous."

I tug my shirt up, wanting his other hand on my skin there. My breasts hang heavy and my nipples ache for his touch.

Nipping at my ear, Cole spins me so I'm sitting on him, my back against his chest, my legs hooked on the outside of his thighs. I pull his hands to cup my breasts, and his hot, heavy breath in my ear is the best sound I've heard all day.

The press of his cock beneath my ass feels pretty good too.

"Sure I can't tempt you…?"

He groans and bites my neck. "Believe me, I'm tempted."

"But no?"

A rough laugh against my skin is answer enough. *Tonight is for me*. I don't understand why, but he's intent and I'm on fire, so I stop fighting, and close my eyes.

Feelings blur the specifics of what he's doing. I don't know where his hands are going, but I like what they do when they stop for a second, how they make me feel. Squeezing, stroking, slapping… with each sensation, I climb higher and feel more free, and then his touch is between my legs again, his arms wrapping around me.

Heat sizzles through my veins, radiating out from each erogenous zone Cole has just switched on, then bouncing back until every part of my body feels connected and on fire and ready to explode.

My swollen skin is so slippery now, his fingers glide over the nerve endings and as his teeth sink into my earlobe, he rocks the heel of his hand over my clit and I combust into a trembling, pulsing, all-thoughts-vanquished puddle of goo.

After the last aftershocks of my orgasm fade,

and I'm slumped against him, boneless and once again, oh so tired, he slowly stands, dead-lifting me as he shoves off the couch, his thighs flexing and his arms straining. I wrap myself tighter around him and he carries me to the bed.

I hold on tighter than tight when he tries to pull away after tucking me in.

"I'm just getting my phone, I need to check in," he says roughly, not looking at me.

I grab his hand, anxious as he moves out of touching range. "Cole?"

He snags his phone and rolls back against me. "Hmm?"

Swallowing hard, I spit out the worry that's been at the back of my head for the last twenty-four hours. "Are we okay?"

I mean it in all the possible ways—emotionally, legally. Relationship-ally.

He grips the back of my neck, his gaze burning me. "Of course."

But when I wake up in the middle of the night, he's gone. We went to sleep together, but at some point, he quietly slipped out of the room.

I don't call him. I'm scared he won't answer, although he's given me no reason to think that.

I don't turn on the television, because I'm terrified of what I might see, although I want to think he'd choose differently now.

He came for me.

I choose to trust him, but it's hard.

It takes me a long time to drift off again. I wonder where he is. What he thinks he had to do. I worry.

In the early morning, I wake up with his arm

around my waist and his face buried in my neck, and I lay there for a long time, silent, relieved tears streaming down my face.

Of course I knew we'd have secrets. And for so long, I'd thought Cole was off-limits for my heart, because he wasn't the guy for me. But then he pushed his way into my life, and I forgot about this side of him, because he was so sweet and we fit just right.

Now I'm remembering everything else. But instead of climbing out of bed and throwing his clothes at him, cursing him and shoving him out the door for only giving me a piece of him, I just lay there, desperately soaking up his warmth, because I love him.

five

Cole

For the second and final interview the next day, Hailey has a lawyer present the entire time.

It goes much smoother, and ends with us getting their blessing to return to Washington, but she's still wrung out when I whisk her into the car, where our bags are already loaded, and we head straight for the airport.

Goodbye Florida. I'll do my best to help you fry Gerome Lively. And if you fail, I'll kill him myself.

— —

Three mornings later, I run from Hailey's apartment to the office. Dawn is breaking, it's cold as balls, and I'm pounding the pavement like it's to blame for what happened to her.

Nope. That's all me. I clench my jaw, owning my responsibility. Hard to pound myself into the ground, though I'm sure as shit going to try.

I own that I'm probably fucked up. Being abandoned at the age of two by addict parents will do that to a kid. The Parkers were good people — are good people, and that I just thought about them in the past tense proves that I'm not capable of the kind of emotional sensitivity Hailey deserves, and needs after what's happened to her.

My adopted parents deserve better, too. I should know, they told me over and over again, until I ran away at sixteen and joined the Navy. Now we live on opposite sides of the continent and I haven't spoken to them in three years. I get polite cards at Christmas and on my birthday, because they're good people even if they don't like me.

A pigeon lands briefly on the sidewalk in front of me, only to take off again in a huffy flutter of feathers when I don't slow down. Fuck you, pigeon, I'm rarely likeable. It's my nature, deal with it.

When we got back to Washington, I wanted Hailey to come stay at my place, but I knew she wouldn't.

"Is my place safe?" she asked me as we drove away from a private gate at Dulles airport. I wanted to lie to her, to tell her she had to stay in my penthouse, but I had to confess to her that I had Wilson convince her downstairs neighbor to move—a fact that did not impress her. But now she has the most secure apartment outside of the White House in all of Washington, D.C., so I don't care.

Much. I care a little that how I deal with problems isn't how she'd want them dealt with. But when she curls into my side, closing her eyes to the outside world, I think maybe she doesn't know how to deal with the horrors of *my* world. Maybe she just accepts that I do what needs to be done, even if I don't like it.

I stayed home with her the first day. I took her to her office that morning and she made me wait in the reception area while she had a conversation with her boss about taking a leave of absence from her internship.

So far, we've kept her name out of the media,

and our Florida attorneys will keep on the courts to ensure she remains Jane Doe, but that might not last forever.

Yesterday was my first day back at work. When I returned to her place at the end of the day, she'd baked muffins, but as soon as I walked in the door, she crumbled. I held her as she cried, then I fed her and tucked her onto the couch with me. I rubbed her shoulders and smoothed her hair until she fell asleep.

I haven't touched her again since that night in Miami. I want to. God, I want to so much. The urge to lose myself in her body is overwhelming, but each day she seems worse, not better. I can't take advantage of her.

I want to tell her I'm working hard to make her world safe again, but that would be a lie. Because of me, her world is never going to be the same.

I stole that from her, and I don't know how to make it better.

— —

Tag and Wilson step into my office shortly before lunch and close the door behind them.

I shove Lively's file, which I'd been poring over for the hundredth time, looking for something new —anything—and cross my arms. "What?"

Tag's face says it all, but he spells out the news anyway. "Lively's been granted bail."

"Fuck." I punch my desk and stand, pacing to the window. "Restrictions?"

"Monitoring ankle bracelet. Passport surrendered."

I glance at Wilson, whose jaw was clenched even harder than mine, and who'd been silent to this point. "And we are…"

"I'm tapped in to the security footage on his Miami home. There are some blind spots, but I can fly down there and try to get inside." He hesitates, his eyes steely grey as he stares at me. "You want this problem to go away?"

Do I want Wilson to assassinate the man who'd had Hailey kidnapped? There has never been an easier answer. Yes, I want that. Fuck, I want to be the one to do it.

But it's not that easy. We're not invisible agents in this. We need to be smart.

I slowly shake my head. "Go. In and out like a ghost. Get us more information, but we don't interfere."

Tag lifts his eyebrows.

"Yet," I clarify, scrubbing my hand up my face. "We don't interfere *yet*. Let's wait until the Feds fuck it up. Give them a chance to do the right thing."

A single knock at the door reminds us we've left someone out of the conversation. On purpose? I look at Tag, who looks at Wilson, who opens the door.

Jason strolls in, his hands in his pockets. Casual as anything. This can't be good. "You forgot to invite me to your tea party," he says slowly, looking at our partners before pinning his gaze on me.

"Just talking."

"We do that together. The four of us. When did we stop being a team?"

I shove to my feet. "When you warned me off of Hailey."

"I wasn't wrong." He stares at me, daring me to claim otherwise.

I take a deep breath, then let it out. "Does PRISM have any thoughts on what's happened?"

He shakes his head. "Not yet. I'm flying to Geneva tomorrow."

"You were summoned?" It's one thing for us to bristle at each other. It's another for Jason to be in trouble—I'll always have his back, like he had mine in the Bahamas, no questions asked.

"It's fine." He lifts one hand and points his palm at me. "Really, it's fine. I need to renegotiate the terms of our service to them, anyway."

"You shouldn't go alone."

"I'm not. I'm taking Mack with me." Jason's brother borders on paranoid. I can respect that. "He'll bring his security team."

I don't want to ask if there's anything he doesn't want us to do while he's gone, because I'm not sure I can stay within any parameter he sets.

Like he knows that, he just nods and glances as Wilson. "You've got news?"

"Lively's on bail, at home. Ankle bracelet."

"You're going down there?"

"Like a shadow."

Jason twists his head back toward me and ghosts me a smile. "Cole read my mind, clearly."

I nod back at him. We may not be in sync any more, but we're still cut from the same cloth. Always have been.

He holds out his fist. "Stay safe."

One by one, we each return the bump.

six

Hailey

I can't blame Cole for thinking I need to be treated with kid gloves. I have nightmares every night, and haven't been able to go to work or leave the house by myself yet.

Every day I lose myself in Ravelry and a long bath and baking muffins.

By the time he comes back, with take out for dinner, I'm ready to crawl out of my skin.

Over and over again, for six days.

Now I need something else, something that will wipe away the humiliation and fear.

The sensible answer is counseling.

I stopped being sensible two months ago, when Cole Parker strong-armed me into his car and accidentally made out with me in my kitchen.

I want sex. It's been over a week, and while what we did in Miami was what I needed at the time, it's not the same thing. I want what happens when we're together in every way possible, that crazy chemistry magic that makes me feel invincible.

My heart starts beating faster as his key turns in the lock.

"I got Vietnamese noodles," he calls out, and I set the lube I'm holding on the bedside table.

"Sounds great," I say with a smile as I join him in the kitchen.

He puts the food down and wraps me in a tight

hug.

"What's that for?"

He kisses my forehead. "Can't a guy just hug his girl?"

"He can, and she'll like it, but that was extra squeezy." I slide my fingers under his shirt and stroke the bare, tight skin of his abdomen, tracing the ridges of his six pack as he flexes for me.

How am I this lucky? He literally saves my life and lets me grope him to my heart's content. I'm done feeling sorry for myself.

"What are you doing?" The question comes out part groan as I go to work on his shirt buttons.

"Getting you out of your work clothes."

Dark amber eyes glow down at me from a rugged face, five-o'clock shadow highlighting all the harsh lines that I've come to love. "If I'm going to be stripped down, I'm going to want some naked company."

I grab his hands and slid them over my hips. "Make it so."

We get each other naked in record time as Cole backs me into my bedroom, and by the time we hit my bed, I'm aching for him to just be inside me, even though I had other plans.

"It's been too long," he says as we fall together as one, his heavy thighs shoving my legs apart. I rock my hips up to meet his throbbing cock, wet and ready for the heavy thrust I know is coming.

I don't know anything.

"Do you know how hard it is to not taste you?" he growls, nipping at my jaw. Desire ripples across my skin, ever-widening circles of awareness as he moves down my neck, rasping his wide tongue

286

across my skin, stretched taut for him as I arch my back. "And now…all I want to do is fuck you so hard I go blind."

"Yes," I gasp. "I want that. Do that."

"I can't." Another growl as he reaches my breasts, cupping my overflowing flesh together as he feasts on my nipples. "I need to worship you first."

"A hard fuck is an acceptable form of worship in the Religion of Hailey." I squirm as he pinches one nipple while tugging the other deep into his mouth. He knows what that does to me. "I'm so wet, Cole. You'd slide in so smooth."

He swings his body up, effortlessly kneeling between my spread legs now, and he lazily strokes my swollen, exposed pussy. "You aren't lying."

"Never," I whisper as he shoves first one, then two, then three fingers into me, stretching me wide. His cock thumps hard and heavy against my thigh, and I reach for him, but he snags my wrists and tugs them over my head, looming over me once again.

"You know why I can't fuck you yet?"

I shake my head, mouth wide, nipples straining for the rough rub of his chest against mine.

"Because I haven't kissed you yet. And you deserve to be kissed from head to toe every single time we make love."

I giggle, because that sounds dangerously close to saccharine, but he just glowers at me. "No laughing?"

"Feel free to laugh—if you can."

He fists himself, coating himself in my wetness, then he rocks the wide head of his cock against my clit as he drops on top of me—our sexes aligned, but not for fucking.

Apparently, he was serious about that kissing thing.

And once he starts, I can't object.

Hard and determined, his mouth covers mine, sucking and licking and teasing. At the same time, his hips press between my legs, moving just enough to keep my blood near the boiling point.

Not nearly enough to make me come, even as he devours me in a kiss that says so much—how hard it's been to keep his hands off me, how much he needs me. I recognize that possession. It pulses through my veins, too.

But he's not marking me. He's giving it to me hard—the only way he really knows how—but he's being careful. No whisker burn, no swollen lips. As he moves south, I'm sure he'll avoid hickies and bite marks, too.

He's just making me feel good. Taking care of me, *again*. Which is *nice*, but it's not what I want.

"Cole!" I plead as he threads his fingers into my hair, tilting my head to the side. "You don't need to be gentle with me."

He grips me tight enough to show he thinks he isn't, and he pulls my earlobe into his mouth. "You have a problem with how I'm making love to you?" he growls, jerking his hips against my sex.

Of course I don't. But...

"I didn't ask you to *make love* to me," I hiss back, shoving against his chest. Since when do we call it that? "I asked you to *fuck* me."

He twists to the side, stunned at my anger. I'm a little surprised at myself. "Hey," he protests, reaching for me, but I shove his hands above *his* head and climb on top of him, centering his cock right where I want it.

"I want *this*," I insist, sliding onto him. And *oh God*, he feels so good inside me. That first breach makes me wide-eyed and breathless, and greedy for more. But it's raw, too, how he stretches and fills me from the inside out, and I feel tears welling.

Oh shit.

He jackknifes up, wrapping his arms around me, pulling us hard together. Holding me tight. And the panic recedes.

"How did you know?" I whisper, rocking my hips, desperate to get that sexy-as-fuck edge back. Despite my momentary freakout, Cole is still rock hard, and now he's moving us, like the waves of the ocean.

"I've been through trauma before, baby," he rasps as he flexes his cock inside me. "It's messy and confusing and surprising. But that's okay. You're strong." His arms tighten around me. "I've got you. Let me love you."

I feel like an idiot for not seeing his restraint — how he held himself back this past week — as loving. I kiss him, desperate to show him I get it now.

And he's still hard. And still moving, ever so slowly inside me.

A new understanding dawns on me as my desire rises again.

Still on the surface, we cling to each other, me straddling him, his arms around me like bands of steel.

But inside our embrace, under the surface...the

pull is intense. One-of-a-kind chemistry. The magic that happens on my skin everywhere his mouth and hands touch me. The tight slide and thrust of his erection inside me. Shallow movements that rub just the right spot.

And if he's the dark water, rushing in toward shore, I'm the tide. I rise on my knees, as much as he lets me as he pins me in place, holding my gaze. But I need this. I need to be in charge, even though I'm not great at it.

Even though I need to be held while I'm pretending to take him.

But maybe that's okay. Maybe I just need to be the force that compels him.

I stroke his face, and he relaxes, skating his hands down my back to cup my bottom—his big hands covering my ass cheeks, his fingers curling into the cleft between them. And then I remember.

"Oh," I say, a breathy sound that's even loaded to my own ears. I lift more on the next rise, almost slipping him entirely out of my body before sinking down.

He grunts and grips my hips tighter. "What?"

"I, hum…" I lean forward and bite his lower lip. "I put out the lube. You know, if you wanted to…"

His eyes darken as he drifts his fingers over the smooth skin around my puckered hole, making me feel beautiful and dirty and desirable all at the same time. "I always want."

As if there was any doubt, he swells inside me and I cry out, riding faster even as it gets harder to lift myself fully off his erection.

"Feel that?" he grinds out the question as he

drives deep inside me, making me scream for him. "That's how much I want to own your ass. But not today. Not when you need to be in charge."

A half-laugh, half-moan rips from my throat as I throw my head back, giving myself over to the dark wave rolling toward me—the heavy, unstoppable, erotic force that is Cole Parker.

"I'm not in charge," I pant, my voice reedy and faint, and he grips my hips tighter as he moves me, changing the angle at the same time as he latches on to a nipple.

Kinda proving my point, I think groggily as I fall blissfully into an orgasm that ripples through my entire being.

He keeps rocking us together, stretching out my pleasure until I grip his biceps in a voiceless plea—*enough*. He stops, immediately, which kind of proves *his* point, and then he falls back, pulling me up his torso before sliding me onto my tummy.

A dark thrill races through me as he mounts me from behind, but he doesn't enter me again, he just jerks himself against my ass—and damn, but that's hotter than I'd ever have imagined.

With his free hand, he smooths over the bare skin in front of him, making me wet and achey all over again. "In time, beautiful. When this is all behind us. I'm going to fuck your ass and you're going to love it." He falls forward, bracing that hand beside my face, his breath coming hard and fast as he gets closer. His next words make me gasp, the rough delivery somehow perfect for the sweet secret. "It'll be my first time. You'll have to be gentle with me."

I'm still reeling as he comes on my back, his

wet shaft slapping against my ass as he loses control at the end, and hot tears prick behind my eyelids.

After he cleans me up, he rolls me into his chest, and he gives me a look that says, *go on, ask*.

"That's true? You haven't done that with anyone else?"

"Yeah." He gives me almost a sheepish smile. "Still think of me as a bad boy?"

I laugh weakly. "I gotta say, I'm surprised."

"It's just never..." He trails off, shrugging.

I squeeze him tight. "You're right. It should be special, then."

I meant it genuinely, but this is such an absurd conversation, it sounds like I'm making fun a little, and maybe that's a good thing, because Cole's eyes are twinkling.

"You haven't either," he says drily.

"I know," I whisper. "But everything about you feels like firsts for me."

He rolls on top of me, his face all serious and his brows drawn. "I could say the same thing. Maybe I should have. I'm not very good at this sharing stuff."

"What? No, that's not...it's fine."

"Don't," he says harshly. "Don't excuse me. I owe it to you to share more."

I frown. "What?"

He shakes his head and strokes my hair, weaving his fingers into the loose strands. "Nothing."

I'm learning not to push him when he says that. He's been more than I ever expected. I can wait for him to open up in his own time.

So I change the subject. "Are you going to tell me what was on your mind when you came home?"

He looks at me, then slowly tucks a loose lock of hair behind my ear. "You weren't supposed to notice that I had anything on my mind."

I prop myself up on his chest, my hands under my chin. "So much for sharing more." He gives me a pained expression and I raise my eyebrows. "Or are you all talk, no walk? What are you doing at work this week?"

"Nothing I want you thinking about."

"Argh!" I poke him with my chin as I settle closer again. It doesn't really upset me that he doesn't want to share, but I can't stop digging. "You think the case against Lively will fall apart?"

"No..." he trails off and brushes my forehead with his lips, taking his time before adding more. "We suspect he'll end up with a deal."

"Can I do something to prevent that from happening?"

"We're monitoring the situation for now. Collecting information, just in case. Nothing to worry about."

We talk for a few more minutes, then climb out of bed when his stomach growls.

That night I don't cry.

But when I wake up sometime after midnight, I'm alone again. I curl myself around Cole's pillow and fight against the rising panic.

He'll be back when I wake up.

— seven —

Cole

Over breakfast the next morning, Hailey informs me she's going shopping. "I assume you'll want me to take a bodyguard with me?" she asks, archly.

I laugh as I look at her over my coffee cup. "Too much of a princess move?"

She sighs. "No. Not if it's smart. Can it be Wilson?"

"Haven't you tortured him enough with the knitting lessons?"

"Why would shopping be torture?"

"Wilson doesn't like crowds," I say softly, and her lips curl into a silent "o".

"Okay, one of the hired goons is fine."

"Maybe don't call him a goon. His name is Scott." She sticks her tongue out at me. "Put that away before I put it to good use."

I'm teasing her, and she's being snarky, but there's an edge to the conversation, like she's running scared from the stuff that came up during sex the night before.

When she gets up to put her cup in the sink, I follow her, pinning her against the counter, my tan hands bracing next to her paler, creamier fingers on the counter.

"You have to go to work," she whispers, biting her lip to keep from smiling as she glances back at me over her shoulder.

I was a fool to hold back this week. My girl doesn't want soft and sweet.

Her hair is loose—long, honey-brown waves with expensive highlights, still damp from her shower. Fucking gorgeous.

"What are you thinking?" she asks, twisting to catch my eyes.

"How good your hair looks wrapped around my fist," I admit, gathering the strands in a loose ponytail. She smiles as she closes her eyes, and I decide work can wait.

Tugging her head to the side, I lower my face to the creamy skin of her shoulder and breathe her in, running my nose up her neck to the spot behind her ear.

I slide my hand up her front, pressing the hard length of my body into her back as I squeeze her breast. "I will never get enough of you."

I taste her, kissing her neck with an open mouth, soft at first, then harder. I bite my way down her neck again, to where the tendon flexes, and I suck there, using my tongue to savor every last inch of her.

My hands roam higher, tugging at her neckline. I rub my thumb along her collarbone, then cover her throat, pulling her mouth to meet mine for an urgent kiss before I move back to her neck.

"Think of this all day today. Think of how hard I get just breathing you in. Tasting your skin." I yank her hair harder and she gasps and smiles and all is fucking right with the world. I cup her cheek with my other hand and rub my thumb along the edge of her lower lip. Her skin's silky soft and she looks at me, her green eyes wide. "Tell me you feel the same."

"You know I do."

"I want to hear it."

She slides her hand between us and cups my throbbing dick. "I'm always ready for you." She licks her lips and closes her eyes, tipping her head back against my shoulder. I brush my mouth against her cheek, nuzzling her. Willing her to continue. "Wet. I want you to think of me, aching for your fingers."

Her voice is barely above a whisper, and her breathing is coming hard and fast now. Like I want to, all over her.

"I will," I growl in her ear. "We're both going to hum with that need, Hailey. And at the first available opportunity, I'm going to fuck you, and you'll be so primed, you're going to come as soon as I drag my big cock through that gorgeous fucking wetness. I'm going to spank your pretty little clit and you're going to scream for me."

"Umphf—" I cut her off as I suck her tongue into my mouth, twisting around her body now like we're one. Kissing her like it's better than breathing.

And I have to fucking go to work.

Breaking off the kiss that I can feel tingling across my scalp and down my spine is a fucking Herculean task. I want a gold medal for keeping my pants zipped.

"More..." she whispers against my lips, and I want to give her the moon. And a thousand orgasms.

"Later. Soon. It'll be worth it."

She thumps me weakly in the chest as she licks her lips. "Hey…I wanted to ask you…"

I reluctantly wipe my mouth and gesture for her to continue with my other hand.

She winces, but keeps her eyes on mine. "Where did you go last night?"

Shit. "You were asleep, and something came up. I wasn't gone for long, and you were asleep when I got back."

"You keep doing that. You did it in Miami, too."

I exhale roughly. I don't know what to say. "I'm sorry. You should have called. I wasn't far away."

Wilson had called and told me he had something, and I'd asked him to come to me instead of me going in to the office. When he picked me up at Hailey's, we circled the block while he told me that Clara Forrester bought a plane ticket last night. It's not for two more weeks, and it's return, but…it's still concerning. We have a guard on her now. That will be hard to maintain in Europe, where Lively has a stronger network than he has here in the States, and that's saying something.

Even from a Florida jail cell, he can make people disappear.

We spent more than an hour arguing over the best course of action.

"Would you believe me if I told you I was with Wilson, convincing him not to kidnap someone?"

With a groan, she crosses her arms. "Sadly, yes."

"It wasn't a serious plan."

"I can't even imagine." She tips her head to the

298

side, her lips pursed and her eyes soft and sad.

"I do a lot of things in the dark of night, beautiful. Most of the time, I'd rather you not know about it."

"You need to stop thinking I'm a heavy sleeper. Just leave me a note or something."

Jesus, I'm a bonehead sometimes. "Yeah."

"Is this about me?"

I can't lie to her, not even by omission. "It's another woman that could testify against Lively. She's running scared."

Hailey's mouth curls into a sad frown. "I know something about that."

How much I wish that weren't true.

She takes a deep breath. "If there's anything I can do..."

I pull her in for a kiss, then press my forehead hard against hers. "I hope to God I never take you up on that. You be nice to Scott today, and if you ditch him, I'll paddle you."

She licks her lips, and I reach around to smack her ass.

"I take that back. If you ditch him, no paddlings for a year."

— —

My right leg won't stop shaking.

I grip my knee tightly and press down.

I don't like leaving Washington, not even for the day, and depending on what happens today, it might be overnight or longer.

It takes thirty seconds for my phone to light up with a text message response from Hailey. Thirty seconds for the tightness in my chest to ease.

H: Nope, not having any fun at all. Scott hates knitting. Who doesn't like a yarn store? Madness.

I laugh under my breath.

C: Sorry I need to go to New York. I'll be back tomorrow. Can't wait to see your yarn.
H: That's just cause you want to tie me up in it, right?
C: Damn straight.

My cock thickens at the thought of strapping Hailey down. Not with yarn. But maybe velcro cuffs, and I'd loop her yarn through the loops—some of that rainbow-hued hippy stuff she has in the basket in her living room, bright bursts of red and yellow and pink stringing between her wrists and her headboard, holding her in place for me.

I'd take my time. Get her warm before putting the cuffs on. Let her get used to the feel of them on her wrists as I lick her pussy. Then I'd weave the wool through the loops, all lazy-like, letting the soft ball of it roll around on her tummy as I tug lengths out for my filthy purposes.

The driver's door opens, breaking me out of my fantasy, and Tag gets in. He hands me a bottle of Dr. Pepper and sets his own drink in the cup holder in the console of his SUV. We're at a truck stop halfway to New York.

Clara Forrester changed her flight to the next day, and Jason got a heads up from a friend in

300

Miami that the Feds were going to stop her from leaving the country.

Excellent idea. Piss poor execution. I can't think of a faster way to make her an uncooperative witness.

"Has Jason talked to you yet about who we're going to bill all these hours to?" Tag asks me as he merges onto the freeway.

"There are more important things in life than billable hours."

He shrugs. "Don't have to tell me that. I'm used to living on a cop salary. We could do this pro bono for all I care."

"Maybe we should." I mean, we already were. It's not like I was going to bill Hailey for any of this. She didn't ask us to dig into Lively. We started doing that for PRISM, the shadowy extra-governmental organization that only concerned itself with geopolitical issues of the highest order. But right now, if they asked us to back off, I'd tell them to go fuck themselves.

Which would be colossally stupid, and probably mean I'd be out of a job, at best, and living with a price on my head at worst.

In my world, we always assume worst case scenarios are the only scenarios.

Tag must be reading my mind. "Is there a way to do that and keep the overlords happy?"

I shrug. Fuck if I know.

"You want to be a gladiator or something?" He snorts. "There aren't any real heroes in this world. The good guys just get trampled."

"I know." I squint through my sunglasses, not liking where this conversation is going. I don't want a reminder that it's just a matter of time before I do something Hailey won't be able to stomach. "Gladiators are just puppets, anyway."

"What?"

Now it's my turn to snort. "Read a fucking history book, man. They look it, all dressed up and sent into the arena for battle. But the stage was set by those in the shadows. Those with the real power. The fights were rigged."

"You're fucking kidding me. Like professional wrestling?"

Laughter thunders out of me. "Yeah. Something like that."

"Got it. No gladiators. Arena masters?"

"Nah." I peel the label off my drink and watch the bubbles bounce against the inside of the plastic. "We gotta think bigger than that. Go back a step. Trojan horse type of thing, maybe."

"Now you're talking in riddles."

"Yeah." I rock my jaw from side to side. There's something there, in the back of my mind, but I can't grab onto it. Not yet. But it'll come to me. I close my eyes. "Wake me up when we get to New York."

— —

"What are you doing here?"

I give Clara Forrester my most charming smile as she glowers at me from the door of her Hell's Kitchen artist loft. It doesn't work. I look at Tag, and he tips his head to the side.

She opens the door.

He laughs at me as he steps past. Pretty

motherfucker. Oversized bear is what he is, and all the girls eat him up.

I roll my eyes as I follow him inside.

"You can't go on this trip," he says gently, pointing to her suitcases piled in front of a bookcase near the door.

"Of course I can." She crosses her arms in front of her, wrapping her floor-length sweater coat thing tighter around her small frame.

We first met this woman before I went to Miami. She'd agreed to fly down there after I talked to the Feds, but of course that plan went to hell in a hand basket after Lively was arrested for Hailey's kidnapping.

From the pained look on her face, that's where her mind has gone. "I agreed to speak to the investigators when it was all in the past. But they came to see me this morning. They told me what happened and why he's been arrested now. I can't..." She shakes her head. "I'm sorry. I need to distance myself from that danger."

I clench my jaw to keep from asking her if she's stupid. "Lively will eventually find out you've spoken to the investigators."

Fear flashes in her eyes. "And I have you to thank for that."

I keep my voice soft and speak slowly as I try to erase her false sense of security. "If we could find you, someone else would have—eventually."

"But nobody else did. Until you showed up, that was just a gross part of my past. Now it's my terrifying present. I'm not okay with that."

"That was luck."

"Well, my luck was pretty damn good until you

showed up in my studio. You don't understand. This is my life we're talking about."

"I do understand. The reason Lively was arrested? The raid they told you about? He kidnapped my girlfriend. This is *my* life, too. This is personal for me."

Over her shoulder, I see Tag giving me a warning look, but I don't care.

"You would be Jane Doe 2," I explain, more urgently now. She can't walk away. Hailey's kidnapping is just one single set of charges. Clara's the witness that blows the entire case wide open. "It wouldn't just rest on your shoulders. Hailey— that's my girlfriend—she's going to testify, too. But together, your testimonies will reinforce each other's."

"There have to be others. Let them come forward," she whispers.

There are others. The singer Tabitha Leighton was a dead end—Wilson and Jason came back from California empty handed—but the FBI has a list and Wilson has another one. None of those women spent as long with Lively as Forrester did, however. None of them saw the inner workings of his organization.

"You're a silver bullet," I say, but words aren't landing. I shove my hands in my pockets to keep from throttling her.

"You can do this." Tag says, moving forward. I step back and watch as he crouches in front of her. He takes her hand with his big, thick fingers and she bows her head like he's broken her with those four simple words.

"I don't think I can."

"If you go to Europe, he will have you killed."
His words are blunt, but effective. She starts to cry
and he leans in, letting her collapse on his shoulder.
"You'll put him away for life. And then you'll get
yours back. And we'll be with you every step of the
way."

Bull in a china shop, getting shit done.

No matter what the cost.

—eight—

Hailey

Cole sends a text message during dinner, saying he wouldn't be home until tomorrow. I spent the entire day running errands, and now I'm at a French bistro with my younger sister, Alison.

"I can't believe you've got bodyguards," she says, staring pointedly at Scott, who's sitting at the next table. He gives her a thousand-yard stare and she rolls her eyes.

"Hey, don't be rude." I kick her under the table. The attitude is totally unlike her, but I get it. There's something about these oversized men that bring out the bitch in us, like we want to see how far we can push them—and what they might do when we've gone too far.

Oh, shit.

My face heats up as I flick my gaze over to Scott, then back to Alison. My baby sister.

No.

She gives me a look of complete innocence.

Which just means that I'm one hundred percent on the right track.

"Bad idea," I hiss under my breath.

"Eat your dinner," she says, her lips turning up in a secret smile.

Oh God. My sister wants to be spanked by my bodyguard. This is unacceptable.

Like I said, I totally get it.

"How's school going?" I say, a little louder than necessary. It would be pointless for me to tell

Alison she can't crush on the guy with the gun, but I can underline in six different ways to *him* that she's off-limits. "Adjusting to university okay?"

She rolls her eyes. "Subtle."

I stick my tongue out at her. It wouldn't be fun if it wasn't a challenge.

"Actually, I have a meeting with an advisor for my senior thesis," she says, emphasizing the last two words. Out the corner of my eye, I see Scott smirk.

"Which won't be until the year after next, right?" I take a sip of my wine, which I can drink and she cannot, because she's only *nineteen*.

"Nope, I'm on an accelerated program, so I'll start it at Christmas. Your baby sister is all grown up now." She smiles sweetly and shifts on her chair. I can feel her crossing her legs under the table, and I don't have to glance sideways again to know that Scott's looking at her miniskirt sliding up her thighs.

Men.

"Blink and you miss it." I mutter under my breath. I was going to ask her if she wanted to sleep over at my place tonight, but with Scott downstairs, that's a terrible idea. By the morning she'd probably have baked muffins and wheedled her way into the apartment downstairs on the pretense of kindness. She'd ask to see his security equipment and next thing I'll know, I'll be an auntie to tiny wrestler-shaped babies.

But I don't want to go home alone, either. Low-level anxiety twists in my gut at the thought of sleeping alone.

Like she can read my mind—at least the

worried part—my sister sets down her water glass and nibbles on her lower lip. "So you're on your own tonight? Do you want to come back to the estate?"

"Nope." That's an easy answer. The harder one is how I'll get to sleep.

"Dad's not there…" He's gone to London—I already know that from my brother. Apparently he's planning on staying out of the States for a while—and the motivation behind his extended business trip makes my stomach turn.

I sigh. "I don't want to deal with our mother, either."

She shrugs. "Okay." Her phone vibrates on the table and she grabs it, reading a message on the screen. She scrunches up her face as she looks up at me. "Will you hate me if I bail after we finish eating? Some people are pulling together a study session tonight for my Critical Methods class…"

As much as I don't want to be alone, I want my sister to go be a university student more. The biggest worry in her head should be acing her exams. "Definitely do that. I'll be fine."

She doesn't look like she believes me, and she's torn. I don't want her to have to carry the burden of my issues—especially because they're in my head. I have bodyguards, for goodness sake.

"Really. Go. Be super smart and make me proud." I smile, then take a sip of wine to cover the tremor that threatens at the corner of my mouth.

The anxiety gets worse as I stand outside my apartment, waiting for Scott to do a visual sweep. When he steps back out and waves me in, my heart is hammering so hard in my chest I don't know how he can't hear it.

Even though I'm under guard, I don't feel safe. I feel like a sitting duck, which only makes that ugly feeling in my gut bigger—naming it as ridiculous doesn't help.

Taking a shower doesn't help. Putting on a t-shirt Cole had left on my bed doesn't either, not even when I text him, because I can't tell him why I'm reaching out.

H: You busy?
C: Little bit, but I can take a minute. What's up?
H: Nothing. Never mind.
C: Hey...I'm thinking about you, remember that. How you taste and feel.

I don't send him another message. What I want to say, *Come home and hold me,* sounds needy even inside my head. And he's busy.

By the time I'm standing in front of my dresser, looking for something else to sleep in, my skin is crawling. Instead of sleep shorts, I pull open my pants drawer. I reach for yoga pants, but when they're in my hand, I just set them aside and grab the stretchy jeans underneath.

Then I strip off Cole's shirt and put on a bra and a long sleeved t-shirt.

I'm not kidding myself anymore.

I know it doesn't make any sense, but I need to get out of here.

In a flash, I remember Cole giving me his key. *No matter what…*

In the weeks that have passed, I've scouted out

his place, even though I've never been inside it. I've preferred to bring Cole into my world, keep as much normal around me as possible.

So it's a big deal that I want to go there now.

I can't go downstairs and knock on the door and ask Scott to take me over. He'll check with Cole, who'll flip out. He doesn't get what it's like inside my head, all these feelings and worries that aren't grounded in real threats.

And then wherever he is and whatever he's doing, he'll drop it all to come to me.

Nope. I can't do that.

So I slip out the fire escape door. The metal staircase goes all the way to the ground floor, so it's not nearly as exciting as it looks in the movies, which I'm totally fine with. I need to be somewhere else. I don't need to do something stupid at the same time.

I dart through the alley and head for the Metro. Five stops away on the Red Line is an entire space filled with his smell and his stuff, that I can touch and breathe in and wrap myself in until he gets back. I don't care about keeping my sense of Hailey anymore, about sticking to my normal world. That blew up a week ago. Now I just need Cole.

I turn his key over and over between my fingers once I'm seated on the train. Ever since that first night he slept over, I've kept this on my keychain.

Even when I hated him, I trusted him.

Even when I thought he'd used me, I kept this small piece of metal as a talisman of hope.

And for that brief week of normalcy, I thought

about giving it back a dozen times. There's an order to normal relationships and it doesn't start with having a key to your boyfriend's apartment before you've ever been inside it.

That's a step that we haven't taken yet—he'd offered for me to stay there when we came back, but just the first night, and hasn't offered again since.

Well, having a panic attack at the thought of being home alone probably counts as a good exception to the normal rules of dating.

I should have just told Scott I wanted to come here. He'll probably notice at some point and Cole will be upset. I pull out my phone to call, then put it away. I'll call him once I get to his place so he doesn't worry.

I get out at Dupont Circle and move quickly through the evening crowd, thinking of what I'll say to the doorman if Cole hasn't put my name on the access list—but in my heart I know he has.

I'm on high-alert, constantly scanning around me, a running commentary going in my head of the people around me. Couple on a date. Guy going to the gym. Guy coming from the gym, and checking out the first guy. Same bag, branded with the twenty-four gym around the corner. Maybe that'll work out for them.

As I walk the final block to Cole's place, my skin tingles with the awareness that I'm on my own. Relatively defenseless and maybe still a target.

But I won't let that stop me from living my life.

As if to underline the point that I'm relatively anonymous, just a girl hustling down the street, a

312

woman walks past me, too closely, and slams her shoulder into mine, spinning me around. My heart slams against my chest, thumping a mile a minute as I scramble to the side of the building, waiting for the next attack which doesn't come.

Nope, just the standard pedestrian rudeness.

Okay, then.

I rub my sweating palms on my jeans, then lift my head just in time to see Cole approaching his building from the other side.

He's not alone.

I was prepared to be alone tonight. Ready to run the risk of ditching my bodyguard and maybe facing something ugly in the outside world.

I never thought it would be my boyfriend, walking into his apartment building with his ex-girlfriend, their heads close together.

But of course it's not that simple. Of course he doesn't just disappear inside and I go running off into the night, because there's this thing between us. A magnetic connection.

Cole's head snaps up and he looks around.

I'm right here, I think, frozen to the spot. When he finds me, his entire face darkens and he strides toward me, scanning behind me for my shadow.

"You're not in New York," I say as he reaches me and slides his hands up my arms to hold me just below the shoulders.

"What's wrong?" He rakes his flecked amber gaze over my face, then around me, his jaw flexing as he takes stock of the fact that I'm alone.

"I was..." *Coming to cry myself to sleep in your bed* seems like a silly answer now. "Nothing."

"Where's Scott?"

"I assume still at my place. I went out the fire escape."

Cursing under his breath, he yanks out his phone and taps a furious text message. Then he slides the other hand over my shoulder and cups the nape of my neck, like he's going to move me toward the building.

Nope.

I stand my ground as he starts to move, and his arm snaps straight. He doesn't let go of me, he just turns back and stands there, having a stare-down with me.

"Hailey, come on." He scowls.

"Look, you're busy. This was a mistake." Not because I don't trust him, but because I don't want to know what's going on. He's clearly in the middle of something—and for my own sanity, I'm not going to think for a second that it's personal. "I'll go back home. Really, it's fine."

"Fine is the last fucking thing it is. Scott's lucky if he doesn't get fired for not noticing that you dodged out of there, and what the hell were you thinking?"

I swing my hand up between us and swat his arm away from me. He just rolls his eyes and snags my hand, entwining our fingers—which also serves to yank me closer to him. I can feel his heart beating quickly through his dress shirt, and I resist the urge to pet him comfortingly. That might give him the upper hand.

Ha.

Who am I kidding? He always has the upper hand. All I can do is hold on for dear life.

He huffs a frustrated breath and shakes his

head, his gaze burning me. "You were *kidnapped* one week ago. Ditching your guard is not an option."

"You told me you were *out of town* and I was just coming here to sleep in your fucking bed," I spit back at him. "And I got to your building, so obviously it was fine."

His lips tighten as he searches my face, looking for...I don't know what. "Come upstairs."

"No, I don't want —"

"You said if you could do something to help, you would."

I frown at him. "What are you talking about?"

"Come upstairs," he repeats, turning and sliding his arm around my waist. Point, Cole, because while I tense up, I let him propel me toward where Penny Kristoff is standing.

She smiles at me. I manage something that approximates a grimace in return. Ugh. I try again, this time channeling my inner Amelia Dashford Reid. Having a soulless socialite for a mother has some advantages.

Without another word, Cole guides us through the lobby and up the ornate staircase.

We stop on the third floor and walk silently across plush carpeting. The hallway is lushly decorated, with gorgeous wallpaper and expensive light fixtures. His apartment is a corner unit, and it's surprisingly big. And modern. Cold, sleek furniture decorates the space, an interesting contrast to the traditional lobby and hallway.

Also in the space are Tag Browning and another blonde who looks a lot like Penny. Well, let's be honest — all thin, beautiful blondes look the

315

same to me. I shove back that little bit of self-loathing and glance at Cole. Is this an orgy? I regret not discussing hard limits before, because if I'm going to have group sex, I don't think I want any skinny blondes involved. Which probably isn't fair to them, but I'm feeling kind of fragile.

"What's going on?"

"Hailey, meet Clara Forrester. She's an artist from New York who spent some time with Gerome Lively a few years ago. Clara, this is my girlfriend, Hailey. And that's Penny, the agent I mentioned who will help us."

Agent?

I whip my head to my left and glare at Penny. She gives me another bland look.

I feel like an idiot, and maybe I am, because I open my mouth and the stupidest shit comes out. "So…this isn't an orgy."

Tag chokes on his gum, and Clara shoots her eyebrows straight into her hairline.

Cole keeps talking like I didn't say anything at all. "Penny's here to talk you through your options for extended protection."

"I'm sorry," I say, wincing in Clara's direction, but Cole is practically shoving me out of the room.

"What the hell is going on?" I burst out as soon as he shuts the door behind him. I look around. So this is Cole's bedroom. More modern stuff. No piles of laundry. It doesn't smell nearly enough of him.

I hate it.

"It's a long story," he says as he jams his hands in his pockets, shoving his jacket out of the way. He hangs his head for a moment, looking at the

316

floor, and when he glances up again, his face is ragged—there's more emotion in his eyes and around his mouth than I've ever seen before, but it's not all good. "How much of it do you want?"

"I don't know," I say quietly. Only a few feet separate us, but it's too much. I step into his space. He keeps his hands in his pockets. I ignore that and touch him anyway, finding some comfort in the tensing ridges of his abdomen. He holds ever-so-still, heat radiating off him, as I wiggle my fingers up his torso. When I've grounded myself in the reassuring solidity of his tall, broad, and delicious body, I grab a fistful of his shirt in the middle of his chest and scowl. "Let's start with the fact that Penny is an agent of *what?*"

"She works for the Department of Justice."

"As…"

"A Federal Marshal."

"She looks like a socialite!"

"She's that, too."

Processing that takes a minute. I breathe in his sweet, spicy cologne, remembering how it used to drive me crazy. It still does, but now it's also… there's this promise with Cole, that he'll always be there for me. He's going to piss me off and hurt me by accident, but he's always going to try to make it right.

"So she's not just an ex-girlfriend." I release his shirt, and like a shot, one of his hands is out of his pockets and wrapped around my wrist. Holding me to him.

"I should never have called her that," he says roughly, dragging my hand to his face. He presses a kiss to my palm and closes his eyes.

"But you did."

"I did. Just to you."

"Why?" I already know, but I feel like we need to recap this, just in case I've been dreaming all this time.

"To push you away."

"It didn't really work well, did it?"

He laughs and shakes his head, still pressing his face into my palm.

"But she's still in your life."

"This is the first time I've seen her since that night at the opera. It's only because I needed to introduce her to Clara."

"So your relationship before was just professional?" He freezes, and my stomach flip-flops uncomfortably. "Uhm, forget I asked that."

"No." His jaw clenches against my fingers, and he opens his eyes, fixing that bright amber gaze right on me. Unwavering. "I want you to know."

"Why?"

Cole just stares at me. "Because I love you."

I blink up at him and burst into tears.

— nine —

Cole

"Fuck me," I mutter under my breath. Shit, I suck at this. "Is that bad?" I bend at the knees, bringing us face to face as Hailey furiously wipes away the tears on her cheeks. "Hailey?"

"I love you too, you asshole." She glares at me and it's the best thing in the world.

I laugh and pull her close. "That would be more believable without the last bit."

The tension I've been holding in my chest eases as she slides her arms over my shoulders, burying her face in my neck.

"You love me?" she repeats, her words muffled as she burrows deeper into my skin. That's okay. It's where she belongs.

"Yeah." I clear my throat. "Didn't really know how to say it. Never have before."

She shakes her head at me.

"What?"

"That's how you make everything right. You make me melt, Cole."

I can't help but grin. Damn, I like the sound of that. I like how she kisses my throat and along my jaw even better, and when she finds my lips with hers, I don't care that there are people on the other side of the wall. I've got decent insulation. I push her lips open with the tip of my tongue, just a tease because we've still got stuff to talk about, but enough to remind her of our conversation this morning, and how I kissed her neck and pulled her hair.

From the way she's curving into me, I know she's thinking about it too. I want to ask her if she's wet, and if she remembered my promise to take her at the first opportunity.

Instead, I nip at her lower lip, then suck on it gently to sooth the sting—and then I pull back.

"Hey, keep doing that," she breathes, and fuck, but I want to.

"Still got stuff to talk about, beautiful. Gotta air it all out, get it out of your head."

"I didn't think…when I saw you and Penny. I didn't get all jealous." She pauses. "Okay, just a tiny bit. But I knew you wouldn't."

"I wouldn't." It needs to be repeated.

She hesitates, then asks, "Are you still close?"

"We've never been close."

"But you dated, for real. Had sex."

"Dating was mutually beneficial. I could trust her. Sex was functional. Fun, even." She scowls at me, but I've got a point to make. "I'm not going to lie. The occasional thirty minutes of banging or watching each other bang other people was a half-way decent way to pass time."

"Thirty minutes?" Her eyes go all soft. She gets my point.

God, this feeling in my chest…the tension has been replaced by something so much bigger. It's hot and and uncomfortable and I think I like it. "At the most."

"Damnit, Cole, tales of your exploits aren't supposed to melt me."

I stroke a finger down her nose and over her lips, taking my time. "Do I need to spell out how

320

what you and I have is different on every level?"

"No." She's still pouting, but her eyes have gone all warm now.

"Do you want me to anyway?"

She nods, and I slide my hand back into her hair, gathering it in my fist. I give it a tug that gets my blood racing again, and hers too, from the look on her face. She licks her lips, leaving them wet and juicy, and I want to drag her onto her knees and slide my cock over them. Instead I hold her close and try to explain how what we have and how we have it is so much more than anything I've ever had in the past. "Physical release, then leave me the hell alone. That's all I ever wanted until I met you. Then I spent six months running scared from how you made me feel, what you made me think. Now I'm all in, because when I'm with you? I just want more. Always. When I take you fast, it's just so I can do it again. When I take you slow, it's because I can't get over how good you feel. Taste. Sound. I don't want to miss any of it and I never want it to end, so I stretch it out. And it's still not enough."

"Because you love me…"

I nod roughly, leaning over her, backing her up until she bumps into my bed.

Hailey Reid in my bed. Fuck, I fought this for so long. Such an idiot.

She nuzzles my jaw, my stubble scratching her cheek, and she makes a whimpering sound that takes my half-chub to a full-blown, aching erection. "I love it when you do that."

"What?"

"When you're heavy," she whispers, opening

her mouth against my cheek. She licks me, tasting my skin, and it makes me press against her even harder. "I can't explain it."

"I love it when you lick me," I grunt, working at the button on her pants. "Don't need to explain it. It's just…" *right*. Fuck, I'm such a sap for her.

And she's fucking soaked for me.

"Your ex-girlfriend is in the next room," she hisses as I slide my fingers between her pussy lips, but she still rocks into my touch. Because we can't help ourselves.

"Want me to stop?" I don't. I just slow my strokes, coating my fingers in her juices. Spreading them around.

"We should. Don't you have to go out there?" She gasps as I rock my fingertips over her clit. "Seriously, Cole…"

"You think I'm not serious about bending you over my bed and fucking you?"

She giggles, then moans again, pressing her lips together to keep it inside. "Noooo…"

Fucking taunting me. I drag myself up and look down at her, splayed out on my bed, her jeans open and her shirt sliding up on the pale skin of her belly.

She looks like the university student she was mere months ago. In my suit and tie, I feel like the big bad wolf, older and more grizzled than my thirty-one years, and while I know we could do this—in another moment, would both get off on the semi-publicness, the secret moment—I don't want to.

Because I'm not such an asshole that I can't remember she was scared tonight, and my first responsibility is to protect her. "You feeling better?"

She nods, slowly, her golden brown hair spread out beneath her on my bed.

"I should have told you I was in the city. I just didn't know how long we'd be here tonight." It's already close to midnight, and I don't know what Penny's plan is for moving Clara to a safe house.

Hailey slides her hands over her mid-section, her fingers teasing at the open space where I just had my hand. My blood, already simmering, starts to boil. "You have to go out there."

A statement. She's not wrong.

"Yeah."

She hooks her thumbs into her jeans at the waist and wriggles them down her hips, revealing her basic black underwear. Never seen anything hotter. "Then go do that. I'll be waiting here when you're done."

—ten—

Hailey

Cole's in the living room for an hour, maybe more. I doze off to the drone of voices, curled up in his bed. There's no part of me that wants to be involved in whatever plan they're doing. Keeping a witness safe, that's all I need to know.

But when he opens the door, I roll over, suddenly awake again. The lamp beside me is the only light in the room. I watch as he moves around the room, stripping off his clothes. Jacket, pants, and shoes in the walk-in closet. Shirt, boxer briefs, and socks dropped in a lidded hamper by the bathroom.

I can't breathe properly as he prowls toward me, totally naked. Tattoos crawling over one shoulder. Scar tissue decorating the other. Hard, lean six-pack dancing just out of stroking range as he climbs on top of me, shoving my shirt up my body as he moves.

His mouth lands on my stomach first, hot and wet. His tongue slides up between my breasts, then his entire mouth covers one nipple, sucking me hard through my bra. The mesh and lace barrier changes the sensation, holding the damp heat next to my skin and allowing him to be rougher.

I cry out as he sinks his teeth around my tender flesh, tugging my nipple deep into his mouth. Against my legs, his cock hangs heavy. I want him in my hands, want to cup his balls and pull him up higher on my body so I can swallow his length and have his musky taste on my tongue.

I want him inside me, too.

I want it all.

"They're gone?" I ask, twining my limbs restlessly, urgently around his body.

He doesn't look up from where he's devouring my skin, making me burn. "Do you want them gone? Or do you want me to take you, knowing there are people on the other side of the wall? Knowing that if you scream, they'll know I've just shoved my cock inside your wet, hungry pussy?"

His heated words brand me and I whimper, rocking my pelvis against his hand as he cups my mound on the outside of my underwear.

"You'll have to be quiet. I'm gonna take you hard and fast."

"So you can do it again?"

He grins, one hundred percent predator, and spins me around, turning me as he crawls backward off the bed. I yelp as he grips my hips, moving me right off the bed, then folds me forward. Ass in the air.

And my pussy squeezes, wishing it had him inside to feel it.

"I haven't even had a chance to tell you how much I hate your apartment," I whisper as he rips off my underwear. "And I don't have another pair of those here."

"You don't need them. If I had my way, you'd be naked all the time."

"Sounds cold."

He lazily spanks first one ass cheek, then the other. "We need to talk about how naughty you were, ditching Scott earlier."

"I came straight here."

Another swat. My nipples ache and I rub them against the blanket, the wet lace of my bra reminding me of Cole's mouth there, stretching my arms in front of me like a cat.

"That was dangerous," he growls.

"I'm sorry." But I'm not. It was fine and now I'm here and this is perfect.

"You should have called me."

I'm glad I'm not looking at him. I close my eyes and press my forehead on to the bed before admitting, "You would have told me I was being silly."

Instead of answering, he nudges me with his erection, and thrusts into me as soon as he finds my opening. Sounds spill out of me as he drags himself out and does it again, each surge more intense than the last. Deeper. Sweeter. More filling.

Swat. "I will never think you're silly." *Slap*. The bite of each open-handed tap instantly fades into a lasting, erotic warmth that soothes and arouses me. "You're amazing. Strong. Honest, Kind. Human." He folds over my back, fucking me so hard it steals my breath. "So fucking beautiful, Hailey. Never silly."

I can't think straight. No, I can't think at all. There are things to say, arguments to be made, but I don't have them. I just have Cole's words filling me up as surely as his cock stretches my pussy. As his hands brand my ass.

Against my ear, he's talking again. "You need me, you tell me."

Sometimes I can't.

His mouth is on the back of my neck now, his

teeth against my skin, and I want his hands on my breasts. I try to lift up, but he's got my hips pinned against the side of the bed, and all that does is rock my clit against the edge of the mattress.

"Oh my God," I moan, spreading my legs wider. I want that again, and when he rocks into me again, I get it. "Oh yeah. Do that…"

He bites me, and I realize he thinks it's his mouth on the back of my neck. Okay, that works too. Jesus, my mind is spinning in twelve different directions.

And Cole keeps fucking me, hard and fast. "Gorgeous," he mutters against my back. "So tight. Can I come in you?"

Holy shit. I wasn't even thinking about that. He pulled out yesterday. "Uhm…"

He chuckles against my back and slams into me, holding himself deep as he slides one hand beneath me, across my belly. Going straight for my clit, but I'm good there.

"Nipples," I gasp, and he changes direction.

"Come for me. Be a good girl and have a fucking orgasm all over my dick. Make me feel it."

He's got both of my tits out of my bra, and he's squeezing them together with one hand, his thumb working one nipple, a slow roll, and maybe his ring finger one the other. I don't know. I can't see it, I can just feel it, but I'm feeling a lot of things.

Inside me, I'm coiling tight. My core is throbbing, all the way from my clit, through all the nerve endings he's rubbing deep inside me, to the top of my effing womb.

And he's still biting my neck and shoulder, little nibbles that make me gush each time his teeth sink into my flesh.

I'm going to die. Or come, I'm not sure which.

"Mmphf," I say, not even a word, but that's okay because now Cole's grunting too. His legs brace behind me, nothing but two pillars of muscle, pistoning his hips as he thunders into me. Around my torso, his arms are bands of steel, biceps bulging as he pins me down and works me over.

I'm sweaty, panting, aching…and over the moon happy. Deep inside me, the thick head of Cole's erection rocks over the perfect spot, shifting my body forward, making my clit rub against the blanket at the same time as he pinches a nipple, and I tumble headlong into an earth-shattering orgasm.

This is one of those climaxes that keeps going, probably because he's still going. I arch my back, my clit suddenly too sensitive to touch anything, and Cole somehow climbs onto the bed, getting me up on my knees as he keeps screwing me, and now I'm full-on moaning with each deep penetration as the ripples of sensation start all over again. I'm clawing at the blanket, my thighs shaking, and it feels like I'm full of jello.

Orgasms are weird.

With a strangled cry, Cole pulls out and comes on my back. I'm starting to think he likes that. Like he's marking me. He slides beside me, tugging me down, flat on my belly, and I can still feel it on my back.

I'll give him a minute before I ask for a washcloth.

Maybe he's not the only one who likes it. God, he's turning me into a deviant.

I twist my head and look at him. "They're not still out there, are they?"

It's not really a question, but maybe it sounds like one, because he looks at me with real surprise on his face.

"Uh...no." He grins. "But I liked that you didn't know and still let yourself go."

"At some point you're going to want to explore that more, aren't you?"

"Your closet exhibitionism?" He kisses my shoulder and gives my butt a pat as he gets up. "Only if it works for you."

When I'm turned on, I think I'll do anything with this man. It's after the sex is over that I crawl back into the good girl shell, carefully constructed by years of private school slut-shaming, and doubt slips through the cracks.

As he cleans me up, I remember the casual way he asked where he should come and I bury my face in the pillow. I feel the bed shift as he tosses the washcloth in the direction of the bathroom, then he hauls me against his chest—where I promptly hide my face again.

"What's with the sudden shyness, beautiful?"

I blush. "I was just thinking about how you asked about coming inside me."

He kisses the top of my head and I blush harder. "Well, yeah..."He strokes his hand over my shoulder, then keeps going, touching me all over, his long arms meaning that no part of my body is out of his reach. He squeezes my breasts and strokes my hip. "I thought you missed a day or two of your pills in Miami."

"Oh." I try to think back. "No. I took the next

day a bit late, but I didn't miss a day."

"I hate using condoms with you, but I would. I should have, I guess."

I shake my head. "No, it's okay." But I obviously wasn't thinking about that, which makes me kind of stupid. "We're safe."

"Do you ever think about kids?"

Holy shit. I freeze, and he notices, because he pauses his lazy circuit over my body for a second before resuming. "Do you?"

"I asked you first." His voice is rough, and he's not looking at me.

That's okay, I don't think I can look at him either. "Uhm, yeah. I mean, in a *sometime in the future* kind of way. I want kids."

Thud. My heart slams in my chest. *Thud thud thud.* What if he doesn't want a family? He's not close to his parents, and I don't know how he feels about being adopted—if that's affected him or something.

"What do they look like, when you think about them?" His voice cracks as he asks me, and I lift up, forgetting to be nervous.

"Hey…" I touch his cheek with my fingertips, pressing just enough to get him to look at me. "You," I say softly. "They look like you."

His chest moves at that, a quick inhale as we hold each other's gaze, then he's on top of me, pinning me down and kissing me, and I'm pretty sure we're about slam into round two, hard and fast all over again.

"I don't deserve you, Hailey," he mutters against my lips once he leaves me breathless. "But I want everything with you, when you're ready."

331

"Okay." I explore his face with my fingers, not wanting to break the moment, but my inner snark can't help itself. "Maybe we should wait until I'm not under armed guard twenty-four/seven."

"So cheeky." His eyes narrow and he rubs his thumb over my lower lip. "Soon this is going to be behind us, beautiful. And it's just going to be me and you, and you can do whatever you want. I promise."

Right now, I just want him again. I swipe at his thumb with my tongue, and he groans—so I pull his blunt digit into my mouth and suck.

He curses under his breath.

I smile.

He shoves it roughly over my tongue. I kind of asked for that.

I still bite down around his knuckle, which he doesn't seem to mind, because he reaches between us and fists his cock, rubbing it in my newly wet again sex.

My eyelids drop, heavy with hunger for him as he takes me again. Slow this time. He braces his arms on either side of my head and starts moving, a liquid wave of pleasure between my legs and over my body.

His gaze, always on me.

This man loves me. He wants forever. With *me*.

I can't even…

"I love you," I whisper, pulling him for a hungry, drinking-until-I'm-drunk kind of kiss. "I'm yours."

"Mine." His eyes gleam at that.

"All yours." My courage is stoked by that dark golden pride. "Every last inch. Every last…hole."

I can't breathe as he dips his head, looking between our bodies where he's sliding in and out of me. His cock must be shiny with my wetness, but we both know he's going to need more for what I've just suggested.

"Do you have…" I trail off, my heart pounding a mile a minute as he looks back up at me.

"Yeah. You sure?"

"Oh yeah." I want him to take my ass more than anything else, ever. It just feels right.

Time slows as he eases out of me. He kisses his way down my body at the same time as he reaches blindly for the bedside table. Snagging a bottle of lube, he tosses it on the bed next to me, then follows up with a condom.

Interesting.

I'm in an altered state, like I've taken a sex drug or something. I lick my lips. "Do we need that?"

He blinks up from between my legs. His breath is hot on my now swollen flesh. "I've heard it helps. I want it to be as comfortable as possible for you."

My butt clenches—in a good way. "I want it." I reach down and tangle my fingers in his hair as he starts to lick me. "I'm not just offering for you."

"I know," he murmurs before sucking ever so slowly on my clit. I can feel it getting hard and swelling against his tongue, and when he lifts up again, his face is wet. That just makes me hotter. He reaches for the lube and grins at me. "I'm mostly just reminding myself."

"Because…" I pant.

Now his grin is huge. Like his erection, I'm sure. "I've been thinking about this for weeks.

Your ass is my number one fantasy."

"I want whatever you want."

"Dangerous words."

"Turns out I'm a dangerous girl." I slide my hands up my torso and cup my breasts for him. "How do you want me? Should I roll over?"

He rears up, all of his muscles flexing and straining in the lamplight. "Not this first time. I want to see your face as I sink into you." He hisses in a breath. "God, you're going to be so tight."

A helpless little whimper slips out as he spreads my legs wider and squeezes some lube onto his fingers. His hand disappears between my legs and I curl up, wanting to see more. I prop myself up on my elbows as the cold gel hits my skin, followed by his warm fingers. He doesn't go straight for the bulls-eye. Like last time, he circles over my skin, wide at first, then narrowing to where I'll take him, and I give up trying to watch because the sensations are already enough—I want to fall into the illicit touch.

Stop thinking and just go with it.

I close my eyes and sink back against the bed, arching my back as just the tip of one finger penetrates me. *Yes.* It's just as good as I remember. Dirty and powerful and the most private touch imaginable.

"That's it, take it." Cole exhales slowly as I relax around his touch and he slides inside easily with the lube. He strokes the back of my thigh with his other hand, still talking quietly. *Beautiful. Sexy. Hot.* I'll never get enough of the words he fills me up with when we're making love and fucking like animals and everything in between.

He pauses on the next withdrawal, and a second finger joins the first.

"Oh…"

"Push out."

My eyes widen in alarm as I jerk my head up. "That's the wrong thing to say in that area."

He laughs. *Laughs.* Oh my God. "I've done my research." He looks at me, his eyes soft liquid gold, and he says the magic words. "Trust me."

I bite my lips and pulse a little bit, bearing down against his fingers, and suddenly he's got two digits inside my ass. And his cock bobs in the air. Okay, he likes this. Ahhh. I like this, he likes this… good stuff.

My clit throbs. My nipples are tight with anticipation. My breasts feel heavy and my mouth is watering.

Cole scissors his fingers inside me and I squirm hard against the ache of it. It's going to stretch a lot more around his cock. I swallow a panicky reaction about *that* and think about how it feels once I'm stretched. How forbidden and intense that first finger felt.

How he's never done what we're about to do, and how much I want to experience that. Have him inside me, everywhere.

"Ready?"

I nod, and he pulls out crazy slow, then rolls on the condom. I watch hungrily as he strokes himself roughly, his eyes rolling back in his head as he applies more lube. Not needing instruction, I slide my hands under my thighs and pull my knees up, curving my back.

And I try to keep breathing. "I might say no…"

335

I swallow hard. "It probably won't mean no."

Cole leans over me and kisses me hard on the lips. "I'll know the difference, and if I don't, let's use Jason as a safe word."

I let out a watery "Ha". Yep, that would stop pretty much any sexy times on a dime. "Deal."

I love watching Cole move. His naked body is a sculpted work of art, and until the fat head of his cock actually rubs against my rear entrance, I'm sufficiently distracted by the bunching play of his arms and chest.

But that first brushing contact zeroes my attention back on Cole, and his feral grin. "I'm gonna go slow, gonna be gentle, but I'll have your ass tonight. All of it."

I can't wait.

The next contact is more…insistent. Like he's not going to stop pushing, but he's not really. It's just…there. Firm. And ridiculously big. *That thing is never going to fit there*. Even as I think it, though, I can feel myself opening for him.

The burn starts right away. My eyes get really big and I squeeze my hands into tight fists to keep from waving them uselessly in the air, but I can't keep the twisted reaction off my face.

Cole stops, but he doesn't pull out. And then he presses again, and I realize there's another level of burning, inside. And I cry out, "No, no, no, no," and this time when he stops, I don't think he's going to continue.

I flash my attention to his face, and I'm surprised to see that his eyes are closed.

"Do it," I plead, my voice weak, and he blinks down at me, and shakes his head.

"Not like this." He slides to my side, rolling me so he's spooning me. "I think I might hurt you the other way."

My pulse is skipping like a triple beat right now, so I just nod.

"Hey, come here." He curls his hand around my neck and gives me a slow, drugging kiss that soothes my hammering heart better than any self-talk. Point, Cole. All the points to Cole tonight. "Touch yourself. Get yourself off, okay?"

This is so much better. The burn is the same, but Cole's warm at my back and he's kissing my shoulder, and this time when I arch my back, I'm pressing into the penetration and then all of a sudden, I'm full.

So fucking full.

I groan as I slide my right hand between my legs, because I'm so wet. And I think if I touch myself, I might go off like a firecracker, but I can't *not* touch myself.

Cole squeezes my hip and rocks against me, and the burning is back. "That's it, take my cock. God, you're so tight. And hot. Holy…" He trails off into a quiet string of curses against my skin.

I hadn't taken it all? Holy shit. I open my mouth to say something, but I can't. A keening wail is all I manage, then I'm panting as his pelvis presses hard against my bottom.

Inside me, he flexes, and black spots start dancing at the corner of my eyes. I can't breathe, but I can move my fingers. I stroke myself, and as my fingers slip through my folds and over my clit, my lungs start working again.

I press my hips back, urging him to move. He

337

doesn't need any further invitation.

Being fucked in the ass is different than regular fucking. Not better. Definitely not worse. Even as I'm spinning out of my mind, I'm sure I want to do this again. This feels…God, I don't even have a word for it. It just *feels*.

Cole starts slow, sliding in and out, but with each lubricated thrust, it gets a bit easier. He's palming my ass, spreading my cheeks. *Is he watching me there? Watching me take his cock in my ass?*

All the fucking feels.

"God, yes." He groans as he slams into me, as he makes me scream into his pillow, and I realize I've started coming already. It's like the type of orgasms I have when I touch myself, little ones that I can almost control, except I'm not doing it. I'm touching myself, and each time I do, I spark another little tremor, but Cole's the earthquake, deep inside me. I give in to that feeling, give in to my body just being one crazy erogenous zone, and let myself slide into this muzzy space in my head.

"Jesus, I can feel you coming." He wraps his arm around me, his muscles engulfing me as he surges into me, over and over again. My hand is drenched and I'm just cupping myself now, spun out completely as he chases his own climax.

When he shoves me forward, falling on top of me as he buries himself in my ass one last time, I can feel his erection twitching inside me and I come again.

It takes him a minute, maybe two, maybe more, before he slowly pulls out. I'm instantly cold and aware of my butt, but then I hear the shower come on and he's back, rolling me over and lifting me up.

338

I wrap my arms around his neck, breathing in his skin.

He sets me down just outside a glass shower, and I cling to him as he walks me backward into the steamy spray.

Cupping my face, he gives me a sweet, doe-eyed, just-fucked look before slanting his mouth over mine and sliding his tongue into my mouth. Sweet and not sweet at all.

Us in a nutshell.

"You okay?" he asks as he rests his forehead on mine.

I nod, curving into his body. He grabs a bottle off the shelf and tips some liquid soap into his hand. As he smooths it over my shoulders and down my back, I recognize the scent. Vanilla and jasmine.

I twist and stare at the shelf. "That's mine." He has my body wash, my shampoo and conditioner... even a bottle of the serum I only use once a week. "How...?"

His hands slow as he reaches my ass, carefully smoothing the slick soap over the tender spot between my cheeks. "I have my ways."

"Did you go to a mall?"

He laughs and kisses my neck, sliding his mouth tantalizingly slowly to my ear, where his breath blows hot against my damp skin. "I would, for you, but no. I took a picture in your bathroom and had Ellie go shopping."

"When?"

"So nosy." He nips my earlobe as he reaches for the shampoo. "A while ago. As soon as she knew about us—that was her punishment for being nosy.

You women never learn."

"Mmm. But I like your punishments."

"You get very different punishments than Ellie does, I promise you."

He uses more than I would, but I'm not complaining as he carefully massages my familiar products into my hair. First shampoo, then conditioner. He blushes when I joke about him using the latter to jerk off, and a dull heat pulses in my belly when I realize he actually has.

Reaching for him, I stroke his length, bringing him closer to me with each tug until the swollen head is brushing against my wet belly as I jerk him lazily.

"So you fucked my ass," I say languidly, leaning back against the glass tile wall. He falls forward, bracing his forearms on either side of my head.

"Sure did." His breathing picks up and I feel a drop of pre-come roll under my thumb on my next stroke. "You drive me crazy," he mutters, cupping one of my breasts. "And now I want to fuck your pussy again."

"So do it," I pant, spreading my legs for him. I'm ready again. I'm always ready.

He hoists me in the air, high enough for me to slide down on his cock, then he takes me, hard and fast in his shower. I didn't think it was humanly possible to have this much sex in one night—and maybe it's early morning now, I've lost all sense of time—but time and again, Cole proves that everything I thought before was nothing.

Right here, Cole dragging his cock in and out of me, his mouth on my chest and his strong, capable hands holding me up under my thighs... this proves that anything is possible.

A bad boy can be so very good.

A good girl can get really dirty.

And two lonely people who find each other can finally be happy.

"I still don't like your apartment," I whisper as we finally curl up together in his bed. "But I think I like your shower more than mine."

—eleven—

Cole

When we wake up late in the morning, it doesn't take much to convince Hailey we should go for a leisurely brunch at Birch and Barley, a modern restaurant with dark wood, exposed brick and funky lighting. I approve of the first two and tolerate the last because they have amazing sticky buns, which Hailey teases me over quite a bit until she tries one.

"Now who likes the sticky—" I laugh as she chucks her napkin at me and I snag her fingertips, pulling them across the table for a quick kiss.

After we eat, we walk back to my place and grab my vehicle. I have a meeting I've been putting off, but it can't wait any longer. I drop her at her place. Scott's off today—and Hailey whirls on me, thinking I've fired him. I haven't, although I considered it. Instead, I leave her in the very capable hands of Aki Yamashita, a freelance operator Jason and I have known forever, who's recently moved to the east coast.

"You want me to babysit your girlfriend?" he'd asked me last week when I offered him a spot in the rotation on watching Hailey.

"She killed one of Gerome Lively's girlfriends." No further response needed. Not that Lively had enough feelings to care one way or another, but Hailey is on people's radar now.

I drive north through Bethesda to the Reid estate in Potomac. Fifteen miles and a world of

343

privilege separates Hailey's new home from where she grew up, and my anger grows the farther I get from the woman who had the misfortune of simply being born to the wrong parents.

No amount of comfort or privilege makes up for not being loved.

I know we've just really started our relationship, but I want give her everything she missed out on. Not just love and affection, but a real home. Her place isn't big enough for the two of us, and apparently she hates my condo.

One step at a time. First I need to make sure she's safe. Then I can tell her we're moving.

My dick pulses at the thought of that fight. Maybe she'll be okay with it if I tell her she can bring the stripper pole.

I turn onto the long lane that curves through the front of the estate, the Potomac River glinting in the distance. After parking my SUV in front of the grand entrance, I climb the steps. Before I get to the door, it swings open, and Amelia Dashford Reid herself is standing in the entranceway. She doesn't invite me in.

I walk in anyway, brushing past her. I don't see any staff, but they're around somewhere.

That's fine, I'm not hiding my visit.

From behind me, she clears her throat. "My husband isn't here."

I spin slowly, cocking one eyebrow. "Oh?"

"He's on a business trip."

"For an extended period of time?" I let out a single humorless huff of laughter. "That's smart, sending him away."

"Excuse me?"

344

I slowly button my suit jacket and stretch to my full breadth and height. Crossing my wrists behind my back, my fingers curling around my pistol grip in the hidden holster there, I lean forward slightly. "I know who you are."

One elegant brow curves, matching my expression. "Yes, I imagine you do, as you have worked for my husband for the better part of a year and you are currently seeing my daughter."

She's good. Cold as ice, unwavering presentation as a woman of society. Which she is. They all are.

"Your father is in Geneva right now."

She shrugs. "Perhaps. I don't know."

"Yes, you do. You've spoken to him almost a dozen times in the last three days."

That gets a flicker of surprise in her cold green-blue eyes. I'm struck by the thought that I've never seen a similarity between Hailey and her mother, but they share many features. Their eyes, although Hailey's are greener. Their hair and nose. But Hailey's mouth curves in genuine happiness and her soft curves make her lush and beautiful.

Amelia Dashford is a monster. Not to be trusted.

I whip out my gun and aim it at her chest. Center of mass. Maximum damage.

She laughs. "Put that away, Mr. Parker."

"You don't think I'd hurt a woman?" I slowly release the safety and aim my weapon at her forehead. "I'll *kill* you. Without breaking a sweat. Are we clear?"

She stares at me, her eyes wide enough I know she's thinking now. After a beat, she nods slowly and sits down. I don't follow suit. "What do you want?"

"Insurance."

"I don't follow."

"Hailey was kidnapped because of your world. Because of the games you and your father play. Because of Gerome Lively and your husband, but you and I both know that's just one layer of depravity in a world of murky ugliness, don't we? There are people who might want to silence Hailey because she doesn't play by the rules."

Amelia swallows hard, but she doesn't break or drop character. Her hands flutter together. "This is quite the fantasy, Mr. Parker. But I have no idea how I can help. Of course I wouldn't want anything to happen to Hailey. I'm sure Morgan has never—"

In two quick strides, I'm in front of her and I have the barrel of my Browning pressed against her forehead. "Why is Gerome Lively still alive?"

She blinks up at me from beneath the black steel. "Because you haven't killed him yet? Isn't that what you wanted? A chance to play barbarian hero? We would have ignored a bit more bloodshed, you know. You had a chance and you blew it. Don't get pissy with me."

Jesus Fucking Christ. At least Wilson's hunch wasn't wrong. I'm glad Morgan Reid's phone wasn't the only one I bugged. "My best friend thinks that PRISM is the good guys. But we know differently, don't we?"

Nothing. The ice queen just blinks at me, and I want to blow her brains out. The fact that those are Hailey's eyes is the only thing that saves her, and

346

that's probably a mistake on my part.

Since she's not talking—although she's already shown me more of her hand than I expected—I move on to Plan Two. Jerking her by the arm, I shove her ahead of me down the hall and instruct her to walk to the library. I make her sit on the couch in the corner where she can see the portraits of both her husband and her father. Her two lovers, although I'm not sure she's ever loved either of them.

I sit across from her, my back to those paintings. I don't want to see either of their faces. I don't want to see hers, either, but this won't take long. I pull out my phone and start recording a video.

"When did you start sexually abusing your children?"

"I've never," she spits at me, all pretense gone now.

I ignore her. "Was it about the same age as when your father started touching you?"

She glowers at me.

"Maybe Daddy didn't corrupt you, but the other way round?" I shake my head. "I don't really care. All that matters is that you're still screwing him—"

"Turn that off." The fury in her voice is a thing of beauty. I love it when people get pissed off. They stop thinking.

I click off the video and put my phone away. "Tell me how I've got it wrong."

She pulls herself up tall through the spine, her head perched just so on top of a neck so tight it looks like it might just snap itself.

If only I were so lucky.

"What do you have?"

I snort. "Everything."

"You're lying."

"A suite at the St. Regis. We have photos of the last three visits."

She blanches.

I lean back against the couch and stretch my arms wide, lazily tapping my gun against the overstuffed cushion. "When he's huffing away on top of you, do you ever wish you'd gone in a different direction with your life?"

Her nostrils flare, and an angry flush is growing up her neck. "He's not really my father."

The power imbalance there is a million types of fucked up, and why she did it...well, I don't need to know that. I just need some fucking insurance to keep Hailey safe. "I hardly think that will matter to the tabloids."

"And what do you want?" She picks at imaginary lint on her arm and stares just over my shoulder.

"Have you ever touched your son?"

"No."

"Your daughters?" The thought fills me with rage, and if the answer is yes, I will kill her. "Did you groom them in any way?"

A tremble gives her away, and I raise my weapon, but she yelps and starts talking. "No. Not...intentionally. It's possible that Taylor may have picked up on something, a vibe or a moment...but you have to understand, I was never abused. Morgan and I don't have a...loving relationship. And the man who raised me knew

348

what it was like to be married to someone for reasons other than love."

"Your mother had affairs."

"Many. I was the product of one. My father was unable to have children."

"So he raised you as his own." I sneer. "And then turned you into his mistress."

"No. It's not like that. We have an equal relationship. It's unconventional but we…support each other. Make business decisions and—"

"You use Morgan."

"For good. I know you don't believe me, but PRISM…there are people in the organization who can predict things happening ten, twenty steps down a path. Chaos theorists."

"At what cost?"

"I never—"

I stand, forgetting that I wanted her to keep talking and storm over to her, leaning over the couch. She shrinks back, terrified of me. Good. "Your daughter was kidnapped by a man that PRISM actively kept out of jail. They're probably interfering in a federal investigation as we speak. That needs to stop, do you understand me?"

"Yes."

"I don't give a damn about some mathematician's idea of what might happen. I'm telling you what *will* happen if you don't make sure that Hailey is nobody's concern. Not just now, but forever. Are we clear?"

"Yes."

I pull out my phone and tab to the browser window I've got waiting. It takes a minute for the video to buffer, then the black and white feed from the cameras in the corner of the room flicker to life. She looks at herself, looking at herself on my phone, and sucks in a horrified breath.

"Right now, that video is private. But if something were to happen to Hailey, if she is threatened in any way, shape, or form…that video and much, much more will instantly be released. Be afraid, Amelia. I'm your worst enemy. You can tell your friends that The Horus Group is no longer their puppet."

In the distance, we hear the front door open and heels click across the marble of the foyer. "Mom?"

Amelia jerks her face toward the door. "That's Alison," she whispers.

"I'll take her with me to Hailey's," I say, standing. I don't care that I've broken this woman, that I've pushed her to detail depravity and hint at crimes she thought she'd buried deep. All I care about is forever severing the ties that bind the woman I love.

"She's not in danger here," Amelia pleads, grabbing at my arm.

I shake her off, needing to be away from this woman and everything she represents. "Of course she is. It's a miracle they all turned out relatively unscathed."

The library door swings open, and Alison steps inside a second after I re-holster my gun. "Oh! Hi, Cole."

"Hey. I came to pick you up for the sleepover at Hailey's," I say smoothly.

"Uhm…" she frowns, looking between me and her mother. "Well, I have a car, so if I was staying at Hailey's, I could just drive myself over there, but I didn't know we were doing that."

"Might be a surprise. Come on."

I don't look back, and Alison doesn't ask any more questions.

352

Hailey

I haven't had Cole in my bed for two long days. He hasn't been far—on the couch—but he's moved my sister into my apartment and shaken off my suggestion that we leave her there and go back to his place.

The man must have hit his head, because I'm climbing the walls wanting to have sex and he's organizing pajama parties.

On the second night, after Alison falls asleep, I sneak out of my room and curl up next to him on the couch.

"Can't sleep?" he asks absently, kissing my temple before going back to scanning news stories on his tablet.

"I miss you."

"I'm right here." He frowns at me, then raises both brows as my meaning dawns on him. "Oh." He grins. "Yeah, I miss you, too."

"Not enough to go back to your place."

"It's complicated."

I don't ask for details. "How long is it going to be complicated for?"

"Not much longer. I just need to assemble a second security team, and since this isn't something that we ordinarily do, it's going to take some time to hire the right guys."

"That reminds me..." I fill him in on the flirtation between Alison and Scott, and he wrinkles his nose. "So maybe not..."

"In my experience, there's not much point trying to keep apart people who want to get naked together, but sure. He can stay on your guard."

I wrap my arm around his shoulders and read the news over his shoulder for a minute before asking the question I've been wanting to put out there for days now. "How much is all of this costing?"

"Don't worry about it."

"Can't help it. I mean, I have a trust fund, but I'd prefer not to touch it."

He laughs. It's not a good laugh. "Yeah, I don't want you to touch it, either."

"But professional bodyguards can't be cheap. Is it even still necessary?"

He clicks the power button and slides the slim tablet away. His fingers graze the side of my face as he gives me a painfully serious look. "I don't want you to know how necessary it is, but yes."

"Wouldn't it be better if we went to a hotel or something? Instead of stacking in here like sardines?"

"Not secure enough." He slides his hand into my hair, holding my head as he leans in to kiss me.

"I *miss* you," I repeat, whispering between licks.

"Soon. I have a surprise for you tomorrow."

"Is it alone time?"

He laughs and kisses the corner of my mouth. "Something like that."

— —

When Alison gleefully skips off to class with

354

Scott in tow the next day, Cole takes me across town to Capitol Hill—the neighborhood. He drives in his usual slightly-too-fast, totally-got-this way, and refuses to answer any questions about where we're going.

He parks on a residential street lined with townhouses on one side and a renovated school-turned-lofts on the other.

He ignores my curious look and guides me inside the loft building. He knows the door code. Why am I not surprised?

Inside, we find Wilson in one of the top floor lofts. They have a wordless man conversation that's just shrugs and grimaces, and ends with a fist bump before Wilson leaves.

Oooh-kay.

It's a really nice loft, polished redwood floors and muted walls, thick white trim around crazy-tall windows and black steel fixtures. I poke around a bit. The main room has an open-concept kitchen and living room. At one end, the room opens onto a deck with a view of Capitol Hill. *Wow.* There are three bedrooms, two on one side of the living room, the other down a short hallway. That one is *sweet*, with two walk-in closets and a bathroom just as nice as Cole's, with the big-ass glass shower, but it has a tub as well.

Definitely an improvement over his old place, if he's thinking of moving. But given the neighborhood, I'm guessing he's just going to use this as a safe house for my sister.

Lucky brat.

"So what do you think?"

I glance back at Cole over my shoulder and

smile. "Depends what it's for."

He gives me a weird look. "Well, I've put a deposit down on it."

My smile gets bigger and I turn to face him. "Yeah? I like the tub. But I have to help you decorate, because that cold stuff from your place really will ruin the warmth—"

Laughing, he shakes his head and steps closer. He shoves his hands in his pockets, hulking up his shoulders. He looks big and rough and entirely uncomfortable, now that I'm really looking at him.

"Wait, do you...If this isn't your type of place, then why are you moving?"

"It's my type of place, don't worry about that. But there's a potential problem."

"Oh no!" I give one last longing gaze at the bathtub and walk toward him, sliding my hand into his as I tug him back to the living room space. "What's the problem?"

"I'm worried the condo board might not accept my application. They're quite particular about who they let move in. I doubt Parker is a name they recognize."

"Surely they know The Horus Group."

"Not always a selling point." He winks at me and spins me around, taking me fully in his arms. "Maybe I should become a senator or something."

I make a face. "You need a better plan."

"I was hoping you'd say that." He looks down at me, his smile slipping into a more serious expression. "I don't have a lot going for me, really. A decent job, although that's in flux. A good pile of savings, but I just dipped into that for an investment."

"I don't care about any of that." I press my hand to his cheek. "Okay, practical question. Can you afford it?"

"Yes."

"I gotta say, it's really nice. But..." I stop myself from saying it's too expensive. I actually don't know what Cole can afford. Maybe I should have taken Wilson up on his offer to share those details a few weeks earlier.

"Your place is too small for both of us, and you don't like my place."

He's not wrong, but I figured that eventually we'd move into a place together. Maybe I was silly to think that far ahead. "Well, I don't really care where you keep your stuff. I never should have said anything about your place, I'm sorry. It's nice. Maybe you just need a warm painting or two."

"It's a bit late for that, I've already sold it."

"Cole!" I gape at him. "When did that happen?"

"Yesterday some time. I mean, I still have it for two more months, but it's a done deal."

"Shoot. Well, okay, what I can I do to help you get this place?"

He takes both my hands in one of his and reaches into his pocket, pulling out a small white envelope. "Can I get your opinion on this investment I just made?"

I resist the urge to roll my eyes. One time he sees me following stocks and now I've gotta make a snap decision about —

Oh. Three gorgeous diamonds, none of them small, one bigger than the others, spill into my turned up palm, and now Cole is down on one

357

knee.

Sugar. All the blood in my body rushes to my head.

I can't breathe. I'm definitely going to cry. And he hasn't even started talking yet.

"Hailey Dashford Reid, since the first moment I laid eyes on you, I've known you were mine. I fought it for a long time, because I'm truly not good enough for you. You deserve white picket fences and chubby children with handfuls of wildflowers. A nice man with a good job and a briefcase."

I'm shaking my head and laughing and crying, because he's so damn earnest about this and I just want to throw myself at him and scream yes. I bite my tongue.

"One day, maybe soon, we'll move to the suburbs and get a fence. Maybe before that we can have some of those chubby children, if you promise they have your hair and your smile."

"I like your smile just fine," I whisper, then shush again because I think he's got more.

"But I'm never going to carry a briefcase. I wouldn't even know where to find one. I'm going to try to be a better man for you, beautiful, but I'm always going to piss you off. Some of the time, I'm going to do it on purpose just so you spit fire at me, because I love that. I love you."

"I love you, too," I mouth, wet tears plopping on my lips.

"I have no idea what kind of ring you'd want. We haven't had those conversations yet. I wasn't even sure what kind of condo you'd want, but I think this one has lots of room for the stripper pole

358

and good lighting for knitting, and it's warm, like you."

"Okay."

"Wait, I haven't asked you yet."

"Okay."

He spreads his hand over mine, his fingers tracing mine as he closes my fist around the diamonds. When he looks up at me, I could swear his eyes are shiny and bright, but if they are, I'll never tell anyone. That little piece of Cole is just for me. "Will you remind me every day what love is? Give me a reason to be a better man?"

"You don't need a reason—"

"I need you." He pulls my hands to his mouth and kisses my knuckles before taking a deep breath and finally asking the question. "Will you marry me?"

"Yes." I smile through my tears, vibrant relief coursing through my entire body. This is happiness. "Yes! Yes, yes, yes."

He surges to his feet, picking me up and spinning me around as I wrap my arms around his neck, the diamonds squeezed tight in my hand. "Really?"

"Yes!" I lay a big, smacking kiss on his cheek. "Did you doubt?"

"Well, not when I was putting a bid in on the condo, but then…" He slows to a stop and lowers me to my feet, his gaze searching my face for some kind of confirmation. "It's hard to imagine you can see a future with me."

"Oh, baby." I pull him in for a slower, sexier, hungrier kiss. His hands skate over my hips and up my back, and I want to touch him, too. "Where can

I put these blingy rocks?"

"I was thinking a ring, but…"

I laugh and twist out of his arms. "I meant right now." I carefully put them in the middle of the kitchen island, then turn around. Cole's right there, looming over me. "They're beautiful."

"Like you." He's staring at me like he can't believe his good luck.

I loop my fingers through his belt and slide our bodies together. "That right there. That's why I see a future with you. Forever with you. Because you see the best in me, always."

"I could say the same thing," he says gruffly as I move up his body, getting in some gratuitous groping of my fiancé before kissing him again.

We both deserved more, and now we finally have it. I can't be all *poor me* about my life, but I shouldn't be the first person to love Cole unconditionally.

That's just wrong, and I tell him that when I'm finally done tasting his ridiculously fine mouth. He tries to brush it off.

"Hey," I say, forcing him to look at me, to see how serious I am. "Your first parents made selfish choices that meant they were taken from you. Your second parents had…I don't know, but some kind of messed up expectations or something. All of them should have loved you for the terrifying little ball of energy I'm sure you were."

"I think I was a pretty quiet kid, actually." But he smiles.

"Sure. You didn't climb trees or build weapons out of cardboard boxes?"

"Well…"

"Cole, when we have kids, I'm going to plant trees and pick up bonus boxes at the grocery store for them."

"I think a good climbing tree is more mature…"

"You're missing the point!"

"Okay. We both deserved better parents," he says. "At least you've got your siblings."

They're okay. But they don't always have my back. "You've got Jason and Tag and Wilson."

He nods slowly. "I do. They're good. But they're not you."

"And my brother and sisters aren't you." I trace his lips with my index finger, loving the way his eyes darken and his cheeks flush. "You're *mine*. You're my first and last thought every day. You're already my primary family, really. I want to run decisions past you and tell you about new knitting patterns and share all my secrets. I want to plan a future with you. I can't share any of that with my siblings because there's all this…other stuff that they bring to it. Worry and doubt. They're always cautioning me, you know. Like I should be less brazen and brash. And then there's you, wanting me to spit fire at you."

"'Cause it makes me hot for you."

That's a great reason. "Speaking of which, are we going to be interrupted here?"

He shakes his head no, and I go to work at his buttons. I want this man naked. Stat.

"I forgot to tell you the other thing," he starts to say, but I'm not listening, so he grabs my wrists and hauls my arms in the air. "Hailey!"

"What?" I blink up at him.

"Other news."

361

"Pretty sure nothing is going to top that we're getting married." I grin up at him.

"I'm stepping back from my previous role in the firm."

"You're quitting?" What? That's crazy. And maybe good. But… "Is this your decision?"

He nods, then shakes his head. I blink at him, not understanding his mixed answer. "Not quitting. I'm still a partner. But I'm only doing pro bono work. No clients. No hobnobbing."

"And Jason is okay with that?" I can't wrap my head around this. "This is for real?"

"Yep. I didn't really give him much of a choice. I want to be a ghost in the background." His gaze drops down my face, and he dusts his fingertips along my collarbone. "It's safer that way. But we're all in agreement. As of this week, The Horus Group's mission and vision statement is changing."

"Wow. What does this mean?"

"We're still sorting that out. Tag's taking point on the new branding. And in the meantime, that leaves me with lots of time to fuck my fiancée."

"Really," I murmur as his mouth follows the path his fingers had just blazed. "Tell me more about that."

"Fuck her so hard she can't walk straight. Make her scream so loud the neighbors blush."

"Sounds romantic," I say, fighting back a smile.

"Is that a challenge?"

"Damn straight. I double-dog-dare you to make me swoon with your filthy ways."

We stay in our new condo until dusk falls, and on the way back to my place, we stop at the jewelers Cole bought the diamonds from and choose a ring setting.

It turns out, he knows me better than he thinks.

Cole

Three weeks later

My phone vibrates as I round the corner a block from work. I duck into a doorway and pull it out. It's a message from Jason.

J: 911 sit at office. Shark has a new request.

We have code names for all our clients. Shark is Morgan Reid. Fuck me.

C: Thought he was out of the country.

J: Apparently not.

Thirty seconds later, I'm in the stairwell taking the steps two at a time.

"What is it?" I bark out as I storm into the boardroom.

"Mr. Parker." Morgan stands and holds out his hand, which I ignore as I fist the front of his three thousand dollar suit and shove him into the wall.

"Did we not make ourselves perfectly clear? We're not in the business of cleaning up your messes any longer." We haven't made a formal announcement yet, but we've spent the last few weeks disentangling ourselves from the clients we no longer want to work with. Morgan Reid was my first call.

He smirks at me. I'm a fucking monster, and he's not scared of me in the least. That's terrifying. "I didn't do anything this time."

This time. Again, I swear under my breath and release him, but I don't step back. "Then what is it?"

Jason clears his throat from the other side of the room. He didn't stop me when I charged in, which means he's unimpressed as well.

Morgan adjusts his tie. "It's Taylor. She's gone missing."

"Not missing," Jason says drily. "Just in hiding."

I flex my hands at my side and watch Morgan swallow and press his lips together before answering. He's nervous. I lean in and let fly the obvious question. "Why is she hiding from you?"

He jerks back. Not as smart as he'd like to think. Asshole. "You need to talk to her. Convince her to…"

"To what?" Fear is now rolling off him and he avoids my gaze.

Behind me, Jason interjects. "There's a leak. It's on a blog."

Blogs are a dime a dozen in Washington now. I glance back at him. "A real one?"

He shrugs. "It's not A-level, but it's big enough that tweets have started."

As if summoned by the now painful tension levels in the room, Wilson strolls in with his phone in his hand. "You've stepped in it now, Reid."

Tag joins us, and I realize they all must know more than me if we're all here at quarter to seven in the morning.

"Will someone fill me?" I glance around, then back at Morgan, who's turning a vile shade of green. "Did you hurt her?" The words are barely out of my mouth before I grab him and spin him around, slamming him face first into the conference

366

table. He groans as I wrench his arms behind his back.

"I didn't touch her," he whispers pleadingly. "I swear!"

I can't breathe. Rage fills my chest, and maybe air is optional. I thought I was done with Morgan and Amelia Reid. Wishful thinking. I lean into the hold, enjoying the strain of his arm under my hands. "If you think we're going to help you cover anything up, you're fucked in the head. You narrowly missed being arrested in Miami for the kidnapping of one daughter, and now—"

"You have to," he says with a groan. "Not for me. For her. This is a mistake."

I let go, because touching him makes my skin crawl, and there are three other men in the room who can take turns bouncing him off the walls like a tennis ball if he tries something stupid. Like leaving. He's definitely not walking out those doors until we know the whole truth, however disgusting it may be.

It wouldn't be the first time we've heard something vile.

But hopefully it'll be the last time we hear it from a guilty client.

Wilson clears his throat. "Has the Vice President ever been a guest of Gerome Lively at one of your disgusting rape parties?"

He asks it like he's wondering if anyone wants coffee or tea.

Reid blanches. "This is a mistake," he repeats, sounding dangerously close to losing his morning martini on our conference table.

"That doesn't answer the question," I growl.

His face is white and sweat is popping all over the place. "If she persists in telling people that, she's going to end up dead."

"Because it's the truth or a lie?" Both would be powerful motivators to silence Hailey's sister.

He nods, jerkily. "Truth. Not with her, but she found out about it and approached him." He glances at me. "I'm not sure why this is happening."

I am. PRISM.

I glance at Jason. He nods and jerks his thumb toward his office. "Excuse us for a minute."

"What do you know?" I demand as soon as his door closes behind us.

"Can you stop treating all of our conversations like they have to be a come to Jesus moment? I've come. I'm converted, even if I'm not a true believer yet." He rolls his eyes at me and slowly undoes his suit jacket so he can sit at his desk. "Let's start with what I don't know, which is a lot." He narrows his eyes and chews on his lower lip as he stares at the neat row of papers on his desk. "What's the end game?"

"A shot across the bow?" I shake my head and throw myself into the chair across from him. Lively's network is running for cover already. A power play isn't necessary and doesn't make sense. "Righting a wrong?"

"At the expense of Taylor Reid?"

"No..." I trail off, staring at the wall, as if I could actually see Morgan Reid sitting at the conference table. "He thinks she's in danger. But what if she's not? Her reputation isn't smeared any further by this, not really."

Jason nods. "Not with the Vanity Fair spin that young women were taken advantage of."

"It's not spin."

"You know what I mean."

Yeah, unfortunately I do. All that rape culture bullshit that means Lively and Company were given passes for being dirty old men when they were really terrorists. At the end of the day, he'll go down for kidnapping, not the rapes he should hang for.

I think of Miguel, my contact in Miami. *My* guy, who owes *me* a favor. Not us. If Lively goes free, it won't be a decision by committee that determines what happens to him. It'll be a single call from the burner phone I bought that night we met in the shadows of a disco, the night after Hailey was taken and rescued and saved from a fate worse than death. The day she saved herself because she fought like hell.

"So we don't interfere." Jason frowns. "That doesn't sound right."

My laugh surprises us both, and then he joins in.

It might not sound right, but it feels...good. "Yeah. Bit of a mind fuck, just letting shit be."

He tosses a pen in the air. "You're going to find the girl?"

I nod. I already have an idea where she might be.

"Then let's go kick that asshole out of our offices, yeah?'

"Fuck, yeah."

Tag is more than happy to escort Reid out of the building when Jason delivers his cold-as-fuck

369

denial of service message. While they're doing that, I slide Wilson a note. **Taylor. St. Regis Hotel?**

It's just a hunch.

And frankly, if I'm wrong, I don't care.

I don't care if I'm right, either.

I'm done with all the fucked up Reids.

All I care about is the one who's going to take my name. Hailey Parker.

And just like that, I'm hard as nails.

Only one thing for that. I head for the stairs, shaking hands with each of my partners on the way out.

"Taking a sick day," I say to Jason.

Tag winks.

He's not wrong.

—epilogue—

Cole

I sprint up the stairs to our new apartment. It's hot and sticky outside, the height of a typical D.C. summer, but I still prefer to run the fifteen blocks between our house and the northeast community center where I volunteer a few times a week. They have a good boxing ring now, thanks to Hailey, and it's a clean, safe space for youth to hang out.

The punching bags are a big draw, too. My gut tugs at the haunted look at the new kid's face as he unleashed himself on one tonight, ineffectively whacking away at it. By the time we were done, he was powering it into my shoulder as I held it on the other side.

I'm not the guy who invites confidences. Nobody ever spills their guts to me unless I'm making them, and those days are behind me—for the most part. But I can teach kids how to punch right. How to channel that fury and harness their own power.

Elijah's face as he promised to come back again —that's why I go back.

And the woman inside this apartment gets the credit for me going in the first place.

She's in the kitchen, cleaning up, still in the tank top and shorts she was wearing when I left. She gives me a slow, appreciative up and down, then flicks her gaze to the oversized clock on the wall.

"You're all sweaty," she says, licking her lips.

"It's hot out there." I prowl toward her, pulling

off my shirt. I maybe flex my abs a little—anything for my girl.

Giggling, she turns her back to the counter and hoists herself up. "It's getting hot in here."

"We've got some time?" I fit myself between her bare legs and tug down her tank, baring her lush tits.

She nods, leaning back on her hands. "Gonna get me dirty?"

"Filthy." I lean over her, almost kissing her before dodging to the side and tasting her neck.

"Get back here," she demands, sliding her hands into my hair. She's not the only one who likes to be tugged around. She drags our mouths together, our kiss suddenly desperate and slightly clumsy as I knead her breasts, the rub of her nipples against my palms making me rock hard.

I drop one hand to tease at her waistband, and she lifts her hips. *Get me naked*. The order is clear, and I'm happy to comply. I strip her bare, settling her ass right on the edge of the counter. She leans back again, her pale, luscious curves begging for my touch, the trim brown curls above her pussy pointing to the pink lips I never get enough of.

I drop to my knees and run my nose up her thigh, breathing her in. She spreads even wider as I get to the good stuff—shiny, pink, and warm, her cunt is beautiful.

"We do have an engagement party to get ready for," she whispers, and I lick her for being silly. I know we do.

"Pretty sure the party starts when we get there."

"You—ahhh!" The argument ends with me sucking her clit, then it's just warm moans and panting little breaths from her as I wind her up until she's begging for my cock.

Fuck, I love that.

Shoving to my feet again, I notch the fat head of my cock into her soft, wet folds and ease into her tight channel. I love this, too, the way her pussy clutches me, like I need to be a little rough to get all the way in.

The way she claws at my back when I get there and doesn't let me go.

"So hot, so tight," I growl, wrapping my arms around her waist, sliding one hand up her back as I press the other against her pelvis, low in her back, holding her in place as I set a blistering pace.

It doesn't take long. Her legs tighten around me as she humps back against me, rocking her clit where we join each time I slam into her. As soon as she seizes up, trembling in orgasm, I let myself go. Three thrusts later, I'm spilling myself inside her, my come spurting out so fast it almost hurts.

We're both breathing fast, dragging ragged breaths into our lungs as we cling together. I press my forehead against hers and whisper that I love her.

"I love you too, more and more every day."

"We should do something about that—like get married."

She grins at me. "Sounds like a plan." Taking a deep breath, she slides her palms down my sweat-slicked chest and pushes me away from her. "And now I'm sweaty too, so let's have a shower, yes?"

Once we're clean again, Hailey sits at her dressing table and starts putting on her makeup. I slowly put on my boxer briefs and dress pants, but

I keep getting drawn back to my fiancée, perched on a stool in a black slip.

I quietly come up behind her, leaning over to kiss her shoulder before she can stop me. "You're breathtaking," I tell her under my breath, and she smiles.

"I'm not even wearing my dress yet."

"It'll be stunning, too." I want to kiss her again. There's nothing I like more than seeing Hailey breathless and aching. She licks her lips, and I get it—I want more, too. "Come on, beautiful, we're going to be late."

"You're so mean," she says with a smile, turning her attention back to the mirror.

I cross our new bedroom to my closet and pull on my shirt, buttoning it neatly before sliding on my jacket. "Tie? No tie?"

"Tie," she calls out. "Let's pretend we're civilized tonight."

Overrated, but maybe I'll use it to tie her up when we get home.

We're going to a restaurant with her friends from work—she's now a full-time junior employment counselor at the agency she did her internship at—as well as my partners, and her younger sister and brother.

Her older sister has moved to Los Angeles, but they're slowly rebuilding a relationship of sorts. I'm not sure Hailey and Taylor will ever be close, but everything is different now.

Almost normal. It's weird and kind of wonderful.

"What are you thinking about?" Hailey asks as she hands me her necklace. She's wearing a dress now, black silk, and my diamonds flash on her left hand. The necklace is a hand-crafted twisted metal piece she bought at Eastern Market a few weeks earlier for twenty bucks. That's Hailey in a nutshell.

"How lucky I am that I have no will-power when it comes to resisting you." I kiss her cheek, and offer her my arm.

When we get to the restaurant, we run into her friend Tegan at the entrance. There's some squealing and ooohing and ahing over outfits, then we head inside, where everyone else is gathered. Everyone except one of my co-workers.

Once I've shaken hands and accepted congratulations from Hailey's friends, I find Jason and Wilson at the bar. "Where's Ellie?"

Jason's clenching his jaw so hard I think he might crack a tooth. Wilson's the one who finally answers. "She quit. Left a resignation letter on her chair at the end of the day today."

"What?" Well, shit. That puts a damper on things. "Any clue why? Can we get her back?"

Wilson opens his mouth, but Jason interjects before our hacker can say anything else. "Leave it alone."

"But I don't want to get a new receptionist if we can woo her back. Is it money? When was the last time we gave her a raise?"

"That would just make it worse," Jason mutters, shoving his hand through his hair. His top button is undone and his eyes are a bit wide.

"Are you drunk?" I don't mind, as long as he doesn't make a scene, but Jason rarely drinks, and never to excess.

He pins his gaze darkly on me for a minute before reaching for his glass again. He raises it in the air. "Only a little bit, my friend. We're celebrating."

I exchange a look with Wilson, but there's a limit to how much digging I'm going to do at my engagement party. "As long as we do it safely."

He gives me a look as if to say, *yes Dad*. The role reversal isn't lost on either of us.

Tag joins us next, and we have a more genuine toast to my future bride, but even as we all sit for dinner, I can't shake that look on Jason's face. I know that look. I've worn it before.

Things for Jason are going to get worse before they get better.

— —

One week later, Tag and I are standing together just off the dais at the Washington Club. He's going to give a keynote address to a monthly luncheon put on by the Chamber of Commerce. A pretty regular event, but Tag's no public speaker. Jason was supposed to do it, but he's such a fucking curmudgeon again, he can't do it—when he flew to Dallas for work, we all let out a sigh of relief.

I should do it, I'm more comfortable up there, but I just don't want to anymore. I shrug at Tag as he stands in front of me. He looks older. We all do, I'm sure. "It's a good speech."

"You should know. You wrote it. You sure you don't want to deliver it?"

I nod. "Never been more sure of anything in my

life."

He gets it. Maybe if things had gone differently with Kendra, he'd be doing the same thing.

I pat him on the shoulder. "This was never the life for me. We probably should have seen that from the beginning."

I'm not quitting. I'm just stepping back—into the shadows. Most of the time I'll be looking for clients. Sometimes I'll draw on my old skills, and strike when I'm needed. I'll do it anonymously, and I'll do it for good.

The rest of the time, I'll be Hailey's.

I'm no longer a gladiator. I'm not sure what I am, yet, but my battles aren't for public consumption.

Tag makes his way to the podium and I slowly walk to the back of the room, listening to the words I know by heart. I look at the faces of Washington's business people, watching them react. And when Tag pauses before delivering the last line, I stop watching them and I zero in on him.

His shoulders are square, his head is tall, and he looks determined as fuck. It doesn't matter what anyone else thinks. We're all in on this.

He looks around the room, then finds me and nods. His voice rings loud and clear, hopefully striking fear in the hearts of our former clients. "The Horus Group is no longer for hire by the wealthiest and most powerful. We're no longer in the business of making excuses. We're here to make things right."

THE END

(keep reading for two bonus epilogues in **the postscript** — and at the end of that, there are some clues about future Horus Group books)

HATE F*@K

Cole and Hailey

the postscript

—in the middle of the night—

Hailey

His palm drifts under my t-shirt, light strokes on my belly the signal he wants me to wake up. I will, but I'm warm under the duvet and sleep feels too good to shake off completely. This is part of the game, anyway, so I wiggle back against him, letting him play, but ignoring his shifting movements to get me on my back. I know that if I roll over, my hand will wrap around his cock, and that would nice, but instead we'll do this and it will be even better. He chuckles in my ear and I bite back a smile.

"Are you awake?"

It's more fun if I don't answer. It doesn't matter, because we both get off on the fact that he's touching me, stroking me with fingers that don't care if I'm awake or not as long as I'm getting wet. Sometimes I'm able to stay still until after he thrusts into me, and I pretend to be confused and scared, but it's hard to stay passive that long. Hard to keep my hands off him. My mouth.

He pulls me tight against him, settling me in the crook of his body, his cock long and hard against my panties. I wore pajama pants to bed—he must have taken them off before I woke up. I want to wiggle again, I love the feel of him flexing between my ass cheeks, but that's not tonight's game, so I hold still, hoping for that twitch to happen on its own. When it does, I almost gasp out loud from how much it turns me on, that simple wordless communication of want. Of need.

His hand cups my left breast, his thumb grazing my nipple and I feel myself swell in response. I know my pussy lips have parted, a sliver of space created for my swollen clit. If his fingers move south, he'll feel the moisture even before parting my pink folds, and I'm sure he knows that, but he's only just started with my nipples. I know he won't finger me until I give in, until I'm wet and panting, begging to be fucked, desperate for penetration.

He drags his thumbnail around my areola, leaving a trail of goosebumps in its wake. I can't help but shiver and his low, deep laugh reminds me that while I'm slowly being spun out of my mind, he's still fully in control. The next swipe of his thumb is softer, fleshy pad down, directly on my erect nipple this time. Almost a flick, but slower, up and down. From below the nipple, pausing at maximum stretch of my aching peak, over the top and then back down with another pause, the flat of his thumb pressing my nipple as if it was my clit and I can feel it so acutely between my legs it might as well be. He reaches across my chest with his ring finger, his thumb never ceasing its ministrations, to tweak my right nipple in a matching pattern. I groan under my breath.

"You must be so wet for me. You can't help it."

I nod. My eyes are still closed, but I'm about to start rocking back against his cock, I know it. My body is aching for more all over. I give in to the urge and press my ass into his lap, my neck into his mouth, my breasts into his hands, my pussy into...and as if he knows that I've run out of points of contact, he rolls me onto my stomach, his left hand still in constant motion against my tits. With his other hand, he jerks my hips into the air, or where the air would be if he wasn't pressed flat on top of me. He arches his back to make room and slips behind me to press his erection solidly between my legs.

"I'm going to take you like this tonight."

I don't know if he means my pussy, my ass, or both, and I don't care, I just want him inside me. I grind back against him and he slides his hand out from beneath my body. I'm so wound up I don't care, the sensation of my heavy breasts moving against the fabric of my shirt and the bed beneath me enough to keep me spinning. He pushes my shirt up my back, then slides his palms down my spine, to my panties, and with a hook of his thumbs, he takes those over my hips and down to my knees. Sometimes he leaves them there, binding my legs together, but tonight he encourages me to kick them loose. He drags his hands back up to my ass, his thumbs brushing my pussy between my legs before tracing up my crack to rest just above the pink pucker of my anus. I twitch, wondering if one of his thumbs will return there now or if I'll have to wait.

"You want something in your ass, beautiful?"

I nod, my face buried in my pillow. He circles my anus twice, then pauses. I feel a cold squirt of lube next, just a bit, not enough to get messy, and I know that this is just a tease. He eases the tip of a finger, maybe his thumb, into my dark hole, and I focus on the muscles that control that sphincter. I push back against him, knowing that will actually pull his finger in further. He pumps in and out, slow at first, then faster, and I rock up to meet his hand, eager for the invasion.

"That's so fucking hot," he grunts, and I know he means it both literally and aesthetically. "Love that you open for me, baby."

And I was. As if to prove the point, he slowly pulled out, then pressed again at my opening, this time with two firm pads. Oh god, yes. The muscles fluttered, welcoming the touch, and this time the invasion was smooth and quick.

It steals my breath and shuts down my brain. Sometimes I can't believe he hadn't done this before me, but I love that it's our secret pleasure. That neither of us have had this primal connection with anyone else.

Sometimes he lets me play with his ass when I'm sucking his cock, and I love it, but we don't do that in the middle of the night. When he wakes me up like this, I'm his to fuck and suck and lick, to come in or on, and I get off on it in a way I never would when I'm fully awake. Of course, I am awake now, totally, but I woke up in this altered state of arousal and it makes me a different person, frees the baser part of myself to submit without thinking too much about it. Without limits or concern. The truth is that it isn't *what* we do that's different at night, but how we do it.

When we have sex in the evening, or morning or afternoon when given the opportunity, there's a lot more talking. What we like, what we don't like, how we feel about each other. At night, it's reduced to the purest form of communication. His action, my reaction. When he wakes me and takes me, it's with a unique confidence that I will like it, and that pleases us both.

That's the thing about depravity. Once your mind is open to it, it's not so depraved after all. It's just delicious.

His cock knocks up against my pussy, like a silk wrapped homing missile, and I reach for it blindly between my legs. I gasp as my fingers slip effortlessly into my folds. I'm so fucking wet it might be embarrassing if it wasn't so hot. I moan into the pillow and rock against his length.

"Yeah, baby, I feel it. You're so ready for me. Dripping for me." He eases his thumb out of my ass and I whimper at the loss. "God yes, you want to get fucked, don't you?"

I nod again and arch my back, presenting both options to him.

He chuckles and shifts behind me, and I'm about to beg, or try to impale myself on his cock, when I feel him press into me, placing himself just inside my pussy at first, then the inexorable cleaving that makes me cry out. "Ohmigod," I breath, as he sinks fully into my warmth. "Oh, god. Fuck me, please."

He flexes inside me, his cock nudging at my cervix, and I can just imagine it kissing his head, asking ever so nicely for a warm bath of sperm. I arch my back, folding my hips as much as possible, until my clit rubs against the bottom of his cock. I wiggle back and forth until his palm slaps down on the side of my ass.

"Stop moving. You don't need to come right away."

I cry out, because yes, I think I do. "Please," I

whisper.

Please put your finger back in my ass. Please pinch my clit until I buck against you like a rodeo horse. Please make me come so hard I pass out and can't remember where you finished. I promise I won't care.

"Stop thinking about what you want." He folds himself forward over my back, his breath drifting over my shoulder and along the crest of my ear as he rocks his cock in and out of me slowly. "Say it, or hold still and let me give it to you."

I whimper and bite my lip. I want him to give it to me.

"Good girl."

The praise fills me up and gives me strength. I can be patient. He'll make it worth my while.

He pulls himself off my back in a single smooth action. I can see in my mind's eye his abdominal muscles contracting, the only indication that it would take him any effort to move so fluidly. With the same balance of strength and care, he shifts my body up, lifting my hips up into the cradle of his pelvis. My knees are off the bed, but he's holding me securely with his large, rough hands and his cock is rubbing a spot inside me that drifts me into an altered headspace where he could twist me into a pretzel and I wouldn't care. As he can sense that I'm lost in bliss, he holds me there, fucking me just hard enough to ride over that spot, using his words to twist my mind up and over the final crest toward my first orgasm.

I know it's coming, and I know it's just the first, because he's not in any hurry to join me. He loves coming in my pussy, and he loves doing it at the same time as my walls clench hard around him. He swears his come spills right into my womb that way, and if he says something like that when it happens, it makes me so fucking hot I could go again right away. And sometimes we do.

But other nights, he holds off, wanting to see how many times he can make me fall apart before he loses himself. Those nights, he might come on me, marking me, white ropes of him shining on me in the dark. Or he might, on rare occasion, come in my ass, but usually he he pulls out and spills on my back, liking how I shudder at the loss of him.

He likes everything about fucking me, and I love that.

I love him.

I always have, but now that we have this, this no-holds barred connection, this *honesty*, I love him more than I ever thought possible. And I don't think I could ever find the words to tell him how much this means to me, so I show him instead. I give him my body. I give him my trust.

"Your pussy is so tight, baby. I could do this all night, rocking in and out of you. Do you feel how hard you make me? Do you feel that cock, filling you up? You do that. You turn me on that much. I love fucking you. I love rolling you over and having my fucking way with you while you're still sleeping. And you're such a good girl, you spread your legs for me even while you're sleeping, don't you?"

And that's what does it. That's what rips me apart, knowing there's never a time I'd say no to him, because he needs me as much as I need him. I seize up hard around him, and he slows his rocking, not stopping, but gentling enough to give me a chance to recover before he's going to ramp us both up again.

"You get so sloppy after you come, baby. It's hot." I wish I'd known that. I wasted ten years after puberty being embarrassed about the awesomeness between my legs. Of course, if I'd slutted it up before, then I wouldn't have discovered this with him. And I love that he's the only person who's ever known this side of me. The only one who's met my inner hedonist. In some ways, he didn't just meet her. He made her.

I shiver, and he pulls out. "No..." I moan, and he chuckles.

"Hold still, I just need to get something."

I shift, trying to see what he's doing through the darkness, and I heard the air part a split second before his palm connected sharply with my ass.

"Hold. Still."

I know better than to shift again. If I do, I won't get another spanking, I'll get put away wet and needy. He rarely spanks for fun, and never if I try to manipulate it. He's right, of course. It wouldn't make my pulse jump if he gave in. Wouldn't make my pussy drip with excitement, or my skin itch with need.

He's back. He places something at the far side of the bed, then he's over me again, and his hands at my sides, gently shifting me. Turning me over.

"I fucking love fucking you, baby," he whispers.

I smile, and he lowers his face to cover mine, his lips gentle but demanding, his tongue right there, teasing, then right here, inside me, and it's hard to tell where he ends and I begin.

388

The kiss reignites our need, and I feel his cock stiffen between us. I reach for him, but he stills my hands and pulls them up above my head, pinning them together with one of his large palms.

His eyes are dark and heavy, boring into me as he knees his way between my thighs and thrusts hard, his cock somehow finding its sure way to my core. "Just getting wet, baby."

Fuck. He's going to take my ass like this. Oh, fuck. We've tried this facing each other only once before, and while the idea turned me on like nothing else, the sensation was overwhelming and he didn't get more than the tip of his cock into my tight rear hole.

I must have made a noise, or a face, because he grins wolfishly and nodded. "You're gonna take all of me this time."

My head isn't sure, but my pussy squeezes tight around his shaft, my body telling him in no uncertain terms that it's on board. Warm anticipation floods over me as I surrender to desire. My lips part and a quiet sound of encouragement slips out.

He rears up and slides his hands to the back of my thighs. With a firm press, I'm folded in half, and his cock pops out of me with a loud squishing sound. I revel in that sound because I know he does too. He makes me that wet, just as I make him...*ooooh. That hard.*

He's fisting himself, teasing me, rubbing his engorged head at the entrance to my ass. I focus on the sphincter there, and breath out, willing myself to relax. To open. He presses just a bit, *just enough*, and like the scantest of kisses, he slips in.

389

It burns. He's only in maybe half an inch, and it fucking burns. But I love it, and want more, because I bear down, without any thought, and my ass pulls him in a bit more, until I cry out and he eases back, not fully out, but just to the tip again. *Just the tip*. That phrase makes me blush so hard now.

Ahhhhh. "No, don't pull out..." It's the most I've said since he woke me up, but when he pulls out completely, it leaves me unbearably empty. It honestly makes me want to cry. I crave him inside me again. Need to see that look in his eyes as he has me folded over, completely open to him. To his cock.

"Shhhh, baby. Just need more lube." A cold squirt, a touch of his fingers, and then the burn is back and it's so good.

"Going in all the way this time, slow and steady. Breathe deep, push out, yeah. Oh fuck, yes." He slides in, reaching the second muscle with ease this time, and I try to keep my breathing steady as he leans in with his hips, but the burning floods my mind and my eyes roll back in my head. "Breathe."

His voice is sure and deep, commanding and utterly sexy. I drag a reedy breath into my lungs and push it out again, and again, until I feel his hips firm against my ass cheeks. He holds there, as I adjust to having all of him inside me. He flexes his cock, involuntarily, and we both groan.

"You get so wet," he mutters, his right hand trailing between my legs. This is why he's always wanted my ass from this angle, so he can see my pussy.

"Touch me," I whisper. "Feel yourself in my ass."

He grins, his teeth flashing white in the dim room, and he slides two fingers into my pussy with ease. I buck against his hand, already on the edge, and he starts an easy rhythm, moving just a bit in my ass.

He pulls his fingers out and holds them in front of my mouth. "Suck."

I do so greedily, both wanting to taste myself and have any part of him in my mouth. He hitches his thumb under my chin and presses firmly there for a moment before trailing his wet hand back down my body, entering my pussy again, this time with this thumb, leaving his fingers to rock almost accidentally against my clit.

It was almost too much, and not enough at the same time. I whimper and twist, wanting him to hammer hard. The burn has eased off, and now I just feel deliciously full.

"So tight, baby. I love that you give this to me. You're beautiful, and so fucking dirty. No one knows that you love getting your ass pounded. Just me. My ass. My pussy. Mine. Mine. Mine." His fingers flutter faster between my labia, around my clit, and I know he's getting close, and he's going to take me with him. "Fuu-uuhh-ck. Fill you up. Fuck. Here it comes. Oh. Uhhhhhhh--uh!"

He jerks hard, around me and inside me, and I shatter into a million pieces too as he slides his palm flat against my pussy. His head is thrown back, his thighs hard and tight behind my legs, and his hands tremble against my skin.

I let out a weak sigh of contentment, and he

shifts his attention back to me. I'm floating now, drifting on a sea of endorphins and bliss. The loss of him as he moves away makes me sad on an elemental level, but then he's back, with a warm washcloth, and he's taking care of me. Cleaning me up, then holding me. He always holds me and pets my hair, lets me ride the bliss right back into dreamland.

—wedding day—

Cole

Being late for my own wedding would be a terrible idea.

Too fucking bad it's unavoidable.

I twist the wheel hard to the right and accelerate through the turn. When I got the tip about Amelia Dashford Reid landing at Logan, I needed to see it with my own two eyes. We'd picked this week for our courthouse wedding because Hailey's socialite mother—and secret sociopath—was supposed to be in Paris for Fashion Week.

Hailey didn't want her family anywhere near our wedding day. The last time I saw her mother, I threatened to kill her—so a secret wedding works for me, too.

But Amelia has her ways, and her reasons, and I don't trust either.

So I followed her from Logan to her estate in the country. Then further, all the way to West Virginia.

Right behind me was another to take over the tail once I was confident she wasn't back in the country to ruin the day that Hailey finally, officially, becomes my wife.

Now I'm twenty minutes away from city hall, and it's just ten minutes to the top of the hour.

I pull out my phone and tap out a quick message to the most beautiful woman in the world.

C: I'm going to be late.

H: Stop saving the world for a second, okay?

C: Deal. Twenty minutes out.

H: I'm marrying the first handsome man to walk through the doors.

I laugh and flip my phone onto the passenger seat. Funny girl. Like I wouldn't kill my replacement with my bare hands. At least she wasn't alone. Her friend Tegan and her younger sister, Alison, had met her at the salon—ostensibly for a girl's day, only to find bridesmaids dresses waiting for them.

And my partners would be there, too.

And the judge who'd agreed to marry us.

Fuck. I stomp on the gas.

If she knew about her mother… that would be different. I could have explained why I needed to disappear just as she was waking up.

Our last kiss as an engaged couple had been long and slow and full of secrets.

I'm an asshole.

But for every secret that I'm keeping, there's probably a dozen truths that I don't know yet. I have no clue how deep Amelia is in PRISM. Or what that means. Or what the hell she's doing in a historic little town in West Virginia right now when her daughter is having a secret fucking wedding day because, even though she has no clue her mother is a monster, she still doesn't like her.

The truth is, I hope I never have to tell Hailey what I know. I hope I take the knowledge of how fucked up her mother and grandfather are to my grave.

I seriously doubt I'll be that lucky, because things have been quiet. Too quiet.

Every cell in my body vibrates, an early alert system that shit's about to get real again.

Not today, universe. Not today.

The fates are kind to me as I approach Judiciary Square—traffic seems to speed up, suddenly going Cole speed. Small miracle.

Whipping into a parking lot with valet service, I toss my keys and a hundred bucks to the attendant, then shrug on my jacket. Three button, slim fit black Hugo Boss.

Hailey picked it out. My woman has exceptional taste.

A quick tap on my breast pocket confirms I've got the rings. The judge has our license—we picked it up a few days earlier and delivered it to him together.

I dash across D Street, and then I see them. The men who are, for better or worse, my brothers.

Wilson's got his phone out, and it looks like the asshole is taking my picture. I flash him the finger, then bust out a grin. "You our backup wedding photographer?" I call out as I slow down and slide my hands into my pockets, doing my best GQ impression.

"We weren't sure you were coming," he responds with a smirk.

"Shut up. You know I had to make sure—"

Tag snorts, interrupting me. "Yeah, we know you're the world's greatest fiancé. Don't need to brag about it."

Jason doesn't say anything. He just gives me this look, a solemn nod that says it all. End of an era, but we've survived the transition. What we were? That's long gone, and now we're ready for the next fight.

Bring it on.

After this weekend.

It's Friday afternoon. Spring is blooming all around us, and inside, my bride has cherry blossoms in her bouquet. A little nod to the city that brought us together, she said.

"You ready?" Jason finally speaks, a hint of a smile tugging at the corners of his mouth.

Like there was any doubt. "One thousand percent."

They fall in step beside me, and we stretch out across the sidewalk, four big men in black suits. People look at us, and for the first time in months, I don't care. I'm flying high now, and a hundred feet away is the courthouse.

Hailey.

Tag dashes ahead to grab the door and in we file. Swagger, maybe. Fuck, I never thought I'd actually do this, and now I'm proud as a fucking peacock.

There's a room we're going to, where the ceremony will take place, and I thought that was where we decided to meet, so it takes me a second to realize she's in the lobby.

Half a second, maybe.

I can feel her laughing at me, a sparkling warmth that gets straight under my skin. Laughing with me, really, because I'm chuckling as I turn in a slow circle. And there she is on the far side of the security checkpoint.

I mutter something about being the late groom,

and the uniforms shake their head at me as they wave me through.

Fuck me, she's beautiful.

I haven't seen her dress before this moment, and it's perfect. White, knee-length, strapless, curvy to the max—this is a dress that celebrates every inch of her luscious body, and I can only imagine what amazing contraptions she's wearing underneath it to lift her tits like that…

Is it wrong to drool over your soon-to-be-wife in such a solemn building? In front of maybe hundreds of people?

Doesn't feel wrong.

"Beautiful," I murmur as I reach her, spinning her around in my arms. "You didn't find a more prompt husband?"

"Are there other men here?" She winks at me. "I've only got eyes for you."

"I like the dress." I swallow hard as I take it all in. The world's tiniest piece of tulle floating off a comb in her upswept hair, like a mini-veil. Pearls, the same colour as her satiny lips, shining softly around her neck and dripping from her ears. Just enough bare skin to keep me distracted. "Your legs look fucking amazing."

"Don't swear during our wedding, baby," she whispers, her eyes twinkling with amusement. Her bouquet is between us, so I can't haul her hard against my body like I want to, but I settle for leaning over it and kissing her on the cheek.

"I'm sorry," I whisper against her ear. "Not for swearing. For being late."

"It was important, right?"

I hold her gaze as I pull back, and nod once.

"Then don't worry about it." She grins, wide and bright, and holds out her hand. "Come on. Let's get hitched."

As we walk hand in hand to the private room where the judge will meet us, I can't stop looking at the woman who's become my life. I'm suddenly worried my vows won't say everything that's in my heart—everything that she deserves to hear.

I try to live every day like my deeds are my vows to her. I don't always succeed. Sometimes she needs to poke me.

"What's got you frowning?" she whispers as we stop outside the closed doors. A sign indicates another ceremony is in progress.

I brush an imaginary strand of hair off her cheek. I just want to touch her. She's fearless and determined when it comes to getting me to open up, so there's no point lying. "Worrying I'm not good enough for you," I admit, my voice rougher than I expect. "Might pack a few extra promises into my vows."

Hailey glances past me, then tugs my hand, pulling me down the hallway a bit. Once we're out of earshot of our friends, she presses up on her toes and wraps one arm around my neck, her bouquet tickling my ear. She brushes her mouth softly against mine, then parts her lips just a little as her tongue darts out to tease me. It works.

I take over, restraining myself enough so she doesn't get mussed up, but she's giving me her mouth and damn it, I'll take it. Hard, soft, fast, slow. Over and over again.

"Don't ever think you're not enough for me," she mock growls at me when I finally let her up for air. "You're my rock, you get that? I don't need you to be anything else, because you anchor me." Her eyes narrow. "You don't think that I know you shelter me from the storm that is my family? You make it possible for me to live a normal life, Cole. I love you for many, many reasons, but that's number one. Do I really need to remind you of that?"

"Yes," I laugh, finally squeezing her tight for a hug that makes everything better. "No. I'm just being...emotional, I think. It's a weird and confusing state for me."

A whistle interrupts her laughter. We turn around to see the doors open and everyone waiting.

"Hey, you mind giving us a min—" I cut myself off as the judge steps through the doors. Hailey elbows me in the side and I clear my throat. "Your Honor."

He winks at me. I knew I liked this guy.

I leave Hailey standing with her sister, and offer my hand to the judge. He shakes it, then we head inside. Tag hits play on his phone, and Otis Redding's "I Love You More Than Words Can Say" fills the room. Hailey picked it, and it's so fitting, a chill runs up my spine.

I might be her rock, but she's my conscience. She knows me better than I know myself, and she never stops showing me how I can be better. And the kicker is, I'm not even sure she knows she does it.

Tegan comes in first. I like the blue stripe in her hair. Funky.

Then Alison is next, her eyes already wet. I'm

glad Hailey's got her.

Hailey pauses in the doorway for a few beats, her smiling growing for a polite debutante curve to a full-on grin. My. Fucking. Girl.

I mouth *I love you* in her direction, and she sticks her tongue out at me before her lips spell out *I love you, too*.

She starts walking on the last refrain, and I realize she's timed it. You can take the woman out of the society rules, but you can't take the society rules out of the woman.

I give her my hand as she reaches my side. Can anyone else hear my heart thumping like that?

"What a special afternoon," the judge begins, but any worry on my part that this was going to be overly sentimental disappeared in his next words. "Cole Parker is in the courthouse without police escort."

Next to me, Hailey gasps, then shakes with laughter as she sees my face. Maybe not all the society rules stuck. I glower at Wilson, who shakes his head and points at Jason. That fucker just gives me a bland look of denial. I'm remembering this for when he finally tracks Ellie down and drags her back to his cave by her hair—or whatever his plan is there.

The judge claps me on the shoulder, then draws in a sobering breath. "No, today is a good day because two people have decided to join their lives together, and build something bigger than either one of them could accomplish on their own. Today we see Cole Parker and Hailey Dashford Reid join in matrimony."

Those words sound so damn good. We waited

longer than we wanted for this moment, and now that it's here, I need to shake off any residual fear.

I'm only doing this once. Gotta be present for it. I'm going to want to tell my grandkids about how pretty their grandma was when I put a ring on her finger.

"Marriage is the bedrock of our society. With this union, Hailey and Cole, you've begun a family. And it will grow." He gestures at our friends, at Hailey's sister, and I get what he means before he explains it. "It has already grown, hasn't it? Marriage means you've got someone in your corner. And they bring their people. We can all use more people in our corner. More support, more friendship.

But marriage is even more than that. It's the most important friendship of all, with added layers of intimacy and confidences. It is a promise of respect and commitment to a shared past and present and future.

A promise that will be tested. Today, getting married...that's the easy part. Staying married, that's the true measure of a union."

Hailey squeezes my fingers as she beams up me. *We've got this*, her eyes say.

"You will need to listen to each other." He pauses and looks at Hailey. "Listen to his words." He turns to me. "Hear her silences."

Damn good advice. I nod.

"And above all else, support and encourage each other. When you are worried, when you have concerns, be mindful in how you express that. Hold each other's hearts gently. And when you step afoul of each other, give one another space to

401

heal."

We've already tested that, more than once. I search my fiancée's face as he talks, watching as she presses her teeth into her lower lip. As her head tips to the side. As her eyes flick back up to meet mine, and her gaze floods me with heat.

Not just *want to fuck you* heat, but a deeper possession. She owns me, and this ceremony just formalizes that fact.

"Now it's time for your vows. I understand you've written them yourselves?"

We both nod. Fuck, there's a lot of nodding in a wedding ceremony.

I have my vows written on a piece of paper in my pocket, but I wrote and re-wrote them so many times over the last few weeks that I don't need it. And I want to hold her hands for this. I square my shoulders as I hold out my palms, and after she hands her sister her bouquet, she slides both of her hands onto mine.

"Hailey, I give myself to you, to be your husband and your best friend. I promise to love, honor, and cherish you, every day of our lives. I will stand by your side through sadness and joy, sickness and health, hardships and triumphs. I will celebrate your achievements, nurture your dreams, and shield you to the best of my abilities. I commit my life to you."

Her lips part on the last point, and her eyes fill with tears, but she blinks them back. "I like that last part. I'm stealing it."

"It's yours," I whisper back. "Everything I have is yours."

"Ours." She smiles and takes a deep breath.

"Whew. This is hard! I need a tissue."

Alison drifts one over her shoulder and she dabs at the corners of her eyes, then she hands it back.

Lacing her fingers into mine, Hailey locks her gaze on me as she starts her vows. "Cole, we're already life partners and best friends. Today, I promise that will never change. Today I pledge to be your wife for the rest of time. To love, honor, and obey you, unless I disagree with you, then I promise to tell you that you're wrong." She grins as everyone laughs. "I promise to trust you. To walk by your side on new journeys and have your back when you're challenged."

My girl is smart. She knows this is the only time I'll ever let her say that and now pull my caveman routine of insisting that's my job, not hers.

"And I commit my life to you," she adds, an adorable hitch in her voice as she tacks on the last bit of my vows to hers.

I can return the favor. "I promise to listen when you tell me I'm wrong." God, I love the way her face softens there. So I keep the rest of the thought in my head. *But you'll damn well obey me or there will be consequences.*

Her eyes light up, and I realize I probably didn't do a great job of keeping that off my face.

This is a forever kind of love—being able to read your partner, see their most frustrating, stubborn ticks, and still loving them hardcore. I wink at her and whisper how lucky I am.

When we're done making moon eyes at each other, the judge asks for the rings. I pull the soft pouch from my inside pocket and hand them over.

He tips them out into his hand and balances them carefully on top of the black velvet. Two platinum bands, mine plain and Hailey's a sparkly channel-set diamond ring.

"May these symbols of your commitment, exchanged today, remind you of your solemn vows forever more."

He hands me Hailey's ring and quietly instructs me on how to hold her hand. We're both shaking a little bit, and she giggles as I balance the band just past the tip of her ring finger.

He prompts me with the next lines, and I say them loud and clear. "I give you this ring as a token of my love and devotion, and with it, I thee wed."

The ring glides right over her knuckle and nestles at the base of her finger. She'd switched her engagement ring over to the other hand last night, while we were cuddling in bed, and on a whim I reach for her other hand and tug it off, setting it back in its right place on her left ring finger, now tucked against the wedding band.

"And Hailey, it's now your turn…" The judge gives her the same prompt in two parts, and she carefully slides my ring onto my finger.

"I give you this ring as a token of my love and devotion, and with it, I thee wed."

I don't need to be told what comes next. I cup the back of her neck with one hand and use the other to brace the small of her back as I dip her back, sealing our union with a scorcher of a kiss.

"Stand by Me" starts playing as I easer her back to standing, then I kiss her again, picking her up and spinning her around as she wraps her arms tight around my neck.

"Ready for whatever comes next?" she says quietly, her eyes bright and clear as everyone claps around us.

"With you as my wife?" I kiss her again. "Fuck yeah."

THE END AGAIN

(for now...)

Stay tuned for more Horus Group stories by signing up for my newsletter at http://ainsleybooth.com/newsletter/

There will be four story arcs in this series:

Hate F*@k - Cole's story
Love Hate - Tag's story
Dirty Love - Wilson's story
F*@k Dirty - Jason's story

Each of them will be told in their own way. Coming in Fall 2015 is **dirty**, a prequel to Dirty Love. Look for Love Hate in early 2016, told in two parts—like Hate F*@k, that one is going to get worse before it gets better.

The rest? You'll have to wait and see. The story of The Horus Group has really just begun.

~ Ainsley

—acknowledgments part one—

First of all, Sera Bright, for humoring me and understanding me and coaching me way more than she needed to as I blundered my way through writing in first person. Jules, Cher, and Nikki were also faithful first person cheerleaders. Thank you all for putting up with my grumping.

Elle Rush deserves all credit for the name of The Horus Group, and others in the TMI Room weighed in on the names for each of the guys— Kate, Amity, Melanie...thank you for helping to name Tag and Wilson.

Editing thanks to Rhonda Helms, the first person to read the entire thing from start to end, and flagged no less than a hundred things to make better. Be glad she did! Revision suggestions from Kate Willoughby, Annie Nicholas, Amity Lassiter, and Molly McLain were also much appreciated. Dana Waganer's eagle eyes caught all the missing words, and the bonus u's, and any that she missed can be blamed on Cole's dirty mouth—so distracting.

A million thanks to all my Zoe fans for understanding that I wanted to take a break and try something different. Turns out that the cliffhanger was the biggest difference, so I'm sorry about that! But thank you (a million times thank you) for pointing out that Cole and Hailey's love story isn't that different from anything else that I've written...just a bit rockier, maybe. And the pussy-slapping...that's new. Ahem.

(Wow, awkward segue...)

Final thanks go to my family. The Viking, who just looks at my covers and tells to go get it. No matter what else is going on with us, thank you for the unconditional support. My kids, who have no idea what I write but think it's cool *that* I write. And everyone else: my sister, my in-laws, my close friends... I love you all beyond measure because you don't blink when I tell you that I'm writing a book called Hate Fuck. I have the coolest, bestest, craziest peeps ever.

—acknowledgments part two—

All the early Goodreads reviewers who encouraged their friends to request part one on NetGalley. Thank you for taking a chance on me. Thank you for loving Cole and Hailey as much as I do.

Jessica A., Linsday B, and all the other Zoe fans who were early Ainsley fans and had to wait extra long for part two... thank you for your patience. Part three won't be far behind.

The exploding Ainsley's Angels group on FB. Thank you for being so excited about all the Horus Group guys!

My editing team: Rhonda Helms, Sadie Haller (ha! I know you won't hang an editing shingle, but look, I've snuck you in here anyway), Dana Waganer. You guys rock. All remaining errors are mine, either from futzing or stubbornness or both.

The Chatzy crew. Elle Rush, Amity Lassiter, Kate Willoughby and others.

Other writer friends like Molly McLain, Gen Turner, Shari Slade…that list is endless!

All the LOL ladies who just *got* why I had to write this project and cheered me on *so* hard. Julia Kent, Daisy Prescott, Mimi Strong, Juliet Spenser, Harlow Nash, Deanna Roy, Melanie Marchande, Cassia Leo, Bria Quinlan, Brenna Aubrey.

YouTube, for delivering the awesomeness that Sylvia is to me — chapter twelve wouldn't have been the same without the songs "If You Get The Notion" and "Sweet Stuff". Probably iTunes deserves a nod on that front, too. And since I'm talking music, Nine Inch Nails…thank you for "Closer" and "Something I Can Never Have", Kings of Leon for "Beautiful War", and The Stone Foxes for "King Bee".

And my family, always.

—acknowledgments part three—

Sadie Haller and her husband—Sadie because she finds all the little things that don't make sense, and her husband because when one of those things was some kissing choreography, he helped her figure out where I went wrong. Three-dimensional fact checking, people! How amazing is that?

My Ainsley's Angels Facebook group, who held down the fort while I locked myself in the writing cave—thank you for all the entertaining memes and man candy pictures and polite reminders that it was April. I love you guys.

Friends, family, writing buddies all got nods in the last two instalments, so I guess the last thing I need to say is to you, the reader, especially if you're one of those quiet people who isn't on social media a lot, and you found my book and decided to give it a go. Thank you, seriously. You are are why I write books, you are me a few years ago, and I hope Cole and Hailey's love story gave you the escape you were looking for.

There are more Horus Group stories to be told. Thanks to everyone who has asked about Wilson, Tag, and now finally Jason—still an asshole, but maybe there's some hope for him, yes?

~ Ainsley

—copyright—

Made in the USA
Charleston, SC
31 July 2015